The Nature *of* Cacti *and* Satellites

KAITLIN CRANOR

For Evan.
You are the reason this book finally happened.
I love you so much.

Chapter 1

[August 1996]

C ivil disobedience looked so much cooler in movies.

As Rosalee sat between the looming bulldozer and the magnificent cottonwood in front of Picket General Hospital, she listened to the sputter of the idling engine and realized that her initial burst of adrenaline had long since dissipated. The lingering emotion was hard to identify, but it didn't feel like fear.

The only things that truly worried her in this situation were that (a) she might not be able to stop the bulldozer from destroying the tree, and (b) her frail arms might pop out of their sockets like a mistreated Barbie doll, should the operator attempt to drag her away by her ankles. Otherwise, she was a little ... bored.

At least it was a beautiful day. The intermittent wind throughout the morning had left the sky virtually cloudless and the shade of cerulean often featured in vacation brochures for cruises to the Caribbean. The indigo mountain range that trimmed the horizon was more crisp and clear in the blazing sunlight.

As Rosalee contemplated her surroundings, the stocky bulldozer operator ambled back into view, gesticulating angrily and shouting into his cellular phone. Rosalee redoubled her backward grip on the tree trunk and pressed her spine further into the rough bark. The operator stopped pacing for a moment, listening hard to the voice on the other end as the scowl on his face deepened.

"I know, but this goddamn *hippie*—" He shot a nasty look at Rosalee. "—won't get out of my goddamn way. I don't know, some chick with ratty hair. I don't think—I already—great, thanks."

The operator snapped his phone shut as Rosalee inspected the end of the naturally red braid that hung nearly to her waist. Had she brushed her hair that morning? Actually, she was pretty sure she had slept in the braid.

Meanwhile, the operator stomped over to stand in front of her. Rosalee raised her eyebrows, then caught hold of a tall stalk of wild grass growing close to her calf. She yanked it up and stuck the end between her teeth before snaking her arm backward around the tree trunk.

The operator's phone rang and he turned his back on Rosalee again.

"What?" he snarled into the mouthpiece. "No, I didn't ask her yet." He turned back to Rosalee. "You want money or somethin'?" The voice on the other end of the phone buzzed like a hornet. "Well, how the hell was I supposed to say it, then? *What do you want?*" he barked at Rosalee.

"It's pretty simple … *Stan,*" said Rosalee, speaking around the stalk. "I don't want you to doze this tree."

The operator glanced down at his name embroidered on his sweaty work shirt. "She doesn't want me to 'doze' the tree." He rolled his eyes. "I don't know why. Why?" he said, jutting his chin in Rosalee's direction.

"Is that your supervisor?"

"Yup."

"Can I talk to him?"

"Nope."

Rosalee crossed her legs in front of her and sat back again, chewing on the end of the grass. She had no place to be.

Stan listened to his supervisor for several moments, frowning. "No, just—I'll hold." He sighed. "You want money or somethin'?" he said to Rosalee.

"You already asked me that."

"You didn't answer me."

"No, I don't want money. Can I talk to your supervisor, *please?*"

"No ... *thank you,*" Stan said mockingly.

"Rose!"

Rosalee turned a little too sharply and felt bark scrape through the thin material of her worn-out polo shirt. The air shimmered above the asphalt and blurred the outline of her younger sister, Ellie, in a flowered sundress, marching up the hill from the parking lot with a small duffle bag in tow. Rosalee leapt to her feet, then laid her palms quickly back against the tree as Stan dared to look momentarily hopeful.

As soon as she reached her, Rosalee shaded her eyes with one hand to try to read her sister's expression. "Hi. Everything okay?"

Ellie nodded, wiping stray strawberry blonde hairs off her forehead as she handed Rosalee the duffle bag. "Brought you some stuff for your protest. Jeez, it's hot."

"Thanks. How did you know I was here?"

"Aunt Lola. She said after you guys dropped off the chairs, you decided to sit out here and fry instead of coming home."

Rosalee sat down again with the bag. "Well, it shouldn't be long now. I've got this guy right where I want him."

Ellie eyed Stan dubiously. He was still glued to his phone and, presumably, on hold. Hesitantly, she sat next to Rosalee, tucking the skirt of her sundress neatly beneath her. "You're gonna ruin your teeth."

Rosalee ignored her and repositioned the grass so that it stuck out between her front ones, then wiggled it up and down with her tongue. "Remember that tree in Pete's backyard we used to climb and hang upside down in?"

"And then we had splinters stuck in our legs for the rest of the summer?" Ellie smiled. "This one looks a lot like it. Why are they knocking it down, anyway?"

"I don't know, I wasn't paying attention. I was too busy watching the icky, sweaty man freak out."

As if on cue, Stan snapped his phone shut and headed their way, looking more disgruntled than ever. Rosalee saw Ellie stiffen out of the corner of her eye.

"You don't have to stay if you don't want to. No reason for you to get in trouble, too," said Rosalee.

"It's okay. I don't want him to knock over this tree, either."

"Why's that?"

"Because you don't."

Rosalee glanced at her sister, who smiled tentatively back.

"Okay ladies, time's up. Move it." Stan planted his feet squarely beneath him and glowered down at them.

"What did your supervisor say?" said Rosalee, squinting into the sun to look at him.

Stan slapped a fly away from his shiny neck.

"He said that I can ask you kindly, again, to move, or I can call the Sheriff and let him do the honors."

Beside her, Ellie fidgeted nervously, but Rosalee remained unfazed.

"Did you ever think that telling me why you need this tree down might save you some trouble?" she said.

The operator motioned irritably behind him before digging his phone out of his pocket again. "Like I told you, it's blocking that there sign. Now, you've got about ten seconds to move, or it's cuffs for you."

"*Handcuffs,*" Rosalee muttered. "That's what I should have brought."

"*What?*" Ellie said sharply.

"Well, then I could have chained myself to the—never mind," said Rosalee quickly, catching sight of her sister's expression.

Ellie sighed.

"Thinking about Aunties?" said Rosalee.

"Thinking about your bail. Everybody at the bank should be back from lunch now."

"There's money in my sock drawer from that stenciling job last week. But I don't think the Sheriff is going to bother arresting me." Rosalee raised her voice a few decibels for Stan's benefit. "See, we're on pretty good terms with the Sheriff, aren't we, El? What with him coming around to dinner sometimes?"

Stan appeared not to have heard her, although she did notice a particularly juicy vein pulsating in his neck as he punched in a number at the bottom of his phone.

"What's with the accent?" Ellie said quietly as she got to her feet.

"I don't know, it just came out."

Ellie nodded in approval. "Very 'small-town-Southern-y.' Although … we're in Colorado, so … You sure you don't want me to wait with you?"

"Go on. *Git.*" Rosalee shooed her sister away. "Thanks for the care package."

She watched Ellie walk back toward the parking lot, then pulled the duffle bag into her lap to investigate the contents while Stan grumbled into his phone. He turned at the sound of the zipper and ended the call. "Hold on a second, young lady. What've ya got there?"

Rosalee opened the bag wider and dumped several items onto the grass in front of her. "Well, let's see. Sunscreen, sunglasses ..." She paused to put them on. "Mmm, homemade corn muffins, *Vogue* ... good grief." Ellie was relentless. Stan only glared and wiped his forehead with the back of a gritty arm while Rosalee continued through the pack. "Walkman, and—" She stopped to unscrew the top of a plastic water bottle and sniff. "—iced tea. You want some?"

Stan scoffed. "What, so you can poison me?"

Rosalee finally removed the grass from her mouth, tossing it away behind her before taking a long drink from the bottle. She smacked her lips appreciatively. "Just bein' polite," she drawled, unable to stop her charade now that she'd started.

Stan harrumphed and turned back toward his bulldozer. "The long arm of the law'll be here any minute. If you was a sensible girl, you'd stay outta reach of it. Don't say I didn't warn ya."

He stumped away to wait in the cab while Rosalee unwound the headphone cord wrapped around her tape player. She pressed PLAY and was immediately engulfed in pop music so bright and shiny that she halfway expected something pink and glittery to ooze out of the auxiliary port. She stopped the cassette and popped the tape deck to find Madonna's *Bedtime Stories*—not the tape she had left in there. Ellie was no longer allowed to borrow her Walkman. She would have to put her foot down.

———— •●• ————

By the time the Sheriff's two-tone brown and tan Ford pulled up, Rosalee was pretending to read an article about pairing your jean jacket with the quintessential clutch while actually wondering how in the world she was going to manage to save this tree. She waved as he parked, then stuffed the magazine and her Walkman back into the duffle bag.

The Sheriff got out of his truck, shaking his head. Rosalee had known him most of her life and never ceased to be amazed by the calming presence that emanated from his person. In his mid-forties, he was undoubtedly handsome, with smooth bronze skin and shiny black hair that always reminded her of crow feathers. If anyone could turn this fiasco around, it was the Sheriff.

"Ms. Andrews." He touched the brim of his hat in acknowledgment as he made his way toward the bulldozer.

"Hi, Sheriff."

Stan hopped out of the cab, hitching up his waistband as he approached. "You're the sheriff?" he said gruffly. "Martino or somethin'?"

"Martinez, that's right." The Sheriff extended his hand. "You must be Mr. Gallagher. Pleased to meet you."

Stan grasped his hand, looking him up and down skeptically. Compared to Sheriff Martinez, who was sturdy but slender, Stan's ungainly bulk made Rosalee think of a boulder next to a sycamore.

"Ms. Andrews?" The Sheriff turned back to her and the tree. "Would you come over here, please?"

"Sheriff, sir, with all due respect, I can't leave this tree or he'll knock it over."

"Please," he said again.

Slowly, as slowly as was physically possible, Rosalee pushed herself up from the ground and meandered toward the men. Meanwhile, Stan's phone rang and he struggled to retrieve it from the depths of his pocket. He pointed to it unnecessarily. "I gotta take this."

The Sheriff nodded, then waited until Stan was out of hearing range to turn back to Rosalee. "What's with the accent?"

"It just came out." She waved a hand dismissively.

"Rosalee, there's nothing I can do here. This is private property and the hospital has every right to see to its landscaping."

The unexpected tenderness behind his aviator sunglasses caused Rosalee's eyes to well up. She blinked rapidly to clear them. "Because of a sign, though? Because this beautiful sculpture of nature is in front of their stupid sign? How is that okay? You know, we need these things for oxygen—they're not just for decoration."

Sheriff Martinez raised his eyebrows, although Rosalee detected a hint of amusement beneath them.

"Sorry," she said anyway.

"Look, I don't want you to get in trouble, but the hospital called me about potential trespassing charges even before this … fine gentleman."

Rosalee shot a dark look toward the large windows of the hospital, where several patients and employees were staring unabashedly through its windows as though this situation were some sort of zoo exhibit. Several other people sat outside by the entrance on benches and concrete ledges, consuming their lunches with their faces also pointed toward the spectacle. Further around the corner of the building, a man in a button-down shirt and tie and a woman in scrubs puffed on cigarettes, flicking the cherries into a large, concrete ashtray.

"Hey, Sheriff," Stan called, holding his phone away from his mouth, "My supervisor'd like a word."

As the Sheriff walked over to Stan and the bulldozer, Rosalee turned her attention back to the main entrance of the hospital and saw Gwen, one of the HR employees, heading out with a stack of paperwork and a travel mug of coffee balanced precariously on top. Rosalee waved half-heartedly and Gwen made her way toward her, before the fancy smoker in the shirt and tie intercepted her course. Rosalee watched as they chatted and Gwen shifted the stack of papers in her arms to awkwardly shake the man's hand.

Of all of the people she knew from the hospital (and that was only a few so far) Gwen was her favorite. She was short and petite, with wavy, dark brown hair that was almost always tied back in a practical ponytail. Rosalee figured she was probably in her late thirties, but the spattering of freckles across her nose and cheeks would likely keep her looking much younger for years to come.

At long last, she made it to Rosalee. "Hey, honey. I'm heading out. You want a ride?"

"I'm alright. Thanks, though."

Gwen furrowed her brow and leaned closer. "Is everything okay? You're not going to get arrested, are you?"

Rosalee shrugged. "I doubt it. Who was that guy you were talking to back there?"

"Oh, we interviewed him about a construction job on some of the new wings. Nice young man." Gwen glanced behind her, then turned back to Rosalee, not to be deterred from her motherly instincts. "Anything you want me to relay to your aunts? I'm headed over to Lola's class in a few."

"No, thanks, I have a feeling this will be over soon anyway." Rosalee nodded toward the Sheriff, who was finally off of Stan's phone.

"Okay, well, I'm gonna get going, then. Afternoon, Sheriff," she called as she went.

Sheriff Martinez tipped his hat toward Gwen as he walked back to Rosalee. Stan was bobbing along in his wake, looking sickeningly smug.

"Ms. Andrews, Stan's company is going to bill the hospital whether or not this tree comes down today. I'd hate for you to have to pay the invoice, so I'm afraid we'll need to move you."

"You can't *physically* move me, though," said Rosalee.

The Sheriff looked pointedly at Stan, who was practically salivating over his shoulder. "Give us another minute, will you please?"

Stan's mouth worked heatedly before he spat in the dirt and lumbered away again, muttering under his breath.

"Rosalee," said Sheriff Martinez, quietly enough that he wouldn't be overheard. "I know you're going through a lot right now, what with Evelyn and … everything."

Evelyn.

Rosalee wrapped her arms around her body protectively as though it might help to shield her from the sudden wave of emotions threatening to crush her. She struggled to keep her breathing calm and even.

"My hands are tied here, hun," said the Sheriff. "I'm so sorry."

But Rosalee couldn't let it go yet, even if it meant grasping wildly at any straw that might provide a tether to this rapidly unraveling state of affairs. "What if it turns out that this hospital was built on, like … a Native American burial ground or something?"

The Sheriff gave a half-smile. "I'm afraid the historical society would have documented such an occurrence before the structure was even built."

Rosalee slumped in on herself and felt the dreaded tickle in the back of her eyes again. She tilted her head back and blinked against the gathering moisture. "There has to be something we can do. This tree has been here forever. I mean, what if I, like … bought it off of them?"

"What if you 'bought it off of them?'"

"Yeah, like, maybe I could pay to replant it somewhere else, or I could pay for a new, bigger sign so they didn't have to move the tree at all."

There was no way that Rosalee's painting money could pay for bail, landscaping services, *and* a giant tree, but she had to try. Meanwhile, Sheriff Martinez was looking at her with something that looked suspiciously like pity, which made her feel even more pathetic.

She turned away from him to see the fancy smoker approaching them (minus his cloud of smoke), straightening his tie importantly as he came. This close, Rosalee realized that he must be near her age, with dark blonde hair and darker eyes, one of which winked at her so quickly she thought she might have imagined it.

Stan reapproached the little gathering, the vein in his neck throbbing dangerously again.

"Afternoon, Ms. Andrews. Gentlemen," said the newcomer, nodding at Rosalee, the Sheriff, and Stan in turn.

Rosalee stiffened. How did he know her name?

"I'm Alex Conway, Ms. Andrews' attorney, and I'd like to ask you a few questions before you knock down this tree," he said to Stan, pulling a pen and legal pad out of his messenger bag.

Rosalee blinked as a tiny bubble of hope blossomed deep in her chest. Could this possibly be real? On the one hand, she knew she couldn't afford an attorney, but on the other, wasn't it worth a shot? She quickly arranged her features to look as though the introduction and concept were not brand-new information. Out of her peripheral vision, she saw Sheriff Martinez shake his head at the ground.

Stan looked back and forth between everyone as though waiting for a punchline. When none came, he became steadily more purple in the face until finally, he began to shout so loudly that spittle appeared at the corners of his mouth. "NOW LISTEN HERE, YOU ALL, I'VE

HAD ABOUT ENOUGH OF THIS TODAY!" he bellowed, "I'VE ALREADY MISSED AN HOUR AND A HALF OF WORK, IT'S HOTTER THAN SATAN'S GONADS OUT HERE, AND I'M LONG OVERDUE FOR A PISS!"

"I understand, sir," Sheriff Martinez began in a pacifying tone, but Stan had already spun on his heel and was moving faster than Rosalee had seen him go yet. The Sheriff hastened to follow him.

Rosalee turned frantically to Alex Conway, alleged attorney. "What do we do now?"

Before he could answer her, the bulldozer roared to life, making them both jump. He and Rosalee watched in horror as the heavy machine swung around sharply and rumbled toward the cottonwood.

"No!" Rosalee screamed, launching herself back toward the tree.

She could hear Sheriff Martinez shouting at Stan from the side of the bulldozer and braced herself for the impact of the first blow with her heart pounding in her ears—the engine hadn't slowed in the slightest. But before she could relinquish her grip, her legs were swept clean out from under her.

Rosalee struggled in Alex's arms with all of her strength as he heaved her out of the way, shouting herself hoarse until a tumultuous crash rendered her momentarily breathless. Only then did she succeed in elbowing out of his arms, but he caught her again around the middle before she could get the ground properly under her feet.

A resounding crash rent the air and Rosalee sagged, sinking with Alex to her knees, where he finally released her. Then she was sobbing and there was nothing to do but let her sorrow consume and immobilize her. Her body shuddered with the marrow-deep sadness that she knew had very little to do with the tree because truthfully, she had expected to fail from the beginning.

"Shit, shit, *shiiit!*" she yelled into her knees.

She couldn't bear to look at the broken remains of what seconds ago was life and grace and beauty, nor could she pick herself up from where she knelt on the ground, feeling little pieces of herself breaking, too. Eventually, she felt a warm and tentative hand on her back. She threw it off and wiped her eyes furiously on the collar of her shirt before glaring up at the attorney.

"I'm *so* sorry," he said, panting. He was still next to her on the ground, trying to catch his breath.

"Are you *even* an attorney?" said Rosalee. "How the hell did you know who I was?"

Alex nodded back toward the hospital. "I asked Gwen. And no, I'm not."

At least he had the decency to look ashamed of himself.

"I—thought you were trying to help me." Rosalee tilted her head back to stem the flow of tears that leaked out of the corners of her eyes and ran down her cheeks anyway.

Alex wiped the sweat off of his forehead with the sleeve of his dress shirt and gestured toward Stan, who had a manic glint in his eyes as he surveyed the destruction he had rendered. "I was trying to help you not get murdered."

Rosalee shook her head in exasperation and looked over at Sheriff Martinez, who was still yelling at him. "He wouldn't have killed me. He's kind of a dick, but I doubt he's willing to go to prison."

Alex raised his eyebrows skeptically. They watched as Stan threw the bulldozer into reverse.

"Stop!" Rosalee shouted.

She hauled herself up from the ground again and ran back to the tree, then tugged at the duffle bag, which was caught underneath the bulldozer's track. One final heave and the bag ripped free, tearing along the seam. She rummaged inside and was relieved to find that she had at least escaped this odious incident with an intact cassette player. The corn muffins and sunglasses (which had apparently fallen off during her tussle with Alex), had seen better days.

She tried very hard not to look at the mangled pile of sticks and splinters next to her as she shoved everything down to the undamaged portion of the bag. She wiped the last of her tears away surreptitiously before turning to face Stan and Sheriff Martinez.

"Well, I should go. Thanks for trying, Sheriff. And you, *Stan*," she said, infusing as much hostility as possible into the last word.

Stan's answering self-satisfied expression nearly activated her up-chuck reflex. "Ma'am," he said, tipping an imaginary hat.

Rosalee ignored Alex completely as she walked past him toward the road, her Walkman wedged under one arm as she gathered the torn edges of the duffle bag and bound them together with a thick hair tie from her wrist.

"Hold on a minute, Ms. Andrews," Sheriff Martinez called after her. "I still have to take you in."

Rosalee stopped walking as a hearty guffaw erupted from the bull-dozer cabin. She turned back miserably. "You do?"

Sheriff Martinez nodded as he waved the bulldozer away. "And bring your ... attorney."

Chapter 2

Sheriff Martinez insisted on driving Rosalee home, but she was relieved when he didn't have time to come inside. She waved goodbye at the end of the long, dirt driveway until he rounded the corner, then made her way up to the house. He hadn't actually taken her or Alex into the station, although he treated them to a short lecture about the more misguided aspects of their tree-saving attempt.

As she trudged up the front porch steps, her combat boots weighing her down even more in the heat, she lingered by the marigolds soaking up the late summer sunshine. Her Aunt Robin had planted them along the porch railing in every shade of yellow, orange, and red she could find—for Evelyn.

And again, the ever-present lump in Rosalee's throat distended into her airway. Her eyes strayed to the large bay window and the dining room beyond it, and she backed herself up against the railing, hoping the small assembly at the table hadn't seen her yet. As much as she hated crying in front of strangers, she especially hated crying in front of her family. She leaned forward again, enough to catch a glimpse of her Aunt Lola, still in her workout clothes with her thick, blonde hair swept up off of her neck with a scrunchy, and Ellie, sitting across from her. They appeared to be focused on something on the table between them and, thankfully, hadn't noticed Rosalee grappling with her feelings on the porch.

The woman who had practically raised Rosalee and Ellie—who had been more of a mother than their actual mother—was gone from this world, and Rosalee could hardly understand how it kept right on spinning anyway. She wondered if Evelyn could see the flowers that her sister, Robin, had so lovingly sown for her, wherever she was.

It was several more minutes before Rosalee was calm enough to push the front door open and walk into the dining room.

"Well, speak of the devil, there's the felon herself," said Lola.

"Hey." Rosalee flopped down into the chair next to her, then pulled the bottle of iced tea out of her ruined duffle bag and shoved the rest under her seat. She took a long, deep draft. "God, it's hot."

"It's not too bad in here," said Ellie.

She barely looked up, as she was busy picking beads out of a mixing bowl and sorting them into a plastic container with many compartments—like a tackle box, only this one was full to bursting with beads of every size and color imaginable.

"New shipment?" Rosalee asked Lola, who was likewise occupied.

Lola nodded. "I know I shouldn't have, but I couldn't resist. Just *look* at them."

Rosalee held out a hand and Lola dropped several glass beads the size of peas into it. She tilted her palm to examine the effect of a black and white marbled bead next to a deep, bottle green one and a smooth onyx. "Wow. These are kind of amazing."

Robin emerged from the kitchen, running a hand through her short-cropped, salt and pepper hair, damp with sweat. The dirt stains on the knees of her jeans suggested that she must have been gardening in the backyard. She nodded at Rosalee. "How'd it go?"

"Not good. They tore it down."

"They tore it down?" Ellie yelped, scattering her pile of beads and then throwing herself on top of them in her scramble to keep them from rolling off the edges of the table.

Rosalee nodded and bit her lower lip as it began to tremble.

"Oh, honey." Lola reached a hand toward Rosalee's, but stopped just shy of it.

"Why'd they knock it over?" said Robin, leaning against the doorframe.

"Blocking a sign, wasn't it?" said Ellie. "I thought that's what the icky, sweaty man said."

"Stan," said Rosalee. Ellie made a face. "But no one pressed charges this time."

Robin nodded and the lines around her mouth softened perceptibly.

Lola scoffed. "Well, I should think not, after you painted those gorgeous chairs for the hospital for practically nothing."

Rosalee shrugged. She was starting to feel self-conscious with everyone's eyes trained on her.

"How are you feeling?" said Robin.

"Fine."

Although, as Rosalee turned her thoughts inward for the first time since the tree went down, she realized that "exhausted" would have been a more accurate description.

Robin seemed to gather that from her face. "You look like hell. I think you oughta lie down for a bit."

Rosalee was too drained to argue, especially since now that she realized she was tired, it was only getting worse. She took the bottle of watered-down iced tea with her as she nearly crawled up the stairs to her bedroom and fell onto the blue cotton comforter, fully clothed. She didn't wake for several hours.

When Rosalee finally came to, Ellie was sitting at the wooden desk next to her bed, flipping pages in a magazine and chewing noisily on a piece of gum.

"Hey," said Rosalee, feeling groggy.

"Hey. Aunties told me to tell you dinner's almost ready, but I can bring it to you in here if you want."

Rosalee felt herself nodding off again and heaved herself into an upright position, stuffing two pillows behind her to stop the temptation of a much longer nap. "No, I'll eat with you guys." She barely stifled a yawn.

Ellie glanced sideways at her. "Are you sure? You're still pretty flushed."

"Could it be a sunburn?"

"Yeah, maybe." Ellie went back to her page turning.

Rosalee swung her feet over the edge of the bed. "I slept too long as it is. I'll never get to sleep tonight."

"It's not ready, like, right now," said Ellie, turning another page. "We still have a little time. *Ugh* ..." She stared down at an advertisement in her lap for a moment, rolling her lips inward before taking the gum out of her mouth, sticking it resolutely in the middle of the ad, then ripping the whole page out of the magazine.

"Which one?" said Rosalee.

"Premarin."

"Wastebasket is by your feet."

Ellie wadded up the page with uncharacteristic aggression, then sighed, her shoulders drooping. "I forgot what I was saying."

"Okay, well if I keep sitting here, I'm gonna fall asleep again."

Ellie closed the magazine and set it back on the desk. "Well then let's talk about stuff."

"What stuff?" Rosalee said warily.

"Sheriff called."

"What? When? Why?"

Rosalee wondered which party had changed their mind about pressing charges. She really did have other plans for her painting money.

"He called when you were asleep," said Ellie. "To make sure you were okay and everything."

"Oh."

Rosalee felt her shoulders relax, but Ellie's eyes narrowed suspiciously.

"What?" said Rosalee.

"What actually happened after I left?"

"What do you mean? I told you the tree got knocked down."

Ellie nodded, raising her eyebrows so high they nearly disappeared into her bangs.

"What?" Rosalee said again. "You don't believe me?"

"It's just that Sheriff said something that made it sound a *teensy* bit like maybe you were hiding something from the people that love and care about you and I couldn't help but wonder—"

"*What,* Ellie?" Rosalee watched her sister tap her nails on the magazine cover and suddenly remembered the contents of the duffle bag. "Also, where did you put my tape?"

"What tape?"

"The one you took out of my Walkman so I had to listen to your sticky 'Tootsie Roll pop.'"

Ellie rolled her eyes. "You mean 'bubble gum pop'?"

"Yes, that."

Ellie smiled.

"*What?*" said Rosalee.

"Nothing. You seem …"

Rosalee waited, but Ellie just smiled again. "I think it's in my room, hang on."

She returned a moment later with Rosalee's tape. "Are you sure you don't want to borrow the Madonna one? She's not just 'bubble gum,' you know—she's kind of edgy."

Rosalee shrugged. "Sure."

Ellie set both tapes on Rosalee's desk, then plopped down in the desk chair again.

"So, what was your question?" said Rosalee.

Ellie pressed the tips of her fingers together into a tent under her chin. Rosalee was suddenly very aware of her breathing—not because she had anything to hide, but because her sister looked so solemn.

"Okay, I'm just gonna ask it," she said.

"Great."

"Since when do you have an attorney?"

Chapter 3

"**C**'mon, we're gonna be late!"

Ellie's face peered around the door frame and frowned at Rosalee lounging on her bed, perusing paint samples, then withdrew again in a flurry of curls.

"El, it's a picnic," Rosalee called after her. "There is no 'late' unless all the food's gone."

Ellie's voice came through the wall. "I have pies to enter, remember?"

Rosalee sighed, putting down the samples and slipping her feet into the worn-out flip-flops at the end of her bed. "Have you seen my sunglasses?"

"Bulldozed, remember? You can borrow mine." Ellie reappeared and gave her sister's worn-out jeans and paint-spattered T-shirt a disappointed look. "But you're not dressed."

"What's wrong with this?" Rosalee turned toward the full-length mirror, then quickly away.

"You're in your paint clothes."

They looked at each other for a few seconds before Rosalee caved, slouching over to her chest of drawers for a pair of shorts, assuming she had any. She had spontaneously dumped most of her wardrobe at a Goodwill several months ago out of spite. After all, she was never going to be able to go back to who she was before Evelyn—before everything—and it was no good having constant reminders of her former shiny self.

She dug around for a bit, then unearthed some old cutoffs and held them up for Ellie's approval. Ellie studied them for a moment before giving a stiff nod. Rosalee quickly exchanged her jeans for the shorts.

"Huh," she said, moving into the mirror's reflection once more. "Hey, El?"

Ellie was looking properly abashed. "What? I just fixed 'em a little." She moved quickly to Rosalee's closet to search for a top. "My sewing machine was sitting there gathering dust."

"Yes ..." Rosalee nodded sarcastically as she ran her fingertips along the seams that were now much closer to her thighs, "I'm sure that with your sundress-a-week habit, the dust must have been an inch thick."

Ellie stuck her nose in the air and re-immersed herself in Rosalee's closet. "Oooh, what about this?"

Rosalee stared blankly at the floaty green material shoved in her direction. "That's a dress."

"Uh *huhhh* ..."

"No."

"Why not?"

Rosalee turned her back on her sister and resumed ravaging her shirt drawer until she found a *Laurie's Café* touristy T-shirt from the Lauries themselves—a gift for watching their dog once. She threw it on the bed.

"Oh, stop being so dramatic, Rosalee. Not everything you wear needs to be black."

Rosalee looked down at her navy blue shirt. "This isn't black."

"It's still dark. What about this one?"

Rosalee wrinkled her nose at the offending lacy top dangling off of Ellie's finger. It must have been Lola's doing, though she had no idea how it had escaped her thrift store reaping. "El, this is a town event. I'm not dressing for a wedding."

"Yes, but it's a 'Welcome Picnic.' You're supposed to look welcoming."

"Yeah, 'welcome to Rabbitbrush,' not 'welcome to my cleavage.'"

Ellie and Rosalee exchanged a long and stubborn look until Ellie broke eye contact to glance at the clock. Then she sighed and sat down on the edge of Rosalee's bed, gesturing resignedly toward the *Laurie's Cafe* shirt.

Rosalee smiled triumphantly and pulled her painting T-shirt over her head, then reached for the touristy top when she felt a sharp tug at the back of her head. Ellie was attempting to unravel the long braid that hung down her back.

"*Why?*" Rosalee demanded.

"It looks pretty down."

"Who's gonna look?" Rosalee fought her sister off long enough to yank the new shirt on.

Ellie wiggled her eyebrows. "Your *attorney* might."

Rosalee turned to glare at her. "Is *that* what all this is about?"

She wished fervently that she had never opened her mouth about that traitor. She could have lied. Made him disappear. He could have never existed.

Ellie gave a little shrug and continued undoing Rosalee's braid.

Rosalee rolled her eyes. "He may not have even gotten the job and why would he come to this thing, even if he did?"

"Upside down," Ellie ordered, pointing at the carpet.

She waited with one foot stuck out in front of her, leaning on her hip the way Evelyn used to. Rosalee was tempted to laugh, but instead, let her upper body go so that her arms dangled and her fingers grazed the carpet.

"*Ooh ooh,*" she grunted. Like an orangutan.

"Ha, ha," Ellie answered sarcastically, ruffling her sister's hair.

A moment later, Robin shuffled in, looking as forlorn about the evening's activities as Rosalee. However, Rosalee's spirits lifted marginally as she took in her aunt's outfit—an old, black, Joe's Crab Shack T-shirt and a pair of boxy jean shorts.

"Ha!" she said, grinning triumphantly, "We match!"

Ellie frowned. "Oh, for heaven's sake, Aunt Robin."

Rosalee gleefully pushed Robin out the door and skipped with her ahead of Lola and Ellie, before either of them had another chance to argue.

•❖•

Like most outdoor town events, the "Welcome Picnic" was held in a clearing next to an old, red barn that had been a fixture since Rabbitbrush's establishment. The space was surrounded by aspens and ponderosa pines and lay at the foot of one of the best sledding hills in Rabbitbrush. At the top of that very hill, Rosalee, Robin, Lola, and Ellie stopped to marvel at the festivities.

Rosalee's initial thought was that someone had scattered rainbow confetti all over the picnic area. Multi-colored pennant banners adorned the buffet tables like buttercream frosting on the world's longest sheet cake, and bright bunches of balloons stood sentinel by picnic tables and the half-dozen benches surrounding an enormous lighted Ferris wheel.

Ellie immediately spotted the pie table, and Rosalee and Robin shuffled half-heartedly after her and Lola as they led the procession.

Rosalee paused next to the wooden fence running along the clearing's perimeter, struggling to balance the enormous bowl of fruit salad she carried on her hip. She swiped at a long blade of grass growing next to the fence with one hand, then promptly lost her balance as fruit juice flowed from under the Saran wrap and soaked into her shirt. She managed to steady the bowl before any of the fruit spilled out.

"For crying out loud, Rosalee," Robin muttered.

She bent down to pick the piece of grass herself and handed it to Rosalee, who held it between her teeth, farmer-like. "Fanks."

"You're gonna ruin your teeth."

Rosalee continued to chew the grass, cow-like.

Rabbitbrush celebrations were almost worth attending for the food alone. Rosalee and Robin struggled to find places for the fruit salad and giant pan of yeast rolls amid the dishes and dishes of homemade breads, casseroles, and salads. Then there were pans of grilled and fried chicken, succulent slices of spiral-cut ham, and paper-thin shavings of roast beef.

Rosalee attempted to fit some of everything on her plate, being sure to leave room for her favorite dessert. Frog Eye salad was traditionally made with *acini di pepe* pasta, from-scratch custard, halved red grapes, maraschino cherries, and marshmallows. However, Rosalee had done such a thorough job of convincing her sister that it was made of real frogs' eyes when they were little that Ellie still wouldn't touch it. Rosalee suppressed a grin as she watched her spoon a portion of Waldorf salad onto her plate, instead.

Once everyone's paper plates were under significant strain, Rosalee, Ellie, Robin, and Lola managed to find four places near the end of one of the many brightly colored picnic tables. The other end of the table was occupied by two unfamiliar men in business suits, who smiled politely before turning back to their conversation. Robin and Lola sat on one side of the table and Ellie had barely set her plate down next to Rosalee's on the other side before announcing that she was going to find Pete.

Rosalee, Ellie, and Pete had grown up together and remained good friends to that day, although Rosalee had to admit that she hadn't been very good at maintaining the relationship in the past several months.

"I'm sure he'll find us when he's- aaand she's gone." Rosalee watched Ellie vanish into the crowd of people moseying around the buffet table and lingering between tables to chat.

Rosalee looked down at her plate, trying to decide what to try first and finally settling on a golden-brown crescent roll. She pulled the tender dough apart and inhaled the buttery inside before popping a savory morsel into her mouth.

"Rosalee Andrews? Is that *you?*"

An all-too-perky and familiar voice made Rosalee stop chewing at once, closing her eyes momentarily to summon her strength. Robin's sudden fascination with her napkin and Lola's over-bright smile across the table confirmed her suspicions. Rosalee rolled her eyes heavenward before assuming the expression she usually reserved for difficult customers and turning to face her misery.

"Angela, how are you?"

Angela Marsh was the epitome of a Southern belle transplant, with dance team captain and student body president under her belt from their high school days, teeth so white they could blind you, and probably "Mattel" stamped on her fanny. To Rosalee, however, she was the two-faced, Circus Peanut kind of fake sweet that was likely to make you sick. Also, she had lived in Alabama for exactly one year between sixth and eighth grade and had come back with an accent so thick you could rip your toast trying to spread it.

"Oh, it *is* you!" Angela clapped her hands and swooped down to hug Rosalee, who sucked in a sharp breath, tensing her muscles until she was released.

Angela didn't seem to notice her discomfort and plopped down into Ellie's vacant seat."Oh, and Robin and Lola as well? Well, this is quite the reunion, isn't it?"

Rosalee was amazed by Angela's ability to show off all her pearly whites at once, although it tended to lend a psychopathic quality to an already alarmingly pleased expression.

"And how was your ... *art internship?*" said Angela.

Rosalee glanced apprehensively at her aunts. "Oh, great. It was great, thanks."

"Well, you certainly look different. So *free.*"

Ellie had said something similar to describe this new and shabby version of Rosalee, although what others deemed "shabby," Rosalee considered "practical."

"Oh, but where's dear Ellie tonight?" said Angela, looking around theatrically. "I don't think I saw her come in with y'all."

"She said she was going to find Pete," said Rosalee. "They'll probably be back any minute."

Rosalee thought she noticed Angela's eye twitch at this information, but after another round of formal farewells and reminders to cast their votes at the pie table, she finally sashayed away in spotless yellow heels.

"You know, she wears those to my classes, too," said Lola conversationally.

"What, the dresses or the shoes?" said Robin.

"Good lord," Rosalee muttered, turning back to her food and impaling a pea that had escaped from her vegetable casserole.

Just then, Ellie and Pete slid onto the bench next to Rosalee. Pete's plate was half empty, so Ellie had likely dragged him away from another table.

"Well, your timing couldn't be better—you just missed Angela," said Rosalee. "By the way, Pete, if you were planning on dating her at all, you'd better do it soon, before she has a conniption."

Pete's cheeks colored slightly while Ellie looked mildly nauseated.

"She used to be okay, right?" said Rosalee. "Like, we used to like her? Granted, it's easier to like someone before their initiation into the Stepford Wives."

Ellie giggled, then immediately looked contrite. "That's mean, Rosalee. She's not that bad."

Pete's expression seemed almost apologetic. "She's not, Rose."

Rosalee looked between them, waiting for someone to laugh. When no one did, she glowered at both of them and stuffed the rest of her crescent roll into her mouth without bothering to savor it.

Chapter 4

Over the next hour, friends and neighbors stopped by to make small talk, offer their condolences about Evelyn, and inquire about Rosalee's internship. Eventually, Rosalee escaped to the pie table to give her face a rest from the constant fake smiling.

When the coast was mostly clear again, she wandered back to the table with her assortment of pie slivers and a voting slip. All of the entrants had baked two pies each (both the same flavor), under the theory that there would be enough samples for everyone. Rosalee somehow doubted that the results were very accurate that way, but no one seemed to mind very much.

Halfway through a tangy, crumbly bite of strawberry rhubarb, Lola gasped in a way that made Rosalee nearly choke on it.

"What?!" she sputtered, attempting to clear her windpipe.

"We only have an hour before they shut down the Ferris wheel!" Lola gathered her empty plate and cup and tried to grab Robin's away midbite.

"Dud gib be a sebken," Robin said thickly through a mouthful of tapioca pudding.

Rosalee watched in amusement as Lola bounced in her seat and Robin attempted to inhale her remaining pie samples.

"Jeez, Lola, don't kill her. An hour's a long time," said Ellie.

"Ib's oday. I'b dub." Robin's cheeks were still bulging as she tossed her trash into the wastebasket and stood, wiping her hands on her shorts.

"Go ahead, we'll catch up." Rosalee waved them away with her fork, then scooted around the end of the table to claim the empty bench across from Ellie and Pete.

Ellie glanced over her shoulder at the slowly rotating wheel. "We should ride it, too. All of us."

The Ferris wheel had been Rosalee's favorite ride when she was younger, but now it made her a little nervous—she wasn't sure she liked all of the adrenaline. Still, something about the late summer air tonight made her itch for some sort of adventure.

"We'll have to take turns," she said. "Those look like they're only two-seaters."

"Remember when all three of us used to fit in one seat?" said Ellie. "We were so *little*."

"That's my fault, I'm afraid," said Pete, lowering his voice by at least an octave. "What with all my manly ... beefiness."

For a moment, no one said anything. Rosalee shared an astonished look with Ellie. *Did Pete just make a joke?* Then Ellie snorted, which made Rosalee and Pete laugh as she covered her burning face with her napkin.

Pete had always been the approximate build of a string bean, but now that Rosalee was really looking, she noticed with a pang how far he'd come from the little boy that had asked her and Ellie to play on the jungle gym, a lifetime ago. His light brown hair was the same, and he had always been very put together, like he should work at a bank (which he did). But now, she noticed the slight hollow in his cheeks, the strong line of his jaw, and the way his grey eyes looked less like the boy with whom she had gone to school nearly her whole life and more like a ... *man?* When had that happened?

She realized she was staring and went back to her plate. "So, Pete, how's the new roommate?"

Pete swallowed his bite of apple pie before answering. "He's great so far. He works a lot, but when he's home, he's nice to have around."

"When do we get to meet him?" said Ellie.

"Well, he said he would be a little late since he's at work." Pete glanced at his watch. "But actually, he should be here pretty soon."

"Is it weird being, like, an adult?" said Rosalee. "All moved out and grown up and cooler than us?"

Pete laughed, shaking his head. "You could move out too, you know. Although I'm not sure why you'd want to."

"Me and Rose started looking for places a while ago," said Ellie, chasing a dark, gooey cherry around the edge of her plate with her plastic fork. "But then, with everything ..."

The atmosphere grew suddenly serious and Rosalee wondered if she could excuse herself quickly without being suspicious before Pete cleared his throat.

"It's weird," he said. "I never realized how expensive it would be to live on my own. Did you guys know that apartments don't come with irons, or staplers, or can openers? I think our parents had to *buy* them."

"See, I never would have thought of a can opener," said Rosalee. "Me and Ellie were fixin' to get you a riding lawnmower for your housewarming party."

Ellie giggled and then became very interested in something over Rosalee's shoulder. She nudged Pete. "Is that him? The blonde guy walking over here?"

Pete followed her gaze and then nodded, waving, as Rosalee turned too quickly and cricked her neck.

She turned back to Pete and Ellie slowly. "*Is this a joke?*" she demanded.

Ellie was becoming a wonderful actress, Rosalee decided, because she looked thoroughly confused.

"Hey, man," said Pete, as Alex Conway approached the table with his plate.

"Hi." Alex raised a hand in greeting. His eyes lingered on Rosalee and he smiled tentatively, but she could only stare back.

"Alex, these are two of my best friends, Rosalee and Ellie," said Pete. "And this is my roommate, Alex."

"Nice to meet you, Alex," said Ellie. She flashed her brightest smile and Rosalee knew her sister was overcompensating for her gloomy demeanor.

"Thanks. You, too." Alex hesitated to sit down since the only open seat was next to Rosalee. "Hey, Rosalee. Nice to see you again."

Rosalee attempted a smile, but her face felt stiff. "You, too."

Pete looked curiously between them and Rosalee watched the dawning realization on Ellie's face, which was transitioning rapidly into something unabashedly smug and gleeful.

"Have you guys already met?" said Pete.

"Um. Yes." Alex sat cautiously on Rosalee's bench, though at least a foot away from her. "That was the whole bulldozer, lawyer, tree fiasco. The 'BLT,' if you will."

Pete and Ellie laughed, but Ellie stopped quickly at Rosalee's expression. "It's awful that they tore down that tree," she said.

Alex nodded. "I agree. Totally unnecessary."

Rosalee glanced at his face, then quickly away before he could meet her gaze.

"This is your first town event, right?" said Ellie.

Alex speared a cube of watermelon on his fork. "How did you guess?"

"You look a little too happy," said Pete. "Once you have a couple more under your belt, your eyes will kinda glaze over a little more."

Ellie laughed. "That's not true. Rosalee and I still love them, don't we?"

Rosalee raised her eyebrows and Ellie frowned at her.

"Fine, well, I do." She sighed, looking around her. "All the amazing smells, all the floral prints, the fireflies."

If Rosalee was being honest, she liked these town events for the same reasons as Ellie, although she wasn't quite as emphatic about the floral prints.

"So, Rosalee," said Alex, with the air of addressing someone in a loosely fastened straitjacket, "Have you heard anything more about the tree?"

Rosalee stared blankly at him.

"I mean, are they going to plant a new one, or ...?"

"Oh." Rosalee stabbed at her pie crust as though it was a deserving bit of convicted murderer, "I don't really know."

Alex nodded and struggled to cut a piece of grilled chicken with his plastic knife. After a few moments of awkward silence, Ellie laughed at something over Rosalee's shoulder.

"What's so funny?" said Pete.

"The sign next to the Ferris Wheel says that it will be closed *for* one hour for pie judging and the Welcome Speech. Lola doesn't read things very thoroughly when she's panicking."

"What's a 'welcome speech?'" said Alex.

"To thank everyone who's working on the hospital. Kind of a support thing," said Ellie.

"... Wow. That's really nice."

"Well, it's also nice having a hospital in the next town, instead of fifty miles away," said Pete.

"The next town?" said Alex. "This isn't Picket?"

"This is Rabbitbrush," said Rosalee. "Didn't you figure that out when you changed your address?"

Ellie kicked her under the table. Rosalee scowled.

"Guess I haven't done that yet," said Alex, looking sheepish.

"Let's go ride the Ferris wheel, Pete," Ellie said suddenly, pulling him up from the table by his elbow.

Panic expanded in Rosalee's chest like a balloon at the idea of forced small talk alone with Alex. "Wait, what? We were gonna ride it together."

"Well, then hurry up." Ellie wiggled her eyebrows as she steered Pete away. Rosalee glared after them.

Alex appeared to have finally cut his chicken into manageable bites. "I'm sorry about the other day," he said.

Rosalee stood to clear her plate. "Don't worry about it."

"I'm almost done. I mean, I can eat fast and ride the Ferris Wheel with you if you want."

Rosalee sighed.

"Or … not," said Alex.

Rosalee felt a pang of guilt as he went back to his plate. She turned away from him, determined to ignore it. And yet, the pang persisted. Why was she being so mean?

She turned back to Alex. "Um, actually, why don't I meet you there?" She needed a few minutes alone to collect her thoughts.

Alex nodded as he chewed, then raised a hand against the setting sun to look at her. "Deal."

•●•

It was kind of peaceful watching the Ferris wheel lights weave a stationary firework in the quickly darkening sky. Lola was clearly having the time of her life, whooping every time the wheel arched downward and completely oblivious to poor Robin, who had the dazed, almost saggy look of someone about to be sick.

After a few minutes, the Ferris wheel slowed and couples climbed out of their seats. Ellie motioned frantically for Rosalee to take the seat in front of her and Pete, but Rosalee pointed at her iced tea and shrugged sadly, feigning disappointment at her dilemma. Meanwhile, Robin clambered over the side of the railing and hurried to the nearest bench, where she sat with her head between her knees.

"You can put the drink *down* Rosalee," Ellie called, her eyes narrowed.

Rosalee smiled, shrugged, and took another sip of tea as the operator prepared to start the ride again.

"Hold on!"

Rosalee turned to see Alex running toward the ride, his hair ruffling in the breeze.

"Gettin' on?" said the operator.

"Yeah, just—if you could hold on *one* second."

Alex jogged back to where Rosalee was sitting and jabbed his hand into the space between them. "C'mon. You're gonna miss it."

Rosalee winced away from his hand. "I changed my mind. I think I just wanna watch it this time."

"'Something persuasive,'" said Alex.

"What?"

"Sometimes when I'm not sure what I want the next line in my screenplay to be but I have the basic idea, that's the kind of thing I'll write. So, 'something persuasive.'"

Rosalee hesitated.

"Rosalee, get your scrawny behind up here!" Lola shouted, provoking several chuckles from surrounding passengers.

Now, both of Alex's hands were extended—one toward Rosalee's hand and one toward her cup. She ignored both of them but set her drink down under the bench and followed him to the ride like a prisoner toward the gallows. She climbed into the open seat in front of Ellie and Pete and scooted as close to the edge as she could to avoid any unnecessary contact with Alex.

A lurch signaled the start of the ride and Rosalee could hear Lola shouting from her seat. "Wait, wait, Robin's not on!"

Rosalee looked around to see Robin shaking her head resolutely from her sideways position on the bench.

"Oh, go ahead, then," said Lola, disappointed.

Rosalee heard Alex laughing softly next to her before something made sharp contact with the back of her head.

"Ow, what the hell?" she demanded, turning to see Ellie lacing her skinny belt back into her dress. She widened her eyes at Rosalee in what she probably thought was an encouraging gesture.

Rosalee rubbed the spot on her head where the buckle had struck and threw her and Pete a dirty look before turning her back on them. She could feel Alex watching her.

"Still mad at me, huh?" he said.

"I don't know why I would be."

"But you are."

Rosalee sighed. "Yeah."

"I'm really sorry."

Alex reached for Rosalee's hand, but she sucked in a breath and yanked it away as they crested the top of the ride and began the sharp descent.

She clutched the bar in front of her. "Yikes."

"Yikes?" said Alex, "You don't like the Ferris wheel, do you?"

Rosalee pushed her hair away from her face as their seat moved backward and up again. "No, I love it." She realized as she said it that it was still true.

"You said 'yikes.'"

"It was a good 'yikes.'"

Alex laughed again. It was a nice laugh—sort of quiet and to himself.

As they began another downward arc, Rosalee could hear Lola whooping above her. She smiled and couldn't help silently whooping with her as the warm evening air rushed past.

"Do you know her?" said Alex.

"She's my aunt." Rosalee gathered her airborne tresses into a low ponytail and held it firmly over her shoulder "My other aunt is the one dry heaving on that bench."

"And you live with them?"

"For now."

"So, two sets of sisters. That's fun."

Rosalee shook her head. "Lola and Robin aren't sisters. Robin is our biological aunt. She found Lola a long time ago, brought her home to live in our garage, and that was it."

Alex cocked his head.

"*Converted* garage," Rosalee clarified. "We're not hillbillies."

Alex laughed again and Rosalee became absorbed in a stray thread on her shorts. She had already shared more than she meant to.

"You guys seem close," said Alex.

"We are." *Or* were, *anyway.*

"So, who's older—you or Ellie?"

"Me."

Alex raised his eyebrows. "Huh."

"Why?"

"Ellie seems pretty protective of you," he said, then faltered under Rosalee's suddenly accusatory stare. "Just—from—"

"Did you feel sorry for me?" said Rosalee. "Is that why ..." she motioned to the seat, the ride, the universe in general.

"What? *No.* I mean, I was sorry about the other day with your tree and I wanted you to ride with me because you were—"

"Alone? Isolated?" Rosalee felt her skin heat up as Alex scanned her face like an X-ray.

He nodded slowly. "Unprotected. Vulnerable. Easy prey, really." He raised his eyebrows at the look of repulsion crinkling Rosalee's nose. "Different," he said, rolling his eyes.

They looked at each other.

"Different," Rosalee repeated.

"I think it's cool that you push down all the bumps on your soda lid. I do that, too. I can't leave them alone."

Rosalee clicked her tongue. "Everyone does that."

"Alright fine, you caught me." Alex held his hands up in mock surrender. "I hate 'different.' Conformity all the way."

What was *with* this guy?

"What do you want from me?" said Rosalee.

"Pure, unrefined hatred. Radiating from your every pore until I'm cooked like a rotisserie chicken."

Rosalee felt the corner of her mouth twitch upward and quickly forced it back down. "What about the other day? Why were you lurking around your ashtray pretending to be my attorney?"

Their eyes met again and Rosalee looked away first, then stared at the seat in front of them. "Are you stalking me?"

Alex glanced between her and the seat, seemingly unsure about which of them she was addressing.

"No," he said slowly, "I told you—I was there for a job interview."

"Oh." *Right.* "So you got it, then?"

"I did. Do I scare you?"

Suddenly, Alex's eyes seemed to take on a different kind of concern than his apparent remorse about Rosalee's lingering anger. One of the lights above them shone on his face and Rosalee realized that his eyes were a warmer shade of brown than she had noticed before. They reminded her of the fancy, mahogany coffee table in Angela's sitting room, ages ago. They were also full of something all too familiar to her, although she couldn't quite identify what it was.

Did he scare her?

Rosalee tuned in to the little voice inside her and finally shook her head.

"Good," Alex said softly.

He sat back, studying her from under a piece of hair that fell just above his eyelashes and she was suddenly very aware of herself. She turned away from him and prepared to get out of her seat.

"One more time!" someone yelled above them.

Before Rosalee had a chance to escape, the ride lurched into motion and she was hurled backward into her seat. "A little warning would have been nice!" she complained to no one in particular.

She tilted her head back and glared at the seat above her. Then several things happened at once: First, a gust of wind came out of nowhere, once more blowing her hair all around her. Then, a sharp pain zinged through her skull as one of the loose strands caught in something next to their car and began to pull.

That was about the time she started screaming.

She struggled to rip her hair loose, but was jerked sideways against her seat. She could feel little fiery pops as her hair follicles disconnected themselves from her scalp at the roots.

"Stop the ride!" Alex shouted.

Rosalee heard the command echoed several times around her. Then the gondola lurched as Alex lunged across her. His fingers combed quickly through her hair to find the section that was ensnared. Then, with one swift movement, she was free and gasping into her knees.

She stayed that way for several long moments, desperate to keep herself from sobbing in front of a mostly complete stranger.

"Hey." Alex nudged her gently with his shoulder. "Time to get off."

Rosalee jerked, then straightened slowly, readying herself for the piteous looks from fellow passengers. "Hey," she said, orienting herself. "We're still at the top. We're not even moving."

"I know. I thought you might want a minute. You know, to—"

"Right." Rosalee wiped under her eyes with her thumbs, then swept her hair over her shoulder again.

"We're good!" Alex yelled down to the operator.

Rosalee inspected her handful of hair, expecting a giant, knotted mess. Instead, a long, half-inch wide chunk seemed to have been sliced clean off.

Alex opened his hand, revealing a Swiss Army knife. "It was caught in the, uh … trunnion. I figured quick was better. Sorry."

"No, it's okay." Rosalee thought she might be in shock. "Thank you."

"No sweat. Are you okay?"

Rosalee shrugged as her lungs stopped a full breath. "How many people saw that, do you think?"

She glanced at Alex, who was looking distinctly put on the spot, as though she had asked him to please recite the Pledge of Allegiance in Mandarin. Then there it was—unbidden laughter making its way up Rosalee's throat. Alex paused, confused.

"I—don't—know," Rosalee gasped, helpless against the mirth that had her bent double.

Alex chuckled. "Adrenaline, I guess."

Rosalee laughed all the way down.

Chapter 5

"**B**reakfaaast," Ellie sang, flouncing into Rosalee's room and hopping onto the end of her bed.

Rosalee squinted against the bright sunlight streaming through her window.

"You made breakfast?" she croaked.

"No, Laurie's made breakfast. C'mon."

Rosalee groaned and rolled onto her stomach, burying her face in her pillow. She was vaguely aware of Ellie's weight disappearing from the mattress as she drifted off again, before the unmistakable sound of her sister digging through her closet startled her awake once more.

"Time's a-wastin'!" Ellie dropped a top on Rosalee's bed, then moved over to her dresser. "Where are those shorts from last night?"

Rosalee snuggled deeper into her pillow without answering and felt another piece of clothing add itself to her covers. Then it was quiet.

"Up!"

"Argh," Rosalee grumbled, rolling onto her side, seriously misjudging the edge of her bed, and toppling onto the floor.

"Thank you." Ellie came around to where Rosalee lay tangled in her sheets. She held up her newly altered cutoffs (even though Rosalee had stuffed them behind her hamper the night before) and a lacy top.

Rosalee stumbled into a semi-standing position. "No."

Ellie pursed her lips. "Why not? I thought you liked the shorts."

Rosalee dodged her sister, kicking her sheets from around her ankles as she went. She shuffled quickly into Robin and Lola's room and crawled between them on their bed, shoving her head under one of the pillows. She didn't care if it was childish. Sleep was sleep and she loved it.

"Save me," she muttered. "Save me from The Ellie."

Robin chuckled and rolled onto her back, eyes still closed. Lola patted Rosalee's arm sympathetically. "What time is it?"

"I don't know," said Rosalee, her voice muffled by the mattress.

Ellie appeared in the doorway with an armful of Rosalee's T-shirts. "We're throwing these away. I don't even think a thrift store would take them."

Rosalee emerged from the pillow to glare at her. "I was going to wear that one to breakfast."

"Which one?"

"... All of them."

"Aunt Robin, this is *your* doing," said Ellie, sweeping out of the room again.

Robin yawned and stretched, planting her bare feet on the wood floor and rubbing the sleep out of her eyes as Lola wandered into the master bath closet.

Several moments later, Lola threw an unfamiliar piece of clothing at Rosalee. "Get a move on, girlie. If we don't leave in the next half hour, Robin and I won't be able to drop you off on the way."

Rosalee sat up. "On the way to what?"

"That loan officer at First Federal agreed to see us at nine o'clock about the B&B," said Robin.

"Oh, good." Rosalee unfolded the garment Lola had thrown at her and was pleasantly surprised to find a T-shirt. Not any of *her*

T-shirts—this one was teal and a v-neck—but not bad. "Where did this come from?"

"It's mine," said Lola. "I think it even fit me once. Yours if you want it."

—••—

Rosalee and Ellie waved as their aunts departed for their meeting, then made their way up the long driveway leading to Laurie's Cafe and Lakeside Restaurant.

About three-quarters of the way up, Rosalee stopped. Suddenly, the thought of being surrounded by people and their questions, in an enclosed space, seemed unendurable. At least at the picnic, they had been outside.

"You okay?" Ellie called, having reached the top of the drive without her.

"Yeah." Rosalee thought her voice sounded far away, even inside her head.

Ellie walked back down the drive to meet her, flip-flops slapping against the asphalt. "Do you wanna sit on the bench for a few minutes? Or the dock?"

Rosalee nodded toward the latter and they walked to the end of the pier, then sat with their toes dangling in the cool water. Rosalee watched the reflections of boats bobbing up and down in the glassy surface of the lake, surrounded by the fluttering yellow-green leaves of aspen trees.

Ellie followed her gaze. "Pete and I were gonna come back here and hang out on the shore later today. It's supposed to get up to eighty-two degrees."

"Jeez, already? I mean, about the temperature."

Ellie nodded. "Do you want to come with us?"

Rosalee hesitated.

"You don't have to," Ellie said quickly, tucking a stray curl behind her ear and looking back across the lake.

"No, I want to. But ... why are you being so nice to me?"

"What do you mean?"

"Just ... all the crappy things I said to you before I left? I thought maybe you would still be mad."

"Oh. Well, did you mean them?"

"Of course not. I was just ... *so* angry."

Ellie shrugged. "I knew that."

Was it really that simple?

"I'm still sorry."

"I know that, too."

Ellie offered a tiny smile, but something palpable still hung in the air between them.

"But?" Rosalee prompted.

Ellie glanced sideways at her. "I just ... wish I had known every-thing."

"Everything?"

"Like what you were thinking, what you were feeling ... what you were taking."

Rosalee stiffened. "What do you mean?"

Ellie stared straight ahead, kicking at the water and sending the spray arcing over the surface of the lake. "Where did you even get those pills?"

So she knew. Now there was no way around it.

"Um ... Connor Mitchell."

Ellie finally abandoned her tunnel vision and looked at Rosalee with an expression of overt revulsion. "What, from high school? Connor

Mitchell, who will forever work at the movie theater and reek of weed?"

"That's the one." Rosalee stared at her knees as she straightened them, then let her legs dangle again.

"God, is that why he called you so much?"

"Probably." She hoped her lying was getting better, but couldn't tell if her sister bought it.

"Why, though?" said Ellie. "I mean, why would you take them?"

"I didn't want to care about anything anymore. Or ... feel anything."

Ellie appeared to be chewing her tongue—a habit she only ever adopted when she was trying not to form angry words with it.

"What, El? Just say it."

Ellie clenched her jaw. "I don't want to fight."

"Well, maybe we need to."

Ellie shook her head and then looked over her shoulder, away from Rosalee.

"So then ... what do you wanna do?" said Rosalee.

Ellie stood up suddenly and brushed off the back of her shorts. "I want to eat. Something with a ton of calories and fat, and *waaay* too much chocolate."

She didn't turn to check if Rosalee was behind her, but Rosalee stood, too, following her sister back up the dock.

Thankfully, the usual Laurie's crowd seemed to have slept in. Rosalee and Ellie ordered a huge plate of chocolate chip pancakes and Rosalee hoped that it would have all the healing effects she had come to expect from such a breakfast.

"I'm sorry, Ellie," she said after she couldn't stand the silence anymore. "I never should have kept those things from you. I just wanted—"

"To protect me?"

"Well ... yeah."

"Thanks," Ellie said to the waitress who delivered their giant platter of pancakes and Ellie's orange juice.

"Thanks," Rosalee echoed.

Ellie frowned and dug her fork into the edge of the stack, then stared at the bite. "Have you done it since?"

Usually, she didn't press the subject of Rosalee leaving, but Rosalee realized that she was probably being very brave. Maybe she could be brave, too. She took a deep breath. "You mean since I've been back?"

"Yeah."

"No." Rosalee cleared her throat as her voice threatened to waver. "I guess I should have noticed the pills were gone, but I haven't really wanted to look."

Ellie chewed slowly, evidently pondering. "I guess that's good. So, did it help you? Going away?"

"Yeah, it totally did. I mean don't I seem ... better?"

"I guess it's hard to tell. Everyone's been a little off ... since Evelyn—"

"Right." Rosalee paused to take a sip of ice water and winced as it hit her teeth.

Ellie cut into another chocolatey edge of pancake with her fork, then let the bite hover over her plate. "I missed you, ya know?"

Rosalee wrestled with the lump in her throat. "I know. Me, too."

"Were you really mad at Aunties, or ... all of us? For sending you away?"

"At first. When it felt like you didn't want to deal with me anymore."

"That was never why."

Ellie put down her fork and put her hand lightly over Rosalee's. Rosalee flinched but fought the urge to yank it away. She blinked rapidly and looked up at the ceiling. "So, I guess you found my stash. You didn't … *take* any of them, did you?"

"I thought about it. Just to understand you a little better." Ellie moved her hand from Rosalee's to brush her bangs out of her eyes. "But no, I didn't."

Rosalee nodded, unsure of what else to say but relieved beyond measure. Ellie seemed relieved, too, and Rosalee watched as her usual effervescence gradually returned.

"I can't believe this still works," Ellie said, tucking into the pancakes with new enthusiasm.

Rosalee wiped her eyes with her napkin. "What does?"

"Chocolate chip pancakes. They're, like, magic."

Rosalee grinned across the table and Ellie snorted into her plate.

"What?" said Rosalee.

Ellie shook her head and dragged her bite of pancake through a puddle of maple syrup she had poured on her side of the plate. Rosalee quickly swiped at her nose with the back of her hand, feeling paranoid. She picked at the pancake stack with her fork, throwing occasional dirty looks at Ellie, who continued to snigger.

"Now *that* is what I call breakfast."

Rosalee started, then promptly gagged as she realized she was eye-level with Alex Conway's very-toned-through-his-shirt abdominal region.

"Hi, Alex!" Ellie said, waving a chocolatey fork.

Rosalee was still distracted by the food blocking her windpipe. After a few good coughs, she grimaced at Alex and brushed her hair out of her face, taking in his apron and bus tub. "So you work here, too?" *Fantastic.*

Alex stared at her. Rosalee stared back, then glanced sideways at her sister.

"What?"

"You have … something," said Alex, the corner of his mouth twitching.

Rosalee glared at her sister, then wiped randomly at her face, all the while wishing the bottom would drop out of her seat and through the restaurant floor.

Ever the happy helper, Alex grabbed a napkin out of the dispenser on the table. "Here, hold still a sec."

"No thanks, I got it." Rosalee ducked under his arm and pushed past him toward the restroom.

Once inside, she turned the lock and dropped the tear-stained napkin she was still clutching into the wastebasket. She ran her hands under cold water and glanced in the mirror, and that's when she noticed the thin line of chocolate all the way around her mouth—like badly applied lip liner.

"Figures," Rosalee said to her reflection.

She wiped all traces of food and tears from her face, then dried her hands the rest of the way on her shorts. Her first day back at Laurie's in months and she already had a new reason to avoid it. She waited a good five minutes before reemerging from the bathroom and was relieved to find that Alex had migrated to another vicinity of the restaurant in her absence.

She plopped down across from Ellie again. "Well, that was *awesome.*"

"Sorry. I would've told you sooner if I'd known he was here."

Ellie looked far more repentant than Rosalee wanted her to, especially considering the emotional hurdles they had so recently cleared.

"It's fine. It's not a big deal," she said.

Still, Ellie continued to look apprehensive, swirling the remaining juice around the bottom of her glass.

"El, what?"

"I kind of ... told Alex about the movie thing tomorrow night—please-don't-hurt-me," said Ellie, cowering in her seat.

Rosalee imagined cement blocks forming around her feet as she stared at her sister. "You *what?*"

"I'm sorry! I didn't know what else to do because he asked me what we were doing tomorrow and I said we were going. Plus he's Pete's roommate, so I didn't want to be rude."

Rosalee took a calming breath and a deep swallow of ice water before folding her arms in front of her and looking across the table. "El, aren't you back at school tomorrow night?"

Ellie stared back at Rosalee for a moment before sudden realization made her eyes widen again.

Rosalee groaned and laid her forehead against the smooth wood top of the table, keeping it there until the waitress came over with the bill.

Chapter 6

As eight o'clock approached the next evening and the sun sank below the horizon, Rosalee squinted against its final rays to appreciate her surroundings. The light filtering through the clouds made them bright flamingo pink, juxtaposed against a navy sky and mountain peaks of deepest plum. She opened her eyes as wide as possible to take it all in until they watered ... then tripped over a wooden trail marker before she had looked her fill.

Lola reached out to steady her. "Easy there, space cadet. You okay?"

"Yeah." Rosalee drew her attention back to her feet, as well as her trepidation for the evening ahead. She sighed heavily and continued to lead the way down to the barn, where a massive white tarp had been draped on one side for the festivities.

"Why the long face?" said Robin. "You were the one who suggested this movie."

"I know, I know." *That was before Ellie and her big mouth.* Rosalee stopped abruptly and Robin nearly walked into her. "Where are the chairs?"

Rosalee looked from the makeshift movie screen to the projector several hundred feet back from the barn, and the long stretch of bare lawn in between.

"Honey, why did you think you were carrying the picnic blanket?" said Lola, looking a little worried.

Rosalee glanced down at the bundle in her arms. "Right."

"*Oh ma gawd,* is that the gentleman from the Ferris wheel?"

Rosalee looked up, startled, then turned to shush Lola, who had apparently stopped being worried and adopted her favorite Southern accent. In fact, it wasn't far from the one her niece had used not even a week before. Lola fluttered her eyelashes at Rosalee and fanned herself with her pamphlet.

"I'll leave right now, don't think I won't," Rosalee hissed.

Lola snickered, leaning in closer to her. "He's looking at you."

Rosalee batted her away. "Quit it. You two find us a spot."

She had hoped that she wouldn't have to talk to Alex at all. It wasn't like Ellie had invited him to watch the movie *with* them—she only reported that it was happening. Still, it felt a little too rude to ignore him completely when they had so openly spotted each other. With that in mind, Rosalee took a deep breath that never quite reached the middle of her lungs and forced her leg muscles to cooperate with the forward motion that her brain reluctantly suggested. Alex, of course, did nothing to slow the inevitable but hastened to meet her.

"Hello," Rosalee heard herself say when she reached him.

She was relieved to find that the green, plaid shirt he wore over a white T-shirt was far less distracting than his Laurie's uniform.

"Hello." Alex smiled in a sort of self-satisfied way that made Rosalee very tempted to roll her eyes. Instead, she turned her attention to a black, marble-patterned notebook with red duct tape on the spine, which he held in one hand.

"What's that?"

"Notes," Alex said quickly. She noticed his fingers twitch compulsively, as though afraid she might tear it out of his grip. Then he shook his head. "I don't know why I said that. It's a movie I'm writing."

Rosalee felt a faint flutter of interest through her stubbornness but quickly smothered the impulse to ask any follow-up questions.

"Do you like movies?" said Alex.

"Not really."

Rosalee wasn't sure why she was lying, except that she was definitely not in the mood for a date, which was usually the only reason boys ever asked you if you were interested in movies. Meanwhile, Alex looked like he had been sucker-punched in the gut and was trying valiantly to ignore it.

Rosalee decided to take advantage of the momentary silence. "So, I wanted to thank you for the other night. I'm really grateful not to have had my neck snapped."

Alex blinked. "I'm grateful, too. That would have been unsettling ... and gross." His mouth twitched like he was trying not to laugh.

"What?" said Rosalee, a little more sharply than she intended.

"Why are you being so formal?"

"I'm not. I just thought I should come thank you. So, *thank you.*"

"That's a lot of 'thank-yous' so far. Wouldst thou like to sit down?"

"No." Rosalee shifted uncomfortably, wishing she hadn't tied her boots so tight. "No, I'm gonna go sit with my Robin ... and my ... Lola."

"Hey, don't run away," said Alex, "I want you to meet someone."

Rosalee grimaced.

"C'mon, it'll be fun." Alex shoved his notebook under one arm and grabbed her elbow to steer her before Rosalee sucked in a breath and yanked her arm out of his grip.

"Sorry, I'm sorry," said Alex as Rosalee cringed away from him. "I get a little overenthusiastic sometimes. But I promise you'll like this. Really."

Rosalee sighed, tilting her head back so that her long hair brushed the top of her waistband. Alex waited patiently for her to finish her mini-tantrum, then smiled and started walking.

Before long, they came upon a group of professional-looking people and Rosalee couldn't help but feel a tad inferior in her casual getup. As they approached, a woman in a fancy blouse and French roll hairdo looked up in recognition and flashed Alex a smile as bright as the delicate pearls dangling from her earlobes.

"Mr. Conway," she said, as the rest of her colleagues turned to acknowledge them politely. "I'm so glad you made it."

"I would never pass up an opportunity to learn about native birds of the Rocky Mountain region," said Alex. Rosalee wondered if his apparent enthusiasm was just show, or if he meant it—*not that she cared.* "By the way, this is my friend, Rosalee."

Rosalee felt her face growing hot as she smiled and grasped hands with Ms. FancyBlouse (she had already forgotten her real name out of sheer panic) and her colleagues.

"Rosalee is an amazing artist," said Alex. "She's practically painted this whole town."

"Is that right?" FancyBlouse looked interested.

"I don't know about that," said Rosalee.

She tried not to look too surprised or stare at Alex too hard. Did decorative cutting boards and TV trays scattered around Rabbitbrush really count as "painting the whole town"? And would it kill him to let her in on his plans, *just once?*

"Well, you know," said FancyBlouse, "Mr. West (She indicated the fancy man next to her.) and I have been scouring the state for someone to paint a mural in the new children's wing of Picket General. Would you be interested in submitting some of your work?"

"Oh. Wow," said Rosalee, "Yes, I would love that."

Now, Alex was smiling a little too widely as FancyBlouse gave Rosalee a business card and instructions for her submissions. As Rosalee and Alex thanked her and walked away, Rosalee felt a little like her legs wouldn't support her and didn't realize that Alex was talking to her until he stopped and raised his eyebrows.

"Sorry," she said, gradually resurfacing. "I can't believe that actually happened."

"Are you excited? I mean, you seem excited."

Rosalee stopped, her earlier questions catching up with her. "How did you know that I paint? I'm sure I never told you that."

"No, you didn't. Pete did. I saw that painting you did for his birthday."

"Oh ..." Rosalee racked her brain for a second. "Oh, you mean the farm landscape? God, that had to have been six years ago."

"Well, it must mean a lot to him—it's right over his desk."

"... I hadn't noticed."

In fact, she couldn't remember the last time she had seen Pete's desk. Eighth grade for their history project couldn't possibly be the most recent memory.

"So, I guess I should let you get back to your aunts." Alex gestured toward Lola and Robin, who had found an excellent spot near the front and were lounging on the blanket.

"Where are you sitting?" said Rosalee before she could stop herself.

"Uh, it looks like they've already set up behind the projector." Alex shook his head and waved as a flashlight beam swiveled in their direction. "I'll make sure to confiscate that before the movie starts and make him sit on his hands."

"Who's 'they'?"

"Oh. Just my coworker." Alex shoved the hand that wasn't cradling his notebook into his front pocket. "I misspoke."

He looked suddenly uncomfortable and Rosalee felt her inhibition sidling in. Her feet were already pointed in the direction of her aunts, so she started to move that way, prompting Alex to lift a hand in farewell before walking in the opposite direction.

"Hey ... Alex?"

He turned back.

"Thanks," said Rosalee. "Thank you. *Really*. For ..." She hooked a thumb over her shoulder, where the fancy folks still stood.

"Yeah, no sweat." Alex thumped his notebook lightly against his palm and appeared to suppress a smug look with effort. "Enjoy the rest of your night."

"Oh, sure. You, too."

— • —

Rosalee tried to pay attention to the movie and give coherent whispered responses to Lola's incessant questions, but despite her best efforts and the numerous things that could have occupied her thoughts, they kept circling back to the eighth grade.

— • —

The next day, Rosalee stood in front of Pete and Alex's apartment for at least five minutes before summoning the courage to knock tentatively on the aluminum storm door. By then, she was almost hoping that Pete wouldn't be home and more afraid that Alex would be. But almost immediately, she heard the floorboards creaking toward the front door and Pete answered in jeans and a button-down shirt. His face betrayed a flicker of surprise, but he seemed happy to see her.

"Hey, Pete. Am I interrupting anything?"

"Not at all," he said, stepping aside to let her in. "I was just putting some things away."

Rosalee followed him into the kitchen of the two-bedroom apartment, trying to soak up as much detail as possible to make up for lost time. Her eyes traveled over the pine finish of the wainscoting and the grey and white striped wallpaper that reached the ceiling. She marveled at the spotless condition of the white laminate countertops and then remembered that she was at Pete's.

"What are you listening to?" she said, picking up a CD next to his answering machine. "Sarah McLachlan? Wow, Pete, you *have* changed."

"It's Ellie's," Pete said quickly. "She thinks I need to relax."

"Well, I can't argue there. What are you making her listen to?"

"The Smiths."

"Attaboy. Although she's going to tell you they're depressing."

The corner of Pete's mouth lifted briefly. "I could say the same about her choice. Do you want something to drink?"

"Water would be great, thanks."

Rosalee sat down on one of the bar stools as Pete took a glass out of the cupboard and filled it at the sink.

"So, Alex told me about the mural," he said, sliding the water across the counter to Rosalee. "You must be excited."

"Excited, nervous ... dying inside."

"Sounds about right."

"Speaking of which," said Rosalee, "I was, um ... I was wondering if I could borrow the painting I did for you? Of the farm? I need to take a picture of it for my submission."

"Oh, sure. I'll get it right now."

When Pete returned several seconds later, Rosalee couldn't help staring at the canvas. "I can't believe how long ago this was. It's like we're completely different people now."

Rosalee watched as Pete made his way back around the counter, tidying things as he went.

"Pete," she said tentatively, "Does it feel ... *weird* between us now?"

He paused his straightening and braced himself against the counter to look at her. "I guess a little."

Rosalee nodded and took a tiny sip of water, tucking her chin to keep it from sliding down the wrong pipe. "I think that's mostly my fault ... I'm sorry."

Pete hesitated for a moment before rounding the counter again and sitting on the other bar stool, facing Rosalee.

"I'm not mad or anything," he said, his grey eyes still more guarded than Rosalee liked. "And after ... everything ... I get it."

Rosalee shifted her attention to her hands clasped in her lap. "You're so different around me. Somehow."

Pete nodded and ran his palms up and down his jeans. Maybe Rosalee wasn't the only one who was nervous. "I wish you could have talked to me," he said finally. "I didn't think there was anything we couldn't talk about."

"I wanted to. I *really* wanted to. I just couldn't. I'm sorry, Pete."

"Sorry" seemed to be all she was lately. Maybe she should make it into a T-shirt.

Pete shrugged. "You're here now, right?"

"Right."

Pete smiled the first real smile Rosalee had seen the whole visit before walking to the cupboard and bringing out a large Ziploc bag containing an open package of Fig Newtons. He removed the package and pushed it toward Rosalee on the counter.

"Thanks," she said, plucking a cookie from its crackly plastic slot. "Although I'm supposed to be cutting out wheat ..." She stared at the cookie for a moment, then shrugged, biting off a corner.

"Is that supposed to help?" said Pete. "Cutting out wheat, I mean?"

"And dairy, according to Robin's newest hippie dippy book. But I blew it with all that food at the picnic the other night, anyway. And pancakes the other day ... oh well. Aren't you having one?"

"Oh, no, I just had—"

"—two with lunch." Rosalee smiled. "How could I forget?"

Pete smiled, too, and came to sit next to her at the counter again. Rosalee looked at him thoughtfully. "You know, if I eat mine, your count's gonna be off."

Pete paused to consider this. As Rosalee had learned early on, he wasn't a big fan of odd numbers. He sighed and fished another cookie out of the package, tapping it against Rosalee's before popping it into his mouth. "Cheers."

"Cheers." Rosalee finished hers, as well. "So, how's the bank?"

"Good. I finish my loan training soon, so that's ..." Pete brushed a stray crumb off of his jeans. "Well, it's not exactly *exciting,* but it's where I was headed."

"Pete, that's awesome. Really, that's great. We should celebrate."

"Oh, I don't know." He shook his head, but Rosalee thought he looked pleased. "Maybe if I actually get the promotion. By the way, I saw Lola and Robin talking to Sharon about their bed and breakfast on Saturday."

"Yeah, they're really excited about it. They wanted to talk about it with me and Ellie as soon as Robin gets home tonight."

"Good."

"Definitely."

Rosalee couldn't believe how much she missed talking to Pete. How many other parts of her life had slipped past without her noticing? They eventually ran out of small talk, but she decided that that was okay for today.

Baby steps.

That was all she could ask of anyone right now, including herself.

Chapter 7

Rosalee had three favorite smells in the world: burning leaves curling into a crackling fire, lavender hand cream, and freshly cut lemons. The third one was the main reason that getting up at five forty-five in the morning to work at The Goose wasn't completely nauseating.

Rosalee checked the clock over the back deli counter and tossed the ends of a lemon rind into a compost bucket next to the trash. Somehow, it was already six thirty, which meant that she only had another half hour before the store opened and daily customers infiltrated her otherwise peaceful morning of brewing coffee for the bakery, replenishing various department supplies, and restocking shelves. She usually liked to organize the majority of her department duties so that by the time eleven AM rolled around and business was in full swing, she could hole up in the grocery department and bury herself in orders.

By eleven fifteen, she was halfway through pricing a soup delivery when Robin backed in through the swinging door with a hand truck.

"Hey," said Rosalee, sweeping her hair off of her neck and twisting it into a messy bun with the elastic around her wrist. She hadn't realized she was so warm until the air from the open door hit her damp skin.

Robin surveyed the sea of orders stacked around the room before motioning for Rosalee to stand up. "Switch with me."

Rosalee turned to hide her face as she lifted the next box of soups off of the pallet. "I'm okay."

"You're going to overdo it." Robin stepped over several boxes of salad dressings and jerked her head toward the crackers and tea at the other end of the room.

"Fine," Rosalee muttered, although secretly, she was relieved.

She knew the boxes were too heavy. She knew that. But somehow, the only way she could feel less guilty about not moving them was if someone else knew that, too. She switched places with Robin and took a box cutter out of her back pocket to free the crackers from their generous layer of Saran wrap.

"There's too much plastic on this planet," she grumbled, hacking through it like an explorer through the jungle.

"Don't I know it," Robin agreed. "I'm trying to work with more local suppliers."

"Well, that's something."

Rosalee bundled the wrap into a tight ball and shoved it as far down into the garbage can as it would go.

Robin sat back on her heels. "Well, it *could* be something, but then Monday comes again and I remember that I was too lazy to actually make the calls and the plans, and then here we are again."

"Well, you've had a lot on your plate. Also, you might be the *least* lazy person I've ever met. Huh." Rosalee stopped as the word sparked a memory. "What was that thing Aunt Evelyn used to say?"

Rosalee glanced over at her aunt pricing the cans of soup and stacking them on the hand truck. She watched Robin's mouth tighten and hated herself for bringing up the subject. *Too soon.* She turned back to the crackers and set about swiveling the number knobs on the price gun, all the while racking her brain for another topic.

"Something about an ass," said Robin, pausing with one hand on her hip.

Rosalee looked up again and felt the knot in her stomach loosen slightly as Robin tapped a cardboard box with her fingertips, thinking.

"Oh!" said Rosalee, "Oh, it was … 'that kind of busy makes for an ass like a flapjack.' Or something."

"Yeah, well …" Robin smiled as she resumed pricing. "She had a way with words, my sister."

"Yeah, she did." Rosalee wondered when thinking about Evelyn wouldn't make her chest ache.

"So, when do you hear about the mural?"

Rosalee felt a surge of anxiety as she began to pile newly priced cracker boxes into a shopping cart. "I don't know, hopefully sometime this week."

"You nervous?"

"About getting it or not?"

"Both."

"… Yes."

Robin stacked her last can of soup and looked over at Rosalee. "I bet you get it."

"Maybe. I didn't even ask you, though—is it okay if I take a couple hours a week off here?"

"Oh, yeah, it's fine. A little change of scenery would probably be good for you."

Rosalee felt her grip slip on the box she was holding and nearly dropped it as she overcompensated. Hadn't she just gotten *back* from a change of scenery? It suddenly struck her that maybe Ellie wasn't the only member of her family questioning whether her time away had been beneficial.

She decided to change the subject. "That Snapple order for Laurie's came in about an hour ago. I told them to put it in the produce cooler for now. Not much room in here."

"Oh, good, good."

Robin seemed to have retreated into her head and Rosalee wondered if she was just distracted, or trying to figure out how to pursue the "change of scenery" topic further.

Rosalee glanced at the clock behind Robin and pretended to be surprised. "Wow. Didn't realize how long I'd been back here. Guess I better check on the cashiers soon."

"They're okay—we're not too busy today. And as soon as you're done with the payroll this afternoon, you can head on home. Nel is closing tonight, so I'll be right behind you."

"Okay. Wow, it's weird to have nights off during the week."

Robin nodded and smiled vaguely as Rosalee made her escape.

———— •●• ————

As Rosalee moved on to the tea and spice orders, then slogged through payroll, she had to keep rechecking her math. Her family wouldn't really send her away again ... *would they?* She thought she had been doing so much better lately, but maybe from the outside, there hadn't been enough of a change.

She finally resigned herself to the fact that she couldn't think about it anymore as she wobbled precariously on a rickety wooden ladder braced against the counter by the cash registers.

"Hey, how's it going?"

Rosalee jumped and nearly lost her footing, but someone reached out to steady the ladder just in time, apologizing profusely with a voice that was almost familiar now. She let out a forceful breath as adrenaline coursed through her body, then brushed a few stray strands of hair out of her face while Alex Conway looked up at her expectantly.

"How's it going?" he said again.

Rosalee pointed over her head. "I'm changing a light bulb."

"Cool," said Alex. "Are you free soon?"

"I—what?"

"For lunch. Could you be free for lunch? I mean, I thought we could ..."

"Oh. Um ..."

Rosalee's brain was making very slow work of inventing excuses. Alex continued to look up at her with a hopeful expression.

"Yes," she said carefully. "Yes, I can be free for lunch. In a while."

You owe him your life, Rosalee. And the mural. Maybe.

Alex grinned. "You could sound a little more excited."

"Sorry."

"Maybe lunch will cheer you up. I'll be outside."

Rosalee glared at the ceiling and then glanced over at one of the cashiers, who was shuffling receipts into a neat pile. The cashier secured the stack with a paperclip and winked as she caught her eye. They both watched Alex walk out to the picnic area in front of the store and Rosalee wondered how long she could possibly drag out returning the ladder to the storage closet.

By the time Rosalee joined Alex at his table, he was already finished with his lunch and painstakingly picking the seeds out of an apple core.

"Hi," he said as Rosalee sat down.

"Hi."

Rosalee watched him and debated asking what he was doing, but that would be pretty friendly, so instead, she unscrewed the top off of her bottle of water and drank deeply, not realizing that she hadn't stopped for a break all morning.

"Busy day today?" said Alex.

"I guess so. Mostly orders."

Alex nodded. "So, how long have you worked here?"

"Um ... forever, I guess. Robin owns the store, so ..."

In fact, Rosalee had worked at The Gooseberry Patch (AKA "The Goose") since she was fifteen years old—the same age as Robin in 1961. Back then, Robin had tagged along with Evelyn, who worked at The Goose as a cashier during her breaks from college. At first, Robin had only been allowed to bag and carry out groceries and break down boxes, but by the time she graduated college herself, she was a pro in every department.

In her early twenties, Robin left the store and Rabbitbrush to work at IBM in Boulder but moved back in her mid-thirties and eventually bought The Goose. She had been running it ever since and Rosalee had been promoted to assistant manager several years before. For the most part, she was content there.

"Well, I like it," said Alex. "It's so different from other grocery stores. Cozy, or homey or something. Maybe it's the colors."

"Yeah, maybe ..."

"Cozy" was precisely the argument Rosalee had used to convince Robin to let her repaint the store two summers ago, in a PowerPoint presentation that had taken her a week to prepare. She could definitely kill some time telling Alex about that if she wanted to. He would probably even be interested in the history of The Goose.

Instead, she took a Tupperware bowl and fork out of her paper lunch sack and set them down in front of her. "I don't know what to talk about," she said.

"Ask me anything. Let's get to know each other."

"Why?" Rosalee realized too late that that was probably rude.

"Humor me." Alex flashed another grin that caught her momentarily off guard.

Rosalee frowned.

"You're so full of sunshine," said Alex. "Sometimes I can't take it."

Rosalee rolled her eyes. "I'm not a mean person, you know. I'm just not used to playing Twenty Questions every time I see someone. You *make* me be mean to you."

"Or maybe I make you nervous."

"Excuse you?"

"You heard me."

Alex took his eyes off the apple core long enough to study the effect of his words.

Rosalee wasn't going to take the bait.

If she was the old Rosalee—the one right before she left—she probably would have. She would have done her signature hair toss and watched Alex's eyes linger too long on the places where it fell. Then maybe they would have gone behind the store and shared a cigarette and—

Stop.

Rosalee dragged herself back to the present and watched as a light breeze tousled Alex's hair. Then the breeze turned into a gust, sending her empty lunch bag skidding across the table. She pinned it under her elbow, then winced.

"What are you doing?" she said, gesturing toward Alex's handiwork and trying to ignore the throbbing in her funny bone.

"I wanted to plant the seeds." Alex's tongue was between his teeth as he pried out a particularly stubborn one.

"Well, you can't just stick them in the ground."

Alex got the seed free at last and added it to the tiny pile in front of him, then looked at Rosalee.

"I mean, have you thought about how the cross-pollination is going to happen?" she said.

Alex shrugged. "I guess not."

"Well, it's complicated."

Rosalee smoothed the paper bag flat and set her lunch firmly on top of it.

"Maybe you can teach me," said Alex.

Crap. She hadn't bargained on that backfiring.

Alex wrapped his napkin around the seeds and stood to shove the bundle into his front pocket and that's when Rosalee saw it—a thin and jagged scar puckering the skin inside of his wrist. The line was bright red and didn't look very old. He probably wouldn't mind if she asked about it, but what was the point? They weren't friends.

Alex sat down again and watched as Rosalee prized the lid off of her Tupperware.

"What's for lunch?" he said.

"Salad."

"That's way more vegetables than I've ever seen in a salad."

"Well, what kind of salads do *you* eat?"

Alex smirked. "I knew you knew how to do this."

"Do what?"

"Be friends."

Rosalee pursed her lips in annoyance.

"And I like Caesar," said Alex. "Preferably with chicken."

Rosalee shook her head and poked at a piece of spinach with her fork. "That's not salad. It's basically a sandwich."

Alex leaned back on one leg of his chair. "Mmm-*mm*. Just the way I like it."

Rosalee tsked. "So are you off already? From work?"

"No, but I get an hour for lunch and it doesn't really matter when I take it."

Great. Rosalee didn't like the idea of this becoming a habit.

"Don't worry," said Alex, reading her expression before she could wipe it off her face, "This isn't a frequent stop. I had to pick up the Snapple order."

"I didn't mean—"

"It's cool, I know you're a loner. Lone wolf."

Rosalee supposed she shouldn't be surprised by that assessment.

"What's that song?" said Alex.

The question didn't seem to be directed at Rosalee, so she didn't answer. Alex screwed up his face and muttered to himself for a minute, beating his fist lightly on the tabletop. "Lone wolf. Lone-iest wolf," he said, then looked at her. "C'mon, you know it. Duran Duran? Something about a wolf?"

The song title floated into Rosalee's head almost immediately and she blinked in surprise. She wasn't used to things coming so easily anymore.

"Well, I hate to break it to you, but that wolf wasn't '*lone-y,*'" she said.

"Oh, so now you're just not going to tell me what it is?"

"No, I think I like it better this way."

"*Ugh.*" Alex pitched forward on the table in a mock fit of frustration.

Rosalee smiled in spite of herself.

Chapter 8

By five forty-five on Wednesday morning, tempers in Rosalee's household were running high and rampant.

"Look, I'm just gonna walk to the store," Rosalee called down the hall, where Lola and Robin were still bickering in their bedroom. A walk would be a nice prequel to the chaos of the coming workday.

Lola stormed out of the bedroom so quickly that Rosalee had to flatten herself against the wall. "You don't have to walk, Rosalee. We just need to convince your aunt that it's not the end of the world if she's ten minutes late."

Rosalee followed her down the stairs as Robin hurtled past both of them and into the kitchen, snatching her keys off the counter.

"I told you we needed to be out the door by five thirty so that I could drop you off, then come back and pick up Rosalee. I did not say 'Please be in the shower by five thirty so that we can be *fifteen* minutes late.'"

Rosalee was extremely reluctant to let her aunts' bad moods make her day any more unpleasant than she already anticipated and took a calming breath before repeating herself. "I'm walking now, *goodbye.*"

"It's going to be a hundred degrees by the time you get off, Rosalee," Robin snapped. "You can't walk home in that."

"I'll be fine," said Rosalee, gritting her teeth. "Besides, I would have had to walk anyway—I'm not gonna ride your motorcycle home."

Rosalee noticed a muscle in Robin's eye twitch as she watched Lola slowly pour coffee into a travel mug. "I'll give you a ride and then head back to the store."

"Well, Jesus, I'm not an invalid," said Rosalee.

"Honey, no one said you were," said Lola. "Robin was just—"

"Look, I'll take my bike, okay?" Rosalee yanked the door to the garage open and jabbed at the button on the wall to trigger the automatic door. "It's faster, so I won't be out that long."

The garage door opened jerkily to reveal gradual strips of daylight and Rosalee squinted against them to look for her bike. She found it in all its dusty glory, leaning against the lawn mower.

"Oh, for god's sake, that thing probably doesn't even have air in the tires," said Robin from the doorway.

Rosalee ignored her, swinging one leg over the seat. She coasted down the driveway, letting the toes of her tennis shoes drag and scuff along the dirt.

"Rosalee, just hang tight for a few minutes," Lola called. "We'll be back in no time."

"See you guys later," Rosalee yelled over her shoulder before either of her aunts could call her back.

She was an *adult,* for god's sake.

—•❦•—

As it turned out, though, Rosalee's bike tires were flatter than Kansas.

While she walked her bike down a gravel path she was sure would be a shortcut to the store, she had to marvel at the racket she was making. In normal circumstances, the gravel crunching under her shoes would be nearly drowned out by the sounds of rustling grasses and leaves on the trees, not to mention the birds calling to one another and the scuffle of squirrels' toes along the fences that lined the path. But today, here she was, plodding along next to tires relentlessly abraded by their wheels and squawking like two giant balloons mercilessly rubbed together. Rosalee alternated between hoping she wouldn't run into anyone she knew and hoping that she would—so long as the person that happened along was also carrying an air pump.

She hitched her backpack higher onto her shoulders and noticed that the fabric was already damp—it had to be close to seventy degrees already. It was lucky that she still even had this backpack because she couldn't remember the last time she'd used it. In the little front pouch, she had discovered a crumpled bookmark from a Scholastic book fair and a mechanical pencil she had likely borrowed from Pete in high school and apparently never given back (probably because she had chewed the eraser). She had also exhumed the remains of the sort of flower chains Ellie used to weave from clovers along the path to and from school while Angela thought up flamboyant poster ideas for Rosalee to execute in Angela's latest leadership campaigns and fundraisers, plus spare change from lunch money and numerous Capri Sun straw wrappers.

Rosalee had tossed the flower residue and straw wrappers in the trash, but kept everything else—after all, you never knew when you would need a pencil, spare change, or a bookmark. Then she shoved her keys, wallet, lunch, and water bottle into the main pocket, and slipped on some old Converse tennis shoes because they were closest to the door. This was a decision she largely regretted now, as sharp gravel dug into the cardboard-thin soles and tortured her tender feet.

———·•·———

Rosalee was nearly as late to work as Robin, and her mood was not improved when Alex arrived around noon to pick up another Snapple order. However, after several unsuccessful attempts to make herself extra busy to dissuade him, she found herself once more sitting across the picnic table from him.

"What are you having today?" he said, balling up the paper bag from his lunch.

"Salad again." Rosalee felt as bored saying it as it was going to be to eat it.

"Why?" said Alex.

"Because I'm boring."

The sentence hung in the air for a moment before wrapping itself invisibly around Rosalee's throat, making everything heavy. She swallowed against the make-believe noose.

Alex squeezed the paper ball as tight as it would go before lobbing it toward the trash can, which he barely missed. He got up to retrieve the ball, then brought it back to the table so he could try again. After two more shots, he finally sank it, then turned his attention back to Rosalee. "Do you even *like* salad?"

"I don't know, it's salad. It's whatever."

Lately, Rosalee's lies came so easily that she barely felt guilty for them. Mostly. The truth was that she had always loved salads. Robin grew produce fifty times better than anything you could find in the store. But lately, Robin's heart hadn't quite been into gardening and the vegetables could tell.

"I also have nothing to say, so you should talk," said Rosalee. "About something."

She wished Alex would turn his attention away from her and find something else to lob at the trash can, or at least watch other people. The front patio of The Goose was an excellent spot to people-watch.

This lunch, however, was a bad idea. Rosalee was in a bad mood. This was going to be a bad conversation.

"Or …?" said Alex.

"Or what?"

"Or you could ask me things."

Rosalee set her fork down on her napkin and unscrewed the lid of her water bottle. "We're doing this again?"

"I figured it was either this or the License Plate Game. Although I should warn you, I'm undefeated at that one."

Rosalee sighed. "Why do we even have to play a game? Why can't we talk … or *not* talk?"

Alex shrugged. "Your call."

They fell into some kind of silence then, but Rosalee wasn't sure she would call it "comfortable," *per se.* It seemed like the air between them was charged, somehow. It was enough to make her need to fill the silence.

"What's your favorite color?" she said finally.

Alex rolled his eyes. "You can do better than that."

Rosalee almost strained a muscle not rolling her own. "Fine. What's your favorite … movie?"

Alex smiled. "*The Princess Bride.* Good one. Now we're getting somewhere. But I know you can dig deeper."

"*The Princess Bride?* Really? You want me to ask you 'deep' questions and you won't even answer them honestly?"

Alex ignored her. "Keep going."

"What's your … sign?"

She looked up when Alex didn't answer and watched the grin slide off of his face. "C'mon, now."

"Is that not a good question?" Rosalee impaled a halved cherry tomato, then scowled as most of the pulp and seeds oozed back into the salad.

"*Horoscopes?*" said Alex, "Those things they sell next to the tabloids? I barely know you and I know you're not into that stuff."

"How could you possibly know that?"

"The 'gag me' look when you asked me that question was a dead giveaway."

Rosalee shrugged.

"Fine, we'll make it my turn," said Alex. "What's your favorite planet?"

"My favorite planet? Do *you* have a favorite planet?"

"Yes. This one."

"Convenient," Rosalee muttered.

Alex waited.

"I'm sorry, I'm not good at this," said Rosalee. An unpleasant warmth was rising from her torso and radiating across her chest as the combined heat of Alex's spotlight and the afternoon sun intensified. "Plus I really need to get back to work." *And I want to be alone.*

Alex continued to watch her and Rosalee shifted in her seat, twitching her hair forward so that it covered most of the splotches across her pale collarbone.

"Fine, I'll leave you alone for today," said Alex, "After you ask me a *good* question."

"I've already asked you tons of questions."

"Just ask me a question that's not for a three-year-old!"

Rosalee watched as several customers enjoying lunch on the patio looked around before dropping their eyes hastily back to their plates.

"What did you do to your arm?" she said.

The vivid red of the jagged scar could only have been a few months old and Alex turned it now so that the sunlight made an even greater contrast between the wound and his skin. Rosalee was startled by her boldness, but even more so by Alex's hesitancy.

"I'm sorry," she said. "I didn't mean to ask that, it just ... fell out."

She unscrewed her water bottle again to have something to do, then risked a glance at Alex. He didn't seem mad, although he looked more serious than usual.

"Rabid dog," he said finally.

Rosalee immediately swallowed the wrong way and choked.

"Fishing trip, it was a fishing trip." Alex laughed. "Rogue hook, lots of blood. You okay?"

"Great," Rosalee gasped, struggling to clear her windpipe.

"That was good, though, good question."

Alex was smiling again, but Rosalee only nodded awkwardly, stuffing her Tupperware back into her paper lunch sack and standing to leave.

"*I* have a question," said Alex. Rosalee turned back, looking wary. "That town thingy coming up?"

"Oh, the Rabbitbrush Festival? What about it?"

"Are you going?"

"I don't know yet."

In her mind's eye, Rosalee could already see Ellie dragging her bodily from her room, looking like some sort of makeover experiment. She shuddered inwardly.

"Well, would you go if I asked you to?" said Alex.

"... To go, or to go *with you?*"

Rosalee hated feeling stupid and had an inkling that this was something that could easily make her feel stupid if she misunderstood it.

"Well, to go," said Alex. "But also to go with me."

"I—Well, I usually go with my family. Plus, I don't ..."

"Date?"

"Dance. Or ... date."

"Okay. Well, I guess I'll see you there if you do go. Or before then, since it's not for a few weeks."

Rosalee nodded and waited to see if there was more. Alex seemed satisfied for the time being. When she was almost to the door, she hesitated, then called over her shoulder, "Don't forget your Snapple."

—•◆•—

By the time Rosalee was finally able to clock out for the day, it felt like the eve of the first day of summer vacation—not that she would ever get one of those for real again. That was one of the worst parts of growing up, she decided. Still, two days off and no pending painting projects felt freeing enough that she might have skipped if her feet didn't hurt so much. From now on, her Converse would have to be saved for special occasions.

She stopped by the main office to retrieve her backpack before heading out and was pleasantly surprised to find a single lemon wedge in a plastic condiment cup, sitting in a little divot in the fabric like a bird's nest. She smiled and lifted the cup, inhaling deeply as someone knocked softly on the office door.

Gloria had worked in the deli since before Rosalee or Ellie were born and Rosalee (and Robin, for that matter) had always hoped that she would want to take on the role of assistant manager someday. However, Gloria was the type of person who could be content—truly happy where she was—without any sort of negativity indicating that she was somehow settling.

"Lo siento, Rosalita," she said then, "Didn't mean to startle you."

"That's okay," said Rosalee. "Thanks for the lemon."

She smelled it again. It was such an unexpectedly nice end to a mostly stupid day.

"I hated cutting them without you this morning," Gloria said, her deep brown eyes concerned, but not probing. "I know it's your favorite."

That was one of the things Rosalee loved about Gloria—she cared fiercely about people, but she never forced them into talking about things. Instead, she laid the groundwork with the expertise of a mason worker until people were ready to climb on up and start venting.

"I saw your *bicicleta* outside—did it break down on the way?"

"No," said Rosalee, "My tires are flat and I totally misjudged how long it would take me to walk here."

"*Si*, well it's pretty hot out." Gloria puffed out a little breath for emphasis. "I think a lot of us folks move slower in it without even noticing."

"Yeah, maybe ..." Rosalee couldn't help but think that *she* was slowing down—with or without the heat.

"*Pues, chica,* I'm leaving for the day. You want a ride?"

Rosalee glanced out the window where the harsh afternoon sun was beating down without mercy. "Yes, please. If you don't mind."

Chapter 9

The first day of what Rosalee dubbed her "Two-Day Freedom Extravaganza '96" was nearly perfect, except for the fact that she forgot to turn off her regular five AM alarm. Still, she enjoyed lying in bed for an hour, listening to the birds chirping outside her window and luxuriating in the crisp morning breeze coming in through the screen.

The house had never had air conditioning—only a swamp cooler—so Rosalee and her family habitually opened the windows as wide as they would go at night and shut them early in the morning to trap the cool air inside. Rosalee always cheated a little and left a tiny sliver of window open in whatever room she happened to be, as a way to hold onto the outside noises and stave off the claustrophobia of being indoors.

This particular day, since no one was home to suggest that she eat grapefruit or oatmeal for breakfast, Rosalee had a doughnut and coffee on the back porch and watched the morning sun rays disperse steadily over the horizon. After living in a place as vast and open as Rabbitbrush, Colorado most of her life, she had no idea how people survived anywhere without mountains—especially those fancy, new developments with fragile, baby trees and too much concrete.

Alex was from that kind of city, she thought. Hadn't Ellie said he was from Denver? It didn't matter. It was Rosalee's first day off and she had already decided *not* to think about Alex. If she was going to fixate on anything, it should be her family and convincing them that she was well enough to rejoin them. She hadn't quite worried that to death yet and fully intended to.

After breakfast and light dishes, Rosalee took a stroll around Robin's prized garden. To the untrained eye, Robin's cultivation was as magnificent as ever, but to her family, it looked nearly as sad as Robin. Only the perennials had come up so far and Rosalee doubted that her aunt would introduce anything new that year. Still, Rosalee admired the translucent, vibrant red clusters of currants and the dark green leaves of the hydrangeas, the periwinkle flowers of which had bloomed at the beginning of summer and would return in the fall. She walked along the side of the house and knelt in the grass to thread clematis vines through the weather-worn wooden trellis under her bedroom window. She worked carefully so as not to squish the hard, tightly closed buds as she pushed vines through and back again to allow their leaves and muricate tendrils to grab hold.

The sun beat down on the back of her neck as she made her way around to the front of the house, yanking up long, snaking bindweed and a patch of buttonweed by the front porch. Rosalee particularly hated buttonweed because it always broke off far above the root and came back with a vengeance. What she really needed was a digger-style weed cutter, which was in the shed. But she wasn't ready for that sort of commitment today.

By the time Rosalee wandered back into the house, it was at least twenty degrees hotter than when she got up, so she changed into a one-piece bathing suit that probably only still fit because the elastic was shot, slathered sunscreen onto her mostly paper-white complexion, and headed back outside to lay in the sun. The Russian Hawthorn and white ash trees in the backyard offered a cool enclosure before noon, so she whiled away her time before then flipping casually through some of Ellie's *People* magazines and sipping iced tea as the creek that ran beyond the backyard fence gurgled past. When it got too hot, she moved inside to lounge some more.

At some point, Rosalee fell asleep on an article about somebody famous' breakup with a famous somebody else and only woke up when Lola came home from the gym, where she taught six jazzercise classes per week. She waited until Lola came downstairs again, freshly showered and carrying a cardboard box under one arm, then followed her outside and into the converted garage that used to be Lola's bedroom. Now, it was her workshop for hand-made jewelry and easily one of Rosalee's favorite rooms of the house, even though it wasn't technically attached.

It was amazing how that little room held so much of all of them—as though their essence was entrenched in its very walls. Edison-style bulbs hung from the ceiling to give the space a farmhouse feel, and Robin had built wooden counters and shelves for Lola's many supplies. Evelyn and Ellie had sewn bright, floral curtains and cushions to replace the tattered, thrifted versions, and Rosalee had painted a colorful rooster, which hung next to a windowsill full of potted plants. Whenever she and Ellie moved out, Rosalee knew she would miss Lola's studio even more than her own bedroom.

Now, she scooted a bar stool out from the counter where Lola had dropped her most recent supply shipment. "How was your class?" she said.

"Oh, it was good." Lola smiled as she slit the box open with a pocketknife and pulled out numerous small plastic bags.

As Rosalee watched her, she breathed in the wooden, tree house smell of the whitewashed walls and was happy to see that the workshop was in pretty good shape this week ... so far. When it came to organizing Lola, it was a family effort. The thing about Lola was that although she was ambitious, creative, and bubbly, she was also full of self-doubt, unable to make a decision to save her life, and likely to be living under a pile of rubble if Robin, Ellie, and Rosalee didn't come in once a week to put her back together.

As soon as Lola had dumped the new bags of beads onto her workspace, Rosalee confiscated the cardboard box and broke it down. It was a habit now, especially since she was so used to doing it at The Goose. Plus, it was good to head Lola off early before she started stacking things in corners and feeding the clutter.

"By the way, Gwen's been coming to class a lot, which is nice," said Lola, "Thanks for telling her about me."

"No problem. I figured you would get along." Rosalee surveyed the tiny bags of necklace clasps and jump rings, plus a large plastic bag of new, metallic beads. "You need help putting these away?"

"Not yet. I wanted to make sure I got the right beads, in case I need to return them."

Rosalee wound fishing line back onto its spool and hung it on a pegboard hook above Lola's work table. "How do you know if they're the right beads?"

"Well, I got this cord," said Lola, grunting as she reached for a box on the top of one of her shelves, "and I don't know if it'll fit through the holes or if the colors will go—that kind of thing."

"Let's see."

Rosalee cleared a space for the box and set the new bag of beads in front of Lola. She watched her separate one of each color out and thought about how to broach the subject she was pretty sure almost came up in the storeroom with Robin. Somehow, "I know you're all conspiring against me" seemed abrupt and unwarranted, so she decided to try a different approach.

"Hey, Lola?"

"Hm?"

"Is ... Robin ... ya know, okay?"

Lola unraveled a length of cord and threaded the first style of bead through the end, holding it up to the light. "What do you mean?"

"That looks cool," said Rosalee, nodding in approval. "I like the copper with that brown."

"I like it, too." Lola took off the first bead and picked up the next one. "But what did you mean about Robin?"

"Oh, I just noticed that she seems ... tense."

Lola glanced at Rosalee and then held up the next bead, which they both studied before nodding.

"We're still figuring out some stuff about the B&B," said Lola, sliding that bead off and replacing it with the last style. Rather than holding it up to the light, though, she set the spool of cord and the bead down on the counter and turned to Rosalee, biting her lip. "I'm not sure how much I should say about it right now."

"That's okay. I wasn't trying to pry, I just want everybody to be okay." Rosalee shook her head. She wished so much that she could come right out and say what was on her mind, but she knew how that would make her look—more unsteady. Less reliable.

Lola smiled and reached up to tousle the messy, red bun Rosalee had piled on top of her head like a bird's nest. "Everybody will be okay. Starting a business can be tricky."

"Yeah, that's true ..."

All at once, Rosalee was struck with an unbearable thought: Could it be that her aunts had used Robin's inheritance from Evelyn's death to send Rosalee away, only to discover that it hadn't worked the way they hoped? And now there was no money left for the B&B? She felt the blood drain from her face.

Lola, oblivious, held up the last bead on the cord and raised her eyebrows for Rosalee's approval.

"Perfect," said Rosalee, without looking.

———•●•———

By three o'clock the next afternoon, Rosalee was already looking forward to going back to work the next day, if only to get away from the fresh, raw coating of unease corroding her insides. She had refused Lola's invitation to her morning jazzercise class, but later wished that she had gone to alleviate her nerves.

Instead, she moped around the lower level of the house, half-heartedly de-cluttering and tidying. As she passed her usual place at the kitchen table, a corner of glossy paper caught her eye. She slid it out from under the placemat with one finger and sighed as she read the pale yellow Post-it Note stuck to the front:

> *Have to go for my re-certification. Want to come?*
>
> *Lola* →

An arrow under her aunt's name pointed to the inside of the pamphlet, but Rosalee removed the note first to read the title: *Healing with Food: A Nutrition Seminar for Chronic Diseases and Illnesses.* Rosalee's nerves prickled as she opened the pamphlet to find another Post-it. This time, there was no note, but an arrow to a long list of conditions, where, right between "Lung Cancer" and "Osteoporosis," Lola had highlighted "Multiple Sclerosis."

Rosalee closed the pamphlet and folded it, stuffing it in her back pocket. Later, she would shove it in the junk drawer of her desk, where a small collection of clippings and booklets about new medical trials and research, information about support groups, and the like was steadily growing. She knew her family was only trying to help. In the meantime, while she still had energy, she decided to take out her frustration on the remaining dishes.

Sometime later, Robin came home, kicking her sandals off by the front door and setting the mail on the end of the kitchen counter. "Someone left a video in our mailbox."

Rosalee paused her assault on a pan with a stubborn crust of tomato sauce from the night before and dropped it back into the soapy water. She dried her hands on her pants and took the video from her aunt.

The front cover of the cardboard case featured a loving couple framed by a brilliant blue sky, clearly about to profess their undying love for each other. The woman had long, flowing blonde hair and the man was dressed all in black, with a sword in his belt. *The Princess Bride.*

Rosalee shot a "Why me?" look at the ceiling.

"Someone you know?" said Robin.

Rosalee turned the cardboard case over to glance at the synopsis on the back. "Unfortunately, yes."

Just then, Lola bounced into the kitchen, still riding her post-gym high from her second class of the day. "What's unfortunate?" she said, opening the refrigerator.

"I have a stalker," said Rosalee.

"Rose ..." Robin said in a tone as close to a reprimand as she ever heard from her.

"Well, what else would you call it when someone constantly interrupts your life to force you to have lunch with them and then asks you a million questions?" said Rosalee. "And shoves movies in your mailbox to force you to watch them?"

"Sounds like a friend to me." Lola rummaged in the silverware drawer for a spoon. She peeled the lid off of her favorite flavor of yogurt and then paused. "Wait, is this your *lunch pal?*"

Rosalee shot an accusatory look at Robin.

"Not *just* her lunch pal." Ellie wandered into the kitchen with her reading glasses pushed up into her hair. "He also saved her life. Twice."

"Well, that's a little dramatic," said Rosalee, although she privately agreed. "And that's beside the point when he's *UH-noy-ing.*"

"He. *Likes.* You." Ellie opened the door to the pantry, presumably to look for mid-studying sustenance. "You could at least be nice to him."

Rosalee was beginning to feel cornered. "I *am* being nice." *Ish.* "Why aren't you at school?"

Ellie finally decided on a bag of pretzels and carried them to the counter, where she plopped down on one of the bar stools. "My Friday class was canceled."

"Anyway, he's the new kid, Rosalee," said Lola. She scooped a spoonful of yogurt and looked at it sadly. "It's hard to make friends when you're new. There are a lot of days when I *still* feel new."

Rosalee exhaled forcefully, letting her breath drag against the back of her throat on the way out. "Okay, but this isn't elementary school. He's a big boy and I'm sure he'll manage to find other people to harass."

"Ya know, I'm starting to think no one ever really grows up," said Robin. "Maybe we all look older, but underneath, we're all still in elementary school."

Lola nodded earnestly beside her. Rosalee frowned and set the tape back on top of the mail while Lola and Ellie drifted off to the back porch with a bottle of nail polish, Ellie apparently having given up on studying for the time being.

Rosalee stared at the several remaining dishes in the sink while Robin sorted through the bills. Rosalee watched her for a couple of seconds before her aunt offered her signature, tight "Robin" smile and then glanced out at the back porch, lowering her voice. "Do you really think he's stalking you?"

Rosalee hesitated and found it difficult to look directly into her aunt's hazel eyes. Robin seemed to misinterpret her uncertainty in herself.

"Have you told him to leave you alone?" she pressed.

"No," said Rosalee, guilt pooling in her gut from her liberal use of the word "stalker."

The fact was, though, that Alex *was* annoying, and tended to show up wherever she was. Small town or not, Rosalee refused to believe that was a coincidence, and so ... *Could* he be stalking her? Suddenly, Alex's words from the Ferris wheel floated back to her: *"Do I scare you?"*

Robin was still watching her, a crease in her brow.

"No," said Rosalee again, this time addressing Robin's question and reaffirming her answer to Alex's, "But he would leave me alone if I asked him to." Somehow she was sure of that.

"And you'll ask him? If it gets to be too much?" Rosalee nodded and Robin smiled a more comfortable smile, the crease from before disappearing to leave behind a fine line perfected over the years. "Well, the kid has good taste," she said, patting the cardboard cover of the tape as she passed the counter to join Lola and Ellie outside. "This is a great movie."

Just then, Rosalee noticed a sliver of notebook paper poking out of the cover and slid the tape out to find a note attached:

Rosalee stuffed the note in her pocket as Ellie wobbled back into the kitchen on her heels to avoid messing up her toenail polish. "We're watching that tonight, whether you like it or not." She nodded toward the movie before making her way, stiff-kneed, to the bathroom down the hall.

Chapter 10

By the time Friday came around, Rosalee contented herself with the fact that she had at least *tried* to call Alex, even if that meant that she actually called once and hung up when the answering machine picked up, then dialed again (and hung up again) when Pete answered.

Later, she kicked herself for not relaying her excuse to Pete instead of worrying about all the ways Alex might guilt her into hanging out with him when he answered, but she couldn't bring herself to lie to Pete—not when their relationship was still so fragile. Rosalee registered another pinprick to her conscience as she realized how much work she still had to do to mend their friendship and how little she had done since borrowing the painting, before her thoughts were diverted to the sound of someone struggling with the latch on the front screen door.

"Ellie, is that you?" she called.

When no answer came, she wandered out of her room and leaned over the banister, peering down the stairs into the kitchen. From there, she could see her sister's feet in purple platform flip-flops (a great way to twist an ankle) and the bottoms of an extraordinary number of plastic grocery bags.

"Jeez, do you need help?" Rosalee hurried down the stairs to meet her.

Before she could relieve Ellie of any of the bags, however, several of them dropped to the floor. Rosalee chased a red onion across the kitchen as it left a trail of crispy skin flakes in its wake. Meanwhile, Ellie dropped her shoulders, letting the rest of the bags fall around her.

"Should've made two trips," she said, pushing her sunglasses into her hair, then hanging her purse and keys on their hooks by the coat closet

"You should have yelled from the driveway so I could carry something." Rosalee helped her sister pile the groceries onto the kitchen counter. "What is all of this?"

"Oh, Pete got that promotion so I thought we could surprise him." Ellie's face was alight with the glow that always accompanied planning parties. "I got Alex to take him out while we set up. You're not working tonight, right?"

"No, I'm not," said Rosalee distractedly.

If she was being honest, she was a little surprised that she was the last to know Pete's news. Sure, she knew that the promotion was hopefully coming, but she also thought that their talk the other day had unblocked their lines of communication a little. Another reminder of the work she still had to do.

Then the other piece of Ellie's information clunked into place.

"I didn't know you and Alex talked," said Rosalee. "I mean that you were—or *are* talking?"

"Oh, yeah, I didn't know how else to make it a surprise. I felt like a creep because I had to try to catch him on his shift at Laurie's. It took me three tries." Ellie paused. "You don't mind, do you?"

"Why would I mind?"

Rosalee said this mostly to herself because when Ellie planned parties, she became like Tinker Bell—only room for one thought or emotion at a time. At this particular moment, she was surveying the nearly overflowing counter with a worried expression. "I hope I got enough food."

Rosalee looked between the counter and her sister. "Are you kidding?"

"Well, Alex is buying all the meat. You know, the *manly* stuff, and he said he'd grill it and everything, but I thought we should have vegetables, and chips, and soda, dip ... Oh! Do you know where Evelyn's yellow cake recipe is?"

"I'll ... look for it."

Rosalee probably needn't have answered the question at all, as Ellie had since been reduced to a brightly colored blur rocketing around the kitchen. At least she had finally kicked off her platform instruments of death.

———•●•———

By a quarter to seven, Ellie was fuming.

"I'm *sorry*," Rosalee said for the umpteenth time since they left the house to head to Laurie's. "The Goose is never out of cakes—how was I supposed to know? We still got one."

"I don't know, call ahead, maybe?" Ellie unbuckled her seatbelt so hard that it bounced off the window and made them both duck. "We needed *two cakes.*"

"Why?"

"Because it's Alex's birthday, too."

Ellie got out of the car and slammed the driver's side door with unnecessary force, then jabbed at the key fob to unlock the trunk.

"*What?*" said Rosalee.

"Yeah, it's not a surprise party anymore because somehow, Pete found out, and then he wanted to make it Alex's birthday party, instead, but we're still secretly doing a 'Congratulations Pete' party, so ... *two cakes.*"

"Wow, okay. You could have told me that."

"You could have made Evelyn's yellow cake like I asked you to," Ellie snapped, finally succeeding in opening the trunk by holding the fob button down.

"Ellie, hold on a sec."

Rosalee swung an arm out to block her from the contents of the trunk the way Evelyn used to do to whoever was sitting in the passenger seat when she slammed on the brakes too fast. Ellie was chewing her tongue again as she turned toward her.

"Look, I tried to make Evelyn's cake, okay? I seriously did. I messed it up," said Rosalee.

She purposely left out the part where she had to lay Saran wrap over the recipe card to keep her tears from smearing the ink, or how she made herself pretend to be a robot so that Evelyn's handwriting and little notes in the margins wouldn't stimulate her overactive tear ducts. And honestly, she probably could have saved the batter and just picked out the eggshell that embedded itself when she became too impassioned to crack the egg properly. But she didn't. Instead, she dumped the entire bowl into the trash and listened as the thick mixture dripped glutinously onto everything below.

"It's not about Evelyn's cake, Rosalee."

Ellie ducked under her sister's arm to grab multiple bags of chips, dip, and the veggies that had been cut up and speared on soaked bamboo sticks for grilling.

"Okay, well, I already apologized about the store."

"That's not it, either. It's that you don't notice things anymore. Or think about them."

Rosalee balanced her cake box on one hip and reached with her free hand to grab one of the bags with soda. "What do you mean?"

Ellie batted her hand away and grabbed it herself. "Just forget it."

"El, I didn't even want to come to this thing. I was trying to help you."

Ellie was still struggling with the bag handles. "I thought you wanted to show Pete that you were still his friend."

"Okay, fine. That, too."

"Well, if you're someone's friend, you notice things, Rosalee. Dang it, how are we gonna close the trunk?"

Rosalee waved her still-free hand and slammed it shut, then wrestled the bag with soda out of Ellie's fingers. Ellie huffed and turned away.

"Ellie, come on."

"Look, we're already late and Angela's already here with her—oh, for goodness' sake."

Rosalee followed Ellie's gaze to two picnic tables that had been pushed together for serving next to a grill on the lawn below Laurie's. Several surrounding tables had been decorated with elegant tablecloths, candlesticks, and flowers, with equally refined place settings. It was actually very pretty, but maybe a little fancy for the occasion.

"I put her in charge of plates and cups and stuff after she twisted my arm out of its socket," said Ellie.

"I think it looks nice."

"*Tsk.* Oh, sure, *now* you take her side."

"I wasn't trying to—"

Ellie walked away mid-sentence and Rosalee followed her to the party area at a snail's pace. She deposited the cake box on one of the long tables and the soda on the ground by her feet, then tugged self-consciously at the blouse that Ellie had somehow managed to coax her into before their fight. This one was black, with a square neckline, eyelet lace, and bright embroidered flowers around the neck and sleeves. When Rosalee had tried it on, it reminded her of carefree summers, but now it seemed a little dramatic. She had tethered her wavy hair at the nape of her neck in a bun, but several strands had already come loose around her face.

While Angela and Ellie raced around like overworked waitresses in a crowded restaurant, Rosalee poured chips into bowls, piled vegetable skewers into a pan to be grilled with the meat, and finally resorted to arranging the soda bottles into rainbow order to avoid having to do anything else close to Angela. Ellie's accusations rang in her head as she worked.

Had she stopped noticing things? She didn't think so.

She looked up at Laurie's Cafe on the hill and admired the lights Mr. Laurie had strung on the outdoor patio for summer. They were the tough, all-weather kind, but he always took them down during the winter. Luckily, by then, it was almost time for Christmas lights, so their absence wasn't quite so jarring ... Or were they merely mixed in with the Christmas lights? Suddenly, Rosalee couldn't remember. Either way, now they served as an elegant backdrop to what was looking more and more like a wedding reception than a casual surprise party.

"This better earn me brownie points, Pete," Rosalee muttered, slinking into the background as the guests began to arrive.

— • —

"So, congratulations to Pete *and* Happy Birthday to Alex, even though it was technically two days ago," said Angela, raising her plastic cup. "Here, here!"

"Here, here," everyone chanted, imitating Angela.

"*Speeech!*" someone yelled through cupped hands.

Alex shook his head, but Angela pushed him and Pete between the shoulder blades until they were both standing awkwardly in front of the buffet tables, Pete flushing a deep shade of crimson at being the center of attention.

Alex ended up speaking for both of them and looked more or less at home addressing so many people. As he talked, everyone laughed appreciatively, but Rosalee hardly took in a word he said. Instead, she felt herself shrinking down to the size of a very small person. The kind of person who bailed on other people on their birthdays. *Two days ago.*

Ellie materialized suddenly in front of her. "What's up? You look sick."

"Not sick." *A little sick.* "Just a terrible, terrible person."

"Why?"

Ellie helped herself to more soda, and Rosalee knew from her stiff posture that their earlier argument was far from over. But if her sister was playing nice for now, there was no reason not to play along.

"Because Alex wanted me to hang out *two days ago* and I blew him off."

Ellie paused, her cup halfway to her mouth. "Oh."

"I know."

"Oh dear."

"I *know.*"

"Well, go say something to him, then!" Ellie hissed. "Quick, before Angela sinks her manicure into his poor, unprotected skin."

"Right."

Rosalee got up slowly from the table and made her way to Alex, who was surrounded by people slapping him on the back and joking. Pete was nowhere to be found and Rosalee suspected that he was hyperventilating behind a tree somewhere. She stood uncertainly at the edge of the group to wait, but to her great relief, Alex spotted her right away.

"Hey, I'll catch you later, okay?" she heard him tell a waitress she had seen at Laurie's but never met.

Rosalee tried to smile as Alex approached her, but her smallness was still dragging her down toward the dock and collapsing her spine like a retracting Slinky, and she had a feeling the corners of her mouth were following.

"Hi," she managed to say when he stopped in front of her.

"Hey, I'm glad you came." He looked genuinely happy to see her. Maybe because he was a genuinely nice person—not a small person.

"Of course," said Rosalee brightly, as though the thought of bailing had never crossed her mind. *Small.*

Alex smiled at her again and then shaded his eyes against the setting sun to survey the little gathering. "This was an *insane* surprise. I'm not sure I deserve Pete as a roommate."

"I'm not sure anyone does." Rosalee stopped, realizing what she said. "I mean, except—I'm sure you—"

"It's all good. I knew what you meant." Alex took a sip from his plastic cup and smiled, almost as if he knew that Rosalee was trying to bolster her nerves for something.

"So ..." she said.

"So?"

"I'm sorry about the other day. I had no idea it was your birthday. Otherwise, I never would have ..."

"Blown me off?"

Alex raised his eyebrows and Rosalee felt herself going red. She ducked her head and stared at her pale toes in her flip-flops, then realized that Alex was laughing. "Rosalee, I wasn't trying to make you hang out with me because it was my birthday. That was just weird timing.”

“Still. It was a crappy thing to do. I’m really sorry.”

“It’s *really* okay. I get it.”

“Okay.” Rosalee imagined awkwardness oozing out of her pores and twisted her torso back toward Ellie. “I guess I should ...”

“Sure,” said Alex. “Well, thanks again. For coming. And for helping to set all this up.”

Rosalee nodded and hoped her flip-flops would stop catching every godforsaken, uneven nail on the way back to her table.

“Hey, Rosalee?”

She turned back.

“You look nice tonight,” said Alex.

He said it like he could have been talking to a date, at her house, before he took her to dinner, but there was no way to know that for sure. Maybe that’s how he always said “nice.”

“Thanks,” said Rosalee, “And ... Happy Birthday.”

“Also ...” Rosalee turned back warily for a second time. Alex seemed to be enjoying himself. “Not that there’s anything for you to make up, but if you felt really, *extra* guilty about the other day, I know how you could make it up to me.”

Rosalee felt her mouth twitch toward a smile. “Yeah? How’s that?”

“Have lunch with me next week.”

Rosalee heard herself agree before her brain caught up and suddenly her pocket was vibrating. It was a page from Robin:

CALL THIS NUMBER, MURAL

“Oh my god.” She scrolled down to a phone number she didn’t recognize.

“Everything okay?” said Alex.

"My aunt sent me a phone number and she thinks it's about the mural." Rosalee ran a hand through her hair, which was only barely staying put in its elastic. She felt overly warm.

"Do you wanna use my cell phone?" said Alex. "I have one in my bag for emergencies and it might even be charged."

"Really? Could I?"

"Yeah, let's go. No one will notice if we're gone for a few minutes."

Rosalee came back to Earth enough to remember where she was and who she was with. She shoved her pager back into her pocket. "I'll wait."

"So they can give the mural to someone else? Don't be stupid. My bike is up here, c'mon."

Rosalee followed Alex up the hill toward the Laurie's parking lot, where his bike was parked behind the wooden dumpster enclosure. Alex gulped the remainder of his plastic cup and tossed it over the enclosure, then undid the clasps on a leather messenger bag slung over the handlebars of his bike. Rosalee absentmindedly twisted her hair back into a bun, going through the motions three times before realizing that there was no elastic in her hair and that it must have fallen out. Sighing, she shook it out from its twist and let it fall down her back, trying to clear her mind in preparation for the coherent sentences she hoped to form.

Alex emerged with the cell phone and pressed the power button, handing it to Rosalee. His eyes lingered momentarily on the loose strands of red blowing gently in the breeze and Rosalee wondered if he would misinterpret the change in hairstyle as flirting.

Her hands shook as she took her pager out again and attempted to dial the number, and she pressed the END button before she hit the last digit. She peered around the enclosure at the party still thriving down the hill and blew out a forceful breath. Sooner or later, her sister was going to notice she was gone and, after all, she was supposed to be hanging out with Pete.

Alex laughed quietly as he crouched down by his tire to light a cigarette. "We're good. Try to breathe."

Rosalee stared at the phone number again and Alex offered her his cigarette, which she contemplated for a moment before taking it and sucking in a deep drag. She exhaled a long, smoky "thank you" as she passed it back to him. Then she took one more deep breath of night air and wisps of Alex's secondhand smoke and dialed.

Chapter 11

Rosalee took extra care getting ready on Wednesday morning. This was the first time she would be painting in public, as opposed to scrunched up like a hedgehog in the privacy of her own home. She deliberated over the artist persona she wished to project: Should she go for a carefree flower child aesthetic, or something a little more edgy?

She had saved her good news, despite Alex's attempts to persuade her to share it with everyone the night of the party. She hadn't even planned on telling her sister that night, but Ellie had noticed Rosalee's absence and fabricated her own (much more imaginative) ideas about what she and Alex were doing hiding behind the dumpster. At least the news seemed to soften Ellie enough that she hadn't brought up their argument again.

As for the mural, Ms. FancyBlouse said that Rosalee could start as soon as the wall had been primed, which she expected to be finished within the next few weeks. However, the Tuesday after Labor Day, Rosalee got another call that the construction crew was ahead of schedule and she could start at her convenience.

After twenty minutes of digging in the back of her closet for black tights to wear under her jean shorts, Rosalee settled on shorts and boots without the tights and an already paint-spattered T-shirt. It was probably just as well that she couldn't find the tights since the temperature was supposed to reach almost ninety degrees. She also wasn't sure if the particular wing where she would be working was air-conditioned yet.

She passed the mirror, then doubled back, looking harder at her reflection than she had let herself look in months. It had been a while since she had worn any makeup besides a quick coat of mascara, so she dug in a drawer until she found a stick of black eyeliner, too. She tested the line on her palm, then leaned toward the mirror and poised the point at the inside corner of her right eye.

Her hand shook.

Rosalee struggled against the sudden panic that gripped her at the thought of what progressing tremors could do to her painting. Granted, she wasn't hoping to make a living as a world-famous artist or anything, but not being able to sketch or draw without shaking was not ideal. Hopefully, she was getting ahead of herself. Maybe she was just nervous. Or dehydrated.

She hurriedly filled the cup next to her toothbrush with water from the faucet and drank, choking on the first few gulps. That seemed to be happening more often, too, but she tucked her chin and braced herself against the bathroom counter, which allowed her to finish the cup with no further seepage into her windpipe. She wiped her mouth on the neck of her T-shirt and stared down her reflection again. Determined, she laboriously lined her right eye, then her left. She went in again a few more times to make the lines even, and after approximately four attempts on each eye, stepped back to find a panda staring back at her in the mirror.

Rosalee groaned and glanced at the clock, then rummaged in the medicine cabinet for Vaseline. She dug a scoop out of the jar with her finger and wiped the whole mess off of her eyes with a cotton ball, leaving her eyelids uncomfortably greasy. Then she twisted her hair into a knot and nearly tripped down the stairs in her hurry to leave.

Since Ellie always took Lola's car to school and Robin's car was a motorcycle, Rosalee had to catch the bus. Luckily, the bus stop was about a half mile down from her house, but she still barely made it.

•❖•

Someone should have warned me about this wall, Rosalee thought as she set her things down next to the opposite one.

Normally, when she started a painting project, she didn't mind the blank canvas. However, most of her projects were relatively small, like bright flowers and mushrooms painted on the back of a glass cutting board, or a custom picture frame speckled with stars and galaxies. The vast blankness of this wall, however, was relentlessly daunting and Rosalee gawked at it for a good five minutes before reluctantly pulling her sketches out of her backpack.

After hours and days of indecision, restless sleep, and reflection, Rosalee had finally decided on a rough outline that she would fill in as she went. The idea was simple enough in concept: a garden stretching from wall to wall, divided subtly into the four seasons. She imagined winter vines snaking through brown, dry foliage, then continuing among tender spring buds, past glowing summer petals, and then ending amid brilliant sunset leaves of autumn. FancyBlouse had been delighted by the idea and gave Rosalee free rein to fill the space within that theme, only requesting that she approve it once the sketch had been transferred to the wall.

Rosalee had always found it helpful to make grids when tackling anything larger than an eighteen-by-twenty-four-inch canvas, so she spent the first few hours measuring, staring, standing back, and staring some more. At one point, she stared so hard that the lines sank into the wall, then came back into focus, only to blur again.

She decided to take a break and hunt down the nearest bathroom, wondering if residual Vaseline might, in fact, be impairing her vision. She rinsed her face three times with warm water and emerged several minutes later, blotting her eyes with a paper towel. Her vision still partially obscured, she didn't notice Alex until she nearly ran him over. Luckily, he reached out just in time and caught her by the elbows to keep her from falling backward, although she still managed to step on his foot.

"Sorry," she said quickly as he winced, although she was relieved that the distraction at least made him let go of her quickly.

"No, I'm sorry," he said, "I was coming to find you. Not in the bathroom."

Rosalee realized that she was still holding the paper towel and crumpled it into a tight ball in her palm as Alex watched.

"Are you okay?" He probably thought she had been crying.

"I had ... goop ... in my eye." Somehow, the word "Vaseline" just wouldn't come.

"Oh, okay."

She could tell Alex didn't believe her. He ruffled the back of his hair, which was slightly damp and held out of his face by a khaki green folded bandana. If she hadn't already been thinking about paint colors, she definitely wouldn't have noticed the way the green deepened the maple syrup-y hue of his eyes.

"Are you ready for lunch?" he said. "I have something to show you."

"Well, I've barely even started." Rosalee gestured vaguely down the hall, even though her mural was around several corners.

"C'mon, it'll take two seconds."

Rosalee frowned. "Can you wait, like, fifteen minutes?"

Alex was, of course, as stubborn as ever. "My lunch break is *now.*" They stared at each other and Alex looked away first. "Alright, jeez, I'll wait for you outside. Unless you want me to wait with you and then we can go together when you're ready?"

Rosalee's hand itched to chuck her wadded-up paper towel at him. "No, really, you go ahead."

She waited until he left to wander back to her wall, where she ultimately decided that she needed a break anyway. She stuffed her sketches, carpenter pencil, and measuring instruments back in her bag and hoisted it onto one shoulder to find her lunch pal.

You wouldn't have this mural without him, said the little voice in her head.

As she made her way through the main hospital, Rosalee thought about the way she often found herself enunciating her words around Alex, as though she was talking to a boy, and not a grown man. *A grown man.* Where had her childhood gone and what had transpired, in the haze of adolescence, that bore enough power to transform persons in her relative age pool and of the male persuasion from cooty-carrying, booger-picking, icky boys into *grown men?*

When Rosalee reached the main entrance, she realized that she never clarified with Alex what "outside" meant. It was a big hospital—there was a lot of "outside." She took a chance and stuck with the front entrance, which turned out to be a lucky guess. Alex was sitting at a stone picnic table, rolling the red wax casing from a mini Babybel cheese into a ball between his palms.

Unwillingly, Rosalee's eyes slid over him, noticing the light stubble along his jawline and the subtle way his white T-shirt stretched over his toned and tanned arms. This was certainly *not* a boy. *Stop it,* Rosalee scolded herself. It wasn't as though she was unaccustomed to non-boy men, and this one wasn't any different than the rest of them. Maybe more annoying. She sat down across from him with a huff. "Ya know, some of us have a rhythm going before you ruin it."

Alex looked up. "Did I really ruin it?"

For once, he seemed remorseful for the way he consistently tore her away from her work. Not that stocking soup or changing light bulbs was nearly as interesting as a mural.

Rosalee sized him up, trying to decide how guilty she should make him feel. She knew he didn't deserve the burden of her frustration, but was reluctant to let it go. Alex waited. Eventually, she sighed in defeat. "No. Hard to ruin something I haven't found yet."

Alex smiled, mollified. "You will."

Rosalee took the breakfast granola bar she had forgotten to eat out of the front pouch of her backpack. She had also forgotten to grab her lunch from the fridge.

"Time for another 'Lunchtime Poll'?" she said.

Alex was busy pressing the wax sphere into the table and turning it so that it gradually began to form a cube with tiny indentations from the table's surface. *"Heathers?"*

"You've seen it?" Rosalee unwrapped the bar and bit off the end.

"Only the beginning. 'Bloodthirsty, vindictive freaks' isn't really my thing, movie-wise."

"Weren't you just telling me the other night how underrated *The Lost Boys* is?"

Alex paused, then raised his wax cube in a toasting gesture. "*Touché.*" He grinned. "Get your eye goop out?"

"Just about."

"Need help?"

"No," Rosalee said firmly.

Alex shrugged. His feet were doing a kind of off-beat tap dance under the table and Rosalee wondered if he knew he was doing it.

Somehow, she didn't have the heart to chide him; he looked so content with the remains of his recently inhaled lunch still in front of him, people watching with a song in his head that no one else could hear.

What are you listening to? she almost said, but didn't.

"What's that?" she said instead, nodding toward a small something wearing a tissue shroud in the middle of the table. At first glance, she had assumed it was trash from Alex's lunch.

"A tree," said Alex.

"A tree?"

"Yes, a tree. For you. Since it's kinda my fault the last one was ruined."

He whipped the tissue off with a flourish and Rosalee clasped her hands in her lap to keep herself from grabbing it to admire the three tiny green sprouts.

"What kind is it?" she said.

"Grapefruit."

"No way? Where did you get grapefruit seeds?"

"From a grapefruit, *duh.*" Alex smiled. "They were already half-sprouted in there. I thought you could, like, braid the stems together or something when they're bigger. Make one, big, super-tree."

Rosalee smiled back. She couldn't help it.

"Well." Alex nudged the cup toward her on the table. "Here."

"Thank you. This is so cool."

Alex tipped an imaginary hat and stood up from his bench.

"You're leaving?" said Rosalee, before her brain had a chance to catch up.

For some reason, Alex looked almost sad as he gathered his lunch trash. "Lots of work today. I'll see ya later."

Rosalee nodded, purposely keeping her face nonchalant. "See ya later."

She didn't see him later.

Chapter 12

On the tenth day of no Alex, Rosalee began to worry.

It was Saturday night and she, Ellie, and Pete were watching *The Wizard of Oz* in the living room. Ellie and Pete sat on the couch while Rosalee curled up in an armchair, staring at a plate of Evelyn's chocolate chip cookies that Ellie had so effortlessly baked, without so much as a sniffle. So far, Rosalee had made it eighteen minutes without eating one, but she knew that eventually, she would have to give in to avoid hurting her sister's feelings.

"Pass the cookies?" she said finally. She was determined not to shift too much from her fetal position in the chair as she took the plate from Pete, afraid that it might be the only thing holding her together. Ellie beamed as Rosalee took a tiny bite and nodded. "Perfect, El."

She turned away as her eyes prickled, hoping that if anyone noticed, they would attribute the emotion to Dorothy's abrupt introduction to a world of thriving color, which was always her favorite part of the movie.

She probably could have asked Pete where Alex was, but then she risked Ellie finding out that she a) noticed, and b) cared. She did, however, casually ask Mr. Laurie that morning (while Ellie was in the bathroom) if he'd seen Alex lately. Mr. Laurie had rubbed his bearded chin and gazed off into space for a moment, looking mildly concerned, then shrugged and went back to tightening the feet on one of the tables. "Pat (Mrs. Laurie) didn't seem worried and she usually handles the schedule," he said. "I'm sure she'd know if anything happened to him."

At that point, Rosalee felt a wave of panic roll over her. What did he mean, "happened"? What would have *happened* to him? She shook her head to stop her brain from rolling that word around anymore, but by that evening, the vicious little idea had become an erratic snowball, accumulating mass at high velocity and speeding toward endless horrifying conclusions.

"Oh no, here comes the part," said Ellie, hugging a pillow against her chest and bringing Rosalee back to the movie.

"Here comes what part?" Rosalee looked between her sister, who was cowering behind the pillow, and Pete, who was looking sheepish. "What part?" she said again.

"Uh, so Alex knows a lot about movies. Like, behind-the-scenes stuff," said Pete.

"Okay?"

Ellie lowered her shoulders from ear level. "Oh, maybe it's not this part."

"So, he made the mistake of telling Ellie about a rumor from this movie, where a Munchkin allegedly hanged himself on the set," said Pete. "Apparently, you can see his body swinging out from … that tree." He pointed and all three of them froze to watch.

"I don't see anything," said Rosalee, then she and Ellie gasped at the same time.

"Oh god, oh god, oh god." Ellie scrambled for the remote and pressed the REWIND button.

"*Why* are we watching it again?" said Rosalee. Her sudden adrenaline spike was quickly transitioning into grouchiness.

"Because it's too awful," said Ellie. "It can't be true, it just can't."

Rosalee curled into a tighter ball in her chair as Pete and Ellie moved around the coffee table to rewatch the scene, their faces less than a foot away from the television screen. Ellie groaned.

"Look, Alex said it was just a rumor," Pete said bracingly. "It could be anything making that shadow."

"Yeah, let's just watch the rest of the movie," said Rosalee. She was beginning to feel sick.

Meanwhile, Pete had to wrestle the remote from Ellie to keep her from hitting **REWIND** again. She sank to the floor in front of the TV and looked sadly at her hands in her lap. "I don't think I can watch the rest."

"We'll watch something else," said Pete. "No biggie."

With a considerable effort, Rosalee extracted herself from the depths of her armchair and grabbed the TV Guide from the coffee table. She scanned the listings for September 14th. "*Walker* isn't on for another hour, but we could watch *Funniest Home Videos.*"

Unfortunately, Saturday nights during the summer were pretty slim pickings, unless you had cable.

"Or there's *Touched by an Angel,*" Rosalee said quietly, half hoping Ellie wouldn't hear her.

Of course, she perked up at once and came around to look over Rosalee's shoulder. "Which one?"

"I don't know, but it's a rerun."

Ellie's shoulders drooped again. "Oh, I've seen that one. It's sad, too. There are bullies."

Rosalee was secretly relieved. There were some shows that were *too* sappy, and no matter how many times Ellie made her watch it, *Touched by an Angel* was the sappiest of sap.

"So ... *Funniest Home Videos?*" said Pete, flipping through channels.

They all migrated back to their viewing positions, where it didn't take long for Bob Saget to cheer Ellie up again. Rosalee noticed that Pete was sitting a little closer to her sister than before and felt a rush of gratitude that he had been there for Ellie when she couldn't be. Then the rush turned into a pang and she suddenly felt as though she was peering into her two best friends' new lives from a window where they waved but didn't invite her in.

Maybe that's how Alex feels, said a tiny voice in Rosalee's head.

But that was different. Pete and Ellie had specifically asked Rosalee if she wanted to watch a movie with them. They still wanted her in their lives and were making an effort—although they probably had no idea how much Rosalee needed them in hers. So who did Alex have?

Rosalee squirmed uncomfortably in her chair and glanced over at Pete and Ellie again. *Alex has Pete,* she reminded herself firmly. Pete was a great person to have in your corner. That's why it wasn't really a big deal that she hadn't been the warmest toward Alex—because he still had Pete. Besides, Ellie was polite enough to him for the both of them.

After a while, Rosalee realized that she was rolling a new word around in her head and it took her a moment to bring it into focus: *"bullies."* Ellie hadn't wanted to watch the *Touched by an Angel* re-run because it was sad—because of bullies. Rosalee felt her stomach clench. Was she a bully? Surely not. Didn't you have to go out of your way to be a bully? There was no doubt that Alex got in *her* way, not the other way around.

Still ... she held the word in her mind, kneading it experimentally like soft clay and then squashing it together with the word from that morning: "happened." "Bullies." Bullies happened. There was no way that Rosalee's indifference to Alex and her reluctance to be actual friends with him could have caused anything to *happen* to him ... could they? Then again, she didn't know him very well. Maybe he wasn't as happy-go-lucky as he seemed.

For the fourth time that night, Rosalee opened her mouth to ask Pete if he knew anything, then snapped it shut again, clenching her teeth in frustration. She would just have to wait it out. Pete would know if anything happened. People that actually talked to Alex regularly and let him into their lives a little bit would know if anything happened.

"You okay, Rose?"

Ellie's question startled Rosalee out of her excessive delirium and she realized that she was clutching her forehead. "Oh, yeah, I just have a headache," she lied. "I might go to bed soon."

— • • —

Half an hour later, as Rosalee brushed her teeth and changed into pajamas, she wished she had stayed downstairs. It would have been a nice distraction from the words that edged around her conscious thoughts, circled each other, then spiraled downward before flying back to their distant corners to start all over again.

Alex probably had to visit a sick relative. Or maybe his boss at the hospital had assigned him overtime. Just because he wasn't there when Rosalee was didn't mean that he wasn't still working. After all, she only went to the hospital a couple of times a week, while it was a whole second job for Alex. That had to be it—he was working extra hours at the hospital.

Rosalee shrugged her shoulders up to her ears and dropped them several times, urging her muscles to relax. She took deep breaths until she was dizzy while she brushed out the tangles in her hair and weaved it into a loose braid down her back. Then, as she pulled the accumulated bright red strands out of her brush and threw the wad of hair in the trash, she started a new mantra in her head:

Work, just work. Nobody's hurt. Work, just work. Don't be a jerk.

— • • • —

By morning, the mantra was still stuck in Rosalee's head. In fact, she was relieved to have to fill in for a bakery employee at The Goose who called in with a flat tire, if only to have a few hours of the overhead store music to interrupt the relentless incantation.

Eventually, though, she had to attend to her payroll duties and dragged herself half-heartedly to the office, where there was no speaker. One day, she would remember to bring her boombox.

She worked steadily for about an hour and barely realized that Robin had joined her until she looked up to see her frowning at her.

"What's up?" said Robin.

"Oh, sorry. Nothing. Just tired."

Robin licked her fingers every so often as she thumbed through a pile of receipts and added them up on the ten key. "Let me know if you need an extra break today."

"I'll be okay. I think I'll eat my lunch soon, though."

Robin paused her calculations. "Speaking of which, I haven't seen your lunch pal for a while. Did he finally give up?"

Rosalee winced inwardly, although she knew that her aunt was referring to Alex's relentless attempts to claw his way into her life—not anything morbid. Still, she didn't very much feel like talking about her egocentric Munchkin theory, so she just shrugged.

"Hope he's okay," said Robin, ripping off the tape from the machine and making a scribbled note.

Rosalee only barely refrained from falling forehead-first into her neat pile of signed and enveloped paychecks.

Chapter 13

Alex sat next to a large, plate glass window in the lobby of The Boyle, Sullivan & Cheney Law Firm and looked down at the muted cacophony of Denver. It was easy to forget the chaos of the city when you'd been in the middle of nowhere for a while. The interminable kinetic plaid of cars, buses, and trains seemed almost sacrilegious in its loudness, compared to the occasional car wandering down a dusty dirt road in Rabbitbrush, Colorado. And yet ... he had missed the chaos.

Alex shifted in his chair, slacks rubbing foreignly against his legs and the leather of the waiting room seat. He could feel himself sweating through the dress shirt and sports coat he wore. Outside was a balmy seventy degrees, and he suspected that the firm hadn't updated its air conditioning since the late sixties. He could hear the air buffeting the ancient vents as he crunched on the pretzels his mother had hurriedly poured into a Ziploc bag and pressed into his hands before he left her house that morning.

"For the road," she had said. "And tell Oliver that ..."

"I will," Alex promised, a lump in his throat as he watched Carol's eyes fill with tears.

He pulled her into a hug, and her shoulders felt tiny and fragile like bird bones. She had lost weight in the short time that had passed since he last saw her and that worried him. In fact, both Carol and her house were starting to fray at the seams, and Alex spent most of the week playing Mr. Fixit for the numerous things that had fallen into disrepair in his absence.

Alex wished he could stay longer and told her, before he got in his Jeep, to call if she needed anything. "*Anything*, Mom." He waited until she looked up at him with a watery smile. "And please think about what I said. You might like it out in the middle of nowhere."

Then Carol had nodded and wrapped her arms around herself the way that Alex had seen Rosalee do before—like she was holding herself together—and it hurt. It literally hurt to watch. But somehow, Alex managed to swing his bag over his shoulder, which was heavier now with Oliver's care package of books and snacks, and back out of his mother's driveway like it wasn't breaking his heart to leave her like that.

"Mr. Conway?"

Alex was startled out of his reverie by the firm's receptionist, who wore a neat, brown skirt and sensible shoes and smelled like one of those perfume samples stuck inside of magazines. She smiled kindly at him as he reoriented himself with the tall windows and wood paneling of the lobby. Too far away from his mother. Too far away from Oliver. Caught halfway in between.

"He's ready for you now," said the receptionist, beckoning Alex to follow her. "Can I get you anything? A cup of coffee?"

Alex stuffed the empty Ziploc into his messenger bag and stood. "I'm fine thanks," he said, then changed his mind. The calming effect of the cigarettes he had chain-smoked less than fifteen minutes before had already begun to wear off. "Actually, coffee sounds great."

"Cream or sugar?"

"Both, please."

The receptionist nodded and led him down a narrow hallway with more wood paneling that made him feel as though he was about to be trapped in a maze. Eventually, they came to a corner office, where the receptionist knocked twice on the door before turning the handle.

"Here we are," she said, pushing the door open for Alex.

At once, he could see the appeal of a corner office: windows overlooking the city took up two whole walls. The panoramic view of Denver's skyline and the Rocky Mountains would have been enough to keep him from his work for hours at a time.

"Glen, I'm getting a cup of coffee for Mr. Conway, would you like anything?"

"I'm fine, Sharon, thank you," said the attorney behind the desk. He stubbed out his cigarette in a fancy glass ashtray on his highly polished desk and stood to shake Alex's hand. "Good to see you again."

"And you, Glen," said Alex, feeling the chill emanating from his half of the handshake and wondering if it would transfer to the recipient.

The attorney wore a gray suit and light blue dress shirt. Alex noticed that he seemed more uptight than usual, but perhaps he was simply reacting to being called "Glen."

"So," said the attorney, sitting down again and inviting Alex to do the same, "it's been a while. How have you been?"

"Great. Good. Model citizen."

Alex eyed what he assumed was his file between them on the desk.

"Yes, well, this has been a rather difficult situation," said Glen, shuffling several stray papers and tucking them back inside the folder, "but I think we've come up with a reasonable solution."

Alex nodded, his mouth suddenly dry. Luckily, Sharon returned just then with his pale coffee in a styrofoam cup. He thanked her and took a sip, ignoring the fact that it was roughly the temperature of lava.

"Any plans to go back to school?" said Glen.

Alex winced as the coffee scalded his throat. "Working on it."

"Job?"

"Two."

Glen nodded in apparent approval. "And your mother? Doing well, I hope?"

She's not great, Glen. Thanks for that, Alex thought. "Fine, fine," he said out loud. He studied the frayed skin around his thumbnail, resisting the urge to chew it.

"Good. I'm glad to hear it." Glen opened Alex's file, then hesitated. "Any more trouble with ..."

"Oliver?" Alex raised his eyebrows.

Glen nodded stiffly and Alex couldn't think of a single thing to say that wouldn't get him unceremoniously chucked out of the attorney's office. As much as he hated to admit it (and hoped he'd never have to again) he needed serious help. And if anyone could give him the kind he needed right now, it was the man sitting across from him.

"He's ... struggling," said Alex. "But we haven't given up on him, yet."

This time, he noted a shadow of shame in Glen's eyes.

"Still in that ... place?" the attorney said, shifting in his leather chair so that the hinges squeaked.

"'That place?'"

"Carol told me. Briefly."

"You've been talking to my mother?" Alex willed his fingers to unclench from the fists he was making under the desk. *Chill, Alex.*

"Well, she's—Yes, I have." Alex watched Glen's expression of mild irritation turn to defiance. "She called me after the ... incident. She was extremely worried for you. She had nowhere else to turn."

Alex scoffed. "That's not true, she could have—"

"Could have what?" Glen cocked his head with the hint of a sardonic smile and leaned back slightly in his chair, "Waited to see if you made any legal connections in jail? Taken out a second mortgage to help pay the mounting fines of her unemployed son?"

Alex met the attorney's eyes and looked away first, reluctantly. He knew that Glen was the best chance he had right now, no matter how much he wished he had another option. So, he cleared his throat and sat up straighter in his chair. After all, he had gotten himself into this mess and the only thing to do now was machete-hack his way through to the other side.

"Look, I appreciate what you've done," he said. "What you're doing."

The attorney nodded, opening Alex's file again. "And I appreciate your gratitude. As I say, it hasn't been easy."

"So ..." Alex prompted, taking another sip of coffee, which had barely cooled since the first sip.

"Well, Brenneman still isn't pressing charges."

Alex nearly choked. "You're kidding. That's good news, right?"

"Yes, well ..." Glen riffled in a desk drawer until he located a pair of reading glasses. "As with most things in life, there are strings. For one thing, he's said that in no uncertain terms are you to ever make an appearance or solicit employment at that location or any of the others."

"That's not a problem," Alex muttered, waiting while the attorney shuffled several documents.

"He's also insisting on damages and they're steep."

"Why? What did I damage?"

"He's working to obtain estimates for the wooden post you dented."

"Okay." *Hard to argue there.*

"As well as the alcohol you consumed on the premises, the bottle of '94 Beringer Chardonnay you smashed—"

"They don't even *sell* that wine—they just keep the bottle, fill it with the cheap stuff, and cork it in the back."

The attorney continued as though he hadn't been interrupted. "—shattered backsplash, broken wheels on a stainless steel countertop, a cracked drain pipe—"

Alex felt his mouth fall open with a little *pop,* but Glen held up a hand to arrest his angry protests. Alex raked a hand through his hair in frustration but held his tongue.

"—a broken dishwasher handle, stained grout ... oh, and eight stitches."

As Glen stacked the papers and shut them in the folder again, Alex listened to a *clunk* in the vents and then a *whoosh* as the air conditioning kicked in for another cycle.

"How do we know he's not just using me to remodel the whole kitchen?" he said.

"We don't."

"So, then ..."

"I told you I would negotiate and get you the best deal I could—try to work out a payment plan, at the very least. In the meantime, I would recommend you start working and *saving* as much as possible."

"Working as much as I can ... *plus* the anger management classes and AA meetings?"

"That was the deal."

"That was *your* deal."

"I have to know you're serious." Glen frowned. "Look, kid, you messed up pretty bad. You have no idea how lucky you are that the situation ended the way it did. Charges for assault with a deadly weapon aren't something we want to have to argue on top of everything else."

"I know. I agree." Alex looked the attorney straight in the face and could tell that he was disconcerted by the fact that he wasn't about to be sulky and belligerent about it.

"I certainly hope you've gotten the drinking under control since then?" Glen said, stern again.

"Yeah. Yes." Alex shook his head at the last dregs of his coffee. "But that was never the problem."

The attorney let out a derisive snort. "Well, I wouldn't get too comfortable with that delusion."

"Look, I told you, it was bad timing."

"Unfortunately, that isn't an argument that would hold up well in court."

"So, why *can't* we take this to court? Don't you think they would be more reasonable?"

"Maybe, maybe not." Glen regarded him over his glasses. "With no surveillance cameras, it's down to 'he said, she said.' The court may believe that he threw the first punch, but it could also look disapprovingly upon the way you chose to escalate the situation."

Alex gritted his teeth as the attorney continued.

"Add in court costs and potential damage to your record, and you could find yourself in a harrowing situation, to say the least. I can't say I like the idea of Brenneman throwing his weight around, either. This may be the best offer you're going to get."

Glen waited until Alex met his eyes again.

"Okay," said Alex.

"So, we're clear on your responsibilities from here on out?"

"Yes, sir."

"You have a little less than three months."

Alex grimaced but nodded.

"I may be able to get that extended if you can get written statements from both employers," said the attorney.

"I'll work on it."

"Alright, then I'll have Sharon copy these notes for you and let you be on your way." Glen pushed an intercom button on his desk, which made a harsh buzzing noise before Sharon's voice answered amid the static. "Can I get some copies, please?"

The secretary arrived promptly to retrieve the notes, then left again as Alex re-interested himself in his frayed thumbnail. Glen removed his reading glasses again, making quite a meal of wrapping the lenses in a cloth and closing them securely back into their case. Luckily, Sharon returned quickly with the copies, which Alex stuffed into his bag before pushing his chair out from the desk.

"Thanks again," he said, standing to shake Glen's hand.

Before the attorney stood, Alex noticed that the straw-colored hair on his head had become thinner. He didn't know if he would ever get used to the way that time changed people—all of a sudden and drastically. Or maybe it was only drastic when you weren't paying attention, or when the people it changed had been absent for so long.

"Get me those letters as soon as you can," said Glen, letting go of Alex's hand and sitting back down, smoothing his tie. "Take care, now."

Alex nodded, his hand already turning the door handle. He closed it securely behind him and stood for a moment to let his eyes adjust to the greatly reduced light in the hallway.

"You, too ... Dad."

Chapter 14

Rosalee rummaged through another dingy cardboard box, dimly lit by the feeble flicker of the fluorescent light on the ceiling of the garage. She wondered irritably why she could never come up with artistic inspiration during the daylight hours. This day had been endlessly sunny and yet, here she was, post-sunset, wide awake and bubbling with ingenuity.

She folded the top of the box closed, yanking the flaps into place, then went to retrieve the ladder from the back wall. She propped it against the workbench she sometimes used as a drawing table and began to root around in the cabinets mounted over the bench. She was just about to give up on the first cabinet and move on to the next when a flashlight beam illuminated its interior.

Rosalee felt her pulse and adrenaline skyrocket as she whirled around on the ladder, nearly unhinging her knees in the process.

"Jesus, Mr. Bundy, *must* you?" she hissed at Alex, who had quickly tossed away the flashlight to steady the ladder.

Alex let go of the ladder, raising both hands to shoulder height, instead. Rosalee rolled her eyes, trying to ignore that her heartbeat had migrated to her throat.

"I meant the whole stalking-me-under-ladders bit," she said. "You wouldn't have to save me in the first place if you'd lick that habit."

Alex winked. "Well, it *is* harder for you to run this way."

Rosalee made a face. "How did you know I was here?" *And where have you been?* She clamped her teeth together to keep from saying the last part out loud. "You know, Tom Peepery is sort of frowned upon in polite society."

"'*Tom Peepery,*'" Alex chuckled. He located his discarded flashlight at the base of a hedge next to the driveway and inspected it. "I was headed back from work and saw the light. I hoped it was you in here. What are you doing?"

"I wanted to paint on the back patio, but it's too dark. I thought there was a camping light in here."

"This one?" Alex switched his flashlight on again, aiming it at the top of the cabinets, where an old, green Coleman lantern sat next to bug spray and a canister of camping fuel.

"Oh. Yes, thanks." Rosalee climbed down the ladder and moved it to the end of the bench. "So, is that where you've been—at work?" she said in a deliberately offhand way as she stretched to retrieve the lantern.

Work, just work, nobody's hurt.

Alex didn't answer right away and as Rosalee descended the ladder again, she tried not to imagine him smirking behind her as he possibly misinterpreted her curiosity as *missing him.*

"I had some things to sort out in Denver," he said.

When his voice didn't sound gloating, Rosalee turned back to face him. Despite her best efforts at indifference, she could feel her resolve crumbling, but she also recognized the look on people's faces that meant they didn't want to talk about things. In fact, she was fairly certain that expression had affixed itself permanently to Robin's face.

"Is this okay? Me being here?" said Alex. "I wasn't trying to freak you out."

Rosalee glanced at the house. "It's okay, it's just kinda late."

"You're worried about your aunts?" Alex glanced at his watch, then frowned slightly.

"What time is it?"

"Nine fifteen."

"Oh. Anyway, I guess that doesn't make sense, does it?" Rosalee leaned backward against the ladder. "I think sometimes I forget how old I am. And how young."

"How old are you?"

"Twenty-three. Going on eighty-three. How old are you?"

"Twenty-five. Going on ... five."

Rosalee smiled. "Right. How's that quarter-life crisis coming?"

"Right on track." Rosalee detected an uncharacteristic note of bitterness in Alex's voice as she watched him prod a rock loose from the driveway with the toe of his sneaker. He looked at her. "I'll let you get back to your painting. Just wanted to say 'hi.'"

"You can stay," said Rosalee, then instantly felt light-headed at her impulsivity.

"Really?"

"Yeah. I mean, for a little while."

"Okay." Alex's tentative smile reminded her of the one he wore on the Ferris wheel. "Do you wanna set up your lantern?"

"Yeah. Let's go through the back gate."

Alex wheeled his bike after her, leaning it against the side of the house just inside the gate. He slung his messenger bag over his shoulder, then followed her to the back patio, which was lit by a single porch light and twinkly lights that wound up the banister of the wooden staircase leading to a deck on the upper level. Rosalee set the camping lantern on the table and began to fiddle with the fuel pump valve while Alex appraised the backyard.

"Oh my god, is this a sandbox?" he said, crouching down beside a plastic turtle roughly four feet in diameter.

Rosalee looked back over her shoulder. "Yeah, but I'm not sure what else is in there by now."

"I brought my flashlight."

"What about a lighter?"

Alex walked back to the porch and hung his messenger bag on one of the newel posts, then extracted a Bic from the front pocket of his jeans and handed it to Rosalee. After several more minutes of tinkering, the mantles ignited and Rosalee stepped back to admire the lantern light flickering over the surface of the table and her drawing. She gave the lighter back. "That should work for now."

Alex stuffed his hands in his pockets, nodding appreciatively. "Not too shabby."

"You still wanna play in the sandbox, don't you?"

"Kinda, yeah."

Alex walked back to the box and lifted the turtle shell lid with his foot, then flipped it onto the grass. He dug the toe of his sneaker into the box several times, turning the sand over under the beam of his flashlight until he was apparently satisfied. "All clear."

He sank cross-legged into the grass and began to draw large, looping patterns in the sand with his fingers. Rosalee sat across from him and did the same, careful to keep her circles from touching his. After several seconds, Alex laughed.

"What?" said Rosalee.

"You're so human tonight."

"*... Wow.*"

"Sorry. You know what I mean."

Rosalee felt suddenly defensive. "I'm just tired. It's easier to talk when you're tired."

"Is that right?"

Rosalee nodded. *Plus, I'm happy you're not swinging from a tree.*

"So, what were you working on?" said Alex. "You said you were trying to paint?"

"I was just messing around. I had one of those dreams I couldn't get out of my head, and so I thought maybe if I painted it, it would ..."

"Leave you alone?"

"Sort of."

Alex erased his patterns with several long swipes of the side of his hand. "Did you paint me?"

Rosalee laughed and Alex looked up in surprise.

"Not yet," said Rosalee, feeling a little self-conscious. "And anyway, the only reason I'm telling you any of this is because it's been a long day. Also, my brain is fried."

Alex poked random divots into the sand with his index finger. "Yeah, them paint fumes is a bitch," he said in a thick, hillbilly accent.

"What's that from?" said Rosalee automatically.

"I—nowhere. Me."

"I'm still trying to separate your quoting voice from your normal one." Rosalee noticed the corner of Alex's mouth tick upward as he connected the dots he made. "And I haven't started the painting part—this is just the sketch."

Alex glanced toward the table again. "Can I see it?"

Rosalee met his eyes briefly before pushing herself off the ground to retrieve the canvas. On the way back, she held it as close to her chest as she could without smudging the charcoal before losing her nerve altogether. "I'm—it's not ready."

She hugged the canvas tighter, smudging be damned. Alex watched her for a moment, but he didn't seem disappointed.

"Do you like hot chocolate?" he said.

"Uh ..."

"Hot chocolate?" Alex mimed the act of drinking. "The thing with the hot milk and the chocolate powder—"

"Okay, yes, hot chocolate." Rosalee shook her head. "Sorry, your ADD is giving me whiplash."

Alex raised his eyebrows. "And?"

"And, yes. Hot chocolate is fine. Wonderful. I'm so tired," Rosalee groaned.

Alex laughed, then paused. "Come to the dance with me."

"What?"

Rosalee was beginning to think that trying to keep up with the epitome of the Energizer Bunny at this hour may have been a mistake.

"The dance," said Alex. "The fundraiser town thingy."

The word "no" was already formed on Rosalee's lips when her family's lecture plastered itself firmly to the front of her brain. "Why?" she said instead.

Alex sighed.

"I wasn't trying to be rude, I was just wondering," said Rosalee.

"Because I want to see you. More." Alex shrugged. "And I'm gonna be pretty busy for a while, so it would be nice to have something to look forward to."

Rosalee watched him for several moments, then shifted her gaze just over his shoulder. She realized that she was still awkwardly hugging her canvas and walked back to the table. Alex stood and slid the turtle top back onto the sandbox before joining her, leaning against one of the porch columns.

"*Maybe,*" said Rosalee finally, "But no dancing."

"No ... dancing ..." Alex repeated.

"Yes."

"At the *dance.*"

"Right."

"Why?"

"Because I don't dance."

Alex rolled his eyes so hard that his whole head moved with them. "I've seen you dance, you dirty, filthy *liar.*"

"*Excuse* you?" said Rosalee, indignantly. "*When?*"

"Oh, come *on.* When the hospital asked you to paint that mural, you practically did the 'Snoopy dance.'"

"Oh."

Alex shoved his flashlight back into the messenger bag and took out a thermos, then looked behind him. "Do you wanna sit by the creek for a while?"

"Okay." Rosalee pointed to the thermos. "What's that?"

"Hot chocolate."

"You brought hot chocolate?"

"Why did you think I asked you about it?"

"*Again,* with the ADD."

Rosalee retrieved the camping lantern from the patio table and led the way across the backyard, then through another gate and out to the creek. On the way, she flipped a switch that turned on twinkle lights along the fence and softly illuminated the bank, then stood on her toes to hang the lantern on an oak branch. When she stepped back to soak it all in, she realized how much she took living close to the water for granted. When she and Ellie were little, they spent hours by the creek trying to catch crawdads. Now, she couldn't even remember the last time they came out here, even to dangle their feet in the water.

"This is nice." Alex looked around them at the trees that lined the bank, the closest of which were choke cherry, oak, and willow. "I like the lights."

"Ellie and Lola. It was a team effort."

Rosalee waited to sit down until Alex sat so that she could keep the thermos and a little over a foot of distance between them. Still, he was close enough that she detected a mixture of restaurant smells: coffee, something delicious and fried, a hint of dish detergent.

"So ... the hot chocolate," she said. "Premeditated?"

"Like, somehow I got clairvoyant vibrations telling me that you would be outside painting tonight? Or you're still worried that I'm stalking you?"

Rosalee felt herself flush and was glad for the darkness.

"Alright, I give up," said Alex. "Maybe I didn't plan this, but ..." He turned so that he was facing Rosalee full on, his usual smile replaced by a much more serious expression. The intensity of his gaze started a flutter in her stomach, but it didn't quite feel like the good kind. "Rosalee," his voice was low—almost husky, "This was *destiny*. If you knew how I've dreamt about this ... longed for this moment ..."

He shifted closer and Rosalee leaned stiffly away, avoiding his eyes. "Oh. No ..."

"Please look at me." Alex's voice was barely above a whisper and saturated with something as ooey-gooey as Ellie's pop collection.

Rosalee cringed. "I, um—oh my god, Alex, I think maybe you've misunderstoo—"

"*Shhh.*" Alex moved a finger very close to her lips but stopped before he actually touched them. Rosalee's eyes crossed to keep his finger in her line of sight. "Please don't fight this. Rosalee, I know we're meant to be together. *Orion and Gemini.* A love match."

Rosalee stopped leaning away. "Oh." She let out the breath she was holding, torn between relief and the rumblings of a half-formed anxiety attack. "You're kidding."

"I'm kidding."

Alex moved back into his own space and unscrewed the lid from the thermos. He looked at Rosalee out of the corner of his eye and grinned.

"*'Orion.'* Funny," she muttered.

"You would know, O Wondrous Expert of Horoscopes."

"Don't look so pleased with yourself," said Rosalee. "You play a good creep."

Alex ignored that comment and shoved two cups into Rosalee's hands before she could protest. "Hold these, would you?"

"Two cups. So this *was* premeditated. How did you even fit two cups in there?"

Alex's hand was steady as he poured from the thermos. "It *came* with two cups—don't flatter yourself."

As they sat with their steaming hot cocoa, Rosalee let her feet dangle in the water to her ankles. She imagined that the cool water wasn't wet—that instead, it was the air around her and that she was floating in it. She watched the steam swirl out of her cup and change shape with her breaths. She tried holding the air in her lungs to allow the delicate tendrils to take a more direct, upward course, then letting it out gently to watch them scatter again in front of her.

"What's up?" said Alex.

Rosalee took a slurpy sip of the still-scalding beverage. "Nothing."

"You looked like you were holding your breath."

"I was ... watching the steam."

If Alex thought that was lame, he didn't confirm it out loud.

"This is really good," said Rosalee. "Thank you."

"No sweat. It's not the best kind, but it does the trick."

Normally, Rosalee would have ignored the subtle invitation to advance the conversation, but the gentle melody of the creek and the scent of cocoa and Russian olive blooms down the way gave her a rare feeling of serenity. "What's the best kind?"

"The kind out of hospital vending machines, for some reason. I don't know why."

"I guess I've never tried it. You must visit them a lot to know that."

Rosalee tried very hard not to stare at the mutilated skin knitting itself into thin lines across Alex's wrist and forearm. He made a non-committal noise in his throat, then cleared it.

"I'm sorry," said Rosalee quickly. "That was insanely personal."

She met his eyes reluctantly, but he didn't look angry. In fact, he looked smug.

"What?" said Rosalee.

Alex smirked into his cup. "Nothing."

Rosalee set her cup down beside her, accidentally brushing Alex's fingers. She jumped and he moved the thermos out of the way just in time to save it from the water. "Sorry," she said.

She thought about the brief skin contact. The memory was already fading away. It might have been warm, though.

"I feel like the Canadian national anthem should follow you around like a theme song," said Alex.

Rosalee looked at him blankly.

"You don't need to apologize for everything."

"Oh. Right."

"Come with me. To the town thingy."

Rosalee pulled a strand of hair free from her ponytail and twisted it around her finger. She scooted to the edge of the bank so that her feet were submerged to her lower calves, focusing on the cool temperature of the water again. "I already said I might." She picked up her half-empty cup again for something to do. It was finally the perfect temperature and she savored it for a moment, then frowned. "You came from work, but you have hot chocolate?"

Alex laughed. "Good *lord,* you're paranoid. I made it for the ride home. Laurie's has one of those hot water spigots in the kitchen, so I bring the cocoa packets."

"Not a coffee drinker?"

"I'm a *rabid* coffee drinker—just not before bed."

"Right."

Rosalee heard something rustling in the grass and looked over to see Alex running his fingers back and forth through the blades. "Can I ask you something?" he said after a bit.

"Bet you can."

"You don't like to let people get close to you."

Rosalee waited. "Was that the question?"

"I don't know, I could be completely out on a limb here. I just wondered if maybe that had something to do with ... your parents?"

Whatever Rosalee expected him to say, it wasn't that. She almost laughed. "What are you, a fake attorney *and* psychiatrist now?"

Alex looked embarrassed. "No, I'm sorry. I just wondered why you live with your aunts."

Rosalee gazed out across the water, where tall grasses rippled in the breeze on the opposite bank. It wasn't exactly a painful subject—on the other hand, she tried not to think about it very much. She also grew tired of the pitying looks she tended to get when she explained that Ellie was planned and she wasn't; that her parents had decided to put aside their entomological aspirations for a few years to give the whole "family" thing a go after the accident of Rosalee.

Ultimately, the allure of exotic insects in faraway places won out, and they dumped Rosalee and Ellie on their father's sisters more and more often, for longer periods at a time. Through the years, the letters became increasingly sparse, and eventually, the Christmas cards stopped, too. Rosalee and Ellie still received a birthday card apiece every year, though, signed "Mom & Dad," with a crisp fifty-dollar bill. Rosalee knew for a fact that most of Ellie's cards remained stuffed in a drawer somewhere, unopened.

"Okay, too personal, I get it," said Alex.

Rosalee wasn't sure how long she had been lost in her thoughts but decided not to correct him for the misinterpretation of her silence. She watched him tip the last of his cocoa into his mouth and stare straight ahead, his eyes momentarily unfocused as a nerve flexed in his jaw. "Have I told you about my brother yet?"

"I don't think so." Rosalee waited for him to say more. He didn't. "Is … your brother okay?"

Alex shook his head and swallowed. He still wouldn't look at her directly and Rosalee found that this new, quieter Alex made her more uncomfortable than the chatty, probing version.

"Look, Alex, we don't have to do this. Like, talk about things we don't feel comfortable talking about. We don't have to get to know each other *that way.*"

Alex made a noise in his throat that sounded both impatient and irritated.

"I didn't mean it like that," said Rosalee. "I wasn't holding it over you, I'm just saying we don't have to force ourselves to, like … *know* each other. We can still be friends or whatever without getting into all the deep stuff."

"So, like, acquaintances?"

She could feel Alex's eyes on her and finally decided to stop pretending to be too absorbed with looking at her feet in the water to notice. She ignored the fact that her cheeks were on fire as she stared back at him.

"Is that what you want?" said Alex.

Rosalee's mouth felt too dry to get out any actual words. She shrugged.

Alex clicked his tongue. "Okay, well then I guess I better be going."

He stood at once and gathered the empty cups, stacking them in the thermos and twisting the lid back on. Rosalee listened as he passed through the gate to the backyard and then collapsed over her knees, cursing herself silently into oblivion.

She had worried about Alex for over a week. Days upon days of her life, she spent wondering where he was. And then *here* he was and she ruined it. She could have had a friend—an unconventional friend, but a friend nonetheless—an actual human who wanted to have actual conversations with her, and she had already driven him away.

"*Ugh*, Rosalee," she mumbled into her knees.

"Hey."

Rosalee jumped and nearly twisted her neck to look behind her. Alex was leaning on the fence, thermos swinging from one finger again. He didn't even look mad—just pensive. "Are you working on your mural next week?"

"Um. Yes."

"Then ... maybe I'll see you then."

Rosalee nodded stupidly as she watched him retrieve his messenger bag and exit the backyard with his bike, closing the gate behind him.

Chapter 15

"Alex, man, I get all jittery when it's this quiet. You mind if I bump some tunes?"

Alex and Manny, his coworker, were mudding drywall in a deserted corridor of the new geriatric ward and it was almost eerily quiet.

"Go for it," said Alex. Maybe it would take his mind off of the persistent little hamster squeaking its wheel around and around in his head.

Overall, it had been a good night with Rosalee. All things considered, it went better than any of their other meetings (except for the part at the end, but even then, he was pretty sure she hadn't meant it). Still, just to be sure, Alex decided that it should be Rosalee who came to him this time. The ball was most definitely in her court.

"I got my box in the truck," said Manny, scraping mud off of his knife and setting it down over the container. "Back in a flash."

It took all of Alex's self-control not to toss Manny his keys and ask him to grab his cigarettes out of the Jeep, but he was trying to make his current pack last for at least another day. So instead, he nodded and stared at the off-white drywall in front of him and the uniform pattern of mud over seams and screws that extended down the hall until Manny came back with his boombox and two sodas.

He threw one to Alex. "I didn't know what you drink, but it's getting hot."

Alex adjusted the bandana in his hair to soak up the sweat that had already accumulated due to the lack of air conditioning in this wing. "This is great, thank you."

"Sure thing." Manny located an outlet and pressed PLAY on the cassette deck. "My girl made me a mixtape for our anniversary last week. It's got some good tracks. She has good taste."

Alex popped the tab on his Dr. Pepper and took a swig. He hadn't realized how thirsty he was. "How long have you been married?"

Manny was already unrolling paper tape along its crease for a corner seam. "Oh, no, man, we're just dating. I haven't popped the question yet."

"Do you think you will?"

"For sure. It's been, like, almost eight years."

Alex dipped his knife into the mud to slather into the corner. "Wow. High school sweethearts?"

"Yeah, but rings are *hella* expensive. I gotta save up. What about you? Anyone back home?"

"Nope."

Alex took extra care with the corner and then stood back to let Manny work his magic with the tape.

"What about here?" said Manny, his tongue between his teeth as he concentrated. "Got your eye on anyone?"

Alex shrugged and tried not to focus on the deep maroon of his Dr. Pepper can against the unfinished wall. Did he see red everywhere before Rosalee? He couldn't remember. Not that her hair was actually that color. He wondered if he would have felt the same way about a can of Orange Crush.

"That's probably best at this point," said Manny. "Not getting into it with anyone, for now. Like, I'm not one to preach, but I think the 'one-year rule' is a pretty solid one."

"Yeah, I guess so."

Manny stopped to wipe the sweat off his brow. "You said your old man is making you go, but I bet you still find some value."

Alex frowned at several stripes of mud drying and cracking in his hands. "I agree. Out of curiosity, though, why do you think it's a good rule?"

Manny sat back on his heels and unrolled the tape until it reached the floor, then sliced off the end with his taping knife. "It's like … you know on airplanes when they tell you that in the event of an emergency, you should get your own oxygen mask on before you help someone else?"

"Sure."

"I think in general, people would wanna brush that off. Like, the plane is going down and my kid is right here—obviously, I'm gonna put on their mask, right? But then the parent could already be out of air and not realize. Then it's too late."

"Okay, I guess that makes sense."

"How long you been sober for, again?"

"I don't know, like, the middle of June?"

"Of this year?"

"Yeah."

Manny let out a low whistle.

"I know you don't believe me, but I'm not an alcoholic," said Alex. "It was just something to do. Some way to … cope."

Manny chuckled. "You don't think that's how alcoholics feel?"

Alex hesitated.

"Okay, you're up," said Manny. "Smooth it out good. Make it pretty."

Alex picked up his taping knife again. "God. I suck at corners."

Manny grinned. "Hey, *you* said it, not me. This way, you'll learn." He switched places with Alex. "Anyway, I wasn't trying to put you on the spot. Like, it's not even just alcoholics that sometimes need a break. When we first met, you told me you were going through some heavy shit. Are you still going through it?"

"Uh, yeah. Big time."

"There you go. It's like, all that hardship—it's a kind of grief in itself. The process is grief; the healing is grief. Sometimes it's hard to be everything someone needs when you're that weighed down, and the crazy part is that you may not even notice because you're too deep in it. Also, for addicts, anyway, relationships can be like a new high—just a replacement for the craving, you know? And that's not healthy, either."

"No, yeah, you're probably right." Alex realized that he had stopped working while he listened to Manny and hurried to resume the torturous task of smoothing the tape.

"Man, you know I'm gonna support you either way, right? I'm just kinda obligated to lay it all out for you."

"I know, I appreciate it."

A love song started on the mix tape and Alex cringed inwardly.

"Aw, look at all these sappy tracks she got on here," said Manny, laughing. "She said she wants this to be our song, even though we have about fifty of 'em already. You know Selena?"

Alex was trying not to listen too closely to the lyrics, which were nauseatingly romantic. He was not in the mood to pine. "Is that who this is? She sounds familiar."

"Yeah, man. Died, like, almost a year and a half ago. Her fan club manager killed her."

"Jesus."

"Yeah, twenty-three years old. She was younger than us, man. Like, can you imagine trusting someone that much and then one day ..." Manny mimed shooting a gun at the wall.

"Not like that, no," said Alex distractedly. He was still hung up on the "twenty-three years old" part. For some reason.

Manny shook his head. "Crazy shit ... Hey, since we only have a little bit of mud left, I'm gonna do this seam while you finish the corner, okay?"

"Sounds good."

Alex was still hyper-focused on not wrinkling or ripping the tape, although he was at least near the floor now, so he was getting a little faster.

"*Oooh* ..." Manny bounced his shoulders as the song changed again. "This is my jam, I'ma turn it up."

Alex was exasperated but not surprised that Manny had already finished his task. He still laughed as Manny busted out moves he had seen some eight-year-olds practicing in his neighborhood a few weeks before.

"You don't think the nurses will come yell at us?" said Alex, raising his voice over the music as he scraped excess mud off of his knife.

"Nah, it's just you and me in this wing, plus the quiet girl painting in pediatrics."

"Rosalee's back?"

"Rosalee, that's her name? So you know her?"

"Oh ..." *Busted.* "Sort of."

"Oooh, 'sort of,'" Manny teased, "Look at your face. I knew there was someone. Go say somethin' to her."

"Maybe later. I already took too long on this corner."

"I wouldn't worry about it. We're not supposed to start painting for two days, thanks to you rushing us through the last two hallways to—" Manny stopped to stare at Alex, mouth slightly open.

"What?"

"To get to *Rosalee's* wall." Manny threw his head back and laughed. "Lord, here we go."

———•●•———

By the time lunchtime came around, Alex practically sprinted to his Jeep for a cigarette. He leaned back against the cab and inhaled deeply, then watched through the smoke as a hazy girl with flaming hair walked toward him.

Chill, Alex, chill, he said to himself, which was much easier to fake when you had a cigarette in your hand—like James friggin' Dean.

"Hey," Rosalee said when she reached him. "Is this your car?"

Alex blew smoke away from her and smiled in what he hoped was a very *cool* way. "Sure is. Brought it back from Denver."

"Cool. Are you okay?"

"What?"

Rosalee swung her backpack off one shoulder to unzip it. "You looked like you were about to sneeze."

Alex scowled while she dug through the bag. He ashed in front of his steel-toed work boots, then ground it into the asphalt.

"I brought your movie back," said Rosalee.

She handed it back to him and Alex tried to arrange his face into something a little more naturally himself as he looked fondly at the cover. "Great, what did you think?"

"I think the book is better, but it was still good."

"The *book* is better?" Alex's eyes narrowed as he blew smoke out of the corner of his mouth."No way."

Rosalee shrugged. "Guess you'll have to read it. I can lend it to you if you want."

"Maybe. Only if you watch something. *Another* something."

"Deal."

Alex offered Rosalee his cigarette, but she waved it away. "Thanks—I'm trying to be good."

"Me, too." Alex took another draw. "How's the mural coming?"

"Not great. Lucky for the hospital, they're not paying me by the hour."

"Are they paying you *at all?*"

Rosalee paused. "I'm not actually sure? I think I blacked out after she said I got the job."

Alex smiled. That had been a good night. For both of them.

"So, how's your work going?" said Rosalee.

"It's okay. Got to watch Manny do 'The Macaroni.'"

"The what?"

Alex flicked the ash off of the end of his cigarette again and did a poor imitation of the choreography.

"Um, could you mean 'The *Macarena?*'" Rosalee bit her lip, clearly trying not to laugh.

"Yeah, that's what I said."

Alex finished his cigarette and stubbed it out, then dropped it into a coffee can he kept on the floor in the back of his Jeep. Maybe Rosalee would find his lack of littering sexy. He looked up to gauge her expression and was disappointed to see her looking over her shoulder, her feet pointed subtly away from him.

"I should get back," she said. "I have to work at The Goose tonight, so I only have another hour or so to paint."

"Okay. It was good to see you the other night."

Damn it, Alex.

He watched as Rosalee's expression cleared and wondered if his "cool guy" attitude had come across a little *too* cool—frigid, even.

"You, too," she said. "Definitely changed my perspective on hot chocolate."

"Well, we'll still have to get you the best kind at some point."

Rosalee nodded and did her awkward smile and wave, then turned to walk back toward the hospital entrance. Alex watched her go, tapping the movie against his palm, then realized that it was upside down. He caught the tape just before it slid out of its case, then noticed a sticky note.

He hardly dared to believe his eyes as he stared at Rosalee's email address in what he assumed was her handwriting. Eventually, his stomach reminded him that he was supposed to be fueling up for the rest of the afternoon, so he tore himself away from the note, tucking it securely into his back pocket.

———•●•———

By the time he met Manny at their usual lunch spot—a patio balcony off of another deserted wing—he was still floating.

"What's up with you?" said Manny. He had already finished his lunch and was throwing back another Dr. Pepper.

"Nothing." Alex grinned as he dug into tuna casserole and red Jell-O from the cafeteria.

"Aw, don't give me that crap." Manny watched him closely. "Bro, you're not high, are you? We still gotta finish three walls."

Alex laughed. "No, uh … Rosalee caught up to me while I was grabbing a smoke. *To give my movie back,*" he clarified as Manny arched an eyebrow.

"*Aaand,* what did you give her?"

Alex smiled. He couldn't stop. "Nothing. But she also gave me her email."

Manny stared at him for a moment. *"Hot,"* he said sarcastically.

Alex shrugged and opened the cardboard carton of chocolate milk on his tray.

"Do you even own a computer?" said Manny.

"No, but the library does."

"You're gonna go all the way to the library to email this chick? Why can't she pick up the phone?"

"I didn't ask. Anyway, it's a pretty big deal for her."

Manny shook his head. "Whatever floats your boat, cuz."

Chapter 16

Rosalee awoke in the middle of the night to the sound of tree branches scraping and clattering against her bedroom window as gales of rain assaulted the roof and siding. She rolled onto her back to revel in the sweet, damp petrichor emanating from the gap in her window, knowing she should close it to preserve the sill but unwilling to shut out the rain.

"Rose?" Ellie's face appeared around her bedroom door. "You awake?"

Rosalee pushed herself up to sit against her headboard. "Yeah, are you okay?"

"I can't sleep." Ellie tiptoed into the room, the floorboards creaking slightly as she made her way to Rosalee's bed and perched on the end of it.

"Do you wanna stay in here for a while?"

Ellie nodded and Rosalee scooted over so that she could climb in next to her.

"Remember when we were little and we shared a room?" said Ellie, snuggling down under the covers, "I didn't mind the storms so much then. I still didn't *like* them, but I didn't mind."

Rosalee smiled but couldn't quite relate. She had always loved stormy weather.

Ellie nodded toward the open window. "You're gonna ruin your windowsill."

"I know."

Ellie smiled. "You were always braver than me."

Rosalee slid down again and watched the shadows of tree branches dancing tumultuously across her ceiling. "I don't think that's true. You're the one that suggested finding a place together.I was too much of a wuss to even think about moving out yet."

Ellie rolled over to face her and propped her head up with her hand. "Not even ... before?"

"I guess maybe before. It's just hard to tell when the right time is, now."

"Did you hear them fighting earlier?"

"Robin and Lola? No." Rosalee felt a pang of guilt slide down her stomach wall to settle in the pit. Her thoughts had been otherwise occupied. She had received her first email from Alex mere hours ago—nothing special, but enough to distract her. "What were they fighting about?"

"The B&B, of course. I thought having a project might perk Robin up a little."

"Maybe not when the project has so much to do with Evelyn. I mean, it was kind of their dream since ..."

"Forever," Ellie finished quietly.

They exchanged sad looks and then jumped when a crash of thunder sounded near enough to make the house quake. Then Ellie's round eyes narrowed into slits as Rosalee tried not to laugh.

"It's not funny, Rose." Ellie shoved her lightly and rolled over to bury her face in a pillow.

"I know, I'm sorry. You know ... sometimes I think it will be easier on Robin when we leave."

"What do you mean?" said Ellie, her voice muffled by the pillow.

"I mean, I don't know if Robin ever really wanted to be a parent, ya know? Not that she isn't an amazing aunt—I'm just not sure this is what she bargained for."

Ellie turned her head to look at her. "Yeah. I guess Aunt Evelyn was always a little more … motherly."

They were quiet, listening to the steady drip of rain onto Rosalee's windowsill. Finally, Rosalee sighed and climbed out of bed, digging through her hamper for something to dry the puddle. She located a paint-splattered sweatshirt, which she used to wipe the sill and floor below, then wedged it into the gap. At once, both the sound of the rain and its glorious perfume were muted. She stood staring at the sleeve that hung down the wall for several moments, then pushed the window back open, leaving the garment to catch the drips.

"You'll have to repaint it before Robin finds the ripples and kills you," said Ellie, stifling a yawn.

Rosalee slid the window open a bit further, trying to gauge how far inside the rain would actually travel. Then a light in the backyard caught her attention. "Um … I think Lola's sleeping in her studio."

"*What?*" Ellie yelped. Rosalee shushed her as she hurried to the window. "Oh my *god*."

They looked at each other. Rosalee was sure Ellie's pale face and wide eyes mimicked her own.

"They wouldn't *break up?* God, that sounds weird," said Rosalee, shaking her head.

"She's probably just cooling off. I haven't heard them fight like that for a long time. I'm sure they need a little space."

Ellie took a step back from the window, wrapping her arms around herself to shield the slight chill blowing in from the window.

"You can sleep in here if you want," said Rosalee. "I'm gonna pee, since I'm up."

When she returned to the room, Ellie was already hunkered down under the covers. Rosalee climbed back in and rolled onto her side, facing the window. She shut her eyes and tried to turn off her mind, but the howling wind proved difficult to ignore.

All of a sudden, an almighty crash made Rosalee and Ellie sit straight up, then leap out of bed again.

"What the hell was that?"

Ellie hurried to Rosalee's window and drew back the curtain, peering into the yard below. Her breath immediately fogged up the glass. "I can't see anything besides the big tree."

Both girls stopped to listen as they heard footsteps padding quickly down the hall, followed by a heart-stopping gasp. Rosalee and Ellie stared at each other and then rushed from the room, chasing Robin's bathrobe as it whipped around the corner and down the stairs.

"Robin, what's wrong?" said Ellie, her voice high with anxiety.

Robin turned to look at the girls as though counting them but not really seeing them, then bolted out the back door. Rosalee and Ellie stared at each other, almost afraid to follow, then Rosalee felt her stomach clench as they heard another gasp, followed by a horrible, tortured scream that penetrated straight into her chest.

"LOLAAA!"

Ellie launched herself out the back door and Rosalee followed, nearly tripping down the wooden stairs that were slick with rain. Time stood still as she stared at the wreckage that was once Lola's studio. One of the giant fir trees from the other side of the fence was lying in the mess of broken glass and splintered wood, and Rosalee struggled to draw breath as her throat constricted with panic. This couldn't be happening. Not now. Not after everything her family had already endured.

All at once, the world jolted into a disconcertingly faster pace and Rosalee watched as Robin and Ellie circled the debris, shouting for Lola. As Rosalee ran toward them, the ground tilted and she sucked in a deep, rattling breath to right it again.

"Help me lift this tree!" Robin shouted.

Together, she, Robin, and Ellie scrambled to grip the end of the trunk raised approximately five feet off the ground. They heaved with all of their might, but it wouldn't budge.

"Oh God, *it's no use!*" Robin's voice cracked with barely suppressed hysteria. "Rose, go call 911. I need to figure out how to get in here."

Rosalee nodded and her face felt oddly numb as she stumbled backward, then spun smack into—

"Lola!"

"Who is making all this racket?" said Lola.

She steadied Rosalee and then gasped as she viewed the remains of her beloved studio over her shoulder. Rosalee flung her arms around her aunt and felt Ellie hit her hard in the back a second later. Lola patted them awkwardly, her arms pinned at her sides, then Rosalee heard a dry sob behind her. She detached herself enough from Lola and Ellie to look around.

Robin was standing in the middle of the yard, one trembling hand over her mouth and both covered in mud and debris. Her entire body was shaking with silent sobs, and Lola gave the girls one final squeeze before making her way uncertainly to Robin.

She reached out tentatively to touch her shoulder. "Love?"

Without warning, Robin threw herself into Lola's arms, twisting the fabric of her bathrobe as though trying to tear it. "When—you—didn't come back … I thought—"

"I slept on the couch," said Lola, hugging her closer. "I'm sorry I scared you."

"You *weren't* on the couch," Robin said, suddenly angry. "I *looked!* Don't you think I would've checked that before I ran out here and tried to haul a tree off your shed?"

"I got up to use the bathroom." Lola's eyes widened apologetically over Robin's shoulder.

Robin wrestled her way out of Lola's arms, then stomped toward the house without a backward glance. "Come inside before you catch your death," she snapped as she passed Rosalee and Ellie.

The girls turned back to look at Lola, and Rosalee realized that they were both still breathing as though they had run a marathon. Lola took one last devastated look back at her demolished studio, then put an arm around each of them as they all trudged back toward the house.

Chapter 17

Three days after the storm, Rosalee felt jet-lagged. She wasn't sure if the stress around her quarreling aunts and Lola's smashed studio or the drastic change in weather had caused her latest flare-up, but two days of barely moving from her bed had made her unbearably restless.

Much to Rosalee's frustration, Robin refused to let her resume her shifts at The Goose, insisting that the schedule was full. However, she had a feeling her aunt would have told her that even if the entire store called in sick. So, she caught the bus to the hospital to work on her mural, instead.

By the time Rosalee arrived in her quiet hallway, she was beginning to rethink her rash decision. As good as it felt to be up and moving again, and as much as she hated sitting at home, waiting for the giant globs of energy she lost to come back from their distant corners of the universe, she worried that her body might not cooperate. Even as the thought occurred to her, the idea that she could run out of steam before she made it back out of the hospital and to the bus stop caused her to break out in a sweat.

Rosalee slid down the wall with her backpack and sat with her head on her knees, willing her anxiety to subside. When that didn't work, she awkwardly peeled off her backpack and dug inside for her water bottle. Her hands shook as she unscrewed the cap and took a long drink, then rested her head back against the wall and closed her eyes against the softly buzzing fluorescent lights. After several moments, she remembered the Power Bar she had stuffed in the front pocket of her pack and forgotten to eat on the bus. She struggled with the wrapper for several seconds before ripping off a chunk of the bar with her teeth and chewing slowly, allowing a warm feeling of relief to mingle with the panic. Low blood sugar. Not enough water. Both of these things could have easily contributed to her sudden weakness.

Rosalee finished the bar and refilled her water bottle at the drinking fountain before sitting down again to unpack her supplies for the day. She was still working on her outline, so she didn't have to lug around her paint supplies yet. The short absence from her work had also allowed her to see the whole picture with a little more clarity and grace, so as she began to transfer her ideas from her sketchbook to the wall, her mind was less cluttered.

Just as she began to hit her stride, however, she was interrupted by a harassed-looking nurse who was rounding up volunteers to assist with staff duties. Rosalee agreed to help almost as a reflex before she had time to decide if it was a bad idea.

"The storm damage was mostly on the roof," said the nurse as she walked so fast that Rosalee almost had to jog to keep up with her. "The restoration team basically had to hit and run, so most of the custodial staff is on cleanup duty."

They sped around another corner.

"We can use all the extra bodies we can find," the nurse continued. "Ah. Can I borrow you boys for a minute?"

Rosalee skidded to a stop next to her and looked up to face Alex and a handsome stranger who she assumed was Manny, having learned about him in Alex's emails. She nodded at him politely before getting embarrassingly distracted by Alex's smile. As the nurse recruited

Manny to help her with a task specific to his height, Rosalee had to force herself to concentrate on her own assignment which, thankfully, was only as complicated as replacing the paper towels in most of the bathrooms on that floor. Alex was in charge of music.

"The speakers are blown in rehab and the waiting room on the fourth floor," the nurse explained, "but I think there are a couple boomboxes in the storage closet from the aerobics classes. We just need something besides static."

"No problem."

The nurse nodded her thanks and Alex waited until she and Manny were down the hall and around a corner before turning back to Rosalee. *"Where's the storage closet?"* he said in a stage whisper.

Rosalee smiled and shook her head. "Follow me."

— • —

The closet smelled distinctly of industrial cleaning agents, rubber gloves, and the kind of hand soap that came in bulk and left a lingering scent on your skin for at least a day. Rosalee quickly found stacks of paper towels neatly wrapped in brown paper, but there was no sign of a boombox or any sort of stereo equipment.

"Maybe this isn't the right closet," said Rosalee. She had been so confident that she had remembered all of the interesting places from her brief orientation.

"There's another door down here," said Alex, making his way down one of the cleaning supply aisles. "Do you have a key?"

"Just the one she gave me for paper towels." She followed him anyway.

Luckily, the door was unlocked. Alex fumbled in the dark until he located a light switch. They both squinted as the fluorescent lights flickered and buzzed to life, illuminating shelf after shelf of dusty, forgotten objects with an eerie, greenish glow.

This closet smelled like stale yoga mats and floor wax. Rosalee wandered down the aisles, inspecting rows of other forgotten gym equipment, mismatched free weights, and various partially deflated sports balls.

"I've lost track of which parts of this place are old and which ones are new," she said, running her fingertips along one of the shelf edges. Her fingers came up clean, despite the dusty contents of the shelves.

By the time she reached the other end of the room, Alex had already located an entire sound system. He stooped next to speakers set precariously on upside-down milk crates, then began rummaging through a shoe box full of cassettes and CDs. As soon as he had assembled a small pile, he handed them to Rosalee.

Sade, Michael Bolton, Kenny G, Sting ... Rosalee raised her eyebrows as she looked through them. "Oh, so we're playing them elevator music."

Alex looked up from his sorting. "What's wrong with elevator music?"

"Nothing." Rosalee shrugged. "Maybe they'll feel like they're at the spa. Or Joslins. I'm sure any of these are fine."

"You decide."

It wasn't a request. Rosalee glared at him. "I decide plenty of things."

"Fine, let's play a game," said Alex. "Answer as fast as you can."

"Okay ..."

"Ocean or desert?"

Rosalee thought about cool waves lapping at her toes and closed her eyes. "Ocean."

"Red or green?"

"Green." *Leaves.*

"Fast or slow songs?"

"Slow, probably. I mean fast ... ish." Rosalee was suddenly seized by a sixth-sense tingle as her eyes snapped back open. No way was she slow dancing with Alex, no matter what kind of Jedi mind trickery he used.

There was a pause while Alex shuffled several of the discarded CDs back into his current hand. "Bolton or Kenny?"

"Neither," said Rosalee. "How are those 'fast-ish'?"

"Right, sorry. Oh, what about mix tapes?" Alex didn't wait for her answer, but began to rifle through the cassettes he had uncovered. "Funky or jazzy?"

"Funk, I guess."

"New pop or oldies?"

"Old. New."

"Why can't I touch you?"

"It might hurt."

Time snagged in its forward motion as Alex looked up and Rosalee willed the stinging behind her eyes to subside. She hadn't meant to say it—the trickery had worked. Just not in the way she expected.

Alex grabbed a random tape and slid it into the deck, then pressed PLAY. The armpits of Rosalee's T-shirt were unpleasantly damp as she watched him shove thick, heavy mats aside and scrape metal chairs across the polished concrete floor.

Crap.

"What are you doing?" said Rosalee, as if she didn't already know. Maybe if she asked enough questions, she could distract him.

Alex raised an arm to wipe the sweat from his forehead. "I was trying to clear a space, but there's no room. I give up."

Rosalee let out a breath of relief, but sucked it in again as Alex strode over to the exit door and pushed it open. "Ha!" He smiled triumphantly over his shoulder. "This is perfect."

He wedged the door open with one of the metal chairs, then held a hand out toward Rosalee.

Blood rushed to her face. "I don't dance."

"Ever? Or because of what I said?"

"You mean what *I* said?"

Alex let his arm fall and gripped the back of the metal chair, watching her warily. Rosalee swallowed hard against the lump that was forming in the back of her throat and causing her eyes to fill with tears. Alex took a tiny step forward, his brow furrowed, and a dull roaring started in her ears, magnifying the sound of her breathing.

Over the roar, Rosalee saw Alex's lips form her name and felt a flutter in the region of her abdomen before it clenched in panic. But somehow, it got her moving. She forced her leg muscles to carry her to the boombox, where she cranked up the volume.

"Let's dance, okay?" she shouted over the music, attempting to embrace some part of her former, less inhibited self.

Rosalee skipped past Alex and discovered that the propped-open door led to roof access. She wondered briefly if they were supposed to go out there before letting the music take control, closing her eyes to convince herself that she was alone in this space. It took several measures for her body to respond to her mental pleading, but then the magic was taking effect and the music was her master, and when she opened her eyes, she let it manipulate her strings.

Thankfully, Alex was dancing, too, although Rosalee had a feeling he had started mere moments before she opened her eyes. He moved easily, gracefully, and at one point, he stepped closer to Rosalee, evidently convinced that maybe this time, she could handle it. Instead, she twirled wildly away from him and began a crazy improvisation that she hoped might distract her from the butterflies in her stomach.

Alex shook his head and Rosalee could tell that he was questioning her sanity, but soon, he adapted to her new pace. They spun and whirled around each other like feral forest creatures, Rosalee never breaking time with the music, even when tears flowed unexpectedly down her cheeks. She wiped them hastily away, hoping her untamed mane of hair would hide the rest.

After several more fast songs, Alex sat down while Rosalee carried on like a woman insane. By the time she had worn her anxiety down to a tolerable level, she suspected that she may have also overdone it. She turned toward Alex, who was leaning against the metal railing, the light breeze lifting his dark blonde hair so that he looked remarkably like a Calvin Klein model.

"So ... your pants are smoking," he said casually.

"What?" Rosalee looked down quickly, then back at Alex, who was looking smug.

"From all of the lying. About not dancing."

Rosalee turned away from him and walked resolutely back through the door, squinting as her pupils dilated. Alex stood and followed her, then headed toward the boombox to find a new tape.

He walked slowly back to the door and leaned against the doorframe as Sting's iconic voice wove through "Fields of Gold." For just a moment, Rosalee imagined walking toward him, breathing near him, being in his arms, and immediately, the panic returned.

"I can't go with you," she said. "Not if you're going to make me dance. I tried and I can't."

She watched Alex's eyes narrow. "I'm not blind."

"I *can* dance, that doesn't mean I *like* to."

Rosalee hoped her face wouldn't betray such a downright lie. After all, he hadn't been in her head. She *had* tried. She turned to leave and thought she felt Alex's fingers graze her wrist like a ghost.

"Look," said Rosalee, turning back to face him. "Why is it so important that I dance with you? What do you get out of it?"

Alex cocked his head to the side. *"Me? Not a thing, I—I just came in to get warm."*

Rosalee huffed and turned away, ignoring what was obviously a quote since he suddenly sounded like an old movie.

"No, okay, Rosalee, wait …" Alex walked in a half-circle around her so that they were face to face again. He lowered his voice then, although they were very much alone, and Rosalee watched his expression grow serious. "Look, I don't wanna embarrass you, but you kinda missed your cue back there. You were supposed to say—"

"Damn it, Alex."

"He's making violent love to me, Mother!"

"For crying out loud …"

"Rosalee, I'm sorry, I'm done now. Please come back."

Rosalee took her time doing so. "Why do you *need* to dance with me?"

"What do you mean?"

"I guess I just thought you were different. But I don't know what I was thinking, I mean you *are* male, and like all men, you—"

"*Whoa.*" Alex put up a hand to stem her rant before it gained too much momentum. "That's absolutely *not* what this is."

"Oh, it's not?" Rosalee said in mock surprise.

All humor evaporated from Alex's face. "No, it's not."

Rosalee shrugged and looked away in an attempt to hide the rapidly gathering moisture welling up in her eyes.

"Rosalee …"

"What?"

Alex opened his mouth, then closed it again. He met Rosalee's eyes and she looked away first.

"I'm sorry if I did something to make you feel- that's not how I was thinking about this," he said.

Rosalee shrugged again.

"Don't," said Alex, clearly irritated.

"Don't what?"

"Don't act like you don't care about anything. It drives me *crazy*."

Rosalee didn't know what to say. Of course she cared about anything—she cared about *everything*. But the things eating at her and simultaneously making their way up her throat weren't things she could put into words yet. And anyway, her emotions had become as unpredictable as Colorado's weather lately, so all she really had to do was ride this one out. Even now, she could feel her anger dissipating into its frequent and ugly stepsister: shame.

As Rosalee stared at her shoes, she saw Alex inch closer. She stayed put, but lifted her gaze to something over his shoulder.

"Don't worry, I won't touch you," he said.

"Thanks. I still don't know what I'm supposed to think."

Alex waited for her to look at him again. "About me wanting to dance with you?"

"Yes. Why are you *so* hung up on not being able to touch me?"

The hint of a smile played across Alex's lips. "Well, slow dancing is a lot harder that way."

"And why would you *need* to slow dance with me?"

"I don't *need* to, I just *want* to. Someday. I like all of this cheesy small-town stuff and it's nice to have someone to go with."

"Well, I can't, so you'll have to find someone else to be cheesy with." Rosalee walked over to the boombox and jabbed the **STOP** button before yanking the chord out of the wall. "Maybe Angela's free."

"Rosalee."

"I can't."

Rosalee grabbed the large stack of paper towels from the other closet and headed back toward the storage room door. On the way out, she nearly ran down the harried nurse from before.

"Where have you two been?" she said. "Is that door open? Why didn't the alarm go off?"

Rosalee knew she was being rude, but she ignored the nurse and kept walking, leaving Alex to deal with the questions.

Chapter 18

Alex took one last, long drag from his cigarette and leaned against the back porch railing, exhaling slowly and watching the cloud of smoke drift up toward the roof's apex, then disappear against the early evening sky. He observed a robin edging along a tree branch before it became virtually invisible among the leaves, the only indication of its presence, an occasional flash of red.

He had been so close. *So. Close.* Then he blew it. And why had he pushed so hard, anyway? So that he could dance with someone who didn't want to dance with him? Touch someone who thought it might hurt? Despite his best efforts, Rosalee was still afraid of him. He had written countless emails in his head to try to straighten everything out, but on the actual screen, they seemed feeble and inadequate.

Alex stubbed out his cigarette against the side of the concrete stairs and dropped the butt into the soup can he kept behind a large flower pot. He waved as Pete's red Subaru pulled into the driveway. "How's it goin'?"

"Good." Pete climbed out of his car in dress pants, a dress shirt, and practical tie—his typical bank clothes. "Glad to be home."

Alex nodded, although he wasn't quite sure if Rabbitbrush would ever feel like home to him. "We have wasps," he said instead, pointing over his head at the roof.

Pete sighed. "Fantastic."

"I'll pick up some traps at the hardware store tomorrow."

"Thanks. You coming in?"

"Yup." Alex stood, his legs stiff from crouching so long. He fluffed his shirt to air out the smoke smell as he followed Pete into the apartment.

"What were you thinking about for dinner?" said Pete, setting his briefcase down next to the coat rack and removing his shoes.

"I wasn't sure how late you were working, so I was gonna dig into my leftovers from lunch."

"Perfect. I don't feel like cooking tonight, anyway. I'm gonna go change and then we can hang out, if you want."

"Cool."

Alex shoved the kitchen window open to let the night breeze in through the screen, then opened the fridge and took out his leftovers. He considered microwaving them, then decided he didn't have the heart—a new low.

Pete returned wearing what he considered to be casual, after-work attire but most people would deem appropriate for a church picnic. He surveyed Alex as he sat at the small kitchen table, poking unenthusiastically at his Kung Pao chicken. "What's up with you?"

Alex attempted a shrug that was only halfway successful.

"Okay, so spill," said Pete.

Alex studied him for a moment and stuck both chopsticks in one of the larger chunks of chicken in his container, concentrating on keeping the sticks upright. "I guess I don't know how much I can tell you, since you're so close to the situation."

"Ah." Pete washed his hands at the sink and then set about making a sandwich for dinner. "So, Rosalee?"

"Yeah." Alex seized the end of both chopsticks and popped the whole chicken chunk into his mouth. He chewed slowly, lost in his thoughts as Pete collected bread and fixings out of the fridge.

Watching Pete make a sandwich was nothing short of mesmerizing, just because it was so perfect. He always bought Wonderbread because it was square, and cheese slices that would fit exactly inside the crust. That was generally followed by an "X" of mustard over each slice of cheese, two pieces of bologna (one on top of each cheese slice), and finally, two tomato slices in the middle of the layers. Somehow, Pete made those into a square, too, by cutting two slices in half and then aligning their flat sides with the edges of the bread.

Alex waited until Pete sat down with his masterpiece and a can of Sprite, then shoved his own food away, still barely touched from that afternoon. "I think I pushed her too far this time," he said.

Pete paused warily midbite, then lowered the sandwich back to his plate. "What do you mean?"

Alex glanced quickly at him. "Not like that. Although she seems to *think* that ... who am I kidding? I have no idea what the hell she's thinking."

Pete looked mostly relieved and went back to his dinner.

"Rosalee's, like, your sister, right?" said Alex.

Pete seemed to consider before nodding.

"So, as someone with her best interest in mind ... should I leave her alone?"

"How do you mean?" Pete tapped the top of his soda can before popping the tab and taking a swig.

"I like her. A lot. But I'm starting to think that she's never going to feel that way about me, and I'm trying to decide if I should jump into the friend zone of my own volition before she ... punts me into it."

"Does she know how you feel about her?"

"She *has* to." Alex leaned forward and kneaded the frown lines in his forehead with his palms. "I mean, I know myself pretty well and subtlety has never been my strong suit."

Pete chuckled. "Not really Rosalee's, either. Did she tell you to leave her alone?"

"Not exactly."

"So, what did she say?"

"She said she couldn't go to the town fundraiser thingy if I wanted her to dance, and then she yelled at me, and then she left."

Pete raised his eyebrows and took another sip of soda. "She said *'if'?*"

"*If*… I wanted her to dance, right." Alex looked up, his forehead red where he had assaulted it. "Oh."

Pete smiled and crumpled up his napkin, tossing it on the crumbs of his sandwich and leaning back in his chair.

"So … you think she might still go with me?" said Alex. "If I don't push too hard?"

Pete shrugged. "It didn't sound like an absolute 'no' to me, and Rosalee is pretty direct."

"She is? Are we talking about the same girl? I mean, she's pretty much a walking puzzle whenever I talk to her."

Pete looked amused for some reason. "Huh."

"What?" Alex sighed.

Pete got up to rinse his plate and put it in the dishwasher. "Nothing. But I would go slow. 'No sudden movements' kind of deal."

"Right."

Alex was suddenly ravenous and pulled his leftovers toward him again, attacking the contents with gusto. Of course, part of his brain was still stuck on the part where Rosalee was afraid he would hurt her—*physically* hurt her—but he knew he'd have to wait on that particular insight.

"You wanna watch the game?" said Pete.

"Sure. But can you do me a favor?"

"I'll have to hear it first."

Alex smiled. *Reliable.* Regardless of how frustrating it was that he couldn't talk as openly to Pete about Rosalee as he could with, say, Manny, at least Pete was that—reliable; a reason for Alex to stay in line. He picked up his notebook and shut his pen in it, then handed them both to Pete. "Can you slide this under your cushion?"

"You want me to sit on your notebook? Why?"

"Because I can't write anymore tonight or I'll lose my mind."

Pete shook his head slightly, but slid the journal under his seat and settled in.

Chapter 19

"Do you *want* to dance with him?"

Rosalee and Ellie were sitting on the floor of Ellie's bedroom and Rosalee was watching her sister weave a friendship bracelet out of embroidery floss. It must have been a new pattern because she kept checking an instruction book in between knots.

"Like, in that not-real-life, *movie* kind of way ... yeah," said Rosalee, picking at the threads in Ellie's carpet.

"But you're afraid it will hurt."

"Mm-hm."

"Can't you tell him that?"

Rosalee settled back against Ellie's bed frame. "I did. Accidentally. But that's all I said."

"That you were afraid it would hurt?"

"Yes."

"And then you didn't explain it?"

"Right."

Ellie frowned as she checked her book again, then struggled to undo her last knot. "So, he's probably a little confused."

"Yeah, he probably is. I just don't understand why he won't let the dancing thing go."

"Oh," said Ellie, a look of dawning realization on her face. "That might be my fault."

Rosalee lifted a rainbow-colored plastic pony off the bookcase next to Ellie's bed and combed through its tail with her fingers. "How could that possibly be your fault?"

Ellie watched Rosalee braid the plastic hair strands, looking apprehensive.

"I was … hanging out with Pete one night while you were at work and he found one of our home movies with Angela," she said, twirling the ends of her embroidery floss absently and still watching Rosalee as though waiting for some sort of negative reaction, "And so, we were watching some of them and Alex came home and was watching them with us."

Rosalee grimaced. "Great. Go on."

"Well, I don't know if you remember how much we danced in those movies, but it was a lot. And there was one where we all piled on Pete to get out from behind the camera and dance with us like the Prince in *Cinderella*. Or *Sleeping Beauty*. I don't remember which."

"Probably both."

"So …" said Ellie, "My fault."

Rosalee held the rainbow pony at eye level as she absorbed this information. "Oh … *God*, I'm such a jerk. I basically told Alex he was a pervert."

"Whoops. Well, maybe you can try again."

Rosalee forced her breath out in a huff and watched as the strands of hair hanging in her face blew out in front of it. "I don't think he'll want to after this."

"Hm," said Ellie. "Wanna make a bracelet?"

"Okay."

Rosalee put the pony back on its shelf as Ellie slid over a massive Caboodle of embroidery floss. If Rosalee had to guess, she would say that Ellie probably owned more colors of thread than the largest Crayola crayon box. How could she ever begin to choose? She wondered briefly if Alex wore bracelets. Maybe she could make him a "Sorry-I-Bitched-Out-On-You-Again" peace offering. She would probably never give it to him, but it would be something to keep her occupied for now.

She sorted through the box for nearly five minutes until she finally settled on four colors: a deep, forest green, for obvious, nature-y reasons and because it was close to the color of Alex's overshirt on the night she got the mural; navy blue for his Jeep; mahogany brown; and gold, for the facets in his hair when they caught the sunlight. She stared at the color arrangement long enough that Ellie finally looked over, too.

"Those look good," she said. "Need a safety pin?"

"Thanks."

They had come up with the idea years ago of safety pinning the bracelets to their pants while they worked, which was much less annoying than Scotch tape stuck to a desk or table, since the threads tended to come loose rather frequently from all the tugging.

Rosalee chose a basic "V" pattern because she had done it often enough that she didn't have to focus very hard. Her fingers flew over the knots and she was only aware of counting and the basic color pattern in the back of her mind as she and Ellie chatted about work, Rosalee's mural, and Ellie's classes.

Before long, Rosalee was two-thirds of the way finished with her bracelet. She paused to separate the remaining threads at the bottom and admire her progress when the phone rang in the kitchen. Ellie leapt up suddenly to answer it and nearly tripped on the trailing ends of her bracelet, which was still pinned to her pants.

"What the hell was that?" said Rosalee when she came back several minutes later. "Are you waiting for a call?"

Ellie flushed and sat on the floor again, untangling the threads that had nearly taken her out minutes before.

"*Oooh*, have you been holding out on me?" Rosalee teased. "Is there a *boy* in your class?"

"It was just Robin saying she'll be home late."

Ellie didn't seem to want to meet her eyes and Rosalee tried not to panic for no reason. "Is she okay?"

"She's fine, she just has to close the store after all." Ellie was still staring avidly at her bracelet.

"El, *what?*"

Ellie appeared to be fighting some kind of internal battle before finally meeting her sister's eyes. "Connor's back."

Rosalee felt the sentence resonate through her body. "How do you know?" she said, her voice coming out more fragile than she would have liked.

Ellie looked anxious again. "Robin saw him at the store last week. He asked about you and she almost called the Sheriff."

"Oh, god," said Rosalee, pressing her hands against her eyelids until colors burst behind them.

"He hasn't tried to call yet, I don't think," said Ellie.

Rosalee nodded. Her tongue felt too big for her mouth and her throat was too dry to swallow.

"Rose?" said Ellie cautiously.

"Mm-hm?" Rosalee opened her eyes wide and tried to focus on her knots this time and ignore the way her vision was going in and out of focus. It was the cake-baking fiasco all over again.

Just then, the back door opened downstairs and the girls heard Lola bounce into the kitchen and take the stairs two at a time before she appeared in Ellie's doorway, radiating the sunshine energy that always accompanied her latest creations. She tossed a beaded bracelet in each of the girl's laps, oblivious to the somber mood she had stumbled upon, then skipped back down the stairs to the kitchen. They heard her rummaging through the pots and pans before calling back up the stairs: *"Anyone heard from Robin? I'm thinking I should start dinner."*

"I'll go tell her," said Ellie, slipping Lola's bracelet onto her wrist and unpinning the half-finished bracelet from her jeans.

On her way out the door, she stopped and turned back to Rosalee. "Do you want me to say you're sick?"

Rosalee wiped irritably at the tears that she hadn't noticed until they began to drip down her chin. "No, I'll be down in a little bit."

She waited until she heard Ellie and Lola chatting animatedly in the kitchen before attempting to yank the safety pin out of her jeans without unhooking it. The pin won, however, and Rosalee swore viciously under her breath as she fumbled to undo it the right way, then wadded up the whole mess of thread and shoved it in her pocket. Lola's bracelet was still in her lap and she held it up to the light, blinking several times to clear her vision. Lola had used a lot of beads from her latest shipments—Rosalee recognized the bottle-green and new gold beads against a brown leather cord. It would nearly have matched Alex's bracelet.

That night, Rosalee awoke as suddenly as she had on the night of the storm. It took her several moments to realize that she was in bed, breathing heavily like she had been running, and that her face was wet.

She glanced toward the window where her curtains fluttered gently in the cool night breeze, but it didn't seem to be raining.

Someone knocked softly at her door.

"Come in," Rosalee croaked, still disoriented.

Ellie's dark outline shuffled in and sat on the edge of her bed, fingers twisting guiltily in her lap. "I shouldn't have told you," she said.

Rosalee sat up against her headboard. "What? What are you talking about?"

"I told you about Connor, and now you're having them again. The nightmares."

"Oh." Rosalee couldn't quite remember dreaming, but she felt a vague stirring of the emotions the last one must have evoked. *Fear. Pain. No way out.* All the usual elements that too often contributed to her shouting herself awake. "Did Robin and Lola hear?"

"I don't think so. Their TV is still on."

Rosalee hesitated, sure she should say something, but unable to find the words, then threw back her bed sheets so that Ellie could climb in next to her.

"I wish you could tell me." Ellie settled down beside Rosalee and stared up at the ceiling. "I feel like you almost did this afternoon."

Rosalee scooted down from the headboard to stare at the ceiling, too. Years ago, she had painted swirling clouds against royal blue and dotted hundreds of tiny stars to make it look like her room had no ceiling. She hadn't quite achieved that effect, but she still sometimes found herself getting lost in the brushstrokes that were partially visible in the dark.

Ellie turned her head on the pillow to look at Rosalee. "What are you really afraid of?" Rosalee inhaled and then exhaled shakily. Tears slid into her hair, where they gathered cold and wet. "I'm afraid of what you'll think of me if I tell you."

"Rose, you're my sister. I'm on your side, no matter what." Ellie reached over to give Rosalee's hand a brief, light squeeze.

If Rosalee could tell anyone, it would be Ellie. But she wasn't sure she *could* tell anyone. *It will eat you alive otherwise,* said the little voice in her head, and she knew it was right. But she still wasn't sure she was ready to see the look on her sister's face—it would almost make it too real. Not that the nightmares were any better.

Rosalee sighed and looked toward her slightly open window again, letting the cool air against her damp face calm her. "Remember the stuff I told you about Connor earlier this summer?"

"You mean how he sold you pills?" said Ellie darkly, "Yeah, I remember."

"Well ... he wasn't just selling me pills. We kinda ... hooked up a few times."

Ellie didn't answer, but Rosalee could imagine the look of disgust that was likely twisting her features. Immediately, she felt the need to defend herself.

"He's not bad when he's showered." She shoved a hand into her hair, where her fingers quickly became ensnared in the unbrushed strands. "It was a distraction, you know? Like, I needed to be reckless or whatever. It was stupid."

Rosalee finally risked a glance at her sister. From what little of her face she could see in the dark, Ellie looked like she might be sick but was trying very hard to be polite about it. "Okay ..." she said.

"So, that was when I started having trouble with the rib pain and mood swings ..."

Both of those descriptions were understatements, since the "rib pain" was like a rubber tube tightening around her ribcage, and the mood swings could probably rival the ones she witnessed in Evelyn during menopause.

"Oh, right," said Ellie. "Your symptoms seem kinda better lately. Those ones, I mean."

"Yeah. Maybe a little."

"Anyway ..." Ellie prompted.

"So, I guess we sort of had a routine. I'd go over to his house and we'd get drunk, or high, or both, and listen to crappy music and ... hook up." Rosalee shook her head. It felt like forever ago that she had holed up with Connor in his dim and smoky basement. "So, one day we shared almost half a handle of vodka and were ... um, whatever ... and then the pain started." Rosalee flinched inwardly as she remembered. "I tried to ignore it, but it was like one of those ... old-fashioned dress things ..."

"A corset?"

"Yeah, a corset, and it was squeezing so hard and I needed to stop, and I tried to tell him that."

Rosalee glanced at Ellie's face again and saw what little of her expression she could discern grow stony. When she spoke, her voice was fragile. "You told him to stop?"

Rosalee nodded and swallowed against the lump that was beginning to rise in her throat. "But that's when the laughing started."

"Oh god."

"I could barely breathe to get him off of me and he was laughing, too, because he thought I was messing around, and he's actually really strong for his size." Rosalee hiccuped the shadow of a laugh. "He had no idea. I'm sure he had no idea."

"Oh, *God*." Ellie sat up, her bent knees making a tent with the sheets as she pressed her palms against her forehead. "So, he didn't stop?"

"Not right away. He—"

She broke off and Ellie turned her head against her knees to look at her. Rosalee could almost smell the cigarette smoke that saturated the filthy, scratchy carpet that had pressed into her skin. But she couldn't stomach telling her sister how it felt to be utterly helpless with your underwear around your ankles and someone stronger than you holding you down while you hurt. She took a deep breath, almost expecting her lungs to protest.

"It's not the same. I know it's not the same, but in that moment, it felt like—" Rosalee choked before she could finish the sentence. She couldn't finish it.

"It's okay, Rose," said Ellie softly.

"We were *so* drunk." Rosalee squeezed her eyes shut against the images that stimulated her nightmares. "It's a wonder he even noticed something was wrong. Or maybe I finally pushed him off—I can't remember."

Rosalee heard a sniffle above her and looked up to see Ellie quickly wiping her face with the bedsheets.

"I think he probably feels bad," said Rosalee, "but I haven't talked to him since."

Ellie didn't say anything for a while, so Rosalee looked out the window again. She watched the branches of the remaining trees in the backyard as they swayed and threw shadows against her ceiling by the glow of the partially cloud-obscured moon. She took another deep breath of night air and realized that she felt a little better, somehow—like talking about it had extracted some of the poison from her body.

"And here we all thought he was stalking you," said Ellie.

"I know. I feel awful. On *top* of awful."

Rosalee turned her head away from the window again and saw tears sliding silently down her sister's face. She never meant to inject her poison into someone else. "I'm sorry, El. This is why I didn't tell you. I didn't want you to be upset or ... embarrassed of me."

"'Embarrassed of you' isn't even in the *top five* emotions I'm feeling right now." Ellie slid back down in the bed and turned toward Rosalee, propping herself up on her hand. "Am I the only person you've told?"

Rosalee nodded. "I almost wanted to tell someone at the camp, but I couldn't. So I just pretended I was angry about … everything else."

"Maybe you should tell Aunties."

Rosalee sucked in a sharp breath.

"Not now," said Ellie quickly. "Just eventually. So Robin doesn't file a restraining order or … you know, 'accidentally' stick Connor's arm in the meat grinder the next time he comes into the store."

Rosalee laughed. It wasn't funny but she couldn't help it. As hard as it had been to dig up what she had so diligently stuffed down, maybe the next time she talked about it would be that much easier.

Rosalee settled deeper into her pillow as a cricket began to chirp. It sounded close—perhaps resting on the windowsill just beyond the curtain.

"So, where do you think he was?" said Ellie.

"Connor?"

"Mm-hm."

"I'm not sure. Actually, probably visiting his uncle … in Steamboat Springs, I think?" Rosalee struggled to remember one of her hazy conversations with Connor. "He goes every summer and they fish and camp or whatever."

"I thought maybe prison," Ellie muttered.

Rosalee surprised them both by laughing again.

"Anyway," said Ellie, "are you going to be able to sleep now?"

Rosalee was already beginning to feel drowsy again. "I think so. Are you?"

Ellie shrugged and Rosalee's guilt resurfaced. She had hoped that the burden she had shared with her sister would lift quickly, but she supposed it was still a shock that Ellie would need time to get over.

"You can sleep in here, if you want," said Rosalee.

"Oh, only if you need me to."

Rosalee could tell that Ellie was trying pretty hard to come across breezy and nonchalant.

"Sure, that would be great," she said.

Ellie became far more enthusiastic immediately. "I could bring my TV in here and we could watch something until you fall asleep. Also, why the heck don't you have a TV in here? You're like an old lady."

Rosalee laughed as Ellie left to collect her TV. By now, she was pretty used to hooking it up in Rosalee's room, so it took her little to no time at all. Still, Rosalee's eyelids were growing heavier by the minute and she barely registered what they were watching as Ellie rejoined her. She was just beginning to drift off again when Ellie spoke.

"Rose?"

"Yeah?"

"Alex ..."

"... Yeah?"

"Are you afraid of that happening with him? With the dancing or ... whatever?"

Rosalee opened her eyes again, squinting against the blue glow of the TV. Ellie had the volume at its lowest setting. "Like, when I'm actually with him? No, not really. But then I get in my head later on and overanalyze how he *tries* to touch me."

Ellie stiffened. "He tries to touch you?"

It was different. Rosalee *knew* it was different. "I don't think he's trying not to take me seriously—I think he just forgets. Like, he'll almost grab my arm when he gets really excited about something or try to be ... um ... like, to make me feel better ..."

"Comforting?"

"Yeah, comforting. Like today, when we were dancing on the roof."

Ellie's eyes softened. "When you were what?"

"Just for a few minutes. On the roof access thingy." Rosalee hoped it was dark enough to hide the blush creeping across her face.

"You told me about the crazy dancing and the fighting. I didn't know you actually danced *with* him."

Rosalee flexed her feet under the covers to alleviate the tightness in her calves. "I didn't. The crazy dancing was on the roof."

"So, when did he touch you?"

"After I flipped out. I think he reached out without thinking. I felt his fingers for a second."

"But you *want* to dance with him. Sort of. I mean, for real?"

"... Yeah, I do."

"Oh, Rose," Ellie sighed.

The cricket chirped again from the windowsill.

"I know," said Rosalee softly.

Chapter 20

"Yo. *Earth to Alex.* Man, where's your head at today?"

Alex passed Manny the roll of masking tape he vaguely remembered him asking for several times already. "Sorry, I didn't sleep. Or something."

"Yeah, *or something.*" Manny smirked as he found the end of the tape and began to unroll it, pressing it neatly along the baseboard to prepare the wall for painting. "You get some last night or what?"

"What?" Alex floundered on the opposite wall, failing to match Manny's pace or precision. "Oh. No, I was working on my stupid, *stupid* movie all night."

"Okay, 'Hollywood.' Decided not to go to that AA meeting?"

"No, I went. Then I dug into my movie after that because apparently, I'm an insatiable masochist." Alex tried and failed to stifle a yawn. "Maybe I'll start taking the bus so I can sleep on the way home."

"Wait, how long is 'the way home'?" said Manny. "Isn't there a Y or something by you in Rabbitbrush?"

"They have meetings in the rec room at the church, but that town is *tiny,*" Alex said bitterly. "It might as well be built out of Legos."

"So where do you go?"

"The Y up here. It's fine—just a lot of back and forth."

Manny stopped taping and looked over his shoulder at Alex. "So, is it, like ... a secret? Doesn't your roommate know?"

"Yeah, but that's it—him and you."

Manny hesitated. "I mean, I'm not tryna boss you around or anything ..."

"As my sponsor, I wish you would."

"I don't know, man, if I were you, I'd go ahead and tell everybody who mattered so I could get a decent night's sleep. No need to go driving all over Colorado like a damn zombie."

"Okay, now wait a minute." Alex tore off the piece of tape he was using and pointed the roll at Manny in mock indignation. "I'm not sure I appreciate your overbearing logic as an approach to this complex situation. Like, how dare you, man?"

Manny laughed. "Okay, okay ... so do you have that shy girl all up in your movie?"

"Who?"

"*Rosalee.*" Manny batted his eyelashes.

Alex snorted. "No. Like, why would I—"

"Yo, don't *even* give me that. You are straight-up *twitterpated.*"

Alex scraped his thumbnail against the tape, trying to relocate the end. "I don't know what that means."

"Like, with those two skunks?"

Alex stared at Manny, who stared back, incredulous. "Damn it, have you never seen *Bambi?*"

"Oh. *Oh,* right." Alex groaned. "God, I need caffeine."

"Go ahead, I'll hold down the fort."

Alex stood and stretched. "Thanks. You want anything?"

"Whatever's good, man. I appreciate it. Maybe see if we brought some more tape, too. We still got four more hallways to go."

"Will do."

"And hey."

Alex turned.

"It might help," said Manny.

"What might?"

"Putting that shy girl in your movie."

———•●•———

Alex headed for the soda machines first, then changed his mind and decided that the last thing he needed was a sugar crash in half an hour. Besides, there was a machine that dispensed hot, reasonably good coffee a couple hallways down. The machine was in a small waiting room off of what would eventually be another cafeteria, although smaller than the one in the main wing.

As he dug in his pocket for change, someone appeared out of his peripheral vision and he stepped aside without turning around. "Go ahead, I'm gonna be a minute."

"It's okay, take your time."

Alex only allowed himself a moment of surprise, which he concealed rather well considering the increase in his heart rate, before turning to face Rosalee.

"Hey," she said. "I wasn't trying to be creepy, I just didn't know what to say, so I didn't say ... anything."

"I know the feeling." Alex thought of the emails that remained in his drafts folder, too lame to actually send her. "So ... how are you?"

"Better, thanks." Rosalee absently twirled the end of the thick red braid that hung over her shoulder. "I promise I'm not crazy."

"I didn't think you were."

Something had obviously changed in the couple of days since he last saw her, and Alex was unnerved by the shift. She stood almost imperceptibly closer and met his eyes more often. It also didn't help his word-forming abilities that this particular wing had brighter lights that enhanced the golden rings of her irises, subtly outlined with dark green.

"Well, I know you're probably mad," she said.

Alex managed to tear his eyes away from hers long enough to process that statement and shook his head slowly. "Not mad. Confused."

"About ...?"

"Honestly? Everything." Alex stuffed his change back into his pocket and sat in one of the chairs. Apparently, they were having this conversation now. Before his caffeine buffer. "I just ... I thought that we were getting somewhere, but then I kept wondering if I was just pushing you to hang out with me when you *really* don't want to."

Rosalee watched him for a moment before sitting, as well. There was still a chair between them, but at least she was sitting on the same side of the wall.

"I don't know ... how to do this," she said carefully.

"*'This,'* being ...?"

"You mentioned, a while ago, being friends."

Alex waited.

"Well, I don't know how ... to," said Rosalee.

Alex studied her, tracing the ragged edge of his thumbnail around his mouth. "So, you're telling me that you want to be friends now?"

"Right."

Alex dropped his head briefly into his hands. No sleep *and* no caffeine was a bad combination.

"Unless it's too late?" said Rosalee.

Alex watched as something thickened behind her eyes—as though a layer of translucent onion skin had been peeled away and was now being smoothed back into place. He couldn't let that wall go up again.

"No, it's not." Alex twisted in his chair and leaned over the armrest toward her. "I'm sorry. I'm just trying to wrap my head around this."

Rosalee smiled a tiny smile, which Alex immediately returned.

"So you want to be friends," he said.

He almost sighed out loud. A part of him wanted to stuff a pillow into his face and scream. But somehow, this didn't feel entirely like rejection. For one thing, Rosalee kept catching him off guard by looking at him—directly at him and not just *near* him.

Rosalee nodded. "I used to know how to be someone's friend. I think ..."

Alex had a brief but violent tussle with himself then, begging one half of his brain to calm down and listen to what Rosalee was saying that she wanted, while he bullied the other side to *come* down from the high hopes amid which it was currently bobbing. He yanked hard on both reins, willing himself to focus.

"Okay," he said finally. "When are you leaving today?"

"I don't know, around two, maybe?"

Alex wasn't quite familiar with the look on her face. Relief? Pleasant surprise? Perhaps she had imagined this conversation going badly.

"Perfect. I should be done by then, too," he said. "Manny and I are just prepping for paint today. I could give you a ride home?"

"Okay. Then ... I'll see you around two."

"It's a date," said Alex, then catching the look on Rosalee's face, added, "A *friend* date, Jesus Christ ..."

Alex met Rosalee outside the hospital's front entrance and tried not to read anything into the fact that she had let her hair down, but it was only the second time he had seen it like that and it was distracting. A light breeze kept catching the red tresses while they walked to his Jeep and several times, he felt the ends flutter against his arm and the fabric of his T-shirt.

He glanced up at the sky to distract himself. It was a deep, clear blue for now, but the forecast had called for thunderstorms later that afternoon. Sure enough, he could see the telltale, cauliflower-shaped clouds already making their way over the mountains. He almost commented on them before deciding that maybe he should make a few solid attempts at friendly conversation before resorting to the classic "Looks like rain."

"So, how's the wall prep going?" said Rosalee.

Making the first attempt at conversation—another good sign.

"Good, I mean it's fine," said Alex. "I think I'd go nuts if I was doing it myself, but Manny works really fast, which makes me work really fast, so it goes ... really fast." *Just like that topic. Nice work.* "What about you? How's the mural coming?"

"Good. I'm almost done with the sketch, so maybe I can start painting after that, if FancyBlouse says it's okay."

"Who?" Alex glanced over to see Rosalee looking embarrassed.

"I couldn't remember her name—the lady you introduced me to." Rosalee tucked her hair behind her ear and continued to redden the more Alex struggled to understand who she could possibly be talking about. She waved an arm vaguely behind her, back toward the hospital. "The lady that said I could paint it."

Then it clicked. "Are you talking about Connie Simpson? The hospital director?"

Rosalee opened her mouth in shock. "She's the director? Of the whole thing?"

Alex grinned. "You call her 'FancyBlouse?'"

"Well—I—not to her face!"

"Oh my god."

"It's not funny," said Rosalee, although Alex noticed her mouth twitch while he laughed.

"It's a little funny."

He felt the tiniest twinge of guilt as he unlocked his car and watched Rosalee climb into the passenger seat, but reminded himself that friends probably let friends open their own doors. As he backed out of his space in the scorching hot parking lot, he rolled the windows all the way down. "Oh, wait, we didn't get your bike." He pulled off to the side to let another car pass.

"My bike?" said Rosalee.

"Don't you ride your bike here?"

"Nope. Tires are flat."

"Oh." Alex pulled back out and headed toward the parking lot exit. "So is your car here?"

"I take the bus."

"You take the bus?"

"Yeah, what's wrong with that?"

"I guess nothing, except that they're grimy, and crowded, and smell like piss."

Rosalee shrugged. "Maybe in Denver. There aren't as many people here."

Alex turned onto the main road back to Rabbitbrush. "I could just give you a ride, you know."

"You work way longer shifts than me."

"Sure, but I get a lunch break."

"You know, I really wish people would—I'm fine riding the bus. It's not a big deal."

Something about her tone made Alex drop the subject. Not even ten minutes in and he was already re-racking his brain for topics of conversation. Still, he tried to keep in mind that on his better days—the ones that weren't saturated with caffeine in an attempt to compensate for his bad decisions the night before—he was actually pretty good at talking to Rosalee. Of course now, his thoughts kept drifting unhelpfully back to the fundraiser, but he wasn't stupid enough to bring that up again.

"Alex?"

"Hm?"

"The um ... the fundraiser?"

Alex's pulse quickened and he wondered if he had accidentally vocalized his thoughts.

"Mm-hmm ...?" he said. *Keep it together.*

"It's on Saturday, right?"

"Right." No emotion. He was now the Terminator.

"Well, are you still going?"

"I haven't decided yet."

"So ... you didn't ask anyone else?"

"Nope."

Alex pretended to scratch an itch on his upper arm while actually giving himself a good, hard pinch to make sure he hadn't fallen asleep at the wheel. His skin smarted as he let go, but he wasn't going to ask her again. If Rosalee suddenly wanted to go with him, he was going to make her say it. He could see her twisting a strand of her hair around her finger out of the corner of his eye and gradually, his resolve softened to the consistency of a boiled noodle. Watching her struggle didn't provide him any level of satisfaction.

He cleared his throat. "Rosalee?"

"Yeah?"

"Do you want to go to the town thingy after all?"

Rosalee smiled and something inside Alex crumbled. How in the world could he possibly be just "friends" with this girl?

"Is that a 'yes'?" he said.

"Yes. But still ..."

"No dancing. Got it."

"Well ..."

Alex pumped the brake too hard at a stop sign, throwing them forward against their seatbelts. "Shit, sorry." They waited as a mother made her way across the street with two children and her grocery shopping in tow. "So, you *do* want to dance now?"

"Maybe. A little. *Maybe.*"

The way was clear for Alex to keep driving, but he stared at Rosalee, instead, until the car behind him let out a short *beep.* Alex tapped the gas pedal and dragged half of his focus back to the road.

"So ... okay, hold on, this is making my head hurt. Which part of the other day didn't you like—was it the dancing or the dancing with *me?*"

"What do you mean?"

"I guess it doesn't matter." She wanted to dance with him now, didn't she? *'Maybe.'* "Did something happen between now and the other day to make you ... not afraid of me?"

"I was never afraid of you, *per se.*"

"I wish you weren't afraid of me *at all.*" Alex drummed his fingers on the steering wheel. "Do we need, like ... a code word or something?"

"What?" He could feel Rosalee watching him.

"You know, like, if things get too crazy, one of us can say it and the other one has to stop whatever's ... crazy."

"Huh."

"That was a joke. Mostly."

Rosalee looked out the window again. "It's not a *bad* idea."

"Really?"

Rosalee shook her head, looking thoughtful, and Alex suddenly felt a little sick. Maybe he shouldn't have had greasy takeout three days in a row for lunch. Or maybe he didn't want to think about why a code word would appeal so much to someone so afraid of being touched.

"Well, then we'll have to come up with a good one," he said finally.

They lapsed into a comfortable silence while they pondered, although Alex wished he had thought to turn on the radio before, in case the silence was only comfortable on his side.

"'Dune buggy,'" he said. Maybe thinking out loud was a good idea.

"That's a lot of syllables. But I like it. Deer."

"Isn't that more of a pet name?"

"Deer," Rosalee said again, pointing out the window.

Alex immediately slowed down as they passed a doe grazing in someone's front yard.

"'Yield,'" he said, looking at a yellow sign further down the road. "Maybe too fancy."

Rosalee smiled. "'Halt.'"

"'Bird,'" said Alex as several of them shuffled along a telephone wire.

"'Cactus,'" said Rosalee as they passed a large one in an equally large pot next to a mailbox. "We're not good at this."

"'*Cactus.*' I mean ..."

They looked at each other.

"We'll sit with 'cactus' for now and see how we feel," said Rosalee, settling back into her seat and looking out the front windshield with the ghost of a smile on her face.

Too soon, Alex was parking next to her driveway and Rosalee was thanking him for the ride. "So, when do I get to see you again?" she said.

Sweet lord.

"I mean, when do you work next?" Rosalee amended quickly, looking concerned about whatever Alex's face was doing, and at the moment, he wasn't sure.

On the drive to her house, he had only just crawled to the edge of the point where he was willing to be "friends" with Rosalee forever, as long as that meant that sometimes she was next to him in his Jeep, caressing the breeze with her fingertips as it rushed past the open window, and laughing when it blew her hair around her face and filled the car with clouds of brilliant red. Maybe being her friend wouldn't be so bad—that is, until she got a boyfriend and threw Alex's entire world off its axis, like a basketball to a science fair model of the solar system. But surely, after he rolled away under the table, re-adjusted his rings of Saturn, and licked his wounds, he could forget about her ... *Not.*

"Too soon?" said Rosalee, and Alex realized that he probably looked like he was in pain.

"No. No, I'm just thinking about what a nightmare next week is gonna be."

"Oh. Then I can just see you at the thing on Saturday."

"No, no, no." Alex rubbed the space between his eyebrows as he mentally sorted through his schedule. "What about Wednesday?"

"I work open to close at The Goose. Inventory."

"Okay. Friday at Laurie's? Lunch before my dinner shift?"

"I can do that."

"Yeah?"

"Yeah."

Rosalee gathered her backpack in her lap and reached for the door handle as Alex nearly bit his tongue off to keep himself from offering to walk her to the door. This was not a *date* date.

She smiled as she hopped down from the cab and swung her bag over her shoulder. Alex was still having trouble getting used to that—not the smiling, in and of itself, but the smiling *at him.*

"I'll see you later," she said before closing the door.

Alex was pretty sure he could fly.

— •●• —

Until Friday morning.

"I'm really sorry, Alex," said Rosalee. She sounded like she probably was. You never could tell on the phone, though.

"So you think you maybe caught something?" Alex did his best to curb the disappointment pooling in his stomach and weighing him down. "Like a cold or the flu?"

"No, I don't think it's anything like that."

Alex waited for her to say more and then imagined crickets in the silence that greeted him. "Can I bring you anything?" he said, feeling dull and a little cliche.

"I think I just need to lay low, but thank you."

Alex at least thought he detected a little smile. Sometimes you could tell that, even on the phone. "Okay. Well, I hope you feel better and I guess let me know about tomorrow night."

"I'll be there."

"Really?" Alex felt his pulse jump somewhere near his Adam's apple. "I mean, if you can't, that's cool."

Not cool. Not cool at all. Don't give her ideas.

"I'll be there, Alex."

He definitely heard a smile that time.

Chapter 21

Rosalee hung up the phone in the kitchen, watching the coiled phone cord twist around itself as it retracted.

"I feel like I lied," she said.

Robin looked up from mashing herbs and spices into a bowl of cooked tomatoes. "About what?"

"Not feeling well."

"Well, do you?"

"No. But it's not like I'm sick."

Robin spooned the tomatoes into a glass pan and began chopping zucchini. "I'd say it's a lot like you're sick."

Rosalee sighed, then turned her attention to the abundance of produce on the counter surrounding the stove. "What can I help with?"

"You can wash those mushrooms." Robin pointed with her chef's knife.

Rosalee dug in one of the lower cabinets for a colander and dumped the packet of mushrooms out of their damp cardboard container. As she rinsed, she watched the dirt swirling down the drain and inhaled the earthy aroma. The smell of cooking always made her calmer. Good things tended to happen around good cooking.

Even in the midst of her current dilemma, Rosalee couldn't help but be a little excited that Robin was prepping her famous Italian casserole for dinner that night. Evelyn had a saying about grief; she said that like an onion, it had many layers and was "best served sliced into a hearty stew." She had a feeling famous casserole might also do the trick.

When the water ran clear, Rosalee turned off the faucet and held the colander suspended above the sink to drain. She glanced at Robin. "So ... what do you think I should do?"

"About Alex?"

"Yeah."

"About telling him or not?"

"Mm-hm."

Robin considered a yellow onion before chopping off its root end. "I suppose that depends on what you want the outcome to be. What do you hope to get out of it?"

"I'm not really sure," Rosalee admitted.

She shifted her weight and realized that the bottom of one of her feet had started to feel tingly—like pins and needles, but mostly the fuzzy part. Not a good sign. She handed her aunt the colander of mushrooms and then pointed to a couple of red bell peppers with their stickers still on. "These, too?"

Robin nodded.

"I think I just want to be able to talk to him more like Ellie," said Rosalee. "Or Pete, before I left. Although at this point, I spend more time with Alex than Pete."

Rosalee paused her attempts to scrape off the second sticker as a wave of sadness washed over her. Just as quickly, her eyes filled with tears that immediately spilled over the edge and down her face. She hastily shoved her thumbnail into the pepper—peeling off the sticker and a layer of pepper flesh in one—and then wadded the sticky mess between her fingers. She purposely aimed badly for the trash can, then ambled over to retrieve it. Still, the tears kept coming. She sniffed and Robin looked up.

"I'm gonna go blow my nose," said Rosalee, already headed out of the kitchen. "That onion really got me," she called as she hurried down the hall toward the bathroom.

As soon as she closed the door, she turned on the fan and the faucet, hoping to drown out the sobs that racked her body. She crouched low and put her head between her knees, but her breaths came in gasps and she knew any minute Robin would come bursting in to check on her. She jumped slightly as she heard the back door open. Lola's truly terrible singing voice permeated the hallway and made its way into the kitchen, and Rosalee hoped it would drown her out. Sure enough, Robin joined in, equally off-key, and Rosalee felt her shoulders relax by a degree. It was hard to have a full-blown meltdown with the smell of Italian food and singing in the air. Hers was not a family of *good* singers, but what they lacked in tonality, they certainly made up for in enthusiasm.

Except for Evelyn.

Evelyn had had a lovely, low, soothing voice and as far as Rosalee could tell, she could even carry a tune. Hers was always among the most confidant voices in church when Rosalee and Ellie were younger, and one of Rosalee's fondest memories was Evelyn singing in time with the creak and thump of the rocking chair against the porch planks on nights when she or Ellie couldn't sleep. Sometimes, Rosalee swore that she could still hear her aunt's voice on windy nights, singing along with that rocking chair metronome.

When Rosalee finally pulled herself together and splashed cold water on her face, she returned to the kitchen to find Lola and Robin waltzing around it, still singing at the tops of their voices. Rosalee laughed, taking advantage of their momentary distraction to wipe a couple of stray tears from under her eyes with the pads of her thumbs. She took over tending the ground sausage sizzling in the skillet and hummed along with her aunts, wishing this rare moment of light-hearted normalcy could last forever.

—— • ♦ • ——

"So Lola, how was your seminar last week?" said Ellie, cutting a steaming bite of casserole with her fork and holding it over her plate to cool.

Rosalee was glad her sister was home. Ellie had always been good at carrying conversations, and as Rosalee was too busy fighting off a panic attack to contribute very much, it was a welcome talent tonight. The numbness on the bottom of her foot had traveled up to her knee and was sending zaps down her leg that became more frequent the more nervous she became. Still, she wasn't quite ready to deal with the unnecessary fuss that alerting her family would entail, so she decided to keep it to herself.

"Super cool," said Lola. "They offered it with my aerobics certification renewal."

"What was it about?" said Rosalee. Maybe talking would distract her.

Lola twirled her fork so that a string of mozzarella cheese wrapped around her bite of casserole like white, stretchy yarn. "Healing with food," she said. "A lot of the stuff you're already doing, like cutting out dairy, wheat, and processed foods."

"Well, I haven't been great at those."

Rosalee felt suddenly and deeply guilty for not trying harder. She was grateful that Lola hadn't mentioned the seminar since leaving her the pamphlet over a month before, but felt guilty about not accepting her invitation, too.

"I think it just takes practice," said Robin. "And it's not like you have to do everything at once."

193

"So, is that, like, instead of medication?" said Ellie.

The mood changed perceptively around the table and Rosalee felt another jolt go up her leg. She had steadfastly refused medication thus far, reluctant to put anything foreign in her body, and her family had been mostly supportive, even if they couldn't entirely understand. She suppressed a twitch with difficulty and caught Robin watching her, but to her relief, she didn't comment.

Lola shifted in her chair and popped a large bite of casserole into her mouth without letting it cool, grimacing as she swallowed. "It didn't really specify. I'm sure someone could choose to do one or the other or both."

"Maybe we could try some of the ideas together. The food ideas, I mean," said Ellie.

Rosalee couldn't help but notice that her sister had a manic glint in her eye—similar to her party-planning glint, but more intense. Usually, that meant that Ellie was hurling herself into something she vaguely cared about to distract herself from something she *really* cared about. For example, the summer Ellie had asked for a cat and then come to the devastating realization that Robin was extremely allergic, she had thrown herself into knitting. She knitted hats and scarves for all her dolls, then moved onto miniature sweaters, until her entire room looked like a toy store out of a winter wonderland.

"Well, I'm in," said Lola, smiling across the table as Robin caught Rosalee's eye. Rosalee looked away before her aunt did.

"Rose, what do you think?" said Ellie. She wasn't looking at Rosalee, but swirling a bit of casserole around her plate to coat it with tomato sauce.

Rosalee forced her mouth into what she hoped resembled the upturned lines of a smile, even while everything else in her body attempted to wrestle them down. "Sure. I think that sounds interesting."

By seven o'clock that night, Rosalee was sitting in front of Ellie's vanity while Ellie fluttered around her, chattering about hairstyles, makeup, and dresses until Rosalee was dizzy. She just wanted to sleep. Every cell in her body was screaming its need to be blissfully unconscious for a few hours.

"El, I really appreciate you helping, but can we talk about it more tomorrow?"

"Give me five more minutes to figure out your hair. I'll be back at school, so it has to be something you can do yourself."

Rosalee glanced in the mirror at the messy bun that hadn't moved since she washed her face that morning. "I'll just leave it like this,"

"Over my dead body," Ellie muttered, undoing the elastic and releasing Rosalee's hair so it hung down the back of the chair. She started to brush through it as the phone rang downstairs in the kitchen.

Rosalee winced as every brush stroke tugged at her overly sensitive scalp. "Why are you going back so soon, anyway? Why don't you come to the dance?"

"Eleanor, it's for you," Robin called up the stairs.

Much to Rosalee's relief, Ellie handed her the brush. "Brush that and keep brushing," she said, and Rosalee heard her skipping down the stairs to the kitchen.

Rosalee slumped down in the stiff cushions of the vanity chair and gathered all of her hair over her shoulder. She held it tightly in a ponytail and brushed it with her fist pressed against her head to avoid any unnecessary pulling. The sooner she got this over with, the sooner she could sleep.

Sleep.

Maybe if she laid down for a few minutes, she would feel better. Rosalee scooted off of the vanity chair and climbed onto Ellie's bed, lying flat on her back and parting her hair into two curtains around her face as she continued to brush. Then she flipped over and inched on her front until her hair hung off the edge of the bed and pooled onto the floor. After several weak attempts to brush her hair from that angle, Rosalee dropped the brush on the floor and let her arms flop over the edge of the bed as she breathed in the smell of fabric softener. It felt good to finally be lying down. Now that all of her limbs were pressed against the same surface, she realized that all of them were starting to ache.

———•●•———

Several hours or minutes later (it was difficult to tell), Rosalee jerked awake and lifted her head, swatting her hair out of her face. She gradually righted herself and sat on the edge of the bed for a few minutes, then wandered into the hallway and realized that her legs had turned to gelatin. She kept her hands on the wall and pushed off sideways to cross into her aunts' bedroom. Robin was standing at the bathroom counter, fussing over a succulent whose leaves had gone brown at the ends. She looked up as Rosalee sank onto the bench at the end of the bed.

"*Oh,*" said Robin.

"What?"

"Nothing, I just ..."

Lola emerged from the walk-in closet with the scent of perfume and looked at Rosalee, too. "*Oh.*"

"*What?*" said Rosalee.

"Is that how you're wearing your hair to the dance?"

"I don't know, Ellie told me to brush it."

Lola walked to the sink and beckoned for her to come over, too. Rosalee glanced briefly into the mirror and got a glimpse of a wild lion wearing her face.

"Maybe don't brush it so much?" Robin suggested helpfully.

"Well, what am I supposed to do with it?"

Robin shrugged. "I only brush mine in the shower."

Rosalee found it supremely unfair that she had inherited the mega-curly Andrews hair gene from a long line of ancestors, while Ellie had escaped with bouncy, practically maintenance-free curls.

"What did you do with it when you went to the dance with what's-his-name? Mark something?" said Lola, "That was cute."

"Lola, that was middle school," said Rosalee.

"Okay, so your hair looked *cute* is all I'm saying." Lola dug a packet of gum out of her purse and then turned to Robin. "Love, what time did you say the movie starts?"

"I can't remember. I'll check the paper."

"I don't want it to look cute," Rosalee muttered. She wanted to be a knockout. Was that too much to ask?

"I thought you didn't like Alex that way," said Lola, seemingly reading her mind. "You know, you really shouldn't lead him on."

"When did I—How did you ..." *Ellie.*

Robin shuffled back into the bedroom, looking sheepish. "It starts at nine o'clock."

Lola spun to look at the clock radio on her nightstand. "But it's only seven thirty."

"I know. I must have read it wrong before."

"Well, then I'll help Rosalee with her hair," said Lola brightly.

"No, it's okay," said Rosalee. *Sleep. I need to sleep.* "I'll figure it out in the morning."

"Nonsense, I have just the thing. It'll be quick. Robin, do you have some old T-shirts that we can cut up?"

Exhausted as she was, Rosalee turned to watch Robin's reaction. As predicted, her aunt was looking moderately horrified. Robin's T-shirt collection was treated with the same reverence as fine silk in more refined wardrobes. Rosalee allowed herself approximately five seconds of amusement before diving in to save her.

"Don't worry, I have some."

Nearly an hour later, Rosalee was dead on her feet (or, rather, the edge of the tub, where she was sitting) with her head covered in little knots with cloth poking out. As it turned out, Lola's idea of a "quick" hair fix for the dance was spritzing individual sections of her hair with water and twisting them up in the strips of T-shirt.

"I'm supposed to sleep on these? How?" said Rosalee.

She pressed on one side of her head experimentally. It was definitely more uncomfortable than the brushing had been.

Lola waved her hand in a "no-big-deal" kind of way. "Oh, they're like little pillows. Take them out while you're getting ready tomorrow night to make sure they're dry."

"Well, thanks. You should probably get to your movie."

By now, the numbness had spread halfway up Rosalee's thigh and she got up from her chair carefully to avoid stumbling.

"Are you sure you don't wanna come?" said Lola.

"In these? Are you kidding?"

Lola applied lipgloss and puckered in the mirror. "It's dark, who would see you?"

Robin came into the bathroom and looked at Rosalee's hair. "Boy. If that doesn't bring back memories."

Lola chuckled and moved to stand beside Robin in the doorway, one arm around her waist. "Fond ones, I'm sure."

"What? Why?" said Rosalee. As much as she was dreading trying to sleep in these *Little House on the Prairie* curlers, she didn't want to think about trying to get them all out before the next day, either.

"Nothing ... I didn't particularly like the Shirley Temple look for myself," said Robin.

"Lola, I don't want to look like Shirley Temple." Rosalee's voice, suddenly whiny and half her age, caused something deep inside her ears to twinge.

"Rosalee, your hair is way longer than your aunt's ever was. Relax."

"Are you going to bed soon?" said Robin.

"As soon as possible," said Rosalee. In fact, she decided that if she brushed her teeth at all, she would do it lying down.

"Good, you look—"

"'Like hell,' I know."

"Maybe you shouldn't go tomorrow."

"Let her see how she feels in the morning," said Lola, smoothing a flyaway hair from Robin's forehead.

Rosalee immediately recognized Robin's internal struggle between protecting her and remembering that she wasn't a child anymore.

"Okay, well, be good," said Robin. "Tell Ellie not to wait up."

"Where *is* Ellie?" said Rosalee.

"I think she's still on the phone," said Robin. "Pete called earlier."

"Huh," said Rosalee. "Okay, well, have a good time. Love you guys."

"Love you, kiddo," said Robin, reaching out a hand to mirror Rosalee's, neither hand quite reaching the other. *"And I love you too,"* came Lola's voice down the hall.

On the way back to her room, Rosalee noticed that Ellie's door was closed. She thought about knocking, then stumbled past to Evelyn's room, instead. She located a pad of bright pink sticky notes in one of the desk drawers and scribbled a quick note asking if she was okay, then slipped it under her door.

She wandered back into Evelyn's room and stood for several moments, unsure why she had come back in. Then she remembered that the computer was still running. She pulled out the desk chair and wiggled the mouse until the cursor appeared on a paper Ellie had apparently been writing for her human biology class. Maybe she shouldn't shut the computer down yet. An envelope in the taskbar caught her attention and she wondered if Ellie was off the phone. She could listen at the wall but that would require standing up, so she took the chance and opened Internet Explorer.

She sighed and laid her head on her arm, looking up at the screen sideways while the dial-up connection was established. At long last, she pulled up her email to find a message from Alex sent several hours earlier:

`Hey Rosalee,`

`No pressure, but if you're feeling better do you want to meet me for breakfast tomorrow morning? I'll be up late, so call if you want.`

`-Alex`

Rosalee hesitated, fingers poised over the keyboard—she should really just call. She exited her email and stared at Ellie's paper on the screen, summoning her strength. She let her body become liquid and spill out of the chair, then crawled on her hands and knees across the hall again to use the phone in Robin and Lola's room. She sat on the floor, leaning heavily against their mattress as she dialed and wondering briefly if she would wake Pete. Alex answered on the second ring.

"Hey, it's Rosalee."

"Hey, I'm glad you called. I was worried I sent that email too late."

"No, you didn't. I don't think I'll be ready to go out in public by breakfast, though."

"Are you okay? Still sick?"

Rosalee made her eyes as wide as possible to dissuade the lids from sliding closed. Like the curtains on a four-post bed. *Mmm, bed.*

"Rosalee?"

It took a few seconds for Rosalee to remember she was on the phone. "Sorry, no, I'm ... wearing really stupid curlers from our grandparents' era or earlier. So, you better be *floored* by the results."

Was that too flirty? At this point, Rosalee could barely think straight enough to tell. Alex laughed on the other line, and after agreeing to see her at the dance, Rosalee replaced the receiver on its base and stood. One of her legs had started to go numb again as she hobbled into the hallway. She noticed that her sister had passed the sticky note back under her door and bent to pick it up.

> *OK-ish.*
> *Can talk about it later.*
> *Go to bed.*

Rosalee didn't need telling twice.

Chapter 22

The first thing Alex noticed as he stood on the hill overlooking "The Eighty-Sixth Annual Rabbitbrush Festival" was the lights. There had only been a few lights set up for the outdoor movie back in August, strategically placed to make sure that people got up and down the hill safely. Otherwise, it was mostly the light of the projector and the moon.

This was a completely different type of event. Strings of white Christmas lights illuminated the outline of the barn, while bigger lights were strung along various booths for games, souvenirs, and refreshments. The doors to the barn were thrown wide open and warm brightness spilled from the upper windows onto the dance floor that began inside the barn itself and extended out into the festival. Even more white bulbs twinkled in a criss-crossing pattern over the dance floor outside and Alex was sure that from the floor itself, they would look like extra stars.

Alex had always been a sucker for lights, as dorky as it felt to put it like that, and he could easily recall the precise type of lights present at any of the important events in his life. On his fifth birthday, he had asked his mom for a camouflaged, Army-themed cake to go with his camouflaged, Army-themed birthday. He distinctly remembered admiring all the little plastic army men with their boots partially sunk into the chocolate and Oreo "mud" and thinking it was the coolest cake ever. He also remembered the kitchen, hazy with lingering cigarette smoke from the neighbor lady who watched him when his parents were at work or out for the night, and a big fluorescent light flickering over everything. That had been a superb birthday.

The lights that really revved him up, though, were the floodlights at stadiums. While Alex had never been a jock by any means, his dad had pushed him to try out for everything. Something about the insane brightness and magnitude of those lights cutting through the sky made him feel like something *big* was about to happen. Back when he still cared, it had been the overwhelming potential that maybe, just maybe, this would be the night that his dad wouldn't wish for a different son than the one he had. Of course, after Glen left, Alex's mom didn't have a problem with him quitting all of the sports that she couldn't afford, anyway.

There was something to be said for softer lights, too, though—like the sconces on the walls in movie theaters, which, with their dimming, seemed to promise something extraordinary. Alex was usually pretty good at picking movies, so he was rarely disappointed in that aspect. Then there was the calming warmth of coffee shop lighting, inviting mystery and release from the hardness of other venues. As a bonus, there was also usually hot chocolate there. Alex would also never forget the gentle flame of the vanilla-scented candle he picked up at Kmart before his first time with Daphne Wright, his high school girlfriend. The anticipation, the nerves, and the hormones were something he hoped never to experience at that level again. Still, he always looked back fondly on that night on the rare occasions when he noticed the scent of vanilla.

One day, Alex hoped he might get the "stadium light feeling" from the lights on a movie set. He daydreamed about finding solace under the fluorescent lights between ceiling panels in a stuffy conference room in LA. Bolstered by the aroma of fast food, coffee, and cigarettes, and surrounded by other exhausted writers, he imagined that the magic would seep into his soul and breed unparalleled creativity.

Now, amid the lights of the festival, strolling with his hands in the pockets of the sport coat he wore over a dress shirt and jeans, Alex felt a mixture of all of the noteworthy light-related emotions. The potential of stadium lights stirred his adrenaline, while small-town warmth enveloped him and kept him grounded. Meanwhile, vanilla anticipation unfurled in the form of the irresistible aromatic combination of funnel cakes, homemade apple cider, and roasted, candied almonds. And of course, in a short time, he would be seeing Rosalee. She would arrive in the same space that he occupied, and on purpose.

"*Yoo-hoo!* Alex, honey, over here!"

Alex turned to see Angela flagging him down in a canary yellow dress and sky-high heels. Pete had only reluctantly agreed to make an appearance at the festival as a show of loyalty to his town and the people in it (his bank was particularly big on loyalty and appearances), but Angela had evidently tracked him down right away. He stood beside her as though carved from stone as she clung to his arm.

"Hey, Pete," said Alex, shooting a questioning glance at his roommate.

The longer he looked, Pete looked more than uncomfortable—he looked downright miserable. Pete shook his head almost imperceptibly at the ground in answer to Alex's silent question and Alex turned his attention back to Pete's captor.

"Angela, you're looking radiant, as always," he said. Angela's undeniable Southern-ness tended to bleed into Alex's mannerisms on the rare occasions that they interacted.

"Oh, you're such a tease!" said Angela, "Save a dance for me, won't you? I've already added this *Dapper Dan* to my card and I don't intend to sit around all night."

Alex found himself making a sweeping hand gesture and bow, much like a footman before he offered his hand to a woman in a carriage. "My lady, your dance is my command," he said, then felt immediately like a caricature of himself. "Or, you know, I'll add it to my card. Or you will."

Angela laughed a high, tinkling laugh while Pete continued to look as though he was a convincingly life-like mannequin that she had bewitched to accompany her around the festival. There didn't seem to be very much Alex could do for Pete at the moment, so as he and Angela were approached by a small group, Alex retreated to the background to sit at a picnic table with his notebook.

He kept an eye on his watch and at ten till seven, two large speakers set up on either side of the barn doors crackled to life. Angela and Pete found him at his table and he stood to join them. "This feels like prom all over again," he said.

"It's meant to feel like that, a little bit," said Angela. "The Rabbitbrush Festival is always held on the same night as the Rabbitbrush High homecoming dance. Everybody goes to watch the game, then the kids go on to their dance and everybody else comes here."

"I forgot about the homecoming game," said Alex. "I wish I hadn't had to work today."

"Did you play football in high school?"

Alex barely heard Angela's question. It wasn't often that he found himself stunned beyond the ability to form coherent sentences or keep oxygen cycling through his respiratory system, but as Rosalee walked toward him, any response to Angela fell by the wayside and floated away on the notes of music that had suddenly become slower. Everything—the music, the colors, the very air swirling around him—paused in the wake of the incomprehensible vision moving toward him.

Where normally, Rosalee's hair surrounded her wild and untamed like some otherworldly sea creature (assuming she hadn't bullied it into a bun or braid), tonight, it fell in soft ringlets down her back, scarlet against her ivory skin. Her dress floated around her as though made of actual sea foam and if Alex had been focusing properly, he would bet that it was within a shade of the green that lined her irises.

As she approached their little group, Alex felt his heart rate stutter and shook himself mentally in preparation. *Just. Friends.* He noticed Angela's manicured fingernails clutch Pete's arm a little tighter.

"My goodness, Rosalee, look at you!" she said, "Why, you're simply—"

"Heaven," Alex murmured.

He was pleased to see the single word deepening the color in Rosalee's cheeks. She looked away from him again and waved awkwardly at Angela and Pete. Alex had been too busy to pay much attention to Pete in the past couple of minutes, but now, he was surprised to see him smiling for the first time that evening. Was this the Rosalee that he had been missing for all of these months? As stoic as he was, Alex could see the pain behind his roommate's eyes every time she came up in conversation—almost as though he was remembering someone who died.

"Hey, Rose," Pete said quietly, and for the tiniest millisecond, Alex felt a pinprick of jealousy at the intimacy of that nickname.

A millisecond later, he had scolded himself back into the realm of good reason and common sense. Rosalee's whole family called her that and everyone in this town had known her for much longer than Alex. He would simply have to do his time. Besides, Alex knew that even if

Pete had somehow suppressed a secret, burning passion for his former best friend, it was extremely unlikely that he would ever flaunt it in front of Alex or Angela, or in any way that was impolite or even public.

"Hey," said Rosalee. "You guys look great."

"Aren't you a doll," said Angela. "Shall we all get some cider?"

Alex resisted the strong temptation to reach for Rosalee's hand. She seemed so much more confident tonight. Everything about her glowed. Everything *around* her glowed as a result of being so near her.

"Actually, Alex and I were gonna go check out the music first," said Rosalee, and Alex was sure he couldn't have heard her correctly. "Catch you guys a little later?"

"Sure, honey," said Angela, waving them away.

Alex hurried to keep up with Rosalee. "You know, we don't have to dance first," he said. "We can walk around for a little while and look at stuff, or have some food."

But Rosalee was already making her way through the crowded dance floor. "I wanted to talk to you, first."

She walked quickly until they reached a remote corner of the dance floor near a speaker, which was loud, but Alex supposed it was easier not to be overheard that way. When she turned back to him, he was startled to see her looking defiant.

"So," she said, crossing her arms.

"So ...?"

Suddenly, the air felt chillier.

"*So*, I got your emails."

"My emails?"

Rosalee sighed and unzipped a shiny clutch, removing several sheets of paper that had been folded inside. She handed them mutely to Alex, who only had to look at the top sheet before panic gripped him, churning his stomach. Here were five separate emails, printed out—*from his drafts folder.*

"When did you get these?" he said.

"Does it matter?"

"Kind of, I never meant to send them."

Rosalee paused. "You didn't?"

Alex shook his head as he flipped through the pages and various lines jumped out, mocking him and making him cringe. "These were in my drafts. I definitely sent them by accident."

"Okay, well, I still feel like we should talk about them."

"Okay ..."

Rosalee shifted her weight to the other foot and looked uncertain. Maybe she had expected him to argue. "So, this whole thing—us being friends? I mean, you can see why I would be upset, can't you?"

"Not really. I agreed to be friends."

"Right, but you're not actually serious about it—you're still trying to scheme up ways to seduce me."

"Well, that's a bit of an exaggeration."

Rosalee snatched the pages from Alex and read from one of them at random.

"'If you think about it, this is your stereotypical eighties rom-com ... boy meets girl, girl ignores boy, boy continues to annoy girl until girl sends boy down into the "Pit of Despair," AKA the "Friend Zone," AKA, the "Arctic Circle," then boy freezes to death because girl forgot to throw down a jacket.'"

Alex grimaced. "Okay, well—"

"So, you've been secretly resenting me and thinking I'm this ... impenetrable ice queen this whole time."

"No, that's not even—"

"Well, you're what ... 'freezing to death,' right? Because I want to take things slow and not just jump into bed with you?"

"That was supposed to be funny. I was hoping you would laugh. Not that—*again*—you were even supposed to read it."

"Okay, well, what about this one ..."

Alex tilted his head back and pinched the bridge of his nose. "Please don't read any more."

Rosalee ignored him and cleared her throat: "*'I just wanted to dance with you. I thought that was the way in.'*"

Alex screwed up his face, trying to remember the whole message. "That one was out of context. Read the part before that."

Rosalee huffed. "If you already know what it says, why do I have to read it?"

"If I'm going to be on *trial* for what it says, it's only *fair* that you read it."

Rosalee's eyes narrowed before dropping back to the email. "*'I wasn't trying to make you uncomfortable and I never meant to push you that far.'*"

"So there," said Alex.

"*Not* 'so there,' you also said that it was '*the way in.*'"

"Yeah, to your life. To you trusting me."

"That's not what it sounded like." Rosalee folded the pages in half. "You know, just because I don't like people touching me doesn't mean I'm naive or a ... *prude.*"

"I never said you were."

Alex was sure he had never written, spoken, or so much as thought those words.

"Well, this still proves that you've been trying to seduce me, which means you never respected what I asked, even when you agreed to it."

"That's hardly fair."

"I don't know why it's so important to you that *that's* where this leads." Rosalee gestured toward the general space between them.

"Um, I'd say the cat's out of the bag there." Alex nodded at the emails still in Rosalee's hands. When she only looked at him blankly, he shook his head at the strings of lights overhead. "*I like you.* As more than a friend. I'm sorry, but I can't control that."

"See, I don't think you *do* like me," said Rosalee. "You haven't known me long enough, for one thing. We barely know each other. It's more like it's some ... dare or something."

"A *dare?*" Alex raised his eyebrows. "What, like I made some stupid bet with a bunch of dickwad jocks to take you to the prom and then *take* you in the back of my Camaro?"

"Yeah, sort of."

Alex made a face.

"*What?*" Rosalee snapped.

"Nothing, I just remembered that I left the pig's blood near the punch bowl—you know, while I was spiking it—and I should proba- bly move it before people confuse the two."

"This isn't funny."

"I agree. I think this is the most *unfunny* thing that's happened to me all day."

"Then can you stop making jokes?"

"I'm sorry, I thought we were being ridiculous—I was just playing along."

"Maybe I should go," said Rosalee quietly.

"Don't go." Alex reached out to grab her wrist before he could stop himself.

Rosalee sucked in a sharp breath but even as they both tensed, she didn't yank it away. Alex still let go. "Did that hurt?"

"No."

"Good." Alex exhaled. "Sorry, I panicked. Can we start over? Or, at least, rewind a little bit?"

It had been such a good start to the evening. It had been such a good start to *everything*.

"I'm not sure that's possible." Rosalee held up the emails, then let her hand drop by her side.

Alex reached toward the papers. "Can I? For a second?"

Reluctantly, Rosalee handed them over, then watched as Alex tore the whole stack in half, then into quarters, then crumpled everything into a ball and looked around for a trash can.

"Over there." Rosalee nodded toward one a few yards away, near the other speaker.

Alex hesitated. As much as he wanted to banish these emails from the evening, he didn't want to leave Rosalee alone and risk her slipping away before he could fix things. Plus, Angela wasn't far away, chatting up an entire table.

"I'll just …" He shoved the whole wad in his pocket, where it made a very noticeable bulge.

Rosalee rolled her eyes, smirking as she unzipped her purse again. Alex pulled the ball back out of his pocket with as much dignity as he could muster, then smoothed the papers against his jeans before handing them back in defeat.

The music changed to a fast song and suddenly it felt too loud.

"Can we go someplace quieter?" Alex shouted.

"If we hurry—I think Angela's headed this way."

Alex walked around the other side of the barn, where there was only one light up near the roof. Still, it was bright enough to see Rosalee's expression, which had softened considerably in the past few minutes.

"Look," said Alex, "I'll do whatever you want me to do. If you want me to stay, I'll stay. If you want me to leave you alone, I will. But …"

"But what?"

"I mean, you seemed kind of excited about tonight. Even the dancing part. What happened?"

Rosalee tugged at the hem of her dress. "Well, it was kind of a disaster, wasn't it? The other day?"

"What was a disaster? The dancing?"

Rosalee nodded, her eyes wide.

"Not from where I'm standing," said Alex.

"Well, from where I'm standing, it *bit*," said Rosalee, flaring up again, "I tried, and I crapped out, and it was humiliating. The end."

"You shouldn't feel humiliated."

Alex stepped forward, but Rosalee immediately countered the movement. "Don't tell me how to feel."

So much for rewinding.

"I wasn't telling you how to—"

"You know, just because you think you have this extraordinary power to read people doesn't mean you actually can. Or do." Rosalee raised her eyebrows, daring Alex to challenge her.

"When did I even—I've never said that."

"Okay, well you've implied it, then."

Alex laced his fingers behind his head and turned away from her, taking a deep breath. He had wrestled with the idea of stashing a cigarette in his pocket before he left the apartment, but ultimately decided against it. He seemed to be unconsciously *full* of bad ideas lately.

"I never asked you to fix me, Alex."

"Who said I'm trying to?" he demanded, turning back. Trying to fix and trying to *help* were two completely different things—why couldn't she see that?

"You're, like, *obsessed* with love stories and damsels in distress. What else would this be?" The subtle trace of nausea in Rosalee's voice stung more than Alex wanted to admit.

"Oh, *unclench.* So I have a hobby."

Something deep in Alex's chest recoiled at the word as it left his lips. His writing was as much a "hobby" as moving air through his lungs or blood through his heart. But somehow what he viewed as passion, Rosalee labeled "obsession."

"Yeah, well the rest of us have to live in the real world, Alex. You can't just make up this fantasy girl in your head and pretend that she's me because it isn't fair to either of us. This is it. This is all you get."

She wouldn't understand how the "real world" comment jabbed him—they hadn't gotten that far. Maybe she was right. Maybe they barely knew each other, after all. Somehow, though, he couldn't quite let it go.

"You're—that's all I want, Rosalee."

Alex watched her assess him like some sort of human lie detector before her gaze fell to his shoes. "I don't believe you."

And there it was—the end of Alex's rope. He had felt it coming closer with every contemptuous glance from Rosalee—like the flag on the winning end of a game of tug-o-war, but without the feeling of triumph.

"Alright, *look,*" he said, not bothering to lower his voice this time. No one could hear him over the music, anyway. "You love to dance, and you know it, and part of you had fun up there on the roof, and you know that, too. But you also *love* to dwell on the doom and gloom in your life, so go ahead and do that instead, I guess."

In the stunned silence that followed, Alex could feel a weight driving him into the grass, starting from his shoulders, then pushing down until he could feel his spine radiating from the pressure. He knew better than to open his mouth before letting his brain catch up, but in the throes of such passionate emotions, well, there you had it.

After what seemed like an eternity, he wrenched himself free from the invisible pull of his bones to the ground and marched away from the space where Rosalee remained frozen, her face inscrutable. At that point, Alex didn't even know where he was going, blinded as he was by the bitter disappointment coursing through his veins and mixing with the adrenaline so that he thought he might fly apart. When someone grabbed his arm, he nearly threw them off.

"Alex, wait."

He stopped and looked down at his wrist, barely comprehending the pale fingers that retracted and came to rest next to the folds of Rosalee's dress. Now that they were back underneath the lights, he realized that it was *exactly* the same shade as the green in her eyes.

"Don't go," she said. "Please."

Alex obeyed, but couldn't drag up any words himself. Rosalee opened her mouth to speak again, then met his eyes and shook her head as hers filled with tears. Without pausing to think, Alex moved closer, resting his forehead gently against hers before she could pull away. He turned his head so that his cheek brushed her crimson curls and felt her shudder slightly against him, but kept his hands by his sides until slowly, finally, Rosalee leaned into him. Only then did Alex move his arms to circle her waist, enough to keep her safe but not hold her captive. At long last, she lifted her arms to wind them around his neck.

"Why is it so hard for you to accept the way I feel about you?" Alex said softly.

Rosalee didn't answer.

"Is it because you don't feel that way about me?" Slowly, Alex felt Rosalee shake her head. "Then do you?"

He drew back very slightly and waited for Rosalee to look up. She met his eyes briefly, then shifted her gaze to a spot over his shoulder. "I just wish you wouldn't try so hard to get me to like you, or whatever, when I'm trying to hate you."

Alex laughed and Rosalee struggled in his arms. He released her immediately as she glared at him, then raised his hands in a gesture of surrender. "I'm not trying to get you to like me, okay? I'm trying to get you to 'whatever.'"

Rosalee stared at him incredulously. Alex raked a hand through his hair, laughing softly. "Rosalee Andrews, you are the most infuriating person I know."

Rosalee frowned. "I know."

And with that, she closed the space between them again and pressed her mouth to his. Alex felt his breath hitch and wondered if she would change her mind and push him away. He responded cautiously, preparing for the worst, but then somehow, miraculously, she was pulling him closer. He felt her body bow against him as his arms circled her waist, and then he was kissing her back—slowly and thoroughly—under hundreds of white lights.

"No sign of Rosalee yet, huh?"

Alex started, trying and failing to catch the pen that tumbled out of his hand. He looked up to see Angela sitting across from him at the picnic table and had no idea how long he hadn't noticed her there.

"Yeah, I guess I kinda lost track of time—do you have it? The time, I mean?" he said, shutting the pen back inside his notebook and standing up from the table.

"Nearly eight o'clock," said Angela, clearly disgruntled. "Pete's nowhere to be found, either."

Alex sighed. "*Damn it,* Rosalee."

Chapter 23

"C'mon, Rosalee, where are you?" Alex muttered ten minutes later, exercising most of his self-control not to pummel the faded plastic doorbell next to her front door.

A light switched on in the entryway and he heard footsteps padding toward him before a pretty blonde woman opened the door. He recognized her as one of Rosalee's aunts, but couldn't remember her name.

"Hi, I'm Alex Conway," he said.

"Nice to meet you, Alex, I'm Lola. Aren't you supposed to be meeting my niece at the festival?"

Alex willed himself not to panic. "I was just there. I've been waiting ... she isn't here?"

"Well, I didn't think she'd *still* be here. *Rosalee?*" Lola called, then listened up the stairs. "ROSALEE?"

Robin appeared from the kitchen, wiping her hands on a dish towel. "Didn't she leave already? I just assumed she didn't say goodbye."

"Alex said she's not at the dance," said Lola, and Alex thought he caught a slight tremor in her voice.

Robin cleared her throat and there was definitely something forced in the way she smiled before disappearing up the stairs.

Alex wondered if he should follow. "What's she doing? What's going on?"

"Oh, Rosalee's probably wearing her headphones," said Lola, waving her hand dismissively and smiling in the same tight way that Robin had. "She'll be down in a second, I'm sure. Do you want some lemonade? Fresh squeezed this morning."

Lola had barely succeeded in coaxing Alex into a chair when the sound of a fist pounding on a door started upstairs, followed by voices that became increasingly louder.

"Rosalee Andrews, open this door before I break it down!"

Lola's hostess smile froze on her face as she attempted to drown out the yelling with hospitality. "Can I interest you in some, uh... *some crackers or some* FRUIT, OR—"

Both Lola and Alex jumped as Robin hammered on the door with renewed vigor. Finally, there was the sound of a lock clicking and a door sliding away from its frame.

"My God, Rosalee, WHAT DID YOU DO?!"

Lola only preceded Alex up the stairs by seconds, but it was long enough for her to snap the bathroom door shut before he got to it. He smashed his ear against the door, heart beating out of his chest.

"Is she okay? Is she—" Alex swallowed against the bile that crept up his throat, *"Does she need an ambulance?"*

"No, Alex, honey, everything's okay," Lola said through the door.

Alex listened harder, only catching snatches of an argument and what sounded distinctly like sobbing. He felt the door frame pressing into the side of his face and rolled his forehead along the cool surface of the door itself, trying to soothe the hot panic that was fighting to get out of his chest. He had pushed her too hard, he knew it. He knew it, but he kept pushing because that's who he was. Alex Conway was a pusher.

"Oh, sweetheart ..." came Lola's voice, and a moment later, she was backing out of the bathroom again. Alex craned his neck to look inside, but she blocked his view.

"Alex, Rosalee won't be up for the dance tonight. She's so sorry."

Alex felt every part of himself sag. "Is she okay? What happened?"

"She's just feeling a little under the weather," said Lola, already ushering him out of the hallway.

Then he saw it—a flash of red dangling from a button on Lola's sweater. *Is that Rosalee's hair?*

Lola flinched and tried to shove the strand quickly away in a pocket, but Alex was too quick for her, seizing the end of a violently auburn ringlet. As if in slow motion, the spiral floated and twisted in the air until it lay still—fiery against the off-white carpet. Alex didn't know how long they stared at it, but he looked away when Lola gave a tiny sniff beside him.

"I, um ... I don't understand," said Alex.

He didn't feel quite so panicked now—more like a deflated balloon. The wild rollercoaster of emotions in the past half hour had left him drained and exhausted.

"I wish I could tell you, honey, I really do," said Lola. "But I'm afraid this ... *hardship* ... isn't mine to tell."

———•●•———

"And it was definitely her hair?" Manny leaned against his truck bed and took a swig of Coke. "It wasn't, like, threads from her sweater or something?"

Alex shook his head, which made lighting his cigarette more difficult. He took a few firm draws and inhaled, then offered the pack to Manny.

218

"Nah, my old lady will smell it on me before I hit the driveway. Thanks, though."

Alex tilted his head straight back and exhaled a plume of smoke that was barely visible against the overcast sky. "It was definitely her hair. And it was a long piece—like, a whole … curly cue." He traced a spiral in the air with his finger. "Six or seven inches, at least."

Manny let out a low whistle and readjusted his stance so that one heel was propped up against his truck's back tire. "I mean, maybe she caught it on something."

Alex looked over at him. "I thought about that. She has a lot of hair … I thought it could have gotten caught on a door hinge or something."

"But?"

"But … that wouldn't explain how her aunts reacted. Or how her whole family and Pete act around her in general. They're *super* protective."

Manny set his soda can down on the edge of the truck bed. "Huh. And you can't ask Pete about it?"

"I don't think so."

"Are they, like … in a cult or something?"

Alex felt the corners of his mouth lift in spite of himself. "I don't think so."

He dug in his lunch sack until he found a sandwich bag of Oreos, which he offered to Manny before stuffing one into his mouth whole. They chewed in silence for a few minutes and contemplated the steadily darkening sky.

"So, is there anything else weird, then?" said Manny, wiping Oreo crumbs on his jeans. "With Rosalee?"

Alex was down to the last few puffs of his cigarette before he was smoking filter, but he was determined to extract every last milligram of nicotine. "What do you mean?"

"Like, does anything else seem ... wrong? Weird?"

Alex wasn't sure how he felt about sharing Rosalee's fear of being touched, especially since he didn't know the extent of it. So, were there any other signs? He tried to thumb through the mental Rolodex of everything he knew about her. She liked trees (or at least, the one she tried to save from the bulldozer. For all he knew, the grapefruit tree could be rotting in the garbage). He knew she liked music, although he hadn't quite pinned down what type. She was good at dancing but weird about it ...

"I guess she was sick before the dance," he said finally. He stubbed out his cigarette on the bottom of his boot and dropped it into his empty Dr. Pepper can.

"What kind of sick?"

"She didn't say."

Manny thumbed the tab on his empty soda can. "So she was sick and ... did she get better before the dance?"

"I think so."

"And then her hair fell out."

Alex turned toward Manny again. "So you *do* think it fell out?"

"I don't know—but it was *out*, right?" Manny's dark eyes were narrowed and Alex could tell he was going into detective mode. It was the same look he got whenever they encountered something unexpected at work, and Alex was somewhat comforted by the fact that Manny always seemed to sort things out. He was also glad to escape from his own head for a while.

"Yeah. It was definitely out," he said.

The image of that startlingly vivid shock of hair detached from its owner would haunt him for years, at least.

"You don't think it's ... wow, I don't even wanna say it," said Manny. He walked around to the back of the truck and hopped up to sit on the tailgate.

"What?" said Alex warily.

"I don't wanna jinx it or something." Manny stared out across the parking lot before looking back at Alex. He looked almost apologetic.

"Jinxing isn't real, Manny," said Alex, surreptitiously rapping his knuckles against the wood paneling along the truck's body as he walked toward the back. He hopped up to sit next to Manny.

"I was just thinking about my buddy in high school," said Manny. "About how his mother was going through chemo and he kept finding clumps of her hair around the house. It was brutal, man. Like, really horrific to watch."

Alex felt his blood turn to ice in his veins.

"Yo, Alex. Are you okay?"

Manny reached out to steady him as Alex slumped forward with his head between his knees.

"God," said Alex, his voice muffled by the thick material of his work pants. "You don't think that's what it is, do you?"

"Look, man, I'm sorry I said it. I told you I didn't want to say it."

"No, no, but it all makes sense." Alex groaned as he pulled himself into a sitting position again. "Why everyone's so protective of her, why she's so careful ... Does chemo make you super sensitive? Like, to touch or whatever?"

"I don't know very much about it, to be honest."

Alex noticed Manny watching him with increasing anxiety and frowned. "What's up? Why are you so wound up all of a sudden?"

"Well, we only have about three minutes left on our break and I'm trying to figure out if I can get back in time with you slung over my back."

"What?"

"Are you gonna pass out or what?"

"No," said Alex, although he was a little uncertain as he jumped down from the truck and immediately got a head rush.

Manny followed suit and helped Alex close the tailgate.

"I think you should just talk to her," said Manny. *"'No le busques tres pies al gato,'* as my wise Abuelita says."

"What does that mean?"

"Don't look for three legs on a cat if you know it's got four. Don't look for trouble where there is none."

"Well, we already know there's *some* trouble."

"True. But you could be making it out to be way worse than it is. No sense driving yourself crazy until you know for sure."

Alex nodded and Manny checked his watch. "Ready?"

"Yup. Let's finish that damned wall."

Chapter 24

"How are you feeling?"

Rosalee raised her head off of her arms where she was slumped at the kitchen table to look at Robin. It was already late afternoon and she had only coaxed her body out of bed and into a chair in the last half hour. "Like I have mono all over again."

Robin slid a chair out on the other side of the table and sat across from her with a mug of coffee. "I think we should make another appointment with Dr. Harris."

"Why? That was a train wreck."

Robin wrapped her hands around the mug and straightened her shoulders as though steeling herself.

"Well, wasn't it?" Rosalee propped herself up on her elbow to look at her aunt. "Plus, we saw him months ago and he hasn't even bothered to follow up."

"His bedside manner could use a little work," Robin admitted. "But he seemed to know what he was talking about. There might be someone else in Picket. Lola's going to ask Gwen at her class tonight."

Rosalee sighed. "I don't want to see any more doctors. They'll all be like Dr. Harris—guilting me into medication."

"We don't know that."

"We *probably* know that."

"Okay," Robin said patiently, "Even if that *is* the end result ... Honey, would that be so bad? I mean, wouldn't it be better to get some relief?"

"I don't like putting things in my body when I don't know what they'll do, especially long term."

"Well, you can't keep doing *this*. Can you even walk?"

Rosalee looked away as tears stung her eyes.

"I wasn't trying to upset you." Robin reached across the table toward her, stopping several inches from her hand.

Rosalee wiped her eyes impatiently on the sleeve of her sweatshirt. "I know you weren't. I swear this is, like, a reflex or something now."

"The medication may help that, too."

Rosalee could feel a sob building in her chest. "I've been doing everything right. The diet, not overexerting myself. I'm so tired and everything hurts."

"I know, kiddo." Robin looked close to tears herself. She looked around the kitchen as though hoping to find a solution there. "I'll get you some Kleenex."

Just then, the phone rang. Since she was already up, Robin went to answer it, leaving Rosalee alone at the table to contemplate the autumnal placemat in front of her. She skimmed the burnt orange stitching with her fingertips and remembered Evelyn's sewing machine. It was the same sewing machine that Ellie had learned to sew on and was now sitting in her room. That was one of the differences between Ellie and Rosalee—Rosalee doubted that she would ever be able to sew on that machine, even if she did possess Ellie's burning desire to make millions of sundresses. Like trying to cook her late aunt's beloved recipes, it was just too painful.

After several minutes, Rosalee snapped out of her reminiscence to find herself alone in the kitchen, then realized that Robin had taken the phone into the other room. The spiral cord strained around the corner of the kitchen where the wall mount hung, and she could hear faint snatches of angry whispering. Her pulse quickened. It had to be Connor.

A minute later, Robin walked back into the kitchen and hung up the receiver.

"Who was that?" said Rosalee.

Robin hesitated, then began to bustle around the kitchen, opening cupboards at random. "Do you want something to drink? Tea, or coffee, or something? Are you supposed to have caffeine?"

"I don't know. I'm fine. Was that Connor?"

Robin froze halfway across the kitchen, empty tea kettle in hand.

"It's fine," said Rosalee, attempting a reassuring smile. "Ellie told me."

"Oh." Robin sat again. "Well, I don't think he'll be calling again. Or visiting. I told him if he did either one, I'd take it up with the Sheriff."

Rosalee's insides squirmed with guilt as heat rose to her face. "You should ... you can go easy on him."

Robin's eyes went wide. "'*Go easy on him*'? Rosalee, when someone stalks your niece, you do not go *easy* on him."

"I don't think he's stalking me, I think he's ..." Rosalee squeezed her eyes shut for a moment. This was it. This was the time to come clean. She couldn't let everyone keep thinking Connor was a creep. "I think he's trying to apologize."

Robin looked slightly nauseated but also had the determined look Rosalee often noticed on mothers' faces—the partially translucent mask of calm to distract from the underlying apprehension. "Why would he need to apologize?"

Rosalee swallowed hard against the dry patches in her throat. "We had a ... misunderstanding. While I was having an episode. And I left before we could talk about it."

Robin was watching Rosalee closely, as though trying to watch a movie of the event projected on her retinas. But Rosalee lowered the invisible curtain and looked away. That was all she could muster for now, and after several long moments, Robin cleared her throat and took a sip of her coffee. When she spoke, her voice was strangely monotone. "Did he hurt you?"

"No, he didn't." *My body did.*

"Are you sure?"

"Positive."

Rosalee looked up again and Robin sighed, running a hand through her hair. "I never trusted him. Not when you were in high school, not now, not ever."

"I know."

"I also can't help but think that you would have never been driven to ..." Robin paused and took another sip of coffee. "... *self-medicating* if it weren't for him."

Rosalee felt a zing go up her arm as anxiety squeezed at her chest.

"Lola and I found a couple bottles in the recycling," said Robin.

"I didn't put any bottles in the recycling."

"Well, then maybe it was your sister."

Rosalee felt her panic melting into something icy that settled in her guts. Again, she was overwhelmingly thankful that Ellie had never been tempted (as far as she knew) to follow in her misguided footsteps. Still, the thought of her little sister collecting the articles of shame from her room was almost more than she could stand, especially when she imagined how it must have made Ellie feel—embarrassed? Disappointed? Ashamed?

"I knew that you hadn't been yourself since the diagnosis," Robin continued. "In fact, I could tell that you were trying to get as far away from yourself as possible."

Rosalee could feel her lower lip quivering and smashed it down with her top lip to make it stop. "I'm sorry," she whispered.

"I don't want you to be sorry, I want you to be okay. And if hanging out with Connor again is going to drag you back down where you were before everything, then …"

Rosalee raised the arm of her sweatshirt to soak up the teardrops that gathered below her chin. Robin passed her a napkin, which she dabbed under her eyes before holding it under the table and twisting it in her fingers.

"I'm not planning on hanging out with him. But a lot of that stuff was *my* idea. I just knew I could get Connor to do it with me. Plus he … knew where to get everything."

Robin shook her head and Rosalee instantly regretted sharing that last part. But Connor was innocent—more or less—and she couldn't let him take the fall for her mistakes anymore.

"You know it would be actual *medicine* this time?" said Robin.

It took a moment for Rosalee's brain to catch up with the subtle change of subject. "Right … but we don't know all of the side effects yet, do we? Especially that new one Harris had me try. What has it been, like, four or five months since it came out?"

Robin tapped her fingers lightly against her mug. "That's true."

"So, what if the side effects outweigh the benefits?"

"That's what you need to talk to the doctor about."

Rosalee sighed. "Why talk? He already gave me all those *super* helpful pamphlets so he can collect his promotional cut."

"Just think about it … I have to get ready for work. Unless you want me to call in?"

"Then The Goose would be short *two* people."

"Okay, well I'll have my pager if you can't get me at the store for some reason."

Rosalee bit her lip again before another apology could escape. She could feel the tears coming again and wondered if the salty trails they made down her cheeks would eventually form raw tattoos.

Robin eyed Rosalee's sweatpants and sweatshirt. "Maybe you should put something cooler on. Dr. Harris did say that heat can make your symptoms worse."

Rosalee wrapped the sweatshirt more securely around her. "Everything I touch hurts. This is, like, a buffer."

"Well, then, drink some ice water, at least."

Rosalee didn't know how long she sat staring at the door after it closed behind her aunt, but she eventually felt herself get up out of her chair. She stood for a moment, then unzipped the sweatshirt and shrugged it off, wincing as the material scraped over her skin. She frowned. She had worn and washed that exact sweatshirt countless times and had never once thought about the material as course, but somehow all of the nerves in her skin felt inflamed. She lifted a foot off the ground and then quickly grabbed the kitchen table for support, moving her leg experimentally. Her sweatpants posed a similar issue. Maybe heavy clothes weren't a buffer, after all. Unfortunately, most of her summer clothes were still in her room upstairs, and she didn't have the energy to get them. The rest were in her dirty laundry. She would simply have to make do. Rosalee sat in a kitchen chair again and hiked the elastic ankles of her sweatpants up past her knees. If she started to lose circulation, she could always pull them back down. She sat for several minutes, thinking longingly about a glass of water before she could make herself move to get it.

Eventually, Rosalee found herself across the kitchen, popping the last ice cubes out of their tray. The phone rang and she stopped to stare at it hanging on the wall. If it was Connor again, she should answer it—at least to tell him she wasn't mad at him. Or that she didn't blame him. But would he leave her alone until he knew *why?* The answering machine clicked on while she deliberated. She tensed her shoulders as she refilled the ice cube tray and attempted to drown out the male voice that cleared its throat by cranking the faucet on all the way.

"Hey, Rosalee, it's Alex … again. I'm sorry, I'm not trying to bother you. Just had a little time before work and wanted to see if y—"

Rosalee quickly turned the faucet handle the other way and spilled most of the ice tray as she set it down on the counter. She rushed to pick up the receiver before she could overthink it.

"Hello? Alex?"

"Rosalee?"

"Hey." She smiled without thinking.

"Hey." Alex sounded relieved. *"Are you still sick?"*

"Um … sort of."

"So I probably can't see you?"

Rosalee hesitated, tuning into the persistent ache in her limbs. Maybe after some ibuprofen and cold water, she would feel better. As much as she wasn't ready to let Alex into this part of her life, she wanted to see him. And maybe he would be satisfied with a vague overview.

"It wouldn't have to be for long," said his voice in her ear. He sounded so hopeful. *"I could stop by now on my way to work."*

"Okay," said Rosalee.

"Okay?"

"Sure."

If anything, this would be a test of their friendship. If he could stand to see her like this, maybe they really could be … friends … after all.

"Great, I'll see you in, like, fifteen minutes," said Alex. *"I just have to shower. Why am I telling you that?"*

Rosalee laughed. In the past week, she had almost forgotten what it felt like. "Meet me by the creek."

She hung up, then sopped up the mess on the counter with a kitchen towel, filled the ice tray properly, and slid it back into the freezer. She found a bottle of ibuprofen in the medicine cabinet of the bathroom and shook out one tablet, then stared at the red, coated pill in her hand on the way back down the hall to the kitchen. This was different. This was *actual* medicine. And she was taking the recommended dose.

Rosalee took her glass of ice water back to the table and sat down heavily, wondering if she would even have the energy to see Alex. When was the last time she had eaten anything? She got up again, catching her breath a little before wandering to the refrigerator, but there were no options in there that wouldn't require a plate. She moved to the pantry and found a granola bar, then sat down again. She threw back the ibuprofen, then sipped the ice water through a straw to avoid choking on both of them. As she unwrapped the granola bar and took a bite, she could almost feel the cogs in her brain picking up speed a little. Unfortunately, this led to new and unhelpful thoughts. When was the last time she had looked in a mirror, for example?

Rosalee took another gulp of icy water and carried her granola bar back to the bathroom, then started digging through the drawers and cabinets. The nice thing about living with so many women was that there was bound to be a tube of mascara lying around in at least every bathroom. Sure enough, Rosalee excavated a tube with minimal dust in a drawer full of Q-tips and travel toothpaste. She swiped it across her eyelashes and then gave herself a closer look. Her nose looked a little red from crying, but maybe by the time Alex came over, it would be back to its normal color. Then her eyes landed on her hair and she felt a little jolt of panic. What would he say when he saw what she did? Alex had never actually mentioned her hair, except for the apology when he was forced to cut a chunk of it out of a carnival ride, but on more than one occasion, she thought she saw him looking at it like maybe he liked it. She stuffed another bite of granola bar into her mouth and rolled her eyes at herself in the mirror. Did it ultimately matter whether or not Alex liked her new hair? After all, she wasn't a Play-Doh Spaghetti Factory.

Rosalee shuffled back into the kitchen and grabbed her sweatshirt off the chair. As much as she couldn't stand the friction of the fabric, she didn't want the first thing Alex saw to be the mess she made of her hair. As she threw it around her shoulders, a sleeve caught her glass of ice water and knocked it over. Luckily, it was the type of glass that shattered into relatively large shards, but that didn't stop Rosalee from muttering a stream of profanities as she scrambled to pick up pieces of glass and ice that had exploded across the kitchen floor and into the hallway.

She realized that all of the clean towels were in the linen closet upstairs (having already tossed the soaked kitchen towel from earlier down the laundry shoot) and nearly cried. She looked around her for something else to clean up the water and spotted a cloth oven mitt lying on the counter. She cleaned up the new mess and used the mitt to pick up the rest of the glass shards, then tossed them in the garbage just as the phone rang again. Maybe it was Alex saying he would be late, or that he wasn't coming at all. Rosalee picked up the receiver and immediately heard heavy breathing on the other line.

"Hello?" she said uncertainly.

"Is ... Rosalee?"

"Yes?"

"Oh thank god, please don't hang up."

Rosalee felt a jolt behind her navel and wished she had let the phone ring. "Connor?"

"It's me. Please just listen—don't hang up." He sounded out of breath, like he had been running. *"Robin said she'd turn me in if I didn't leave you alone, but I'm losing it, Rosalee. I have a right to know. It was my baby, too."*

Rosalee felt the cogs in her brain stutter in their rotation. "It was your ... *what?*"

There was a strange sound on the other end of the line—almost a cough and almost a laugh—still punctuated with erratic breathing.

"Why are you so out of breath?" said Rosalee.

Connor ignored her question. *"You should have told me. Okay, you can't just* split *and not tell someone something like that. It's* shitty.*"*

"I don't—Connor, I wasn't pregnant. That's not why I left."

"... Okay then—dammit, there's a cramp." Rosalee could hear Connor panting on the other line. *"Then, was it about the last time we—"*

"Connor, I can't do this right now."

"No, please, just listen," said Connor, his voice urgent, *"I knew something was wrong, but I thought I stopped in time. I stopped when you started crying, Rosalee—I had no idea you didn't want to. I thought—I swear you were laughing before."*

"I know." Rosalee felt the receiver slip slightly in her hand—even a phone was too heavy for her exhausted muscles. She braced herself against the wall and turned so that her forehead was resting against the cool wallpaper. "It's not your fault and I *did* want to. I just ... I can't explain it right now."

"But is that why you left? To get away from me? Or to process what I—"

"No, Connor, that's not—"

"Yo, eat me, you little puke."

Rosalee blinked. "Are—Excuse me?"

"Sorry, this nosey punk is waiting for the phone," said Connor.

"What? Where are you?"

"I have to go, Rosalee, but please just—I never wanted to hurt you. I wasn't trying to hurt you."

"I know you weren't. I should have—*hello?*"

Rosalee stared at the receiver, momentarily mesmerized by the buzzing of the disconnected line, when movement at the front window caught her eye. Alex's Jeep was pulling into the driveway. Rosalee hung up the phone and zipped up her sweatshirt all the way, yanked the hood over her hair, and stood for a moment in the middle of the kitchen. She couldn't shake the ominous feeling that lingered in the pit of her stomach after Connor's call. She thought about calling him back at his house, but she was pretty sure he wasn't home when he called her.She glanced out the window again. Alex was already out of his car and making his way up the driveway. She should at least try to catch Connor and tell him not to beat himself up and that she would talk to him later. She picked up the receiver again and dialed the number she still knew by heart, then waited, slightly nauseated. After four rings, the answering machine picked up. Should she leave a message? She didn't want to clue his parents in to anything suspicious. She glanced out the back door and hung up again when she saw Alex walking through the backyard on his way to the creek.

Surely Connor wouldn't *do* anything ... but why was he so out of breath? And why, oh *why* did her brain always have to go to such dark places? Maybe he was rushing because he was late for work (*Work, just work. Nobody's hurt.*). Rosalee took a few deep breaths, blowing the last one out extra hard before walking to the back door to meet Alex.

Chapter 25

Alex sat by the creek, watching the water rush over smooth rocks and leave behind swirls of white foam and bubbles. The water level was higher than the first time he visited from the rain the night before, although he was surprised that the lingering warm weather hadn't evaporated off most of the excess by now.

He heard Rosalee's back door open and exercised nearly every ounce of self-control to stop himself from vaulting back over the gate and rushing to meet her. Instead, he took a deep breath and decided to feign deafness, at least until she made it to the gate. He was sure that it only *seemed* like she was taking forever to cross the small expanse of grass between them, but in the meantime, he felt like he was coming undone at the seams. At this rate, he could probably run out to his Jeep for a cigarette and still get back before Rosalee reached the creek.

Finally, Alex heard a latch click and risked a glance over his shoulder. Rosalee had her back to him as she closed the gate behind her, and he immediately noticed that the hood of the red sweatshirt she wore was pulled up over her hair. Apprehension gripped him as he wondered how much was missing and how it would affect him. Would he still feel the same way about her, even without the wild and untamed wonder that was her hair before?

He watched her closely as she came to sit next to him. She hadn't looked at him yet, and he noticed that she was moving more deliberately than usual. Gingerly, almost—like maybe something hurt. When she finally turned toward him, Alex peered cautiously into her face, searching for warning signs or *any* signs to guide him toward whatever was supposed to happen next.

"Hi," Rosalee said, blinking rapidly and then dropping her eyes to the ground. Her cheeks were flushed and Alex thought he caught a tremor in her lower lip, although with her hood in the way, he couldn't be sure.

"Hi." In that moment, any lingering frustration toward her, her family, or Pete for leaving Alex out of this secret vanished, because he was fairly certain that he had never seen such a defeated-looking person. It was no wonder they were all so protective of her. "God, Rosalee, you look—"

"'Like hell,' I know."

For a fleeting second, Alex thought he saw the flicker of a smile in her eyes before she averted them again.

"No," said Alex. "I was going to say 'miserable.' Also, a little like Red Riding Hood."

Rosalee met his gaze again with over-bright eyes that nearly spilled over as she attempted an actual smile.

"Wanna go for a walk?" said Alex.

"Actually ... do you mind if we sit here for a little while?"

"Yeah, no sweat."

Alex took off his socks and shoes and rolled up the legs of his jeans before submerging his feet in the cool water. Rosalee's sweatpants were already rolled up and she was wearing flip-flops, but he noticed that she seemed to be taking her time getting her feet wet. Again, and with great difficulty, Alex swallowed the numerous questions he was aching to ask her. Still, they spawned in his head like streaming banners behind beach blimps: Was she afraid that the water would hurt? (Had she acted that way before and he'd just missed it?) Why couldn't he see her hair yet? Why was she still sick? What was she sick *with?*

When at last, Rosalee's feet were submerged in the water past her ankles, she let out a slow breath.

"What's up?" said Alex, unable to stop himself.

"Nothing." Rosalee's tight smile only halfway distracted him from the way she held herself up on her hands, as though waiting for some sort of pain just from sitting. "I did think you were going to be mad at me, though."

"For what?"

"For leaving you stranded at the festival?" said Rosalee, a fresh batch of apologies already brewing in her eyes. "And for my hair-cutting fiasco?"

Alex had no way to gauge what his face was doing. He couldn't be sure whether the emotion coursing through him was better or worse than when he believed that Rosalee's hair had detached itself from her scalp by itself. No, he could. And it was better. It was *so* much better.

"Wait, *you* cut it off?" he said, just to be sure.

Rosalee bit her lip, which was definitely trembling this time, and nodded at her feet.

Alex let out a low whistle. "So ... am I allowed to ask about it, or ...?"

Rosalee yanked her sweatshirt irritably around herself, wincing as she did. "It got stuck."

"What, like in a door hinge or something?" Alex hardly dared to believe that one of his wild theories could actually be true.

"No," said Rosalee, "Those godforsaken, stupid little *medieval torture devices.*"

Alex gave her a blank look.

"The *curlers,*" she said, as though that should have cleared everything up.

Alex was still having trouble connecting two and two and Rosalee's shoulders slumped.

"I'm sorry, I think I'm still in shock," said Alex. "So your hair got stuck … in the curlers?"

"I was *so* tired, and they got tangled, and every, like …" Rosalee motioned pulling her hair.

"Tug? Pull?" Alex offered.

"Yeah. Felt like an electric zap to my scalp."

"So you cut it all off?"

"I cut them all *out*."

Alex stared at her for a moment and then snorted, clapping a hand over his mouth. Rosalee looked offended, to say the least.

"Ahm fahry," he apologized through his fingers. "No, ahm fahry, I can't—"

He began to shake with silent laughter, letting the waves of relief and resulting giddiness wash over him, even as Rosalee showed every sign of leaving. She had her feet back out of the water and into her flip-flops before Alex could calm down enough to stop her.

"No, Rosalee, please—I'm sorry." He reached out to grab the end of her flip-flop before she could stand up. "I'm not laughing at you."

Rosalee raised her eyebrows skeptically, but remained seated, at least. She looked more annoyed than hurt by his behavior.

"Please come back," said Alex, wiping at his eyes.

Rosalee took her flip-flops off again and lowered her feet back in the water, only wincing slightly this time as they made contact.

"Aren't you warm?" Alex nodded toward the sweatshirt that was still zipped as high as it would go. "It's like, a million degrees out here."

It was actually close to eighty degrees, but for Colorado in October, that was pretty hot.

Rosalee shrugged.

"You can take that off, I promise I won't laugh, or stare, or whatever you're worried about," said Alex.

Rosalee hesitated, then lowered her hood.

Alex felt himself suck in his breath (Where was his self-control today?) and Rosalee yanked the hood back into place.

"No," said Alex, shaking his head, unable to tear his eyes away, despite his promise. "No, Rosalee, whatever you're thinking, it's the opposite."

"What?"

"Just take it off."

"Then turn away for a second." Rosalee sounded irritated again, but maybe she was just exhausted. She certainly looked it.

Alex did as he was told and chewed at the abused skin next to his thumbnail. He heard the sound of a zipper unzipping and material discarded next to him, followed by an unsteady breath.

"Now?" he said.

"Mm-hm."

Alex turned back and tried to keep his face neutral this time, but he was sure he was smiling like an idiot. It wasn't nearly as bad as he had imagined—in fact, it wasn't *even* bad. No big chunks were missing and there was still a lot of hair—it was just much shorter. Before, it brushed the waistband of Rosalee's jeans when she wore it down, but now it was a few inches above her collarbone, with a nod toward the vintage flapper style.

Alex realized that he hadn't said anything yet and noticed Rosalee's fingers inching back toward her sweatshirt, which was lying between them. Alex grabbed it before she could and held it firmly in his lap.

"I love it," he said. "Seriously, I do. I thought I would hate it. I mean, you had this crazy mermaid hair before, but this is great, too."

The measure of relief on Rosalee's face was enormous and she final-ly smiled for real.

"Did you honestly think I wouldn't like you anymore with short hair?" said Alex, ignoring the nagging voice reminding him that he had wondered the same thing not five minutes ago.

Rosalee shrugged, then looked down at her fingers twisting in her lap. "I'm sorry about the dance."

"Yeah, me too," said Alex. "But I'm sure there's no shortage of functions in this town. We're bound to make it to one of them."

"That's true ... So, what did you think?"

"About the dance?"

Rosalee nodded.

"It was fine," said Alex. "But I wasn't really going for the ambiance. The lights were cool."

"The lights?"

Finally, something he could blabber about for a few minutes. Alex told her about them in what he feared was excruciatingly boring detail, but if Rosalee was bored, she was good at hiding it. When he was finished, she looked across the creek again.

"It's the smells for me," she said. "Like, the hay ... cubes?" Rosalee drew a square in the air in front of her and glanced at Alex, bewilder-ment surfacing in her eyes.

"Bales?" Alex suggested.

"Bales, yeah. After they've been sitting in the sun all day by the barn. Or that booth with the roasted candied almonds. Rabbitbrush parties are great for smells."

Then, the awkward silence was back and questions were itching at the forefront of Alex's brain again. He checked his watch—still a good fifteen minutes before he had to be at work. Fifteen more minutes to try to delve into the deep, dark secret. (The "DDS," perhaps, without the threat of braces?) *But how?*

"I know you're still afraid to talk to me about stuff," he said. "But I hope you know that you can. Whenever you're ready."

"I know," said Rosalee. "Thank you. It's just ... it's a lot?"

"I get it. Would it help you if I told you something ... 'a lot' about me?"

"Like what?"

"Like ... I lied to you about my scar."

Rosalee's eyes snapped to his again, but he couldn't tell if she was angry. "So it *was* the rabid dog?"

"No, it was ... me."

Alex noticed Rosalee visibly stiffen and wondered if that was the wrong way to say that. He didn't want to backtrack, though. He had already admitted the lie—might as well rip off the Band-Aid.

"I was in a really bad place nine months ago," he said, wiping his hands on his jeans. "Mostly family stuff—I think I sort of mentioned my brother once?"

Rosalee nodded, still tense and fiddling with the drawstring of her sweatpants as she watched him.

"I can get into that part later, but I wasn't handling any of the 'stuff' well ... staying out late, partying, pickling my liver ..."

Rosalee gave a quiet chuckle next to Alex and he smiled. It wasn't exactly a funny story, but it was nice to hear her laugh—rarely as it happened—and even better to hear her laugh at his lame jokes.

"So, then this one week was really bad," he continued. "My mom and I had to make a really crappy decision and one night I drank too much, and I snapped. It was a *huge* mistake and I'm not proud of—what?" He realized that Rosalee was laughing again and looked around them to see what he was missing. "Are you still laughing about my liver?"

Rosalee shook her head and kept her hand over her mouth, curling in on herself.

"Seriously, what?" said Alex, smiling slightly.

"Nothing. I'm ... so sorry." Rosalee sounded close to hyperventilating as she laughed into her knees.

"That's okay, just let me in on the joke."

Alex was pretty sure he hadn't said anything funny, even in the dry sense of the word this time.

"There—isn't—one," Rosalee choked. "I—can't. I'm so—*so* ... sorry."

"I don't get it." Alex's initial amusement faded to bewilderment. "Why are you ... Are you laughing about what I said?"

Even as the words came out of his mouth, he knew there was no way. Maybe he didn't know Rosalee very well—certainly not as well as he would like to—but he couldn't see her being that heartless. She hiccuped next to him, then began fumbling for her flip-flops.

"I have to go," she said, slipping them on before pushing herself up and lurching to the fence, still chuckling. She nearly tripped and grabbed the thick wooden rail for support.

Was she *drunk?*

"I was kind of trying to ... tell you something," said Alex. "Where are you going?"

Rosalee was still leaning on the fence, and Alex only caught bits and pieces of the words she continued to mutter under her breath, but none of them made sense.

"I can't hear you when you talk to yourself," he said loudly, beginning to lose his patience. "And you forgot this."

He stood up, holding out her sweatshirt. Rosalee grabbed a sleeve and tugged, but Alex held on, causing her to stumble. Then she laughed again and let go of her end. Alex reached out instinctively at the same time that Rosalee caught herself on the fence again, hitting the rail hard enough that it vibrated in its post.

"Sorry," said Alex. "I was trying to get you to come back."

"I ... *can't* come back." Rosalee tilted her head back to laugh at the tree branches that hung over them. "I can't—*do* this anymore."

"*This* ... being?"

And then it hit him and Alex couldn't feel his legs anymore or tell whether he was standing, sitting, or dreaming. He only barely registered the red material that tumbled out of his hands and the figure that stooped in front of him to pick it up.

But it was obvious, wasn't it? Why someone would be sick enough to stand you up at a dance, then get a crazy haircut for no reason that actually made sense, and then laugh like a maniac when she found out how hard you fell for the whole thing? It was all too convenient and *cruel* that his own story should come back to punch him in the face. How terribly ironic that this whole time, *Alex* was the one being played by the mean jocks.

He curled his fingers into his palms, then flexed them again, staring at the ground. "So this was a joke? The being friends, being ... sick? All of it?"

Rosalee giggled and Alex felt a queasy, swooping feeling in his stomach. He turned away from her and tilted his head back, staring up at the same leaves that had also recently been laughed at by Rosalee.

"Well, you got me," he said. "I mean, this was an *insanely* elaborate trap. And I walked—no, I *skipped*—right into it. You must be very proud."

"N-no."

"'No,' *what?*" Alex snapped, turning back to face Rosalee.

"No, that's—not what happened."

Still, Alex could see her smiling, even with her hands partially obscuring her mouth. He waited, but when Rosalee didn't say anything more, he gave up and turned to leave.

"Please don't—go."

Alex turned back, his jaw set. He met Rosalee's gaze as she took a deep, shuddering breath, then sank to the ground. The red sweatshirt was still cradled in her arms as she sobbed into the bundle and Alex felt utterly helpless as he watched her. At this point, he could cry, too, depleted as he was from this emotional rollercoaster from hell.

And what exactly was he supposed to do to comfort her—the conductor of the ride itself? The answer came to him quickly enough; if he couldn't touch her or figure out anything helpful to say, he could at least *be* with her.

Slowly, Alex lowered himself to the ground to sit in front of Rosalee, head in his hands until her gasps subsided into the occasional hiccup and her sobs turned into sniffles. Only then did he look up again to find her staring at him, eyes wide—almost scared.

"I'm s—"

"Rosalee, I swear to *God,* if you say that word one more time ..."

"Well, I *am.*" Rosalee wiped at her eyes with her sleeves, which absorbed some of the black makeup that trailed down her cheeks. "It's over now. I'm—it's over."

"What's over?" Alex's lips felt numb. Everything felt numb.

Meanwhile, Rosalee looked more than apologetic—she looked mortified. "The laughing. I'm—"

Alex gave her a sharp warning look.

"I'm not crazy," Rosalee whispered.

Her eyes were pleading and still shining with tears, and the green in them stood out even more with the white parts tinged with red. But as Alex studied them, he noticed something else; like she was waiting—for an answer? Had she asked him a question? Yes. She asked him if he thought she was crazy. How the hell was he supposed to answer that? He couldn't. He didn't *know* anything.

"Do you have cancer?" he said finally.

"What?"

"*Do. You have.* Cancer?"

"... No."

One question down, ninety-nine to go.

"Okay. So ... are you ever *going* to tell me what's going on, or is this it? Because I've gotta be honest with you, Rosalee, I don't know how much more I can take."

Rosalee nodded, her eyes wide again. "I know. You're right. I've been really unfair to you."

Alex closed his eyes. "God, I just—" A mechanical beeping noise interrupted him and he stared at his watch, unable to comprehend the meaning.

"Do you have to go to work?"

"Yup." Alex squeezed the buttons on either side of the watch face to silence the alarm. *"Damn it."*

"It's okay."

Alex kneaded his forehead with his hands. "It's not okay. It's *super* not okay."

"We can talk later."

"Can we?" At this point, would any amount of talking fix anything?

"I promise," said Rosalee. "When do you get off work?"

"Nine."

Rosalee bit her lip, but nodded. Alex nodded too—stiffly—then dug his keys out of his pocket and walked past her to push the gate open.

"Great," he said over his shoulder. "So ... I guess we'll talk later. Bye, Rosalee."

"... Bye, Alex."

Chapter 26

"Well, *that* sounds like a major disaster." Ellie shook her head and took another sip of hot cocoa. She and Rosalee sat on opposite sides of the kitchen table with a steaming mug and coloring book apiece, and a pile of crayons between them. "By the way, why don't we do this more often? I almost *never* think of hot chocolate. *Or* coloring."

Rosalee shrugged. "Kinda chilly today, so ..."

Ellie tilted back in her chair and craned her neck, squinting at the thermometer by the back porch. "It's, like, eighty degrees outside."

"Well, the swamp cooler must be working. It's chilly in here."

Ellie contemplated the unicorn she was shading using every color of pink and purple in the jumbo Crayola box. "Didn't you say that Alex brought you hot chocolate once?"

"Oh, yeah. I think ... maybe."

Ellie smirked. "Uh-huh. So you *have* been thinking about him."

Rosalee sighed. "Maybe."

"And he hasn't called? Since the ... was it a fight? Are you using that gold?"

Rosalee handed her the metallic crayon. "I think it was as close to a fight as we've gotten. And he called last night, but he said he had an emergency and asked if we could reschedule."

Ellie frowned. "How did he sound?"

"Tired? Mad? I don't know."

"Do you think the emergency was his brother?"

"Oh." Rosalee let her olive green crayon hover over the turtle she was coloring. "I don't know. He didn't say."

You should have asked, Rosalee scolded herself—especially now that she realized Alex had tried to tell her about his brother twice now, both times with semi-disastrous results.

"Maybe he had to go home to Denver," said Ellie.

"Yeah, maybe." Rosalee looked past the kitchen to the bay window in the living room. She wondered if it was sunny wherever Alex was.

"Are you gonna try to call him?" said Ellie. "You should probably at least email him."

"Jeez, El, I don't know yet." Rosalee shook her head and sipped her cocoa, which was getting cold. "He may not want me to talk to him at all."

"It sounds like he made it pretty clear that he does."

Rosalee didn't answer, but set her picture aside to focus on her drink.

"Are you nervous?" said Ellie, swapping her gold crayon out for magenta again.

"Of *course* I'm nervous."

"I honestly don't think he'll be as freaked as you think he will."

Rosalee contemplated the mug in her hands. It was the thick kind with a rounded bottom, and that paired with its sunny, golden hue tended to give her a boost whenever she used it.

"I'm not sure if that's what I'm nervous about," she said.

"Then what are you nervous about?"

"What if he doesn't believe me? Like, what if he thinks I'm making it up?"

"Why would he think that?"

"Well ... most people can't tell, right? You guys are the only ones who ever say I look like hell, but that's because you know me and know what I'm *supposed* to look like ... huh."

"Why are you smiling?" said Ellie, her eyes narrowing suspiciously as Rosalee tried to hide her mouth by taking another sip.

"Um ... I forgot that Alex said that. Well, he *almost* said that. He actually said I looked 'miserable.'"

"And that makes you happy?" Ellie said carefully.

"I know, it's stupid, but ... it felt like maybe he would notice—know the difference, I mean."

Ellie's expression cleared. "Well, he obviously knows *something* is wrong."

"I thought I hid everything pretty well until the hair thing." Rosalee twirled a piece around her finger, then let it fall back against her face.

"But why hide it in the first place? I still can't get over your hair, by the way. It's *awesome.*"

"Thanks." Rosalee wasn't sure she shared that sentiment yet, and she definitely hadn't gotten used to how cold the back of her neck felt with her hair down. "I guess it seemed easier that way."

"Easier to hide it?"

"Yeah."

"... why, though?"

"Because if I tell him, then I have to explain it."

"And?"

"*And* I don't want to think about it, or talk about it, or—" Rosalee tapped the end of a crayon against her placemat, avoiding her sister's eyes. "How am I supposed to explain this stupid thing to anyone else if I don't even want to learn about it myself?"

"If you want, I'll learn about it and make you notecards."

Rosalee smiled and shook her head. "Thanks, I'll let you know."

She got up to wash her empty mug in the sink. Ellie still had half of her cocoa, but followed her over to the counter and sat down on one of the bar stools. "So ... are you gonna tell him about Connor?"

"I don't know ... probably not. Maybe eventually."

"It's still a *major* bummer that you didn't get to wear that dress," said Ellie, a pained expression on her face. "Like, bordering on a travesty."

"Yeah. Maybe next year, for something." Rosalee set the clean mug on the drying rack, then decided she might as well tackle the rest of the dishes from breakfast and lunch. "Anyway, what's new with you? How's school?"

"Good. School's fine. Nothing new, really."

"*Oh,*" said Rosalee, a spark in her memory, "You never told me who you were talking to the night before you left."

She thought she saw Ellie squirm on her stool out of the corner of her eye. "Oh, yeah. That was no big deal."

"Aunt Robin said you were talking to Pete."

This time, Rosalee turned to look at her sister, who definitely looked uncomfortable.

"We were talking about the dance, actually. I really wanted to go but I didn't want to go by myself, and so I thought *we* could go—me and Pete, and he wouldn't. I think he gets worn out with all the customer service stuff he does at the bank." Ellie paused to wipe around the inside edge of her mug with her pinky finger, collecting the residual whipped cream. "I was just disappointed, you know? I love town stuff."

"I know you do," said Rosalee, putting down her sponge. "I wish you would have said something. You could have come with me and Alex. Theoretically."

"I didn't want to be a third wheel."

"Still ... Sorry, El." Rosalee felt another layer of guilt affix itself to her stomach lining. "I feel like I've been ignoring you or something. I hope you know it's not on purpose."

"I know. You have stuff going on. *Crazy* stuff."

"I guess." Rosalee reached across the counter to grab Ellie's empty mug and spoon.

"Thanks," said Ellie. "Have you gone back to work yet?"

"I did a couple hours yesterday and this morning. *Ugh.*" Rosalee scowled as a hot jet of water ricocheted off the spoon and soaked into her shirt. "Aunt Robin is afraid I'll overdo it."

"What are you gonna do if this ... whatever-it-is keeps going? Is it a relapse or a flare-up?"

Rosalee dabbed at her shirt with the dish towel. "I'm not sure. I think it has to be new symptoms for a relapse."

"So ..." Ellie prompted.

"I don't know. I've been thinking about medication."

"Really?"

"Well, I can't keep doing *this,*" said Rosalee, echoing Robin's earlier statement. "I can barely even walk."

"True."

Rosalee surveyed the dishes left in the sink, trying to decide if she was likely to drop the glass ones. "This doctor's going to think I'm an idiot for not being able to take one stupid dose."

"I doubt it," said Ellie. "Did you ever get it in?"

"I only tried once. The rest of the month is in my closet. Oh, except I dropped one of the vials and it smashed."

"Maybe they need better instructions. Or not so many steps."

All of the steps were precisely what made the process so daunting. Each dose included a bottle of powdered medicine into which a solvent had to be injected. The powder and solvent were then mixed until the liquid was completely clear. Any cloudiness or off-color liquid had to be tossed, and after all of that, there was the actual injection.

"Maybe they need to come up with a better solution than making people stick themselves with giant needles," said Rosalee.

"Yeah, maybe."

Rosalee attempted to sweep her hair to one side and over her shoulder, then remembered that it was gone and tucked it behind one ear, instead. She was worried about going back to work at The Goose, especially limping. Luckily, there was plenty for her to do in the main office and off of the sales floor, so there was less of a chance of customers or employees witnessing her attempts to walk while one of her knees insisted on trying to move backward.

"By the way, I have an appointment tomorrow with a neurologist in Picket," she said.

Ellie perked up at once. "Do you want me to come with?"

"Really? I mean, it might be kind of boring. But Robin and Lola are coming, too."

Ellie hopped off of her stool and walked around the counter to dry the dishes. "Well, then I'm *definitely* coming."

Chapter 27

Alex's eyes retraced the white letters stamped into the laminated plastic nameplate that read "Constance Milburn, Practice Administrator" for what felt like the hundredth time. The only sound besides the clickety-clack of Mrs. Milburn's keyboard and the whir of the radiator was the rubber sole of Alex's shoe before he realized that he was tapping it against the speckled black and white tile. He shifted in his seat, crossing one ankle over his knee, then glanced over at the single office plant that stood next to a wastebasket and copy machine in the corner of the room.

"Nice plant," he said.

Mrs. Milburn looked up briefly and smiled. "Yes, I think so. I don't even have to water it."

Alex smiled politely back, then felt his face settle into the harder lines that were becoming more familiar. Would it kill people to buy real plants for their offices, real coffee mugs for complimentary coffee, or keep their files in physical file folders? According to Mrs. Milburn, Engelmann was in the midst of "going digital—for convenience and easier access." Meanwhile, it had been nearly ten minutes since Alex arrived and he was beginning to blink in neon colors from staring at the white wall behind her.

"Ah, here we are," said the administrator at last. "Thank you for meeting with me today, Mr. Conway. I thought it might be a good idea to go over Oliver's progress with you since your mother is unavailable. I will, of course, follow up with her by phone."

Alex nodded, his throat dry as he continued to worry the permanently frayed edge of his thumbnail. "So, you think he's gotten worse?"

Mrs. Milburn looked thoughtful as she scrolled through notes on her computer. "I'm not sure I would say *worse,* but he's certainly less agreeable lately."

Alex abandoned his thumbnail and reached up to knead a knot that was forming between his neck and shoulder.

Mrs. Milburn gave him a swift, searching look. "I hope you know I'm not placing blame. I think he's just lonely and maybe a little bored. We have puzzles, but I think he's done them all. Read most of the books, too."

"I brought more from the library. What about his schoolwork?"

"Finishes it right away. Most days we have to force him to take a break so we can get a decent meal in him."

"Does he ever hang out with the other kids?"

"Well, unfortunately, that might be part of the problem." Mrs. Milburn slipped off her reading glasses, letting them dangle by their chain and rest against the front of her blouse. "This is still a relatively new program and now that the summer camps are over at the Y, there aren't as many people Oliver's age to interact with."

"Not even at the main hospital?"

"We have a few long-term kiddos over there. But most of them are pretty fragile, so activities are limited. We did wonder if he would enjoy reading to some of the younger ones."

"I'll talk to him about it," said Alex. "That's a good idea."

Mrs. Milburn replaced her glasses once more, clicking here and there within the documents. "You know, I read Oliver's files from Denver and a lot of these notes don't even sound like the same boy."

"Is that ... good?"

"I would say so. The meltdowns seem to be occurring less frequently here. It looks like quite a few of them happened at school?"

"That's right."

Mrs. Milburn tutted. "I do wish he could find a friend. Did he have many back in Denver?"

"A few." Alex rubbed the back of his neck. "His episodes scared a lot of the parents, though, and most of the rest of the kids were too worried about his bullies to want to get too friendly with him."

"Any chance one of the 'few' could come for a visit?"

"Is that allowed?"

"Well, every case is different, but with consent of both guardians and proper supervision, I don't see why not."

"Great. I'll call my mom."

Somehow, Alex felt lighter. Maybe it helped to have someone else to bounce ideas off of besides his mother, who teetered more dangerously on the edge of a nervous collapse with every conversation. He smiled at the administrator, feeling a great deal warmer toward her, even if she did have a tasteless affinity for plastic foliage.

"Alright, Mr. Conway," she said eventually, closing the files with more clicks of her mouse. "Then you'll keep me updated?"

"Will do. Thanks, Mrs. Milburn."

"Call me Connie," she said, reaching across the desk to pat Alex's hand. She shifted as though about to stand up from her swiveling desk chair, then sat back again. "How are *you* doing?"

Alex paused. "Me?"

The administrator nodded, surveying him with almost motherly concern. "I don't remember seeing those dark circles under your eyes before. Are those Lauries working you too hard over there in Rabbit-brush?"

"Oh, no, the Lauries are great. I've just been busy finishing up construction work at the hospital and ... classes."

"Okay." Mrs. Milburn continued to look skeptical. "Well, listen, I don't want you to make yourself sick. We're taking good care of your brother."

"I know. I appreciate it." Alex grasped her hand over the desk and stood to leave.

"See you soon, Mr. Conway."

"You can call me Alex."

"Alright, Alex, honey. Bye, now."

———•●•———

As Alex pulled into his apartment driveway half an hour later, he barely registered Rosalee sitting on the front stoop. Was it Tuesday already? Somehow, time seemed to be moving at warp speed while he was too busy to pay proper attention. Then, as if some giant in the sky had hit the **FAST FORWARD** button, Alex was leading her through the front door, then down the hall and into his room. Thankfully, he had at least remembered to make the bed. He picked up a couple of stray socks and tossed them into the overflowing hamper in his closet, then slid the doors closed as Rosalee sat down on his navy blue comforter. A week ago, that single image would have distracted him to no end.

"So, this is your room." Rosalee looked around her at the small space, sparsely decorated with a bedside table, dresser, and desk. "No movie posters?"

"Uh, no, most of them are back in Denver."

The rest of them were rolled up and stuffed away in Alex's closet, but he couldn't bring himself to hang them.

"It hardly looks like you live here," said Rosalee.

Somehow, the sad way she said it lifted his spirits a little, although perhaps not enough to buoy him up to his usual, bubbly self. He thought Rosalee might have noticed that, as she seemed to be watching him closely. "So ... are those all of your notebooks?"

Alex followed her gaze to a single shelf mounted over his desk, where a dozen black composition notebooks featured various hues of duct tape down their spines. Some of the tape was dingier than others, but still clung loyally to the cardboard.

"I have a lot more at my mom's."

"Are they color-coded?"

"Sort of."

"Are you mad at me?"

"Sort of."

Alex turned back to her and Rosalee nodded. "I guess I deserve that."

Alex shoved his hands in his pockets and leaned against his desk, too agitated to sit down. "You know, I was really worried about you. I've *been* worried about you."

"I know," said Rosalee quietly.

"I don't even know why I needed to be in your life so bad, but I thought maybe if I opened up, you would feel more comfortable opening up to me, too, and then—"

"I'm sorry I laughed."

"... Okay."

Rosalee flexed her fingers against Alex's comforter. "I don't always have the right reactions to things. I can't control it, either, which is why I cried afterward—because I was ... *angry.* That part was real."

"Okay," Alex repeated. "I'm not sure what to do with that."

"I laughed at my aunt's funeral, too—while they were burying her." Rosalee seemed determined to keep the conversation going. Alex figured he could at least give her credit for that. "It was horrible. I had to sit by myself behind a tree so no one would see me. That was one of the worst times."

"I still don't ... understand. Do you have some sort of multiple personality disorder or something?"

"No."

"Okay ... so, how did you *mean* to react to what I said? Like, how did you feel about it?"

"Sad? Scared? I couldn't stand to think about you hurting yourself. Or how bad your life must have been to *make* you ..." Rosalee trailed off and Alex saw her glance at the scar on his arm and then away again.

"Okay, look, I'm just gonna start asking questions and you can either answer them or not," said Alex.

Rosalee looked disoriented at the abrupt change of topic, but now that she was here and (for the time being) not laughing, Alex found himself unendurably impatient.

"Okay," she said.

"What happened the night you canceled? The night before the dance?"

Rosalee took a deep breath. "I woke up that morning full of butterflies and nerves and everything in between, but none of them could have lifted me out of bed. Sometimes I just hit a wall. I think I got too worked up the day before."

"... That sounded rehearsed."

Rosalee glanced up at Alex. "It was. I've played this conversation over in my head a hundred times, at least."

Alex paused, then pulled out his desk chair and sat in it backward, crossing his arms over the back. "I wasn't trying to kill myself."

"... What?"

Alex waved his mutilated wrist in Rosalee's direction. "I know that's why you got all bent out of shape, but that's not what it was."

"Oh."

"I was aiming at the guy's face, but he moved." Alex shifted in his seat to alleviate the uncomfortable sensation that he was about to crawl out of his skin. "The glass went back into my wrist. They don't always show that part in movies."

"I'm sorry, did you say, the *glass?*"

"From a wine bottle. Although strictly speaking, I'm not admitting that I was aiming. So ... is that better?"

Rosalee shook her head. "I'm trying to absorb the idea of you swinging a bottle into someone's face. Give me a minute."

"Obviously, it was a *massive* lapse in judgment and one of the main reasons I don't drink anymore."

Rosalee sat up again and stared with her eyes unfocused at the carpet in front of Alex's feet, one of which was jiggling in time with his leg. "Okay. Good to know."

"Well, I thought you *should* know," said Alex. "See, friends tell each other things. Big things. They eventually open up and trust each other. That's what our 'friend date' was supposed to be about, so it really sucks that—" He bit off the end of his sentence.

"Well, this isn't the easiest thing to open up about."

Yeah, no duh.

Alex detected an edge to Rosalee's tone and knew he had hit a nerve, but he wouldn't let that stop him this time.

"I get that," he said. "But I wouldn't be here if I didn't want to know, okay? So, if it's not cancer, then what? Are you dying from something else?"

"Not that I know of."

Alex let out a slow breath. "Great, well, then are you, like, sick from exposure to kryptonite? Did a radioactive spider bite you? Maybe feeling a little peckish this close to the full moon?"

He watched Rosalee's mouth twitch toward a smile and felt his frustration lessen as she met his gaze. "Alex, I have this, like … brain disease."

Alex studied her for several seconds before his eyes narrowed. *"Get real."*

Rosalee shrugged and smiled a tiny, sad smile.

"No you don't," said Alex. "That's a sick joke, Rosalee."

"It's not a joke."

"You *just* said you weren't dying," said Alex, his voice loud in his ears.

"I'm not."

Alex glowered at her.

"I'm *not.* Yet."

"So …?" Alex took his arms off of the chair back and let them flop uselessly at his sides. "There's a cure, right?"

"No."

"No," Alex repeated hoarsely.

"I have it under control. Mostly," said Rosalee. "I can still live a long and healthy … *ish* life."

"Huh." Alex leaned forward, arms still at his sides so that his chest was the only thing holding him up against the back of the chair. He tucked his chin and wondered if he was going to be sick.

"I should have told you sooner. I know that," said Rosalee. "And I understand if you need some space or whatever."

Alex looked up at her again. "Why would I need 'space or whatever'? Is it contagious?"

"No."

"Then I don't need space. I don't *want* space, Rosalee."

"Really?"

Alex shook his head irritably but otherwise ignored her question. "Okay, so you have a ... *brain disease*." He shot her a slightly crazed look. "I accidentally dissected my arm. Let's keep this party going. I'm in AA and anger management classes because it's the only way my attorney—who's also my dad, by the way—will help me get out of the humungous mess I made. Your turn."

"I—*wow*, okay." Rosalee tucked a strand of hair behind her ear. "Um ... most days, I think I only have a certain amount of energy, and if I spend too much from one day, it comes out of the next one."

"Is that what happened before the dance?"

"I think so. But then there are some days that I get exhausted for no reason. Or that I still have energy, even though I used it all the day before."

"Coffee doesn't help?" said Alex. "When you're exhausted, I mean?"

"Maybe a little. Naps are more helpful."

Alex nodded but wasn't quite ready to return the tentative smile Rosalee offered.

"I may not have a job soon because we're almost done with the walls," he said.

"Wait, but you still have your job at Laurie's, right?"

Somehow, Rosalee's question lifted Alex's spirits. Whether she just didn't want to see him homeless or she actually wanted him to stick around, he liked that she cared.

"Yeah, but it's barely enough to cover rent," he said.

"Can you ask for more hours?"

"Maybe. Your turn again."

For an instant, Alex saw the look in Rosalee's eyes that usually meant she was about to bolt. He readied himself, but she seemed to master the impulse.

"Sometimes different parts of my body go numb or hurt and I can't tell when any of it is going to happen," she said.

"Is that why you don't like people touching you?"

"Mostly."

They looked at each other and Alex could feel the dregs of his anger and frustration draining off. At least for now, he was satisfied. *Mostly.* After all, he was still keeping a couple of cards close to his chest, too.

"Am I forcing you into this? Whatever 'this' is?" he said.

Rosalee smiled and kept her eyes on his, filling him up with something that felt remarkably like hope.

"No," she said. "You're not."

She pressed her lips together, still smiling, as though enjoying a private joke.

"What?" said Alex.

"I'm glad there's still a 'this.' Whatever it is."

Alex made a noncommittal head jerk and then rolled his eyes at himself. His attempts to not give himself away completely were getting increasingly awkward.

"Do you wanna get out of here?" he said, "Go for a drive?"

Chapter 28

Ten minutes later, they were headed up a winding road leading away from Rabbitbrush and Rosalee was asking Alex about his notebooks.

"So, the colors depend on what's in them?"

"Yup. I thought the duct tape would make them more *edgy* and *original*." Alex swung his head so that his hair hung in his eyes, making Rosalee laugh. "But that was in middle school, and as it turns out, thirteen-year-olds don't tend to appreciate that kind of stuff."

"That's too bad. I think they're edgy *and* original."

Rosalee tried to catch Alex's eye as she said it, but he was focused on passing by an oncoming pickup on the narrow road.

"Well, to most of the kids, they were my diaries," he said, "Which was only partially true."

"What does that mean?"

"I guess I like to twist reality into my own kind of fiction. So when I had the extraordinarily bad inclination to let my classmates or friends read anything, sometimes they would recognize the stories—which didn't always stick to what happened. Sometimes they were what I *wanted* to happen."

"Like what?" Rosalee realized that she was staring at Alex's profile and made herself look out the window instead.

"Like, I added dragons or sword fights, damsels in distress—that type of thing."

"What's so bad about that?"

Rosalee watched power lines cutting through the brilliant sky and smiled at the idea of a dragon's silhouette bursting out of a distant tree line.

"Well, I wasn't always directly involved in the situations," said Alex. "I was usually just in the right place at the right time, but since writing is a pretty solitary activity, I probably came off as a stalker on more than one occasion."

"Yikes."

"I believe 'creep' was another word they threw around." Alex turned into a parking lot overlooking Rabbitbrush in all its glory. "I found this spot a couple weeks ago. I'm sure you've been here a million times already."

Rosalee turned her attention to the scenery around them. Alex had only driven them a little way into the foothills, but from their lofty position, she could see the red barn nestled among silky, golden threads that were wild switchgrass and Indiangrass up close. Further out were the lush pines and the last remaining leaves of aspens and cottonwoods that rippled in the autumn breeze and winked with fiery colors as their smooth sides twisted toward the sun.

Absorbed as she was by her appreciation for her hometown, it took a moment for Alex's statement to sink in. She frowned. "Why would you think I've been here a million times?"

"Because you live here? I don't ..."

Rosalee raised her eyebrows and Alex stared back for several long moments until at last, she saw something click in his brain. "Oh my god. So this is like ... a *spot.*"

"Yup. Kind of a big one when I was in high school."

"God, I feel so *old*," Alex groaned.

Rosalee laughed. "Kinda sneaks up on you, doesn't it? So I'm going to assume that's *not* why you brought me here?"

Alex winked roguishly. "Assume away."

For now, at least, he seemed to be back to normal. He turned the key halfway in the ignition to roll the windows down the rest of the way, and they sat in comfortable silence for several minutes. Eventually, Rosalee looked over to see that Alex's face had grown uncharacteristically serious again.

"Can I ask you something?" he said when he noticed her watching him.

Rosalee nodded, ignoring the subtle twist of panic in her stomach. She really wasn't ready for another fight so soon after the last one.

"How much did my trying to help you make everything worse?"

"What do you mean?"

"Like, would things have been better if I had left you alone? Not tried to help so much?"

Rosalee shook her head. "I don't know ... Can I ask *you* something?"

"Shoot."

"Why do you feel like you *need* to help me?"

Alex tilted his head and rubbed the side of his neck. "... I don't know."

"I guess I'm not sure how I feel about being your project."

"Fair enough."

"But I didn't hate our impromptu lunches."

Alex's laugh was short and artificial. "Yes, you did."

"Well, in hindsight I didn't. And I didn't hate the dancing. What I *really* hated was not being able to go with you that night."

They settled into another silence, but this one felt distinctly dif-ferent—*charged* somehow. This time, Rosalee felt like she and Alex occupied the same space because she wasn't mentally or emotionally somewhere else. And possibly for the first time, she wanted to touch him—not just to prove that it wouldn't hurt her, but for normal, human reasons. She wanted to smooth the lines in his face that made him look sad and brush his hair out of his eyes so that she could see them better. Her fingers inched forward on her seat and she felt her pulse quicken at her daring. The distance between her fingers and Alex's closest hand still seemed miles away.

"I have a couple mixtapes in there if you wanna listen to some music," said Alex, nodding toward the center console between them.

Rosalee tried to suppress her resentment toward her ultimate cowardice. "Oh, sure."

She opened the console and glanced at the titles, quickly choosing one labeled "Oldies But Goodies" and passing it to Alex. He was careful not to touch her as she handed it to him, then turned the key in the ignition one notch again so that the stereo lit up. He pressed the TAPE button and slid in the cassette, and at once, guitars, drums, and piano chords filled the cab.

"C'mon," said Alex, jerking his head toward the open window.

He pushed his door open and hopped onto the hood of his Jeep, lying back against the windshield and patting the space next to him. Rosalee climbed up and lay back, gazing up at the tree branches that hung over the parking lot. She breathed in the sweet, almost spicy scent of the pine and fir needles, mixed with the mulchy aroma of leaves in various states of decomposition scattered over the ground.

The music from Alex's stereo floated out of the open windows and mingled with the warm afternoon breeze and rustling foliage. Rosalee was still kicking herself for missing her chance in the car. To hold his hand would have been such a simple way to show him something she couldn't put into words yet.

Not that she couldn't still do it.

She looked over at Alex just as the music changed and the opening notes of Fleetwood Mac's "Go Your Own Way" sent a jolt through her heart and into her stomach.

"Oh," she said, covering her mouth as it twisted in sudden and unexpected grief.

"What's wrong, are you hurting?" Alex turned toward her at once, one hand hovering over her before he ran it through his hair instead.

"No. I mean yes, but not like that." Rosalee sat up and hugged her knees to give herself better control. "Evelyn used to play this album all the time on Saturdays while everyone was busy with chores."

"Evelyn?"

"My aunt who died."

"Oh, shit. You mentioned her earlier. I'll turn it to something else, hang on."

Rosalee tried to draw calming breaths as the car shifted and Alex got back into the driver's seat, fast-forwarding to the next song. When he joined her again, he still looked apprehensive and sat with his legs crossed instead of lying back against the windshield.

"I'm sorry about your aunt," he said. "How long ago did she die?"

Deep breaths. "Um ... February."

"What, of *this* year?" Alex sucked air through his teeth. "I had no idea. I'm guessing you were pretty close?"

"Yeah." Rosalee was still focused on her breathing. "Evelyn raised me and Ellie before Robin moved back to live with us. She was Robin's older sister."

"So, how is Robin holding up?"

"Alright, considering."

"Was she—I mean ..." Alex frowned, chewing on his thumbnail. "Was she much older than Robin?"

"Only four years. Do you know what Hormone Replacement Therapy is?"

"No. Well, wait, I feel like I've heard commercials for it. But it's called something else—I can't think of it."

"There are a few brands. Estroserin is the one that killed my aunt."

Alex stopped chewing his nail. "Jesus."

"She went on it maybe a year and a half after starting menopause." Rosalee noticed that her head felt fuzzy. It was almost like she was outside of her body listening to the story. "She was having a hard time—just really depressed and not herself. She tried all kinds of herbal remedies and stuff, but she eventually started the therapy. It seemed like it was working, but it turns out that she had this undiagnosed heart condition no one knew about until it was too late. When she started complaining about indigestion, we thought that was all it was, but she was literally having a heart attack and we had no idea."

"God, Rosalee, I'm so sorry."

Rosalee sniffed and wiped her thumbs under her eyes. At least her waterproof mascara was holding up. "That's actually how we found out I had ... Multiple Sclerosis." She let the word trip off of her tongue slowly to counteract the abrupt acceleration of her heart rate, then immediately wished she had abbreviated it. The whole name sounded so dramatic. "I started getting dizzy and half of my body was, like, going numb. I was on birth control at the time and so I started worrying about the hormones or whatever. Obviously, it was different symptoms, but stroke is another side effect, so they did an MRI and ... *voila*."

Alex swallowed. "I don't ... even know what to say. That sucks. All of it sucks."

"Yeah, it does. I think maybe the reason I wasn't so nice to you when you first moved here is because I didn't want you to distract me from putting my family back together. But I'm glad you're here. Now."

"Thanks. I mean, I am too. Glad."

"Oh, good ... You're welcome."

She watched as Alex's eyes crinkled at the corners. This time, their silence was definitely charged, and Rosalee could feel her heartbeat in her ears over the music, just before it sped up and became garbled.

"Damn it," Alex muttered, scrambling off the hood again.

Rosalee followed, opening her door and kneeling on the passenger seat as Alex attempted to extract the cassette from the deck. She winced as shiny black tape unspooled in a tangle and he finally pulled it free.

"Welp, I guess that's it for this one," he said.

"Maybe not." Rosalee took the mangled mess from him and inspected the crimped and twisted ends. She stuck her pinky in one of the cassette hub gears and began to wind it, smoothing the tape gently as she went.

"Thanks," said Alex. "I'm still not sure about sticking it back in *this* tape player, though."

"Maybe not."

Alex opened the center console again. *"Oh."* He grabbed another cassette. "So, I have this cousin that lives in London and she sends me mixes all the time of music we don't have here yet. The latest one is pretty cool if you wanna hear it."

"That sounds great."

Rosalee placed the freshly wound but newly delicate tape back in its original case as Alex slid the new one into the stereo cassette slot. He raised his voice over the music. "I wish I could return the favor, but the nearest music store to Rabbitbrush is, like, Denver." He shot

Rosalee an accusatory look, as though the behind-ness of her town and the surrounding areas was her fault.

Rosalee was immediately indignant. "What, just because we don't have a Sam Goody, we don't have *any* music? Miller's Books & Music is *super* hip. Even if it's a few months behind..."

"Try a few *years.* Thank god your library is up to date, or I'd never have been able to talk to you."

"What?"

"No, nothing." Alex took the repaired cassette back from Rosalee and closed it back inside the center console.

"Alex Conway, do you not own your own thesaurus?" said Rosalee, and Alex grinned.

"Secret's out."

Rosalee smiled back, then became increasingly distracted by the dangerous idea forming in her head now that her hands were free again. *Do it, do it, do it,* she said to herself. Before she could let her cowardice take the reins again, she hopped back out of the Jeep, crunching dried leaves into the asphalt as her sneakers touched down.

She turned back to Alex, biting her lip to keep from laughing at the sight of him frozen inside the car with his mouth half-open. After several moments, he got out, which was lucky because Rosalee was beginning to lose her nerve as steadily as water dripping through the hopeful fingers of cupped hands. He was still watching her curiously as she backed away from him and the Jeep.

"Heads up," he said, nodding behind her.

Rosalee looked over her shoulder at the guardrail that ran along most of the parking lot's perimeter. Except it wasn't so much a guard rail as a rickety old fence—one that she could easily see herself tripping over before tumbling to her death. Luckily, there were also a lot of sharp-ish trees to break her fall.

She stopped walking and stared at the empty stretch of crumbling asphalt in front of her, unsure how to execute her half-formed burst of inspiration. She was waiting for the music to take her but so far, she was alone with her tingling nerves until finally, her deep breath reached the bottom of her lungs. When she felt her shoulders relax, she finally found the courage to look at Alex again, then laughed as she watched him wiggle and strut his way toward her in time with the music.

"This is what we're doing, right? We're dancing?" he said. "Little of this?"

Rosalee laughed again as he shimmied in front of her.

"This part. Wait for it." Alex screwed his face up in anticipation of an electric guitar solo, which he punctuated with wild air guitar moves.

Rosalee smiled as he gave himself over to a dramatic lip-sync performance and felt her body fall into an easy rhythm, just as the song ended and a slower one started.

Alex stopped dancing when he saw that Rosalee wasn't either. "You good?"

Rosalee nodded, although she couldn't completely ignore the panic she felt tugging at the edges of her stomach again.

"Do you wanna stop?" said Alex.

"No."

Rosalee barely flinched when he moved closer. She kept herself calm by humming along to the music, even though she didn't actually know the song and was undeniably tone-deaf.

"I like this song," she said to distract herself. "Who is it?"

"I don't remember. Something about 'sneakers.'"

"Oh, sure."

"Do you trust me?" Alex said quietly, and Rosalee realized that he was much nearer than she would normally have allowed, although still not touching her. She closed her eyes, breathing deeply and focusing on the air, then nodded.

"I think you need to look at me," said Alex.

Rosalee kept her eyes stubbornly shut. "Why?"

"I have an idea."

Rosalee took another deep breath that got caught several times in her throat. She could feel herself getting dizzy from too much oxygen. Still, she managed to look at him, straight in the eyes.

Alex gave a tiny nod and raised his left hand so that he could have been waving at her, then moved his right as if to circle her waist, stopping just short of it. Rosalee tilted her head, watching him, then slowly mirrored him, curving her right hand against the air around his left and stopping her other hand before it rested on his shoulder.

They began to move slowly, careful not to break their precarious positions. Alex's face was a mask of concentration, which Rosalee realized was probably reflected in her features. She could feel his breath against her cheek but resisted the urge to recoil in case their bodies collided in the sudden movement. Instead, she kept her eyes on his and tried to focus on the temperature. It was as though her body had forgotten about the warmth associated with touch. Instinctively, she moved closer. Her breath caught with Alex's as their hands met, then sprang apart again like the wrong ends of magnets.

"Sorry," said Alex, his voice barely audible and an expression of deliberately measured calm etched into his face. "Did I hurt you?"

Rosalee felt her eyebrows contract, searching her brain for the proper words to describe the sensation. "No," she said eventually. "But I need to stop."

Alex nodded, then moved his hands so that they were no longer in danger of touching her.

"No," said Rosalee, changing her mind.

Alex immediately moved both hands to shoulder height in a gesture of surrender.

"I meant, 'no, keep going,'" said Rosalee. Her eyes prickled with the things she still wasn't ready to show him. Despite her efforts, air came shallowly into her lungs.

"Hey, it's okay," said Alex. "Let's take a break. We're just supposed to be hanging out."

Rosalee shook her head, cursing her tears as they flowed down her cheeks. "No," she said again, placing her hands back into their ghostly positions.

Slowly, Alex followed her lead, looking wary.

As they continued their strange new method of dancing, Rosalee focused on keeping her breaths calm and even. She turned her thoughts back to the subtle heat filling the space between them, and could almost see the temperature radiating between her and Alex's empty hands and from the material of Alex's T-shirt. She felt her body tense but was steeling herself, and the next time their hands met, it was on purpose. Alex's hand was much warmer and more comfortable than she imagined as his fingers twitched and then curved gently around hers.

Rosalee glanced at Alex's face again. He looked quickly away from their hands and she realized that his palm was damp—probably from the effort of not startling her. She lowered her hand, letting her fingertips brush the soft, grey material beneath them. Then she closed her eyes, despite the soft noise of protest from Alex, and saw colors. Colors replaced music notes and the space between their bodies, and as Rosalee let her palm rest against Alex's shoulder, orange danced beneath her eyelids. She could feel his breath again and the energy flowing from his hand that still hovered around her waist. She opened her eyes, feeling that the moment had passed, but Alex still held her there, eyes ablaze with a determination she had never seen in them before. Momentarily, she wondered whether she should be alarmed, but she asked the little voice in her head and it didn't seem to think so.

They continued to move in a slow rotation, and when Alex's free hand moved to press gently against Rosalee's waist, she didn't flinch—she laughed. And again, wonderfully and miraculously, the action paralleled her emotions. Alex only smiled, but it was full of as much triumph, and Rosalee suspected that he was purposely calibrating his reaction, just in case.

Slowly, very slowly, he raised his arm to twirl her, and she did, letting herself fall back into his embrace almost as easily as it should have been to begin with. His breath was against her cheek again, then mingling with hers, and she knew that she should be more careful. But maybe she didn't want to be anymore. Alex cleared his throat before her thoughts could go any further.

"Does this hurt?" he said.

"No."

"Good. I hate to say this, but we should probably head back. I need to get to work soon."

Rosalee moved her left hand from Alex's shoulder and flexed the fingers of her right, releasing them from his grip, but Alex caught both of her hands in his before they could fall back down to her sides. He only held them for a second, applying a brief, gentle pressure before letting them go and leading the way back to his Jeep.

Chapter 29

It was mid-afternoon and Rosalee sat on the stockroom floor of The Goose amid a jumble of partially de-constructed cardboard boxes, expelled packing material, and various glass bottles of herbs, spices, and oils. As usual, she was cursing herself for the frenzied way she unpacked orders. Truthfully, Rosalee loved organization—she just tended to make a mess of it first.

"Oh my." Robin came through the swinging door and surveyed the chaos.

"Don't worry, I've got it under control," said Rosalee.

Robin didn't look convinced. "Can you hand me a box of register tape?" She pointed to a shelf behind Rosalee. "I think it's up above the grocery bags."

Rosalee got up from the floor, then stood on her toes to retrieve the box. When she turned back, her aunt was watching her closely.

"You feeling okay?"

"I think so," said Rosalee.

Robin took the box of register tape from her. "I can have one of the cashiers help if you need to go home. We're pretty slow."

Rosalee paused, chewing her lip. As much as she hated to admit discomfort—or, in this case, defeat—in front of Robin, worse was the hypothetical humiliation that overwhelmed her as she imagined knocking all of the delicate glass bottles she had just unpacked to the floor. Although her new medication seemed to have considerably lessened the inflammation that had induced her latest flareup, her motor skills were still a little shaky. Or maybe it was her confidence—either way, she was better off being cautious.

"If one of them wouldn't mind setting up the discount shelf, I could finish labeling these new bottles," she said. She would likely need help stocking those, too, but she couldn't bear to ask it all at once.

"I'll see who's free."

Rosalee didn't look up to see if Robin was feeling sad for her. She didn't think she could stand to see that look any more than she already did. "Preferably Elijah? He's probably the most careful."

"I'll see," said Robin. "I think he's working on a sign right now, but as I say, we're slow."

Rosalee felt a tiny thorn working its way into her chest. She used to be the sign writer and Elijah had always been second fiddle, reserved for her days off.

Robin seemed to read her mind despite her best efforts to keep it off of her face. "You'll be back to normal soon, I bet. Your muscles just need to remember what to do. Maybe you could paint a little tonight?"

Rosalee ripped a strip of packing tape from its box and wadded it up to toss in the trash. "I'm still waiting for FancyBlouse's okay to go any further on the mural."

"I meant just for fun."

"Oh. Right."

"I'm proud of you, by the way."

"For what?"

"I know it must be hard to give yourself shots every week."

Rosalee shrugged. "It wasn't so bad once Dr. Sawyer showed me how to do it. Visual learning or whatever."

"Still ..."

"Well ... thanks."

Rosalee felt her aunt's eyes still on her as she broke down another box.

"Do you feel any different?"

"Maybe less tired. It's hard to tell."

Was this a test? Would they send her back to the camp if she wasn't better?

"Okay, well I'm gonna work on orders in the office for a while," said Robin. "Do you need anything besides Elijah for now?"

"I think I'm good, thanks."

Rosalee had finally managed to pile all of her flattened boxes together and left out the back door to take them to the dumpster. The container had recently been emptied, so the pile made a satisfying series of *clunks* as the boxes assaulted the metal walls. She wiped her hands on her jeans and then turned to see Gloria headed to her car, lunch bag and keys in hand. As soon as she saw Rosalee, she waved.

"*Hola, Rosalita.* You headed out soon?" she called from across the parking lot.

Rosalee wrapped the coat she hadn't bothered to zip more tightly around her to ward off the late October chill.

"Couple more hours to go," she said when she reached Gloria. "Will I see you tomorrow?"

"Yes, but I'm coming in late. Wednesday mornings I watch my grandbabies."

"Right."

Somehow, schedules and days of the week weren't organizing themselves into any sort of useful pattern in Rosalee's head.

Gloria opened the driver's side door to toss her coat and lunch onto the passenger seat, then closed it again and leaned against her car. "You know, my grandmother had what you have."

"She did?"

Rosalee thought maybe she would have known about something like that sooner, although it also occurred to her that she wasn't entirely sure that Gloria knew what Rosalee "had" in the first place.

Gloria nodded solemnly, raising her eyebrows. "And she lived a *long* and *happy* life."

Rosalee looked into Gloria's face and felt the backs of her eyes prickling. She looked away as a tear slid past her chin.

"I hope it's okay that I'm talking about this with you." Gloria lowered her voice, even though they were alone in the parking lot. "Robin told me a while ago."

"Yeah, no, it's okay. It's just ..."

"It's hard, huh? I know it is. But this is why you should tell people in your life what's going on with you—*tu familia, tus amigos.* We're all here to help you."

"I know, thank you." Rosalee wiped at her face with the back of her hand and then tugged her coat sleeve down to mop up the rest.

"You know what my grandmother used to say?" said Gloria, a smile tugging at the corners of her eyes and mouth, "She said it was called 'MS' because it *eh-mess* with her walk and it *eh-mess* with her talk."

Rosalee hiccuped a laugh and Gloria looked pleased. "You see, honey, you just need to find the humor in the situation. Some days are going to be easier than others."

Rosalee nodded and returned Gloria's smile, feeling a little lighter somehow.

"I left a lemon for you on your *mochila.*"

"Thanks, Gloria. I'll see you tomorrow."

"It's late. What are you doing up?"

Rosalee feigned mild surprise as she looked up from the canvas she was finishing at a workbench in the garage to find Alex leaning in the doorway. But the tires of his Jeep against the gravel were a lot louder than his bike. Plus, she always kept her Walkman on a low volume when she was alone so no one could sneak up on her.

"Couldn't sleep," she said, stopping the tape and pulling her headphones down around her neck.

"Can't say I understand that feeling," said Alex.

"No?"

"No, I'm a little afraid I'm going to fall asleep on my way home from work one of these nights."

"I wish you wouldn't."

Alex walked further into the garage. "Don't tell me I'm growing on you. Surely you wouldn't *miss* me?"

"Maybe at first, but I bet I could get you pretty good from here …"

Rosalee loaded her paintbrush with water from a muddy-looking cup next to her and held it with the bristles cocked, ready to fire. Alex raised an eyebrow and took a step back, spreading his arms wide in a dare, but Rosalee dropped the brush back into the water.

"I can guarantee that's not as filthy as what splashes up from the bus tubs at Laurie's," said Alex. He nodded toward Rosalee's painting. "Why aren't you working on the patio?"

"I needed more light for the painting part and Robin changed the lightbulb." She pointed over her head.

"Ah. I thought it seemed brighter in here. So … is it ready yet?"

Rosalee chewed her lip. "I guess so."

She beckoned Alex closer and scooted her stool to the side to make room for him. He sucked in a breath as he took in the painting. "Where is this?"

"The atrium at the hospital, maybe? I'm not positive, though." Rosalee was a little startled by the expression on Alex's face. "What's wrong?"

"No, nothing." He cleared his throat. "Those are interesting chairs."

"Lola had a bunch of pictures developed from after I dropped them off." Rosalee pointed her brush at an envelope of photos at the edge of the workbench. "I didn't get to see where they set them up, though."

"After you dropped what off?"

"The chairs? I painted them. I mean, after Lola helped me sand them down and everything. We found the whole set at a thrift store in Grand Junction."

Alex stared at her as she handed him the photo she had been working from. In the picture, a small boy of around eight or nine years old sat in a chair decorated with a large, bright toucan, his arms perched at an odd angle on armrests that were too tall. He gazed around at five other chairs situated in a semi-circle around him, each of which featured a different exotic animal. The photo had been captured at a distance to accommodate all of the chairs, but Rosalee brought the boy into sharper focus in her painting.

"This was what wouldn't leave you?" said Alex.

"What?"

"The night you were sketching because you couldn't get something out of your head? This is what you were drawing?"

"Well ... yeah. It took me a while to get it right and then I kinda forgot about it."

Rosalee still couldn't understand the look on Alex's face as his eyes flicked between the photo and the painting. She shifted uncomfortably and shoved her hands in her back pockets. Maybe it was just a letdown. Maybe he had been expecting something more amazing from someone who spent a considerable amount of time painting.

"Not my best work or anything," she said quietly.

Alex seemed to shake himself.

"No, I'm sorry, I'm just ... distracted. I can't believe you painted those chairs. They're great. So is this." He nodded toward the canvas as he handed the photo back.

Rosalee gave him a small smile and Alex studied her, looking like he was trying to decide something. "I've been researching MS," he said finally.

Rosalee stiffened. "Why?"

"Because I wanted to see how worried I should be. How worried *you* must be."

"Okay."

"Are you really going to be in a wheelchair someday?"

"Why, will you not like me then?" said Rosalee, then backpedaled. "I meant '*like*,' like a friend."

"That's too bad because that's not how I *like* you."

Alex met her eyes briefly before she turned back to her painting. She tried to ignore the subtle heat that crept across her collarbone and up her neck.

"Look, Rosalee, wheelchair or not, it won't change anything for me. I'll still find a way to dance with you, too, so don't think you'll get out of it that way."

"What are you gonna do, sit in my lap?" Rosalee could almost taste the bitter value that infused her words and immediately wished she could take them back. "I'm sorry. I know we made progress the other day, I just—I'm still trying to hate you."

"So you *have* been trying to hate me," said Alex, almost to himself. "Why, though?"

"Because it's easier."

"Than ...?"

Rosalee looked at him and then away again.

"What are you doing on Friday around two o'clock?" said Alex.

"Friday, as in three days from now?" Rosalee felt her whole brain straining to remember that single fact. "I'm supposed to work in the morning if Robin doesn't have a cow about it."

"Will you come somewhere with me after?"

"Do I get any more information than that?"

"Not yet." Alex adjusted the strap of his messenger bag. "Oh, but I *did* decide what I want you to watch."

Rosalee struggled against the gaping chasm hovering at the forefront of her thoughts.

"You said you'd watch another 'something' if I read *The Princess Bride,*" Alex reminded her, digging in his bag until he found the video.

"Right." Rosalee took the tape from him and then immediately tried to give it back. "*Romeo and Juliet?* Seriously?"

"Have you seen it?"

Alex shifted his bag again so that it hung down his back and out of reach, then shoved his hands in his pockets so that she couldn't give it back that way, either.

"Everyone's seen it," said Rosalee.

"Have *you?*"

Rosalee paused, then rolled her eyes. "No."

"Well, there's a new one coming out in December with Claire Danes and Leo DiCaprio that I thought we could go see. Baz Luhrmann's directing it, so I think it'll be pretty wild, and I wanted us to be able to compare it with the last movie version."

"Baz who?"

"Luhrmann. He's a director. He did *Strictly Ballroom?*"

"Not ringing a bell."

"It's a dance movie. Cheesy as hell. You might like it."

Rosalee finally resigned herself to the fact that she wasn't going to be able to give *Romeo and Juliet* back to Alex and studied the actors on the cover. Both looked very young and the actress had astonishingly large eyes and long, dark hair. "Jeez, they look like teenagers. And she's, like, *crazy* beautiful."

"They *were* teenagers. And Olivia was my first love. I used to talk to the cover and ask her if she was enjoying her spaghetti."

"Her spaghetti?"

"Sure," said Alex, "They always have spaghetti in Disney movies. *Lady and the Tramp, Little Mermaid.*"

Rosalee smiled. "But why *this* story? It's depressing as hell."

"Don't worry, I'll bring *Dumb and Dumber* next time. I just can't get over the writing and the dialogue in this one. It's, like … crazy beautiful." Alex caught Rosalee's eyes for the briefest of moments. "So what about Friday?"

Rosalee paused, stalling as she set the video on top of her envelope of photos. "What were you trying to decide earlier?"

"If I should ask you to come with me on Friday."

"Oh. So it's something important? Not just … hanging out?" Alex shook his head and somehow his expression sobered Rosalee up at once. "What time should I be ready?"

Chapter 30

T he day was crisp and cool as Alex drove them up the winding and familiar road out of Rabbitbrush and toward Picket, past trees stripped nearly bare and rippling golden fields that somehow made the sky more vast for the lack of green. Alex had barely spoken except to ask if Rosalee minded if he smoked, and she still had no idea where they were going. After nearly fifteen minutes of tenuous small talk, Alex asked about music and at least the radio provided some sort of distraction from the obvious tension. The cigarette also seemed to calm him a bit, but Rosalee saw him wipe the palm that wasn't on the steering wheel on his jeans more than once, which only heightened her nerves.

"It's just past the hospital," said Alex as they approached the familiar building.

Less than five minutes later, he pulled into a parking lot for a building cast in the same mold as the original hospital (before its recent renovations). A sign in front read "Engelmann Spruce Treatment Center for Short and Long-Term Care," and for some reason, it made Rosalee feel cold.

"Are we visiting someone?" she said carefully.

Alex turned in his seat to face her straight-on for the first time since he picked her up that afternoon. "My brother."

"Your ... brother?"

"He's been here for a little over two months."

"Your brother's been *here*? Not in Denver?"

"Yup."

Rosalee struggled to calculate time in her head. "So he's been here as long as you have. Is he why *you* came here?" She tugged at the zipper pull on her coat, ashamed that she had never even asked him.

Alex smiled a tight, Robin-ish smile. "I know it's been hard for you to let me in, so I wanted to return the favor. Kinda ... get some of my demons out in the open, too. Not that my brother is a demon." Alex shook his head. "You know what I mean."

"I do." Rosalee resisted the urge to reach out to him with some sort of physical comfort. *But why?* said a voice in her head that sounded very much like Ellie.

She took a deep breath as Alex stared out the window, clearly readying himself, then stretched out her hand just as he moved his from the steering wheel. Her fingers closed on empty air as he got out of the Jeep and then came around to open her door. Maybe she would take his hand this time when he offered to help her down. Maybe she would keep holding it while they walked and she wouldn't have to think of the right things to say because he would know that she was there and maybe that would be enough.

But for the first time, Alex didn't offer his hand, and as Rosalee followed him into the building, she tried not to feel disappointed.

— • —

The similarities between the medical center and the hospital ended as soon as Rosalee and Alex got inside. The front desk was decorated with fake leaves and cardboard pumpkins, and it somehow seemed warmer than the hospital, possibly due to the dark wood laminate wainscoting stretching as far through the facility as Rosalee could see. The wallpaper made a difference, too. Where the hospital walls tended to be white enough to stick to the backs of your eyes if you stared too hard, here, they were a warmer, satin-y off-white. There was also something nostalgic layered under the standard smell of industrial cleaning agents, but Rosalee couldn't put her finger on it yet.

They signed in as visitors and put lanyards around their necks, then Alex led them through the lobby and past several recreation rooms, some of which were decorated with construction paper Halloween decorations and art projects. It was then that Rosalee recognized the familiar scent of washable paints and the sweet, minty-smelling paste that kids often tasted sneakily while the teacher wasn't looking. Eventually, they made it to a corridor lined with multiple doors and hand-made name plaques in a variety of colors.

When they reached a plaque that read "Oliver Conway," they found a nurse backing out of the door with a picked-over lunch tray. She beamed when she saw Alex.

"Well, hi there! We didn't know you were coming today. He'll be so excited," she said, ushering them inside. "And I might need your help with something in a little while, if you don't mind."

"Sure thing," said Alex. He took a deep breath and turned to Rosalee. "Ready?"

The room was small and set up like the rooms at the old folks' home Rosalee remembered from visiting Pete's great-grandfather once. There was a small living area with a sofa under a window, and a twin hospital bed set up in the corner with a small desk and chair at the foot. She and Alex shrugged off their coats and hung them in a closet next to a closed door that must have been a bathroom, judging by the sign that read "occupied." As Rosalee noticed the smooth doorknob, she realized it probably didn't lock.

On the wall opposite the bed and next to the door they had entered, Rosalee was surprised to see a square window through which a small office was visible. An identical window was set on the office's opposite wall, and beyond it was another room set up exactly like Oliver's.

"These used to be private rooms for chemo and dialysis," said Alex. "The nurses can keep an eye on the kids around the clock this way until they can move back into the cabin."

"Move *back?*"

The sound of a toilet flushing and water running made them both turn toward the bathroom door, and although Rosalee had been expecting a teenager, it opened to reveal a small boy that could only have been around eight or nine years old. Oliver was Alex in miniature, right down to his dark blonde hair. His eyes, however, were a lighter shade of brown and he had a smattering of freckles across his nose and cheeks. There was also something extremely familiar about him and the longer Rosalee looked, the more overwhelming the sense of *deja vu* became.

Oliver looked startled when he saw Rosalee, but his eyes immediately softened as they found his brother.

"Hey, bud," said Alex, "How's it going?"

"The nurses didn't tell me you were coming today and neither did you," Oliver said matter-of-factly, with the slightest tinge of accusation.

"I know. I should have called. Is this a bad time?"

Oliver shrugged. "No. My book is boring anyway. Who's she?"

Rosalee smiled at Oliver and was taken aback by the little adult that appraised her in return.

"This is Rosalee," said Alex. "Rosalee, this is my brother, Oliver."

"Rosalee," Oliver repeated, "Don't you mean Rosalyn?"

"What?" said Rosalee as Alex grimaced and made subtle movements toward his neck with his fingers.

"Nothing," said Alex, abandoning his strange and sporadic sign language. "Just a character in something else he's reading."

Rosalee turned back to Oliver. "Well, it's nice to meet you."

"Nice to meet you, too." The response was automatic, as though it had been programmed in. Oliver turned and walked over to the bed, hopping up and sitting with his back to the wall and his stocking feet about a foot away from the edge. "Are you going to come every time?"

Alex frowned slightly. "Oliver ..."

"Was that rude?" Oliver looked more interested than concerned as Rosalee tried not to laugh.

Just then, the nurse returned, carrying a towel and a bar of soap. "Oliver, how you feel about takin' a shower today?"

Oliver promptly stopped taking on the appearance of a little adult and turned back into a child. He wrinkled his nose.

"How long has it been?" said Alex.

"His last sponge bath was three days ago."

Oliver's sour look deepened.

"I can wait on the other side of the curtain," Alex told him. "I'll talk to you the whole time. Nothing to worry about."

"I'm not worried, I just don't want to."

Alex looked thoughtful while Oliver stared stonily over his head.

"Do any of the rooms have a tub?" Alex asked the nurse. Rosalee watched Oliver's posture stiffen.

The nurse tsked. "I tried that yesterday. I turned around to put on the hot water and he was out like a herd 'a girdles. Took nearly an hour to find 'im."

"Where *did* you find him?" said Alex warily.

"Where he always is—just settin' in those animal chairs." The nurse shook her head, then chuckled. "Though he doesn't normally do it stark naked. He especially likes that big ol' bird."

Rosalee stifled a little gasp with her hand and Alex looked around at her. He smiled softly before turning back to his brother. The nurse bustled around the bathroom to ready the shower while Oliver became visibly more agitated

"What about filling a tub with a *few* inches of water?" said Rosalee.

She assumed the water itself must be the cause of his anxiety. Alex raised his eyebrows at Oliver.

"No *tubs*," said Oliver. "I don't enjoy tubs."

"Not even the one in ... what's it called ... Sir Bigdud?" said Alex.

"Bidgood."

"Yeah, Sir Bidgood."

"*King* Bidgood."

Oliver rubbed his eyes in a weary sort of way while Rosalee and the nurse looked on blankly.

"It's this story about a king who won't get out of his bathtub," said Alex. "It's an *excellent* tub, too. The whole palace ends up in there by the end."

Rosalee smiled but noticed a shadow pass in Oliver's eyes. "It's a *little kid's* book," he said.

Alex shrugged. "So what? It's a good one. In fact, I think we read it *while* you were in the tub."

"It's not really very good." Oliver turned his face toward the wall as the tips of his ears flushed red. "And I've never liked baths."

Alex waited for his brother to look at him again, but he wouldn't. "Oliver," he said quietly.

And before Rosalee could prepare herself, Oliver was shouting. *"I'm not a liar! Don't call me a liar!"*

Alex hadn't so much as flinched since his brother started yelling, but Rosalee could feel her heart racing from the unexpected burst of adrenaline.

"I told you how I feel and then you—you just—AUGHH!"

Rosalee started to back toward the doorway, then glanced at the nurse, who gave her a subtle but clear "stay-there-and-don't-move" look.

"Tell me what I did, Oliver," said Alex, "Let's go through it, okay?"

He didn't say it in a threatening manner—he just said it like Alex, with his hands in his pockets, but Oliver was looking more and more like a cornered animal, his breath coming in gasps and his eyes darting toward the door every few seconds.

Rosalee felt a hand cup her elbow and the nurse whispered "I'll be right back" before letting herself quietly out of Oliver's room. She was probably going for backup. Or sedatives. Rosalee felt a decent spike in her panic level, not least of all because she wasn't sure she should be here after all.

Alex slid the chair out from Oliver's desk and planted it in front of the bed. The chair was made for children, so it made him several inches shorter than Oliver when he sat.

"Bud, I know this is a lot," he said, looking up at his brother.

Oliver started shaking his head the second Alex began to speak, digging his fingers into the comforter and pushing himself up so that most of his weight was on his arms. "YOU DON'T KNOW HOW I FEEL, SO STOP ACTING LIKE YOU DO AND THAT YOU KNOW WHAT I LIKE AND DON'T LIKE!" he screeched at the top of his lungs.

Alex shut his eyes momentarily as his brother unraveled, but when he spoke again, his voice was as calm as ever. "Oliver, what did I say? What just happened?"

Oliver was close to hyperventilating now, and Alex seemed to take this development as his cue to move from the chair onto the end of Oliver's bed, although far enough away to give him his space.

"What did I say, Oliver?" Alex repeated. "What were the actual words I said?"

"I—YOU—AAARGH!" Oliver's hands went into his hair, where he twisted and pulled—hard. "I'M NOT CRAZY, I'M NOT!" he howled.

At this point, the nurse reappeared quietly and hovered by the bathroom. Alex shot her a brief and dismissive thumbs-up, but she only retreated to the living area and Rosalee could see the outline of at least one other person outside of the main door. This was a detail that Oliver did not miss. He heaved a giant sigh that ended in a sob and began to cry in earnest.

"*I'm not crazy*," he said, wrapping his arms around his torso and rocking back and forth where he sat. "I don't need the medicine because I'm not crazy."

Rosalee felt an uncomfortable little spasm in her stomach. Poor, patient Alex, surrounded by "not crazy" people.

Alex caught her eye fleetingly before turning back to his brother. "Look at Rosalee," he said quietly.

Rosalee started. "What? Why?"

But Oliver had already obediently shifted his focus to her. Meanwhile, one of his hands was still busy yanking a large chunk of his hair up by the roots. Alex reached for that hand, but without warning, Oliver grasped Alex's arm with his free hand and held it in a vice-like grip. Rosalee noticed a muscle in Alex's shoulder flex, but if it hurt him he gave no further indication.

"What color is Rosalee's shirt?" he said.

"*Blue,*" said Oliver, his voice coming out strained, although at least he was no longer shouting.

"What kind of blue?"

"Dark."

"What color is yours?"

"Light blue."

"And mine?"

"Brown."

Alex pointed to the walls.

"White. Off-white," said Oliver.

"What else is on the walls?"

Oliver's eyes darted between Alex and several framed nature photos. "Birds."

"What do you hear?"

"Air. Through the vents."

"Are you breathing?"

Oliver let out a tremulous breath and sucked in a new one.

"What else do you hear?" said Alex.

"You."

"Me." Alex nodded. "What am I doing?"

"Talking." Oliver zeroed in on Alex's face, his eyes still wild and searching. "Tricking me."

"Oliver ..."

"You're *tricking* me. Into not being mad."

Alex paused for a moment, considering. "Is it working?"

Oliver squeezed his eyes shut and Rosalee saw his grip tighten on Alex's arm once more, the skin bulging under his fingers. His breathing was becoming uneven with imminent sobs, but Alex stayed calm.

"What are you touching?" he said.

Rosalee watched as Oliver's eyes opened again and traveled slowly to Alex's arm, which was nearly purple beneath his fingers. His lower lip began to tremble.

"Stay with me, bud," said Alex. "What about your other hand?" He nodded toward the one still knotted in Oliver's hair.

Rosalee watched as the fingers on that hand loosened slightly. His fist, however, remained clutched on top of his head. Alex held out his free hand and Oliver seized it as if it were a rope appearing miraculously over the edge of a cliff.

"Are you breathing?" Alex said again.

Oliver looked slightly disoriented as his small chest rose and fell.

"*Now* what are you touching?" said Alex.

"You." The helplessness in his voice nearly broke Rosalee's heart.

"Who am I?"

"Alex."

"Who's Alex?"

"My brother."

"Does that hurt?" Alex nodded toward Oliver's nearly white fingers, which were still strangling his arm.

"Yes."

"It hurts me, too, Oliver."

Oliver let out a soft whimper, followed by a gasp as he flexed his fingers and finally released Alex's arm. Then he retreated into himself once more, hugging himself and rocking back and forth as his tiny body quaked with sobs. This time, Alex moved immediately to comfort his brother and pulled him into his lap, where Oliver flung his arms around his neck and cried into his shoulder.

Rosalee and the nurse excused themselves at this point, feeling like intruders upon such a tender moment. Rosalee let the nurse lead the way into a waiting area, considering that she was half-blinded by emotion by then. She sank into a chair with faded pastel flowers that smelled faintly of cigarettes. Nearby, a coffee and hot chocolate machine hummed and emitted tantalizing whiffs of vanilla and hazelnut-scented comfort.

The nurse sat next to her, fanning herself with a magazine from the coffee table. "*Whew!* Hell of a day for you to meet Oliver Conway. You doin' okay?" She peered into Rosalee's face. "I can scrounge us up some Jell-O from the cafeteria if you're feeling woozy."

"That's okay, I'm fine," said Rosalee, embarrassed at her failure to stem her seemingly endless flow of tears.

The nurse sat next to her and covered her hand in a motherly gesture and Rosalee was grateful that her body seemed to be cooperating with her, despite the unexpected touch. Eventually, her throat opened back up and she was able to take air all the way into her lungs again.

"That's it." The nurse patted Rosalee's back in soothing little circles. "Alex is a good brother, isn't he?"

Rosalee laughed shakily and nodded, wiping the last of her tears away with her thumbs and realizing that they were smeared with black. She would have to remember to choose water-proof mascara for the foreseeable future.

"Are you two dating?"

"We're just … friends," said Rosalee, although that explanation seemed insubstantial as soon as she said it out loud.

"*Mmm*-hmm." The nurse looked a little too knowing as she nodded.

A beeper sounded and Rosalee realized it was coming from the nurse's pocket. The nurse glanced at the code and slid it back into her smock, then stood.

"Let's go see what those rascally boys have got up to, shall we?"

Chapter 31

B y the time Rosalee and Alex left Engelmann Spruce Treatment
Center, it was nearly four thirty and the sun had already disappeared beneath the horizon, although the remaining light filtering
through the clouds was enough to leave behind smudges of pink and
purple along the mountain range. Rosalee breathed in the cool air,
which helped to calm her a little from the afternoon's events.

Oliver had refused to take a shower but grudgingly allowed the
nurse to give him a sponge bath while Alex read to him from *National Geographic: Water, Prey, and Game Birds of North America.*
He hadn't quite warmed up to Rosalee yet, but she didn't blame him,
considering. She was heartened to learn that Alex and Oliver regularly
walked along the path behind the hospital while Oliver kept up a
running commentary of birds they sighted. Rosalee hoped her love
and extensive knowledge of nature and wildlife in the surrounding
regions might help her gain rapport with the littlest Conway.

As they pulled out of the parking lot, Rosalee's head spun with
questions about Oliver, but she wasn't sure she possessed the emotional fortitude to ask them all tonight—or, more importantly, hear
the answers. Instead, she made herself useful by checking that the coast
was clear as Alex navigated back to the main road. They traveled for
several miles in silence.

"So ... that's my brother," Alex said eventually.

Rosalee nodded, trying to focus on watching for deer instead of the things trying to climb out of her chest. "You're really great with him."

"Didn't I tell you that was the best hot chocolate?"

Rosalee smiled. The waiting room cocoa had definitely lived up to the hype. "I'll never doubt you again."

"Sorry about the meltdown," said Alex. "If I had known it was bath day, I would have chosen a different one to make you come with me."

"That's okay. How long has he been taking sponge baths?"

Alex alternately tapped his thumb and pinky on the steering wheel. "Um. *Months*, I guess. That's probably a story for another day."

"Sure, I didn't mean to pry."

"You're not, I just ... wanted to see if we could still salvage part of the evening."

"... I don't think it needs salvaging."

Alex grinned. "You're paler than usual. Like, practically glow-in-the-dark."

"Ha ha," said Rosalee sarcastically. "So, how did you get him to calm down after we left?"

"I made him take off his shoes and socks and make fists with his toes in the carpet. Works every time."

"Jeez, where did you learn that?"

"Die Hard."

Rosalee paused. "Wow, I totally forgot about that part."

"Now you won't."

Rosalee returned Alex's smile, then turned her head to watch the utility poles flashing past her window. "How often do you visit him?"

"As often as I can. At least four days a week and my mom calls him at least twice a day. It's still pretty rough on him, though."

"And he can't have a roommate?"

"He has a few, actually. I don't know if you saw the big cabins in the back, but they sleep about eight kids in bunk beds per building."

"Oh right, you mentioned a cabin. So why isn't he out there?"

"Hail damage from the storm. The insurance claim was only recently pushed through so now they have to replace the roof. They moved the kids from that cabin inside for now."

"So, he's ... he gets to be around other kids usually?"

"Yup. Maybe not as much as we'd like, but that's also partly just who Oliver is. He's always preferred more solitary activities."

Rosalee swallowed against the lump in her throat. "I was afraid he was by himself because he ... scared the other kids or something."

"Surprisingly, adults tend to be more startled by his episodes than kids. Besides, he usually only hurts himself."

"Usually?"

The rapidly fading light afforded little visibility in the Jeep, but Rosalee still found her gaze drawn toward Alex's arm. She wondered if there would be a bruise. Alex noticed her looking and cleared his throat.

"He doesn't really know what he's doing," he said. "He's only ever done that with me and Mom, and he doesn't realize his own strength. I'm not sure he can control it. It's more like we're flotation devices and he's—"

"Drowning." Rosalee felt her heart breaking for Oliver—for all of them—all over again.

"Exactly."

"So, then ... it's only you and your mom because he feels safest with you?"

"Two for two. That's our theory, anyway."

Alex sounded relieved. Maybe he had expected Rosalee to be disgusted by Oliver's outburst.

"Well, you obviously mean a lot to him," said Rosalee, cursing her swollen sinuses for making her sound like she had a cold.

Out of the corner of her eye, she saw Alex glance at her before pulling over at the nearest pull-off. "What's up?" His resigned posture made her feel worse.

Rosalee sighed and turned her head against the headrest to look at him, tears coursing steadily down her cheeks. "You're so good. You're *so* good and all I've done is push you away, and make you feel small, and pretend you annoy me, and I'm sorry."

From what little she could discern of his expression, Alex seemed to be struggling to absorb the change of subject. She wondered what he thought she was going to say.

"Okay ... I'll give you the 'pushing me away' part in the beginning, but you've never made me feel small."

"Well, that's nice of you," said Rosalee.

Alex watched her for a few seconds, then reached down to release his seatbelt. "Can I touch you? Is that ...? You just look like you could use a hug."

Rosalee nodded, pressing her sleeve against her mouth to suppress the sob that was building in her chest. Alex reached over her to release her seatbelt as well. Then, cautiously, he wrapped an arm around her shoulder. Rosalee felt her body curl into his automatically. She supposed that the muscle memory of hugs ran deeper than those associated with fine motor skills as she wound her arms around Alex's waist and buried her face in his denim jacket. She could detect various food smells from Laurie's and lingering cigarette smoke in the material, plus a hint of something citrusy as he shifted to wrap his other arm around her.

Rosalee tried to put all of the emotion she had been feeling since her mini breakdown at Engelmann into the embrace and hoped that Alex could at least feel the things she couldn't say. She couldn't tell him, for instance, about all of the ways she didn't deserve him, because strictly speaking, she didn't *have* him. Still, being in the arms of someone so selfless was humbling, to say the least, and when she finally broke away, she felt ashamed again. She also hoped that it was only tears she had left behind on his jacket.

"God, do you have a tissue?" she said.

"I have a wad of napkins from lunch somewhere." Alex rummaged in his glove compartment until he found them.

Rosalee glanced out the window. It was completely dark now, but she could just make out the restroom by the pull-off. She didn't want to blow her nose in front of Alex and she could probably stand to splash some cold water on her face.

The rest of the drive took surprisingly little time and before Rosalee was ready to leave Alex, they were approaching his apartment.

"I have a meeting at six," he said. "Do you mind if I run in and grab my bag before I drive you home?"

Rosalee opened her door. "Actually, I can walk home from here. I could use the fresh air to clear my head a little."

"Give me two minutes and I'll walk with you."

Rosalee's house was deserted by the time they reached it, so she decided to give Alex the tour, flipping on light switches as she went. She led the way to the guest room on the first floor, which was next to the garage and had a window overlooking the front backyard gate. Thankfully, she had remembered to make the bed that morning.

"This is the guest room. And sometimes my room."

"'Sometimes?'"

"It's usually upstairs, but sometimes walking is just—anyway …"

Rosalee turned away to flip on a small lamp on her bedside table, which was much less harsh than the overhead fan light. She felt Alex watching her, but when she turned back, he was examining a short stack of CDs next to the boombox she had carried down from her room upstairs.

"Is this any good?" he said, holding one of them up.

"It's in there." Rosalee nodded toward the boombox and Alex flipped the lever to the CD slot.

"Not bad," he said after several seconds, then lowered the volume again and turned back to her. "Why are you looking at me like that? Should I turn it off?"

Rosalee shook her head and stopped Alex's hand before he could reach the button. She kept her fingers on his wrist, guiding him to her bed, where she switched off the lamp again and sat down. The only illumination now came from the outdoor light next to the garage. As Alex sat down too, Rosalee noticed that his expression was uneasy again. She willed herself to look directly into his eyes.

"Touch me."

"… What?"

She had been thinking about it ever since Alex posed the question in the car. Before that, actually, but his voice attached to the thought made her shiver.

"I want you to touch me," she whispered.

"You don't have to do this," said Alex.

Rosalee took his hand, interlacing their fingers, then moved them both to the flushed skin of her cheek. She let out another shaky breath. "I don't want to fight anymore. I just want to *not* fight with my body and not be careful and not think and I need you to just …"

She moved their hands lower so that they were resting against her throat. Then she untangled their fingers and held Alex's against her skin. His palm was warm and she recognized the lingering scent of the hospital bathroom soap as she willed her breathing to stay calm and even.

"You don't have to prove anything," said Alex. "I get why you were so careful and we don't need to move any faster just because you told me."

"Please..."

Alex maintained his ground, although he was close enough that his forehead rested against Rosalee's as she moved his hand to lay over her heart. Rosalee closed her eyes, melting into his touch. He turned his head to press his mouth against her hair, but the hand on her chest remained still.

"I can't," he whispered.

Rosalee pulled back to study his face. "Can't? Or *won't?*"

Alex stared at her. He opened his mouth to speak, then shook his head and closed it again.

"Don't you want me?" Rosalee said, her voice barely above a whisper.

"Don't I *want* you?" Alex repeated, looking bewildered.

Rosalee held his gaze, her eyes full.

"Look ... Rosalee ..."

She stiffened, then moved away. "Oh my god. Oh god, I'm so stupid."

"What? Why?"

"You aren't ... *are* you?"

"Are I ... what?"

"Oh my god, I'm such an idiot. You really did just want to dance with me. Oh, and here I am, trying to seduce you."

Alex stared at her with his mouth half open. "I don't think I understand what's happening ..."

"So ..." said Rosalee. "Then do you have, like ... a boyfriend?"

Alex's eyes widened. "No? Do *you?*"

"No," Rosalee said quickly.

"Okay then." Alex shook his head. "So because I haven't jumped you yet, I'm *gay?*"

"Just for a second."

Rosalee blushed furiously as Alex stood to switch on the lamp again. When he turned back, he was frowning.

"Rosalee, believe it or not, I'm not ravaging you right now because about a half hour ago, you were crying so hard I thought you were going to hurl in the passenger seat of my Jeep, which is understandable considering that we had a pretty traumatic afternoon with my brother. I'm *trying* to be the good guy."

Rosalee raked a hand through her hair and huffed impatiently.

"And anyway, wanting someone—what does that even mean?" Alex sat next to her again, close enough that their arms almost touched.

"Okay, Mr. Analyzer, could you drop it?" Rosalee snapped. "Just forget that I said that?"

"Well, do you want to know the answer, or not?"

Rosalee hesitated. "Yes," she said quietly.

"You asked me if I want you. So ... do I want you in my life? That should be pretty obvious, but *yes.* Do I want you ... in my car? Also yes, as long as you hurl out the window."

"Hardy har."

Alex grinned, then reached out to brush a strand of hair behind Rosalee's ear. She watched his eyes grow serious and when he spoke again, his voice was lower—more deliberate than usual. "Do I want you in my bed?"

Rosalee held her breath, afraid to look at him.

"*God,* yes," said Alex, staring her down anyway. "But I need you to feel safe with me so that wanting you doesn't feel like I'm hurting or taking advantage of you. You can understand that, can't you?"

When Rosalee didn't answer, he flipped his hand palm-up on the comforter and she only waited a second before taking it. Boldly, she laced their fingers together and immediately felt a tingle go up her arm. She had only begun to tense in anticipation of pain when the deep recesses of her memory offered up the first time she danced with Mark Tomlinson in the seventh grade. These were *good* tingles.

"Rosalee, I can handle the *torment* of all the extra time and space around you, as long as I can be ..." Alex laughed and shook his head, and Rosalee looked up. "In your orbit," he said, rolling his eyes. "Like a ... satellite or something."

"What was that from?"

Alex grimaced. "Nowhere. Me. I know it was corny. It sounded gut-wrenchingly romantic in my head."

"It sounded like a movie line."

"Well, that bodes well for me, I guess. I just need to be around you. Somehow."

Rosalee tried not to let herself get lost in his eyes, but they pulled her in so completely that she had no choice. "It was," she said.

"What was?"

"Gut-wrenchingly romantic. What you said."

"Well ... thanks."

"So ... you *do* want me," said Rosalee.

Alex laughed softly and looked down at their still-entwined fingers. "You have *no* idea."

"So kiss me, then."

"No."

"No?"

"No," said Alex. "You're upset, you're obviously delusional if you're still confused about my feelings for you, even though they're *definitely* stronger than the ones you have for me, and also, your aunts would be apoplectic if they came home to see you sucking face with some guy in the dark when you're sick."

"*Sick?*" Rosalee pulled her hand free. "Are you kidding me? God, Alex I wouldn't have told you any of this if I thought you would treat me like—I'm not *that* delicate."

"You're a little bit delicate," said Alex. "And really, technically, you *are* sick."

"... Okay."

"Why are you mad?"

"Alex, you've been trying to help me help *you* touch me for months and now here we are, alone, and I'm *begging* you to do it and you won't."

Alex stared at her. "*Wait* a minute. I thought we were past this. When did I morph back into Douche-y McFratBoy, out chasing tail?"

"I don't know, I'm just frustrated."

"Is that what you think, though?"

Rosalee studied him briefly and then sighed. "No, it's not. I'm just embarrassed and pissed off because I'm embarrassed."

Alex watched her for a moment. "Go out with me next week. Like, on a date."

"Ugh." Rosalee flopped over at the waist and buried her head in her knees.

Alex waited a few seconds before nudging her back into an upright position.

Rosalee smiled reluctantly. "A date, huh?"

"Why not?"

"You sure like to build things up, don't you?"

Alex shrugged. "I've waited this long."

Rosalee bit her lip. "I just ... I don't want you to get your hopes up, you know? It's like you live for these perfect moments and romantic storylines, and I'm not sure those are what you're going to get with me."

"Is that the grapefruit tree?" Alex nodded toward a plant next to her boombox. The sprouts had grown considerably in the past several weeks.

"Maybe." Rosalee's eyes narrowed as a smirk flickered across Alex's face.

"I'm not saying things have to be perfect," he said seriously. "But I *do* want to take you on an actual date."

"Okay," said Rosalee finally, failing to suppress a smile that was quickly mirrored in Alex's features.

Alex lifted one of her hands and pressed it to his lips. Rosalee watched his eyes close briefly at the contact and felt a surge go all the way up her arm. This time, though, she recognized it as a wave of goosebumps that was still mercifully unaccompanied by pain.

She let out a shaky breath and angled her body toward Alex's, moving her other hand to rest over his heart. Alex tugged gently on her fingers to bring her closer until their faces were nearly touching.

"I can't stay here," he said. "Or I'll risk overshadowing the *perfect* date I have planned."

Rosalee sighed and rolled her eyes. "There's no hope for you. I tried."

"So, Sunday night? Pick you up at seven?"

"Sounds *perfect.*"

Alex pressed his lips against her forehead before standing to leave. With a jolt, Rosalee realized that this was the second time he had kissed her within thirty seconds, and both kisses were over already.

"Hey, Alex?"

He turned back.

"I'm sorry about pressuring you. I thought—anyway, it doesn't matter." Rosalee's voice caught in her throat and she was frustrated to find that her eyes were filling with tears again. "It's just that ... you don't get to tell me when I'm ready or not, you know? Or what I can or can't handle when it's *my* body."

Alex shoved his hands in his pockets. "You're right. I'm sorry."

Rosalee paused, unsure what to do with the anger that had uncoiled and reared so suddenly, now that Alex had already apologized. So, she nodded, wiping away her tears with the pads of her thumbs.

Alex took a step toward her. "Seriously, I am. I wasn't even thinking about it like that, Rosalee. I was just trying to—"

"Protect me?"

"I guess so."

"Okay. Well, I'm, like ... an *adult*."

Alex sighed, his jaw set. Then, before Rosalee had time to react, he was lifting her gently to her feet.

"Wh—"

They both paused to listen as the sudden, distant sound of a motorcycle cut through the quiet. Alex glanced out the window, still holding one of Rosalee's hands, then flipped the lamp switch off again and crossed the room, pulling her with him to shut the door.

Rosalee felt her breath catch as Alex closed the distance between them, maneuvering her gently against the door and tangling one hand in her hair. She wondered if he could feel her heart slamming into her ribcage.

"What are you doing?" she said softly, giving herself time to decide if she felt trapped. She quickly decided that she didn't, but the question was already hovering between them.

Alex rested his forehead against Rosalee's as his fingers in her hair shifted to tuck a strand behind her ear. "Knitting a sweater," he said. He brushed his thumb along her jaw and Rosalee tried to look away, but gave up as his dark eyes captured hers. "And I'm really very sorry because I have no idea how to knit."

Rosalee laughed, then tried to remember how to breathe as Alex intertwined their fingers again with his free hand and pressed them back against the door, too.

"That was Robin's motorcycle," she said, "She's probably only a block away, if that."

"Okay."

Alex's breath on her neck raised more goosebumps, despite the heat.

"She's probably ... almost here ..." said Rosalee, as his lips grazed the skin there, then skimmed over her collarbone.

"Do you want me to stop?"

"... No."

"Then let her find us."

Alex's voice was rough in a way that made Rosalee's stomach flip. He pressed his mouth against the hollow of her throat and they both jumped at the sound of a key in a lock.

Rosalee smirked. "Not as brave as you talk?"

"Shh." Alex squeezed her waist playfully, making her squirm.

"Rosalee?" came a voice from the kitchen.

Rosalee turned her head to avoid shouting in Alex's ear and her eyes landed on the *Romeo and Juliet* tape still lying on her bedside table.

"HI, I'M JUST CHANGING!" she yelled, then struck by sudden inspiration, *"'By and by, I come!'"*

Alex grinned. "Nice."

"Your daily quote-speak is rubbing off on me, I guess."

"Good," said Alex, trailing his fingers down her ribcage.

Rosalee sucked in a sharp breath. "You should ... go," she said, curling her fingers around the material of his T-shirt and pulling him closer.

Alex raised an eyebrow. "Not if you're changing."

Rosalee laughed again. *"Go. "*

"I'll have to walk right past her."

"Use the window. The screen's out."

Alex groaned. "Cue the high school flashbacks."

"I mean it." Rosalee pressed her fingers lightly against the muscles that flexed under the soft fabric of Alex's T-shirt.

"I'm going," Alex murmured against her lips.

Rosalee willed her knees not to give out. She felt her lips part around Alex's and his warm breath fill her mouth, making her dizzy. He smelled like shaving cream and tasted faintly like hot chocolate, and she nearly floated out of her body as he kissed her like she might break.

Then he was gone and sliding the window open. Somehow, the late autumn air that permeated the room felt colder than it should have and Rosalee wrapped her arms around herself in his sudden absence. Alex climbed halfway out the window, then turned back.

"I'll see you next week."

"Bye," she answered faintly, too stunned to move from where he left her.

Chapter 32

Alex sighed in exasperation. He had only just returned home from what would probably be his last day of construction at the hospital, taken a quick shower, and had exactly forty-five minutes to write before his AA meeting. He decided that was probably good timing as he fought the intense urge to rip the page he was working on from his notebook by the threads. Luckily, this was precisely why he only wrote in composition books—it was much harder to follow through with the rage-induced impulses brought on by impenetrable writer's block when the pages were sewn in.

What had begun several months ago as an entertaining story about dragons for his brother had eventually evolved into a screenplay, which was all the more incentive for him to fit its writing into every possible moment. Unfortunately, Oliver predicted Alex's tendency to interweave some sort of love story into the plot, despite Alex's attempts at subtlety, and nearly gave up on the whole thing right there.

As a result, Alex was currently working on one story for his brother and a different one for himself. He hadn't had much success with the latter as of late. He stared at the feeble sentence in the even more pathetic plot hole he was currently attempting to close, then shut his notebook and launched it resolutely across the room, where it narrowly avoided making contact with Pete's startled face in the doorway.

"Sorry, man," said Alex. "Sorry. Writing crisis. Didn't see you there."

"I see." Pete picked up the journal by its woebegone cover and set it on the end of Alex's bed. "Should I come back later?"

"No, no, it's irreparable at this point. Unless I have him agree with her: *'Why, yes, like a harlot. My thoughts exactly!'* Something sarcastic and witty."

Pete hovered uncertainly in the doorway as Alex chewed hard on the end of his pen. "So, that would be ... the swimming scene? At the lake?"

Alex stopped chewing. "You remember the swimming scene?"

Pete smiled slightly. "I'm glad you're writing again. Guess you found your muse after all."

"Yeah, maybe."

Alex was still floored by the fact that Pete remembered any of his screenplay. He felt suddenly guilty that he hadn't spent much time with him lately.

"So, why the rewrite?" said Pete.

"Because I'm not sure gum should exist in that time period. Or bikinis."

"Ah." Pete nodded seriously. "Well, I hope you don't change too much."

"Why's that?"

"It was just such a breakthrough. Like suddenly Rosalyn trusted Alec enough to be a little bit ... vulnerable." Pete seemed lost in thought, almost wistful before coming back into himself and looking up again. "By the way, the names ..."

Alex laughed. "I know. I'm working on that."

Pete shrugged. "She might not mind."

"What, that her crazy, billowing hair inspired a whole screenplay?"

"And that she hunts dragons."

"That, too."

Pete grinned. "I'll come back later."

"No, no, I'm done. I have to get ready for my meeting anyway." Alex tossed his pen across the room, aiming for his desk, but missed. He scowled but forced his attention back to his roommate. "So, you and Angela the other night at Laurie's? Something going on there?"

"Oh." Pete smoothed the back of his hair, looking vaguely uncomfortable. "We were just eating. Dinner."

"Good. She seems cool."

"She is. She's a great girl."

Alex nodded encouragingly, but Pete remained in the doorway, studying the baseboards with almost unnatural concentration.

"Did—Do you want to come in? Talk about something?" said Alex.

Pete was showing every physical indication of retreating. "Oh, no, nothing. I didn't mean to interrupt."

"Well, do you wanna maybe hang out later?" Alex chewed his thumbnail in the absence of his pen. "I'm closing tonight at Laurie's, but maybe we could watch a movie or something after?"

"Sure, sounds good." Pete nudged at the door stopper with the toe of his shoe so that the stiff spring buzzed as it vibrated, then cleared his throat. "Hey, Alex?"

"Yeah?"

"Are you and Rosalee ...?" he trailed off, shaking his head.

Alex sat up straighter against his headboard.

"Are you guys going out? Dating, I mean?" said Pete. Alex thought he detected a trace of frustration in his face.

"I'm not sure," said Alex honestly. "Obviously, that's the direction I hope it's headed."

Pete nodded, still directing most of his focus to the carpet.

"Is that ... are you upset?" said Alex.

Pete had been hard to read for the past several weeks. Granted, they had both been busy, but he seemed even more reserved than usual.

Pete smiled again, but it almost looked painful. "Nothing like that. In fact, you're a *major* step up from ... well, anyway ..."

Alex perked up. He hadn't heard anything about Rosalee's previous relationships.

"I know you're a good guy," said Pete, "and Rosalee ... Well, if you make each other happy, then I'm happy for you."

"... But?"

"Um ... no 'but.' Nothing related, anyway."

Alex tamped down his annoyance. Whatever his roommate was withholding, he was sure he had good reason.

"Okay, well listen, I have to pack up for my meeting, but we'll talk later tonight, yeah?"

Pete was already halfway back to his room. "For sure, sounds good."

Chapter 33

The next day passed with unnerving velocity and before Alex knew it, it was ten-fifteen on Sunday night, and Rosalee Andrews was taking off her coat in his room, then lingering at his desk, her fingertips skimming over the motley variety of duct tape clinging to the spines of his notebooks, and finally sitting on his bed. It wasn't quite the conventional dinner and a movie date that Alex had envisioned (and for that, he wholeheartedly intended to strangle his coworker with his own apron for making Alex cover his shift), but "Plan C" wasn't turning out to be so bad.

"Plan B" never even made it off the ground. Alex's whimsical idea of french fries dipped in Frostys snuffed it as soon as Rosalee pointed out that the only Wendy's in town was actually in Picket, and it closed at nine o'clock. Alex was fairly certain there was another one off the highway, but Rosalee assured him that it was only open until ten. Thus, Alex proposed the current plan: a pint of Ben and Jerry's, a bag of potato chips, and a movie in his room, with the volume low enough that they wouldn't wake Pete.

Unfortunately, he had only thought of "Plan C" in the car and was subsequently underprepared in the way of bedroom-related ambiance. He had half expected Rosalee to say "no" *because* it was his bedroom, but given their last encounter, he wasn't completely surprised when she agreed. So, he left her sitting on the couch in the living room for several minutes while he un-mussed his bed and shoved any clutter out of sight. He hadn't even thought about candles, assuming that a date in his room was lightyears away. Maybe that was best, though. The last thing he wanted after all these months of gaining Rosalee's trust was to seemingly undermine everything he'd said only days before.

He opened the blinds a little to let in slivers of light from the street lamps, then switched on the red and blue lava lamp on his nightstand and a small reading light on his desk. His TV and VCR were stacked on a TV tray in the corner and he scooted the tray up to the foot of his bed, then piled pillows from the bed and cushions borrowed from the living room couch against his headboard.

"Are you sure you don't want anything to drink?" he said as soon as Rosalee was settled on his comforter.

"I'm good for now, but thanks. Groovy lamp."

Alex set a can of Coke on his bedside table. "Thanks. One of the few things I brought from my apartment in Denver."

"How come? I mean why did you leave so many things with your mom?"

"I guess I wasn't sure how long I was staying. And I hate packing."

Rosalee looked at him, a crease appearing between her eyebrows as she chewed her lip.

"What's up?" said Alex. He sighed inwardly, unsure why everyone was having such a hard time talking to him lately. Pete still hadn't come out with whatever was bothering him, despite Alex's attempt several nights ago to bond over pizza and a movie.

"No, nothing."

Rosalee smiled again and Alex sat down next to her on the bed, leaving what he hoped constituted a respectable distance between them. He took a swig of Coke before settling back against the wall of cushions, hoping the sugar and caffeine would be enough to keep him awake. He had already come so close to missing out on tonight and he *really* didn't want to miss out on tonight. He glanced over at Rosalee again and waited until she made eye contact before reaching for her hand.

"I'm sorry this isn't a real date," he said, tracing circles on the back of it as he held it in his lap. "You look amazing."

Rosalee had been watching the invisible patterns he drew but met his eyes again and smiled when she noticed him watching her. "Thanks. You *smell* amazing."

Alex wondered if she meant to say that as her nose scrunched almost imperceptibly. She ducked her head to tuck a strand of hair behind her ear and he wondered if she was blushing in the dark. He wanted her to be comfortable here—comfortable with him.

"I'm glad you think so," he said seriously. "Not everyone appreciates my dedication to soap, even when I eat the whole bar."

Rosalee laughed and then tilted her head back, exhaling the way she had so many weeks ago, blowing out smoke from his cigarette next to the dumpster behind Laurie's. The narrow strips of light filtering in from beyond the blinds cut her silhouette into shadows juxtaposed with porcelain and ruby. He watched the jewel tones in her hair sparkle as the ends brushed the neckline of the long-sleeved top she wore under her dress.

"This is pathetic," she said. "I *swear* I've done this before."

Alex brought his attention back to her face and her eyes, whose usual green and golden tones now reflected red and blue from the lava lamp as she shifted her gaze from the ceiling.

"Done what?" he said.

"*Dated.* I don't know why I'm so nervous."

She turned her head to look at him again and Alex hesitated, then leaned in to brush his lips briefly against hers. When he opened his eyes,

Rosalee's were still closed and he resisted the urge to kiss her again. She was wearing a dress with tiny straps, and tights, and his favorite combat boots (before she insisted on taking them off), and *sitting on his bed.* If she were any other girl, all of the above would be in a smoldering, reckless pile on the floor by now.

"What do you want to watch?" said Alex, wrenching his brain away from that last image with enormous effort.

"Anything is fine."

Rosalee seemed more relaxed already. Maybe it was simply a matter of getting the second first kiss out of the way.

"I'll pick three and you choose from that," said Alex.

"Fine."

Alex hopped reluctantly off the bed and pulled out all of the drawers in his desk to survey his partial movie collection. He had at least brought his favorites from Denver, but that in itself posed a dilemma: could he risk showing her one of his favorite movies when there was a possibility neither one of them would be paying attention to it? Wasn't it a better idea, then, to pick something that *wasn't* his favorite, in case they felt like talking instead? Eventually, he withdrew to the living room to raid Pete's movies and came back with two of those, adding one of his not-as-favorite-but-still-up-there choices. Then he fanned out the boxes in front of him, angled toward Rosalee.

"Okay, choose. Not with your *eyes closed.*"

Alex clicked his tongue as Rosalee swept her hand over the tapes like a magician over the brim of a top hat.

"Take it or leave it," she said, keeping them shut.

Alex saw his opportunity, realizing his mistake a second too late. As their lips met this time, Rosalee gasped at the unexpected contact and Alex yanked himself upright again, immediately furious with himself.

"Sorry. I'm sorry, that was a bad idea."

Rosalee watched him for a second, then raised herself unsteadily up to her knees, balancing herself with hesitant hands that paused at his shoulders and then pressed lightly into the material of his button-down shirt. Alex felt something like a tug on an invisible magnetic field around him, dragging him forward to collide with Rosalee's. Then she was kissing him with far less caution than he had dared to anticipate for their first official date and he wasn't entirely prepared for the way his heart rate accelerated. When they broke apart, Alex sat down on the edge of his bed to avoid collapsing from the sudden head rush.

"You still have to choose," he said as soon as it cleared. "You can't get out of it with dirty tricks."

Rosalee picked at random, never taking her eyes off of Alex's as a slight smirk hovered at the corners of her mouth. Alex slid the tape into the VCR and retrieved the remote from the TV tray, as well as their snacks from his dresser. For the first quarter of the movie, they dipped potato chips into ice cream (which wasn't quite as good as french fries into Frostys) and Alex shared tidbits and behind-the-scenes information every so often, careful not to bore Rosalee.

When they had both satisfied their snacking, Alex set the container and bag on his nightstand and settled back against the pillows. He saw Rosalee hesitate out of the corner of his eye before snuggling down next to him, close enough to make him wonder how far out of her comfort zone she planned to venture that night. He was sure that every hair on his body was standing up, making him hyper-aware of each subtle movement she made, as though they were connected by pure static electricity. Eventually, she shifted to lace her fingers through his and he let out a slow breath as the subtle gesture made fireworks out of his nerve endings. True, they had held hands before, but this time felt different. She turned her head to rest her cheek against Alex's shoulder and he felt her warm breath against the shirt he suddenly wished he wasn't wearing. Then, unhelpfully, his mind's eye presented the dangerously tantalizing image of Rosalee wearing it instead.

Alex forced himself back to the movie and sat up briefly to swig more soda. He was still determined to avoid snoring or drooling in front of Rosalee. When he laid back again, she had slid down past the pillows and cushions and was propped up on her elbow. Alex readjusted to mirror her and watched the fingers on her free hand twitch ever so slightly between them, as though she might reach for him.

"Do you need anything?" said Alex, inching his fingers closer to hers on the comforter. "A blanket or anything?"

Rosalee shook her head. "I'm not cold."

Their eyes lingered and this time, Rosalee leaned in first and Alex closed his eyes to let her come in all the way. She kissed him cautiously, almost waiting for reassurance. Maybe the previous enthusiasm hadn't been *all* her, after all. Alex felt for her hand between them, then moved his hand up past her wrist, following the curve of her elbow to her shoulder and twisting his fingers lightly in her hair to draw her nearer. He tried not to get too carried away by the intoxicating sensation of the remaining lip gloss that turned her lips to satin as they moved against his but felt himself slipping further away from conscious thought.

When he opened his eyes again, Rosalee looked mildly concerned.

"Are you okay?" said Alex.

"Are *you?*"

How long had his eyes been closed?

"I'm just tired. I think I need to sit up again."

He did and Rosalee sat up next to him, her knees tucked up so that they rested partway across his lap. He wrapped an arm loosely around her waist and she snuggled into him, her warm breath tickling his neck.

Then her lips accidentally brushed the skin just above the collar of his shirt and Alex's pulse leapt again as he realized that it may not have been an accident. He felt his fingers curling into the material at the back of Rosalee's dress as she kissed all the way up his neck to his earlobe, which she took briefly and gently into her mouth. Then he was suddenly wide awake and embarrassed by the noise he had made involuntarily.

"What's gotten into you?" he said and they both laughed and then shushed each other to keep from waking Pete. "Have you been holding out on me?" said Alex, his eyes wide.

"Well, *yeah*. I haven't always been a nun."

Alex couldn't keep his eyes off of Rosalee's lips, which were subtly swollen now. "Me either."

Rosalee giggled, which was actually pleasant to hear when she wasn't doing it in response to a painful revelation of his soul. Then she turned in Alex's lap to straighten his collar.

"Okay, so say I'm a normal girl."

Alex frowned. "You *are* a normal—"

"Humor me."

"Okay ..."

"What would we be doing right now?"

Alex raised an eyebrow and Rosalee laughed and kissed him again, briefly, but enough to leave him a little bit breathless and make it that much harder to open his eyes again.

"What about me?" he said as soon as he could manage it.

"If *you* were a normal girl?"

"Right."

Rosalee winked. "Oh, we'd already be on the cigarette."

"Good to know." Alex wished she hadn't mentioned cigarettes. "Can I ask you something?"

"Shoot."

"How long has it been since it hurt? Being touched, I mean."

"Awhile, I guess. But the first time I really remember, it wasn't a person touching me, it was water."

"Water? What, like, after a belly flop or something?"

Rosalee shook her head.

"We were at a Fourth of July employee picnic for The Goose and I thought I had strained something the day before—a muscle in my back or something. It felt like pins and needles all down my leg, so I tried not to walk around too much. Then they got the water guns out."

Rosalee paused and Alex watched the muscles in her face tense as she remembered.

"I felt this jet of water just ... *rip* across that leg and it felt like being snapped by tons of rubber bands, or an electric current or something. I almost expected to see welts on my legs, but it was just my nerves—like they were fried or something."

"That sounds horrible."

"It wasn't great," said Rosalee, "but I think I'd prefer it to the ... squeezing."

"Squeezing?"

"That's what it feels like. I thought I was having a heart attack the first time it happened. It was like something tightening around my ribs hard enough to crack them and I couldn't breathe."

Alex wondered if the memory would make her claustrophobic and want to push him away, but she stayed.

"So, what do you do when those kinds of pain happen?" he said. "I mean what *can* you do?"

"With the second one, nothing. Just wait for it to stop. The first one, too, although sometimes steroids can make it go away faster.

Either way, I can't handle people touching me when they ... when it happens."

Alex watched Rosalee's eyes turn glassy in the glow of the television. He pressed his forehead into the space between her neck and her shoulder and waited while she took several calming breaths.

"I forgot what it felt like to *want* someone to—" Alex looked up at her again and Rosalee shook her head at the ceiling. "When you asked if you could touch me the other day ... I've barely let people hug me for months because I never know when the pain is going to start. And even though I seriously hope you'll forget the way I asked you to do it again—"

"Absolutely not," Alex said quietly.

"—*god,* I needed that." Rosalee squeezed his hand. "So, thank you."

Alex gently flexed each of her fingers as he held them against his chest and watched as her metallic purple nail polish caught the light. "Nothing's changed, you know."

"What do you mean?"

"I mean, you still need to tell me if I'm hurting you."

"I will."

"Yeah?" said Alex, meeting her eyes.

"Yeah."

"And if it's too much, or too fast, or too ... hard ..."

Danger, Will Robinson.

"I promise," said Rosalee, kissing him softly at the corner of his mouth.

Alex turned his head very slightly, felt her breath on his face, and suddenly Rosalee was on her back and pulling him with her. He cursed his shaky, traitorous breath for giving him away as he hovered over her, before Rosalee dragged him down by his shirt collar, claiming his mouth fervently, almost hungrily. Then his button-down was undone and discarded and she was lifting his T-shirt over his head. Alex felt his self-control haphazardly unraveling as Rosalee trailed her fingertips down his bare chest and he fumbled with the buttons on her dress. She sat up to help him, sliding the thin straps down her shoulders and pulling her undershirt over her head in one fluid movement so that finally, incredibly, there was nothing between them but velvet skin and chaotic heartbeats before the color behind Alex's eyelids blazed a brilliant royal blue.

He jolted awake and squinted at the end-of-tape screen. Rosalee was lying next to him, fully clothed, with his arm draped limply around her waist.

"How long was I out?" Alex croaked.

"Just a few minutes," said Rosalee, although she was smiling her private smile again and Alex hoped to baby Jesus that he hadn't become a sleep-talker. "You told me I needed to tell you if anything was ever too much, and then I'm pretty sure you started quoting *Lost in Space,* and then boom. Out."

Alex shook his head. "I'm sorry. I should have made a pot of coffee or something."

"Don't beat yourself up. *I* got to take a nap before our date."

Alex turned his head to kiss her shoulder and drink in as much of the real-life Rosalee as he could. "I should probably get you home."

They decided to make the short trip on foot, mostly because Alex worried that if he drove, he would ultimately fall asleep at the wheel and send them over a cliff. Too soon, they were walking up Rosalee's driveway, where he held onto her hand to keep her from moving up the stairs without him. She was already up the first step but turned back to face him, her head a few inches taller than his. Alex struggled to read her expression in the warm, yellow glow of the porch light at the top of the stairs, but as soon as her mouth curved into a smile, he reached out tentatively to brush her cheek with his thumb. Then her arms were around his neck and she was back off the step and into his arms.

Alex spun Rosalee a quarter of a turn and backed up against the brick wall, reluctant to break the kiss even as her feet hit the ground. He loosened his hold on her waist to cup her face in his hands and felt her hair fluttering against his cheek and tangling in his eyelashes as their lips moved together.

Several long moments later, Alex pulled away. His denim jacket scraped against the brick as Rosalee wrapped her arms around his waist and rested her chin on his shoulder.

"So, how's the hating me going?" he murmured into her hair.

"Not great."

"That's too bad."

Rosalee leaned back slightly to look at him. "Why?"

"Because I'm gonna need you to pinch me right now. Anywhere. Hard."

Rosalee laughed as he held her tighter.

Chapter 34

"T he story isn't all about you, you know."

"Oliver."

"What?" Oliver looked up at his older brother.

"Was that polite?" said Alex, raising his eyebrows.

Rosalee smiled into her scarf as they walked along the path that ran parallel to the creek behind Engelmann. Further down, it connected to the trail behind the main hospital. In fact, it was the same trail that Rosalee could use to travel between home, The Goose, and the hospital, if her bicycle wasn't flat-tired and useless.

"Wasn't it?" Oliver appeared to ponder Alex's question. "What I meant was, the story used to be more about the hero—not so much the mushy, gushy, *true love* stuff this one's into all of a sudden." He rolled his eyes at Rosalee, hooking a thumb toward Alex.

Rosalee laughed. "Is that right?"

She wasn't quite sure what Oliver meant by "the story," but maybe that was simply his way of describing his life with his brother and reminding Rosalee that Alex was *his* first.

"Yeah, well, can you blame him?" said Oliver, "His favorite book is *The Princess Bride,* so ... you get the picture." He pulled a face.

"You mean the movie?" said Rosalee.

"What?" Oliver glanced at Alex, who was trying to convey something to him with his strange sign language again. Rosalee finally recognized it as the "cut it" gesture. "I wasn't rude," said Oliver.

"No, you weren't," said Rosalee, casting a suspicious look at Alex. "But you said his favorite *book* was *The Princess Bride.* Don't you mean the movie?"

"No. I mean, he's seen the movie a lot, but he read the book until it fell apart. And then he taped it back together again. And then it fell apart again."

Rosalee gaped at Alex, who was squinted into the bright afternoon sky as an uncharacteristic blush crept up his neck.

"So much exaggerating," he muttered, still refusing to look at Rosalee or Oliver.

"I don't exaggerate," said Oliver, as though that closed the matter, then skipped ahead of them to lead the procession. "Where are we going, anyway?"

"Whichever way you want, buddy, but don't go too far ahead of us, okay?" said Alex.

He and Rosalee watched as Oliver cavorted through piles of crisp leaves on the path and picked up tree branch swords to brandish at invisible foes.

"So ... I never got around to giving you *The Princess Bride* to read," said Rosalee. "Which means that Oliver was referring to *your* copy, and you actually owe me big."

Alex sighed, shaking his head. "Name your price."

"I haven't decided yet." Rosalee nudged him playfully with her shoulder as they walked. "Maybe I'll demand pictures of you trick-or-treating with Oliver in your *Walker, Texas Ranger* getups."

"Mean. I wish you were coming, too."

"I know. But Robin's working late tonight and I promised Lola I'd help her hand out candy. Maybe next year."

The sound of their boots crunching through leaves and gravel sounded louder today. Everything tended to feel a little more still in the cold. Rosalee adjusted her scarf and jacket more securely around her to ward off the chill.

"Alex?"

He looked at her.

"Why is Oliver here? Like, at Engelmann?" She kept her voice low so that it wouldn't carry on the slight breeze.

Alex glanced at Oliver, still in his own world a little way ahead of them.

"A prank," he said quietly, and Rosalee was taken aback by the acid in his voice. "A stupid prank is what got him here."

He looked lost in thought and Rosalee wondered if she shouldn't have pushed the subject. "You don't have to talk about it. I get it. It's personal."

Alex shook his head irritably. "Stop that."

Rosalee waited, watching Oliver continue to taunt make-believe rivals.

"Oliver has always been prone to ... episodes," said Alex.

"Like the one on Bath Day?"

Alex nodded. "He just snaps. Something sets him off and that's it. He can get violent without really understanding what he's doing. I guess I already told you that part."

"Right." Rosalee couldn't help but glance at Alex's arm before remembering that, once again, he was wearing a coat.

"We were all getting along pretty well for a while." Alex kicked at a loose rock in the path so that it tumbled a foot or so ahead of him before he kicked it again. "Then things got bad again and he ended up switching schools, and the new school was worse."

"Worse how?"

"Everything. No one wanted to deal with him, so they stuck him in special ed. The other schools were out of district, even though they were nearby, so the bus wouldn't pick him up. Anyway, one day some of the kids from his bus got off at his stop, just for fun."

Rosalee felt as though she had swallowed an ice cube and wasn't sure she wanted to hear the rest. "Did they hurt him?"

Alex glanced at her warily.

"I don't think we'll ever know the whole story. Oliver wouldn't talk about it for a long time. We pieced most of it together, though, and somehow they convinced him to play with them. They ended up hopping a fence into someone's backyard to mess around in their empty hot tub."

Rosalee nearly tripped, so intent upon listening to Alex that she forgot to focus on her feet.

"Here," Alex held out his hand and Rosalee took it.

"Then what happened?" she said.

"Well, the tub *wasn't* empty, but somehow, they convinced Oliver to get in. Then they piled cinder blocks on the cover and left him there."

Rosalee stopped dead, a surge of disgust and horror rooting her to the path. Alex grimaced in response, his face pale and set, but tugged gently on her hand, nodding toward Oliver, who was beginning to pull further ahead of them.

When Rosalee spoke again, she struggled to keep her voice from shaking. "How long was he in there?" She glanced at Alex, who seemed to be chewing the inside of his cheek.

"We didn't find him until after dark. Someone heard him when they let their dog out, thank god. That was probably the longest day of my life."

Rosalee shuddered. "I can't even imagine."

"He's doing a lot better now, but I don't know if we'll ever be able to convince him to go back to school. And eventually ..."

"What?"

"Uh, nothing, I don't know what I was gonna say." Alex didn't quite meet Rosalee's eyes. "He's doing a lot better. He's also very perceptive, which is why he's coming over here, so act happy."

—•●•—

When Rosalee got home, she headed straight to the bathroom and cried. How she managed to hold it together in the car on the way home was undoubtedly some sort of miracle, but luckily for her, Alex had to drop her off quickly to head to yet another meeting and there was little time for lingering.

By the time she got up from the bathroom floor, she was hiccuping and a little sore from the prolonged contact of her joints with the tile, but she felt better. Somehow, that simple thought was a comfort. She had eventually realized that her abnormal crying and laughing "episodes" never concluded in a sense of relief. This time, it felt real.

Rosalee cleaned herself up in the sink, then wandered into her temporary room on the first floor. She still hadn't moved back upstairs—partially out of laziness, but partially because she worried that the act would trigger some sort of jinxing energy to bring her symptoms raging back. She stood staring at her bedside table before remembering that she wanted to check her email.

She wandered upstairs to find Ellie sitting on Evelyn's bed, painting her fingernails a deep aquamarine.

"Hey. Do you mind if I use the computer?" said Rosalee.

Ellie shook her head. Rosalee walked past the computer to open the window.

"Rosalee, it's freezing," Ellie complained as the brisk autumn breeze ruffled the curtains and permeated the room.

"Just until you're done, so we don't asphyxiate."

Rosalee sat at Evelyn's desk and waited for the computer to boot up.

"Where were you?" said Ellie. "With *Alex?*"

"*Maybe.* Where are Aunties?"

"Lola's teaching a class and Robin's at church."

Rosalee turned in her chair to look back at her sister. "Since when does she go to church?"

"She used to go all the time."

"Only when Evelyn made her."

Ellie shrugged.

"Also, it's Thursday," said Rosalee, frowning.

Ellie seemed to be concentrating hard as she awkwardly painted her left fingernails with her right hand. "It was some kind of bible study."

"That still seems weird."

For as long as Rosalee could remember, Robin had never expressed a desire to join any sort of church activity (with the exception of whatever volunteer function Evelyn signed them up for). She grappled with the various unlikely reasons that popped into her head before turning her attention back to Ellie.

"Wait, why are *you* home?"

"Weekend. My Friday class was only for twelve weeks, remember?"

"Right."

Twelve weeks. Wasn't that the length of Alex's anger management course? Rosalee was pretty sure.

Ellie capped her nail polish, then blew on her fingernails as she made her way over to shut the window. The slam startled Rosalee and she looked up briefly, then decided that the unnecessary force was probably a result of the odd angle at which Ellie held her fingers to avoid gouge marks in her fresh polish. Rosalee finally navigated to her inbox and felt the little zing of anticipation in her abdomen that she had come to associate with reading Alex's name there. Although she had seen him less than an hour ago, he had apparently sent her a quick message before his shift at Laurie's.

She clicked the little white envelope and wondered if Ellie would read over her shoulder. She decided to take the risk. So far, Alex had not shown himself to be a composer of steamy or mushy emails.

```
Hey Rosalee,

Just wanted to check in after today. I know everything
with Oliver is a lot, but if it helps, he really seems to
like you.

I have a two-hour break between meetings on Saturday. Can
I see you for a little bit? I couldn't remember if you're
at The Goose or doing your mural. Let me know either way
and I'll make it work on my end.

In case I don't talk to you later tonight, sleep well.

-Alex
```

"What happened with Oliver?"

Rosalee jumped slightly as Ellie squinted over her shoulder at the screen.

"I finally asked Alex why he was in there."

"And?"

"And I just finished crying about it. It was horrible."

"Tell me later?"

"If you want."

Rosalee reread the email and then began to draft a response.

```
Hi Alex,

I'm fine—just sad about Oliver. I'd love to see you
Saturday!
```

She stopped and deleted the last sentence.

"Why did you do that?" said Ellie.

"I wanna play hard to get a little."

"Why? Alex doesn't really seem like that kind of guy."

"I know, I just ... feel like I was a little too *easy* to get the other night."

"Whoa." Ellie gripped the back of the chair and spun Rosalee around to face her. "Back up."

Rosalee rolled her eyes. "Not like that." She swiveled back around to try another response.

```
Saturday should be fine. No set time for my mural and I'm
not scheduled for The Goose.
```

"Oh, come on," said Ellie.

"What?"

"*'Saturday should be fine'*?"

"Well, it *should* be," said Rosalee. "I don't want to seem too available, like I have nothing better to do than pine for him. C'mon, Ellie, all of your magazines preach this stuff."

Ellie didn't answer right away, but flopped back down on Evelyn's bed and slid a *Taste of Home* catalog off of her bedside table.

"I know," she said as she began to thumb through it, "I just think that maybe ... honesty is better. Now."

Rosalee looked at her sister properly and realized that she didn't look at all like her usual, bubbly self. Even her perky blond waves drooped.

"Are you okay?" she said.

"Yeah," said Ellie, but as she continued flipping pages without any particular enthusiasm, Rosalee noticed that her eyes weren't moving much and wondered if she was even reading.

Rosalee frowned but was prevented from prying any further when Lola stomped into the doorway, looking flushed and annoyed. She was still wearing her gym clothes and must have just gotten home.

"Did either of you take the chicken out to thaw? I left a note on the fridge this morning."

Rosalee jumped out of her chair, banging her knee on the desk leg. "I'm sorry, I forgot," she said, wincing. "Why don't we have the chicken tomorrow and I'll order a pizza tonight?"

Lola huffed. "Well, I guess we'll have to if we want to eat before ten o'clock tonight. I'm going to take a shower."

Rosalee watched her go, a little shaken. It wasn't like Lola to lose her temper very often—at least, not with Ellie and Rosalee.

"I feel awful. I totally forgot," said Rosalee, turning back to her sister.

Ellie raised her eyebrows coldly and returned the magazine to the side table, then hopped off the bed.

"What was that?" said Rosalee as she passed her in the doorway. "El, come on."

Ellie stopped just outside of Evelyn's room, not quite facing her. "It doesn't matter because it won't change anything."

Rosalee leaned against the door jamb, bewildered. "What are you talking about?"

Ellie sighed, then crossed her arms. "You don't pay attention."

"This again? I forgot a *chicken*. Big deal. It's not like we're having a dinner party or something. Besides, I remembered the Halloween candy."

"That's not the point. You're not *here* anymore. You don't listen."

"Listen to what? What am I missing?"

"Forget it. Call me when dinner's ready."

Rosalee watched her sister disappear down the hall and stood for a full five minutes staring at the opposite wall until she remembered that she was supposed to be ordering a pizza.

Chapter 35

A lex walked back down the path behind Rosalee's house and tried not to let his nervous anticipation of a looming phone appointment with his attorney dilute the perfectly pleasant afternoon he had just spent with her. From now on, he hoped it rained every day he knew her, after witnessing the way it brought her alive.

As soon as the drizzle had started, Rosalee led them a little way off the main path and into the foothills. She finally seemed mostly at ease with him and even swiped a piece of long grass to hold in her mouth at one point. However, as endearing as he found that, he soon discovered that it effectively got in the way of other things he wanted to do to her mouth and found it increasingly difficult to banish the wild thoughts that entered his head every time they passed the inviting shelter of a tree or bushes. Would she forgive him for the thoughts? Was she having them, too? Surely, she knew by now that Alex wasn't a caveman and the ball was still most definitely in her court. That being said, if she had a sudden urge to slam him against a tree and have her way with him, he wouldn't stop her (although he would try to keep the celebratory whooping to a minimum, for dignity's sake).

Too soon after their rainy adventure, they had made it back to Rosalee's house, but she insisted on staying farther down the bank than usual as they said goodbye and kept glancing in the direction of her backyard.

"Are you, like, *grounded* or something?" Alex said finally. "Why are we hiding?"

"Oh. I'm—we're not. Sorry."

Alex resisted the urge to admonish her for her apology. Overall, she was doing much better. "Still rough at home?"

Rosalee had written several emails over the past week about the growing tension between various family members, but he avoided bringing it up when they were together unless she did first. Alex thoroughly enjoyed forgetting his problems while they were together, so he wasn't about to deny her the same luxury.

"I don't know what's wrong with everyone," said Rosalee, and Alex could already see the tension settling back onto her shoulders like a heavy but familiar backpack. "Maybe I *don't* pay attention."

"People say a lot of things they don't mean when they're in pain."

"Yeah, but that's what makes it so bad. I should *know* where the pain is coming from. They're my family."

Alex squeezed her hand.

"Anyway. I'm trying to just be *here*. With you." Rosalee shook her head. "When can I see you next?"

Alex felt a little swoop in his stomach every time she said that, accompanied by his usual fantasies of quitting all his jobs and responsibilities and whisking her off to a remote mountaintop to live out the rest of their days.

"Well, I'm hoping at Angela's party, if we're still going," he said. For now, that would have to do.

"Definitely."

Rosalee smiled at him, but there was something else in the smile. If Alex didn't know better, he would say it was something a little like longing.

"What are you thinking?" he said.

"Nothing helpful."

"Try me anyway."

"I wish you didn't have to work so much. Or so hard. For selfish reasons."

He could give his two weeks' notice that night. Two weeks was plenty of time to get both of their affairs in order.

"Probably best, though," said Alex, pushing those ideas aside. *For now, anyway.* "Maybe I want you to miss me. For selfish reasons."

Rosalee looked at him, all eyes in her pale face before tilting it slightly to kiss him, softly—surely. Alex kept his eyes shut for an extra second after she moved away, then frowned.

"What are *you* thinking?" said Rosalee.

"Nothing helpful."

Rosalee waited and Alex studied the tiny raindrops that clung to her hair, which was now dark and wavy from the extra moisture. He tugged on the sash of her raincoat, pulling her against him, and they were like magnets again—the right ends—and if he didn't leave soon, he was going to be very, *very* late for his phone call.

He broke away reluctantly, heavily. "I have to go."

"Because you have an appointment."

Alex nodded mechanically. "I have an appointment."

"With your attorney."

"With my attorney."

Rosalee grinned. "Sounds fancy."

She was lifting the spell, at least enough for Alex to properly assess his surroundings. Suddenly, the air felt much colder. "I'm using very particular words to make you think that."

Rosalee looked suddenly suspicious. "... You're not meeting with *yourself,* are you?"

Alex smiled. "No, this guy actually passed the bar."

"And I can't do anything to keep you here?"

Rosalee's voice was low and velvety, drawing him in again. She looked innocent enough with her hands in her coat pockets, but Alex was quickly learning not to underestimate her.

"Out here? In the open?" He raised an eyebrow. "Not anything legal."

Now, Alex continued down the path alone, listening to his boots splashing through shallow puddles and the occasional sound of a woodpecker drilling into tree trunks or siding. He tilted his head back and breathed in the lingering moisture in the chill, autumn air, trying to smell all of the things that Rosalee had described. What had she called it—"manticore"? No, that couldn't be right. He would have to email her later to clarify.

The problem was that it was difficult to absorb what Rosalee was saying, especially when she was in her element. There was also a new playful quality that sparked in her eyes when he forgot himself and stared too long. Anyway, Alex was sure that asking her to blindfold him whenever they talked wasn't the best idea—she might think he was some sort of freak. Or, worse, that he didn't *want* to look at her. It was probably a matter of exposure—like a deer caught in the headlights—he just needed time to adjust to the blinding effect she tended to have on him.

Alex arrived back at his apartment and fit his key in the lock just in time to hear the phone ringing in the kitchen.

————•●•————

"Look, it's better than nothing, kid," said Glen.

Alex sat at the kitchen table with the phone wedged between his ear and his shoulder, the cord stretching from the wall mount next to the fridge. He raked his fingers through his hair and resisted the urge to get up and slam the receiver back into its cradle. "I sent *two* letters from employers *and* one from Engelmann," he said, struggling to keep his voice even.

"Brenneman said that one of the jobs was temporary."

"It's construction—*all* of the jobs are temporary."

"Can you get another one?"

Alex leaned on one elbow and pressed the receiver into the side of his head. There were always construction jobs, but he wasn't exactly the most experienced guy and so, not very in demand. Manny was his lifeline there, and he would be gone for the next month at a job in Colorado Springs. Alex might have considered going with him, but it was way too long to abandon Oliver—not to mention the only other income he had.

"I'll try," he said warily.

"In the meantime, I think you'll be pleased to know that I've decided to relieve you of your Alcoholics Anonymous obligations a month early."

"Oh. Well, thanks."

"You know, sometimes you have to take every little victory you can." Glen's voice was suddenly stern. *"I expected you to be more appreciative."*

Alex knew he should have been grateful, but as troublesome as the meetings had been, he had to admit that a part of him found relief in them.

"Besides," Glen continued, *"If you're as busy as you sound, I'd say fewer meetings is certainly a victory."*

"No, you're right." Alex forced himself to sit up straight again. "I do appreciate it. I was just hoping to have made more headway. Minimizing damages and everything." He felt more and more like a sullen child as he narrowly prevented his tongue from shaping the words "This isn't fair."

"And we have been," said Glen. *"We've successfully minimized the amount of additional damage inflicted upon your less-than-stellar record. As for the financial aspect, we're incredibly lucky that Brenneman has allowed you to pay off your debt over a year."*

"And the amount you emailed me is the final one?"

"Not including interest."

Alex bit back a swear word. He was barely keeping his head above water as it was. "Are you sure we have no leverage with the harassment angle?"

"Not without proof."

"They don't have any proof that I swung at him, either," Alex muttered.

"Be grateful for that," Glen said sharply. *"Rest assured your situation would be much more tedious."*

"Alright, okay. So what about statements from other employees?"

"People who may have witnessed the harassment?"

"Exactly."

"I'm not sure it would make much of a difference in the end."

"What, standing up for what's right wouldn't make a difference?"

"Not when what you're talking about is basically defending someone's honor."

"What do you mean?"

Alex heard what sounded like the flick of a Bic on Glen's end of the line, followed by a deep pull and exhale.

"He wasn't in the room, right?"

"He was at first."

"But you didn't have to shove him out of the way or step in front of him to absorb a punch—that sort of thing?"

"No, I guess not."

"So, it's back to who has the most power, unfortunately."

Alex chewed on the skin next to his thumbnail. "And it's definitely Brenneman?"

"As I said before, you were on his property and so was the damage."

"I know. *I know*, I just feel like there has to be some loophole somewhere."

"I'm doing all I can to negotiate for you."

A sharp ray from the sinking sun appeared between the slats of the kitchen blinds, shining directly into Alex's eyes. He got up to close them. "Maybe the looming threat of a lawsuit would be enough."

"Maybe. But not until someone speaks up."

"Yeah. I guess not."

"Well, listen, I've gotta run, but I'll let you know if there are any more updates."

"I appreciate it."

"Bye now."

Alex stared at the phone in his hand, letting the disconnected tone drill into his brain for a long moment before getting up from the table and replacing it on its base. He glanced at the oven clock—forty-five minutes until he had to leave for work. He had expected the call to take longer and had only just decided to take a half-hour nap when the phone rang again. He answered and immediately heard snuffling on the other line.

"Hello?" he said again, struggling to comprehend the confused din on the other end of the line.

Eventually, he heard a shaky sigh, followed by a voice he immediately recognized.

"... Hi, honey."

His stomach dropped. "Mom?" The last conversation he had had with his mother that started like this had ended with Oliver being sent to Engelmann. "What's up?"

"I finally got ahold of the insurance company and they denied the claim."

"... What?"

"They won't extend the medical trial period," said Carol, her voice rising hysterically. *"So that's it."*

"What, just like that? We have to pull him out?"

Carol didn't answer and Alex sat down in the hard kitchen chair again. He tasted blood and realized he was chewing the inside of his cheek. "Jesus *goddamned* Christ."

"Alexander."

"Well? Mom?" Sometimes there were no other words and right now, there were no other words. (Actually, he could think of quite a few, but none were any more polite.) "So, what do we do?" Back into a child, within seconds. The sound of his mother crying on the other line was almost more than he could take. "How much is it without insurance?" he pressed.

"More than the mortgage."

Alex closed his eyes briefly as waves of hopelessness threatened to drown him. "Can we get a loan?"

"I'm trying."

"I'll try, too."

Maybe Pete could swing something, although Alex would probably need some sort of collateral. Would his Jeep be enough?

"He'll have to come back to Denver," said Carol.

"He's not gonna go back to that school, Mom."

"Maybe we can convince the other one to take him back."

It was only in an effort not to break his mother completely that Alex said "Maybe."

A muffled ambulance siren wailed through the phone.

"Mom? Where are you?"

"I'm on my lunch break. I have to go back soon."

Alex glanced at the clock. "You know, if the insurance won't cover him anymore, maybe you should just move up here. Losing your insurance was your whole argument."

"I'd still have to sell the house and get a job."

"I'll help you," said Alex automatically.

Eventually, he would have nothing left. One day, maybe soon, the well would run dry and he would be stuck at the bottom of the barren pit, scrabbling and scraping at the merciless, unyielding stone. Then again, did Prometheus ever run out of livers? Was Alex destined for the same fate (and could he possibly deserve it)? Or were these merely the sins of the father, catching up to him already?

He heard a hiccup on the other line. *"I don't know honey."* Carol sounded every bit as exhausted as he felt. *"I didn't want you to find out before I told you."*

Alex tilted his head toward the ceiling and squeezed his eyes shut. "Okay," was all he could muster.

"I love you and I'll talk to you later. Give Oliver my love, too."

"We love you, too, Mom."

This time, Alex replaced the receiver right away, then paced back and forth across the apartment. It was only three and a half steps from the front door to the edge of the kitchen, but he traced and retraced those steps, hands locked behind his head as he tried to divine an answer or source of calm from the spongy ceiling tiles. His weight on the linoleum made little popping sounds as the vinyl gapped away from the subfloor, and the more he walked, the more hopeless and claustrophobic he became. What he needed was more space. The floor creaked slightly as he made his way over to his coat, hanging on a hook by the door. What he *really* needed was a cigarette.

Alex rummaged in his pockets, then decided that he must have left the new pack in his car and grabbed his keys. Then he paused, glancing at the oven clock again. He had twenty-five minutes before he had to be at work. Was that still enough time for a nap? Not likely. Or a shower? He felt clammy and stale, but a quick pit test proved that his deodorant, at least, hadn't let him down. Besides, what was the point of getting all cleaned up, only to be re-saturated with mop and bus tub water? On the other hand, he always thought better in the shower. In his less responsible days, he woke up in the middle of the day and got ready for work with a shower and a beer.

Did they even *have* any beer?

Alex paused for another fraction of a second before walking back around the island to the fridge and peering in. He spotted most of a six-pack of PBR in the back, likely left over from his birthday party so many months ago, and reached in to grab one just as he heard a key in the front door lock. He took a Coke instead and nodded at Pete as they passed each other, like two ships in the night.

Chapter 36

Two days later, Alex turned a bronze sobriety chip over and over in his fingers as nausea lapped at his intestinal lining. The cold weight of the small metal token had become a source of comfort over the past few months that he had clearly taken for granted. Here, in his room, away from the dusty, fluorescent lighting and dingy, ancient tiles of the YMCA basement, stabs of regret mingled with the shame eating him from the inside. As much as Alex lived for a good plot twist, so far, he wasn't loving the one about the closeted alcoholic coming to terms with the truth after his obligatory meetings were over.

He flipped the coin again, his thumb brushing over the number "3" stamped in a circle and framed by a triangle. Three months in AA, out the window. He gave the coin a final turn before dropping it into a sock, where it clinked with his thirty and sixty-day coins. He folded it with the second sock, balled the whole thing up, and stuffed it in the back of his dresser drawer. Maybe someday, he would start over, but today was definitely not the day, and tomorrow didn't look promising either.

Alex ran his fingers through his hair and wondered how many days it had been since he'd showered. Only one—he was pretty sure—but it felt greasy. As he crossed the hall to the bathroom, he averted his eyes from the kitchen, resisting the temptation of the last can of beer in the new six-pack he had opened after work the night before. In the bathroom, he stripped and turned on the hot water, then surveyed himself in the mirror. He looked rough. He noticed a faint tinge of purple under his eyes from too little sleep and a shadow around his face. He could use a shave and a haircut before he looked like a mangy vagrant. What would Rosalee think?

God. Rosalee.

How long had it been since he'd talked to her? Alex pulled the days apart in his mind through a spike of panic and comforted himself that he had only missed two days of communication with her. Maybe she hadn't even noticed. He would call her after his shower. Or maybe send an email, depending on how soon he had to get to work.

However, with thirty minutes left until he had to leave, Alex couldn't quite summon the strength to stop by the library and bring her into the loop of the personal hell he'd been living for the past few days. While he was sure she would be sympathetic to most parts of the story, and even that she would be kind about his most recent slip-up, he was willing to bet that she wouldn't be so impressed with the fact that the slip-up was becoming a conscious landslide of bad decisions, up to and including the second beer he was enjoying since his shower and before his shift. Granted, two beers were barely enough to get him buzzed (although his tolerance had shifted in the past few months), but he knew it was irresponsible.

"Hey, Rosalee," Alex muttered as he swiped the cordless phone off of its base in the living room. "Sorry I've been *incommunicado* lately. Stuff came up and I didn't want to burden, um … you. Good lord."

It would probably be best to wing it. He dialed her number and waited for several rings before the answering machine picked up.

"Hey, Rosalee, it's me … uh, Alex. Listen, things have been crazy. Won't bore you with details now. Looking forward to seeing you this weekend, though. Talk to you later."

That would have to do, he thought, as he chugged the rest of his beer and rummaged in his desk for the pack of gum he bought with it. He might be irresponsible at the moment, but he wasn't stupid. Right now, his job at Laurie's was his only job, and even though *he* knew that he was perfectly capable of performing his bussing, stocking, and dishwashing duties with a couple of brewskis on board, he didn't trust that his employers would feel the same way. Besides, his only hope right now to bring in more money was to appeal to Mr. Laurie for more hours. *Maybe not tonight.*

Alex kicked himself as he realized that tonight might have been his best opportunity since Wednesdays tended to be a little slower. Maybe if he walked to the cafe, he could work off some of his nervous energy and hype himself up to talk to Mr. Laurie, after all. Or he would show up sweaty and agitated, with alcohol radiating out of his pores. He needed to get a grip. But more hours at work left no chance of resuming AA meetings, and there wasn't really anyone in his life that he could talk to about it otherwise. Pete was too perfect. Manny would be sympathetic, but tell him to go back to AA. But Rosalee ...

Alex still hadn't gotten to the bottom of whatever spawned her fear of being touched—and he was fairly certain that it *was* fear beyond the anticipation of unexpected pain. He had also noticed that she seemed weird about alcohol on the rare occasions they were around it. At the very least, he knew she didn't drink.

Maybe it would be better for everyone if Alex took Oliver back to Denver. That way, his mother wouldn't have to move or try to sell her house, and she and Alex wouldn't have to kill themselves trying to pay for Oliver's residence. On the other hand, he knew that Oliver couldn't and wouldn't go back to either of his previous schools in Denver, no matter how much progress he had made at Engelmann. Maybe he could be homeschooled instead, but with Carol working full-time, who would do it? Once again, it would be up to Alex to hold the family together.

As Alex gathered his keys and wallet and slipped them into his coat pockets, his gaze fell on the front door and he thought suddenly of a wall hanging in his mother's house that had been there since before he could remember. "Take Me Home, Country Roads," was Carol's favorite John Denver song, and those words appeared in cross-stitched letters, with embroidered mountains below. Alex thought of it every time he heard that song—and again, he was struck by the realization of yet another source of comfort he had taken for granted. At twenty-five, he could hardly call his mother's house "home" anymore, although there were certain moments when Rosalee made him feel like maybe he could find it again in Rabbitbrush.

He felt a little lurch in his stomach as he realized how much Oliver was probably also aching for home—although in his case, that home was still in Denver, with their mother. Then again, so many of Alex's fondest memories of his childhood stemmed from school, and Oliver definitely didn't have many of those. Maybe being with their mother again would be enough to ease the ache. Maybe having both of them in Rabbitbrush would feel like home to Alex, too.

Chapter 37

By late Saturday afternoon, Alex felt less like he was lying in an empty well and more like he was anchored to the bottom while torrential rain sent little rivers down the stones to buoy him up and then drown him. The entire week had passed in a blur, which only made the list of things he had to fix increasingly insurmountable. By the time he got home from Laurie's, sweaty and exhausted, he was beyond grateful that Pete wasn't home because he wanted nothing more than to kick back with a six-pack and the rest of his cigarettes.

An hour later, Alex was nearly frozen to the back porch. But far from feeling better, he was only getting more riled up and wished he had something stronger to dull his insides. Luckily, he did. He had been unable to resist driving past the liquor store near the highway on his way home the night before (although it was in the other direction). So, he brushed off the ash that had gathered on his coat and jeans, then stood to go inside.

Pete likely had proper drinking glasses, but he might be home soon and Alex didn't love the idea of his roommate walking in on him indulging by himself, so he dug a plastic Pizza Hut cup out from the back of the cupboard and poured a generous helping of whiskey in. He carried both the cup and the bottle into his room so that he could hide the bottle in the back of his closet, like some delinquent teenager.

———— •●• ————

When Alex got off of his bed and stumbled to the bathroom some time later, he knew he had overdone it. He didn't even trust himself to stand up to pee and sat instead, his elbows digging into his knees and leaving bright red circles in his skin. When he got up and braced himself against the counter, he could feel a tightening in his chest that never meant anything good. He was startled by the sudden clangor of the phone ringing in the kitchen, but by the time he staggered out of the bathroom, the ringing had stopped. Probably Pete calling to say he would be late again. Or that Alex hadn't gotten the loan. As courteous of a front as his roommate had projected at their meeting several days before, Alex could see that his case was hopeless.

He wandered into the kitchen anyway and was a little surprised to find himself there. The tightness was still constricting his breathing, the weight of the past week pressing in on him with the steady and calculated purpose of a pillow to the face.

He glanced at the phone on the wall, then snatched up the receiver and stared at it, feeling lightheaded. Then he sat hard in a kitchen chair, which tipped back on two legs and gave him an unexpected hit of adrenaline as he dialed a number he shouldn't have known by heart.

Glen answered on the fourth ring.

"We have to think of something else," said Alex, his voice raw and pathetically weak in his ears.

"Who is this? Alexander, is that you?"

Alex could feel the moisture building painfully behind his eyes and squeezed them shut.

"We have to think of something because I can't pay for rent, and Oliver, and help Mom sell her house, and pay off that asshole all at the same time. There's another way. There has to be."

"Another way to...?"

"To stahlp it. To stall it, I mean. *God.*" Alex tried to take a deep breath. He couldn't let Glen know he was drunk or he would never agree to help.

"Look, I told you I'd do my best."

Alex could feel the subtle accusation bleeding through the phone again, although Glen never said it aloud: *This is your mess. I could just let you deal with it.*

"I know I screwed up," said Alex, and he was grateful that the words didn't come out high and full of self-pity. They came from where they were supposed to—deep in his chest, where he still couldn't breathe comfortably, but somehow, he could talk.

Except that now he was out of words again. Because what good would it do to confess his regret for the split-second decision that had gotten him into this mess? Glen would be glad to hear about the remorse that twisted Alex's stomach and hopefully taught him a lesson, but the guilt for Alex wasn't about the fight or losing his job—it was the fact that he still drove home. It was that even though the thought of his mother picking him up with Oliver looking scared in the backseat was enough to make him feel sober, he wasn't. The adrenaline didn't mean he wasn't still wasted. He could have killed someone that night—more than that—*people,* plural. The risk in itself was something for which he would never forgive himself.

And now, it seemed that everyone's future was in his hands—Carol and Oliver were counting on him more than ever before. It was all too much to handle and Alex could feel everything that he had been stuffing down for the past week—really, the past few months—fighting to burst out of him. But he forced it down again. *Deep* down again.

"I'm sorry to call like this," he said, wiping his damp palms, one by one, on his jeans, then clearing his throat to keep his voice from shaking. But when he tried to suck in another deep breath, his throat ached in protest. "I just ... I don't know what else to do. I'm doing the best I can, Dad."

Alex felt his voice break on the last word and the heat rise to his face from his slip-up, but at this point, he couldn't afford to be proud anymore. The moments passed slowly and Alex began to count in his head. If he reached fifteen, he decided, he would hang up.

At nine, he heard a muffled cough on the other end of the line.

"I'll see what I can do. Just, uh ... hang in there."

The call was disconnected and Alex felt the air rattle back into his lungs. He set the receiver down on the table and laid his head on his arm before it rang again. His vision swam as he lifted his head and answered to hear Rosalee's voice.

"Hey, are you on your way?"

Alex could feel his brain struggling toward reasonable thoughts like bicycle wheels through mud.

"Angela said we could show up whenever," said Rosalee, *"but I wasn't sure if you had to work a double after all."*

His stomach clenched and then turned. *The party.* He had made plans with Rosalee tonight—how could he have forgotten that?

"Yeah, so ... bad news there." *I'm drunk out of my freaking mind.*

"You have to work."

Alex shook his head, hating himself. "I do." He cleared his throat, pushing against the tightness.

Rosalee sighed on the other line. *"Well, that sucks."*

"I know, sorry. But rest assured, he will be murdered with bare hands or a ... spatula. When he's back."

"Who?"

"That... sonofabitch waiter. New one."

"Okay, well I don't think I'm gonna go, then."

"What? Why?"

"Um, because I was only gonna go if you were going, so..."

"But you want—" Alex suppressed a hiccup. "—to be friends with Angela again, right? And Pete?"

"Yes, but I can figure out some other way to do that without a million people around."

Alex scoffed. "You *won't.*"

Rosalee paused. *"I won't* what?"

"You won't figure out a way. 'Some other way.'" Could anyone afford to wait around for some other way? "Rosalee, you can't just expect people to carry you around through ... what's hard. You eventually—You'll have to climb on that saddle yourself."

"Are you—why do you sound funny?" said Rosalee.

"I just woke up from a nap." Alex was disgusted at how easily the lies were coming. "I'm not awake yet."

"Okay, well, I'm not some spoiled princess who can't ... get on a horse by herself."

Alex sighed and rolled his forehead against the cool wood of the kitchen table.

"That's not—" Another hiccup. "—what I said. What *actually* did I say to you, Rosalee?"

"Stop talking to me like I'm a child. I'm not your little brother, Alex, I'm your—"

Alex raised his head again. "... Yes?"

"Nothing."

"No, go on going, you're my ...?"

"I guess I'm not sure. I thought maybe tonight would clarify that a little bit, but since you're not coming now ..."

"Oh, gimme a break, Rosalee. I said I was sorry."

"It's fine, it doesn't matter."

"Oh, sure. Okay, Miss I-don't-care-about-any-thing-and-you-can't-make-me. Little Miss Rosalee Two Point Oh." Alex felt his misplaced anger inflating rapidly. "Didn't think I'd be meeting you tonight and don't really want to."

"So then don't."

"Okay, so I won't."

"Okay, so I'm hanging up."

"Fine, but wait, Rosalee, listen ..." Alex clutched the phone to his face. "You don't get to just mope in your room because you're mad at me. Go to the dumb party."

"You can't tell me what to do."

"I can and ... I do."

"Excuse me?"

"Everyone tells you, Rosalee. You let them. You can't do anyone—I mean any*thing*—until someone holds your hand."

"Jesus, Alex, are you drunk?" said Rosalee, then more quietly. *"Are you?"*

Alex squeezed his eyes shut, his mouth set in a grimace. "... It was an accident."

"It was an accident that you got drunk and canceled on me by lying that you had to work?"

"Look, people drink, Rosalee."

"Well, you said that you didn't. What about your meetings?"

"Done. Don't have to go anymore."

"Clearly."

Rosalee's dripping sarcasm reignited Alex's fuse. *"Don't,"* he said, "Just because you've never done anything stupid or messed up in your whole life."

"I have too messed up."

"Not for real. You're like that princess with all the elves."

"… You mean dwarves? Snow White?"

"Yeah, her."

"How?"

"You're so naive and pure and sheltered."

Alex heard a *"tsk"* over the phone, then *"Alex … do you need me to come over?"*

"No, I need to sleep," he snapped.

"I don't know if you should *sleep yet."*

"I'm a grown-ass man, Rosalee. I can take care of myself, but I can't take care of you and everyone, okay?"

"I never asked you to, Alex. You're the one who pursued me and you're the one who lied to me and canceled on me tonight."

"You're right, I did. All of it for which … I will take the fault. My fall. I will, and you know what? I'll do you also this favor and un-pursue you, okay? It's all—Is it better?"

"Alex, come on. Just let—"

"And then," said Alex, talking over her, "maybe you can do *me* a huge favor and *grow up.*"

Alex heard a sharp intake of breath before the line went dead. He held the receiver to his chest and groaned, letting his weight carry him down the wall, where he sprawled with his legs out in front of him on the linoleum.

Chapter 38

Rosalee stared at the phone in her hand and had the strange sensation that she wasn't inside of her body. As she hung up the cordless phone in Evelyn's bedroom, she had to try several times to make the metal tabs line up.

Maybe you can do me a favor and grow up.

The words pinged to the back of her brain and then launched themselves forward again to embed themselves in the backs of her eyeballs, making them sting. She tried to remember the last time she had felt a betrayal of this magnitude. Maybe her sweet-tempered rabbit biting her when she was twelve. She wondered fleetingly if her parents' abandonment should have come first on the list and whether or not she was a black-hearted person for deciding that it didn't.

Alex was drunk, she reminded herself. 'Real Alex' would never have said those things to her. *He was drunk.* But she had stopped hanging out with Connor because she didn't want to be around that stuff anymore—at least, that's the story she told herself. But was that even true? Whether or not Connor had access to all of the tools for the bad choices Rosalee had wanted to make at that point in her life, they were *her* bad choices. She also knew that Connor probably would have hung out with her without them.

Either way, Rosalee didn't feel like going to a party. Maybe a walk. It wasn't very often that she was all dressed up with nowhere to go.

Besides, it was a "good energy" day and she was feeling restless. Unfortunately, the downside of having so little energy on a regular basis meant that on good days she had to discourage herself from spending it all at once.

Rosalee laced up her hiking boots, even though they were not meant for the flimsy material of the tights she was wearing and she would undoubtedly rub blisters into her heels, then shoved her keys into her coat pocket. She didn't leave a note—her aunts already thought she was going to the party.

• ● •

As Rosalee walked along the creek, she tried to remember if anything she knew about Alex's world had been bad enough lately to send him over the edge. Again, she felt that jolt associated with being suddenly out of the loop—of staring into a familiar room, only to realize that someone moved all of the furniture in the second it took you to look away. Why were people so reluctant to let her in? Was she really so self-involved that she was missing the obvious signs?

Rosalee heard leaves crunching nearby and looked around to see a small boy about Oliver's age walking along the bank, an off-leash golden retriever trotting dutifully beside him. Every now and then, the boy picked up a branch and poked at the semi-frozen creek, making the thin layer of ice crackle. Rosalee looked around them, a little disturbed by the fact that the boy seemed to be alone except for the dog. While the boy crouched to investigate the underside of a large rock, she lingered nearby, pretending to retie her shoelaces. After several minutes of this charade, Rosalee, the boy, and the dog had moved about half a mile down the bank.

Why wasn't someone worried about the boy—or watching? Rosalee felt a tightening in her chest as she thought about how lucky Oliver was to have a brother like Alex. (*He was just* drunk, *for god's sake.*) But who did Alex have? Anyone? As much as she hoped that he and Pete would be best friends, they didn't see each other very much. A twig snapped next to Rosalee and she was beginning to wonder if she would have to follow the explorers all night when a woman's voice called from somewhere in the distance behind her.

"C'mon, Rufus," the boy said, slapping his leg.

Rosalee thought the command was probably unnecessary, as the dog would have clearly followed the boy anywhere. She watched as they turned back the way they had come, and looked back every so often until she was sure she saw the boy walk up to his back door. There were no street lamps back here, but most of the houses had installed or strung lights of some sort to help illuminate the long path that ran parallel to the creek. Rosalee wondered briefly how long it would take someone to find her if she slipped quietly into the water and let herself float along in the icy current. She tripped over a rock while she was busy admonishing herself for the thought.

Eventually, she reached the edge of Connor's backyard and wondered if that was where she had subconsciously meant to end up all along. The familiar yard was unfenced and fairly small, consisting mostly of crabgrass and weeds, plus a cement slab with a few rusty lawn chairs and a barbecue.

"Rosalee?"

She squinted to see a figure sitting in a lawn chair directly under the porch light. Fighting down the twinge of nervousness in her stomach, she made her way over, stopping as soon as she was close enough to see the figure properly. Connor had one leg crossed over his knee, where he balanced a drawing book with a mini book light clipped to the edge. She could see multiple pencils stuffed into the spiral ring, and he clutched his trusty, once white art eraser in his non-drawing hand.

"What are you working on?" said Rosalee.

She wondered if he would tell her to go away, but Connor motioned for her to sit down, so she sat carefully in the lawn chair next to him, feeling one of the legs lift away from the uneven cement. He looked the same as he always had, with long-ish, light brown hair that hung curly and unkept in his face, mostly obscuring pale blue eyes that looked darker when he concentrated. Rosalee detected the smell of pot that clung to his clothes and the body spray he used to cover it up.

He tilted the notebook toward Rosalee to show her two drawings of a car; the first of the smooth body and the second, what appeared to be a cross-section of the same car detailing all of its inner workings.

"It's a 1958 Plymouth Fury," he said. "That's the Golden Commando engine." He pointed with his pencil toward the cross-section of the hood.

"That's great, Connor. Really." Rosalee leaned closer to study all of the pumps, tubes, and valves that had been meticulously included in the drawing. "You should think about illustrating car magazines or something."

Connor smiled slightly before pulling the book back into his lap. "Sorry if I don't seem happy to see you."

"I figured you might not be."

"No, I'm just, like, pretty baked." Connor brushed his hair out of his eyes. "Sorry."

"It's okay. I could've called."

"My parents said you did."

"Right." Rosalee didn't bother clarifying. It didn't matter. "I sent you a couple emails, too."

"I never check it."

"Oh."

"I got 'em, though."

Rosalee nodded. "Good."

"Kinda missed you, ya know?" Conner erased a stray mark he had made on the drawing when he pointed out the engine.

Rosalee watched him shade a section of the car's hood, then smudge it with his fingers and carve out highlights with his eraser before blowing away the remnants. She wasn't sure she could return the sentiment.

Connor looked up and seemed to gather that from her silence. "Just, like … going from seeing you almost every day to not," he said.

"Oh. Yeah, that was …" Somehow, "nice" didn't seem like the right word, although it had been nice to escape for a while.

"It wasn't just the sex, either. If that's what you were thinking."

"I wasn't."

Rosalee tried not to think about the sex at all, even though it had definitely been her idea in the first place.

"Like, my routine didn't change a whole lot," said Connor. "I still draw and listen to music or whatever, but it was better with you."

Rosalee smiled. "Yeah, that was pretty cool."

"You still draw?"

"Sometimes. I mostly stick to painting now."

Connor began to add reflections to the car's windows. "What kinds of things do you paint?"

"I did some animal chairs for the hospital. I'm doing a mural there, too."

"A whole mural?"

"Yeah."

"On a whole wall?"

"Yup."

Connor stopped drawing and looked out across the yard, eyebrows raised. "That's dope."

"Thanks." Rosalee smiled, letting herself relax a little bit. It was so easy to just *be* with Connor. She never had to think about what to say or agonize over how she looked.

"Thanks for the emails," he said, finally looking at her.

"I figured I should explain. You kinda freaked me out with your phone call."

"Yeah, well, I knew your aunt was out for my blood and I was scared she was gonna get it."

"What?"

"I had to check to see if she was working before I could call you."

"I still don't understand."

"I ran from The Goose."

Rosalee felt her mouth fall open. "Why didn't you find a pay-phone?"

"I *did*."

"Maybe you need to stop smoking so much. I think it's affecting your lung capacity. Oh, and be *nicer* to little kids who need to use the phone."

"What?"

"The kid you were yelling at when you called me?" Rosalee had forgotten how tedious it was to attempt a conversation with someone who was high as a kite—unless, of course, you were, too.

"Oh, right," said Connor, irritably flicking away some stray bits of eraser. "That wasn't a kid, that was a Gremlin."

Rosalee laughed in spite of herself and Connor smiled, the dimples in his cheeks appearing briefly.

"You still smoke? Drink? Anything?" he said.

"Uh ... no. I quit cold turkey before I left."

Connor watched her for several seconds before going back to his drawing. "What was it like?"

"Quitting?"

"No, that hippy-go-ya-ya camp they made you go to."

"Oh." Rosalee stretched her legs out in front of her, resting the heels of her boots on the concrete. "It was cool. Good for learning coping mechanisms and I got to be outside a lot. Plus, there were activities planned for every minute of the day, so there was less time to … get lost in my thoughts, I guess."

"What kind of coping mechanisms?"

"Like … overcoming negative thoughts, clearing your mind and tuning into your breathing … that sort of thing."

"Did you sing 'Kumbaya'?"

Rosalee smiled. "Almost."

Connor contemplated his drawing. "Maybe I should go to one of those camps."

Rosalee watched his brow furrow almost imperceptibly. She had never really talked about deep stuff with Connor, but she always wondered if the reason he spent his days in a perpetual cloud of smoke had to do with the things he wouldn't (or couldn't) say. Had she even given him the chance to say them?

"How are you?" she said quietly.

"Good?" Connor looked a little disturbed by the question. "I was mostly kidding."

"Yeah?"

Connor shrugged. "Sure. You know me—same old, same old."

"Well, you can talk to me." *Probably. Maybe. Who knows?*

"I know. I appreciate it."

Connor met her eyes and Rosalee felt herself shrink a little bit into her shame. "So, you're not … mad at me?"

"For what?"

"For leaving? For not explaining before I left?" *For using you?*

Connor looked up again and Rosalee noticed his eyes soften a little. She wondered if he could see the guilt in hers. "Shit happens," he said, the corner of his mouth twitching toward a crooked smile. "We're cool."

"Okay. Thanks."

Rosalee wasn't sure she deserved that already. She still hadn't apologized for the way she had stormed into his life, with no warning or explanation, then left just as quickly. However she looked at it, she *had* used him.

"You could still come around if you wanted," said Connor. "To hang out or whatever."

Rosalee felt yet another twinge of guilt. That was always how it started. She would feel the need to escape and call him "to hang out," then wind up sweaty and a million miles away from herself, in his bed or wherever else they collided.

"Yeah, maybe I will."

She tried to match his nonchalant tone, but knew that it would probably be best for everyone involved if she stayed away.

Rosalee barely registered the walk home and was surprised to find Ellie waiting up for her at the kitchen table—fuming.

"Where the hell were you?" she hissed.

Their aunts must have been asleep.

"I went for a walk," said Rosalee.

"*And?*"

"And ..."

"You couldn't even leave a note?"

"They already knew I was going out," said Rosalee, gesturing toward the general direction of Robin and Lola's room.

"Yeah, *I* thought you were, too. Pete and I waited for you at Angela's."

"Look, I'm sorry—I thought we were meeting separately anyway."

"We were, but then Angela needed an extension cord and that's when Pete went back to his apartment and found Alex on the kitchen floor, and you wouldn't answer the phone, so then we started getting worried."

"Breathing?" said Rosalee quickly.

"What?"

"Alex. Was he breathing?"

"Apparently. Pete said he started puking as soon as he could wake him up."

Rosalee let out a shaky breath and sank into one of the kitchen chairs. "Sorry. I should have left a note."

"Yeah, you should have," said Ellie, although some of the bite was gone from her voice. "So, did you guys fight?"

"Yeah."

"Are you okay?"

Rosalee looked up at her sister and saw angry red splotches on the apples of her cheeks—always a danger sign. "I—are *you?*"

"No."

"Okay, then what, Ellie? *Spill.*" Rosalee reached across the table toward her, even though her sister's arms were locked together in front of her. "I feel like you're so mad at me lately and I wish you would tell me why."

Ellie was chewing on her tongue. This was it. She shifted in her seat to face Rosalee straight-on and took a deep breath, letting it out in a little huff. "I'm tired of stepping on eggshells around you."

"I didn't realize that you were."

"Just let me get this out, please."

Rosalee clamped her mouth shut.

"Pete doesn't think I should tell you this, but I've been dying to for *months,* Rosalee, and I honestly don't think you're as delicate as people think you are, or even as *you* think you are, and so I'm just going to say it." Ellie paused. "Pete and I are dating. We're dating and we've *been* dating for months, and he told me he loved me tonight and I couldn't even enjoy it because I was feeling so guilty about not telling you. So there."

Rosalee stared at her sister, watching as her eyes filled with angry tears that she brushed away before they slid down her cheeks. Somehow, the synapses in Rosalee's brain weren't firing or connecting, or whatever the hell they were supposed to do, and all the while, a lightness was spreading through her body so that any minute, she fully expected to float right out of it.

Pete and Ellie?

Her Pete with *her* Ellie?

"Oh," she finally managed.

"So? Go ahead. Let me have it," said Ellie.

Rosalee was still fighting the disorientation fogging her brain. "Have what?"

"I know you're mad, so go ahead."

"... I'm not mad."

"You're not?"

Rosalee took a quick inventory of the emotions cavorting around her brain: shock, embarrassment, more shock. But anger seemed to be missing.

"I don't think so," she said. "I'm still ..." She couldn't think of the word and made a whirring motion next to her head with her finger—like a website loading.

"Okay. Well ... should we talk about it later?"

"Okay."

"Okay."

"'Night."

"'Night."

Rosalee watched her sister pad down the hallway and up the stairs, then followed the sound of her footsteps down the upstairs hallway with her eyes, as if she could see through the ceiling. She let out her breath as the door closed.

How did she feel? Did it matter? *Should* it?

An hour later, Rosalee's thoughts were still swirling and confused and her head full to bursting with overlapping thoughts about three separate men.

Pete had always been a constant in Rosalee's life, ever since elementary school. And while there had been a brief period during which she had considered (no doubt, due to an influx of teenage hormones) the possibility of him being more, there was always something shinier in the way of "crush-able" boys. So, eventually, Pete settled into the older brother category, and she had kind of assumed it was the same for Ellie. When she looked back, all the signs to the contrary were there, and now it was indisputable: she really *didn't* pay attention.

And then there was Connor. It didn't matter how many months had passed—it would have been beyond easy that night for Rosalee to step back through the door she had been trying to lock and seal behind her for months. Connor was a guaranteed escape and he indulged all of the darkness inside her with enthusiasm. There was no judgment, and he never asked her to be anyone other than whoever she happened to be when she knocked on his window.

Which brought her to Alex. Alex, who she could feel slipping away from her and was probably the reason her thoughts were straying to Connor—because she knew that if she chose to turn her back on whatever it was that she and Alex shared, Connor would be there, waiting in the wings. Rosalee allowed herself a moment of deepest self-loathing as she turned that thought over in her mind. She could never go back to that. For months, she had been battling with the feeling of being out of control and at someone else's mercy, but all this time, it had been Rosalee manipulating the puppet strings. Connor was the victim after all—she wouldn't make him that again.

So, then, where did Alex ultimately fall on her map of fractured and twisted relationships? Was she using him, too? Rosalee thought about it, but somehow couldn't bring herself to believe that she was. For one thing, she hadn't even wanted to interact with him at first. He just sort of wormed his way into her life and then she started to rely on him. For what? Comic relief? Hope? That wasn't the same thing as using someone, was it? Maybe only if you didn't offer them anything in return, but if that was true, she never really used Connor. But deep down, Rosalee knew that she had, and maybe they could have stayed friends otherwise, just listening to music and trading drawing ideas. It was too late for that now, whatever he said.

Before sending herself to bed, Rosalee crept up the stairs to Evelyn's bedroom to check her email, but there were no new messages, there or on the answering machine. It was also probably too late to call Pete (not that she would know how to act around him now), so she could only assume that Alex was sleeping off his drunkenness and that Pete hadn't let him drown in the toilet.

God, what a mess.

When Rosalee finally made it to bed, she tossed restlessly under her blankets, unable to regulate her body temperature. Things had been going so well. Somehow, through all of the recent chaos in her life, everything was better when Alex was there. He was the difference between the cave she crawled out of when they first met and wide open plains. And as much reason as she had given him to give up on her in the beginning, he hadn't. So maybe now wasn't the time to condemn their whole relationship—whatever it was, because of one stupid, drunken night.

Again, Alex's words came rushing back to her, but this time, although a tinge of humiliation bled into them, she also felt empowered. Maybe he wasn't entirely out of line—maybe Rosalee *did* need to grow up a little. If only there was a handbook for how to start something like that. She would have to scour her sister's bookshelves for some of her favorite Judy Blume reads—that is, if Ellie would even speak to her again.

Chapter 39

G. R. U. M. P. I. E. S.

G - Ground yourself.
R - Remember to breathe.
U - Understand triggers.
M - Mantra repetition.
P - Practice meditation.
I - "I'm not bad, I'm just mad."
E - Excuse yourself from the situation.
S - Stay away until you're calm.

Alex started. He must have drifted off again. He looked down at the pen dangling loosely in his hand, then redirected his gaze to the facilitator of his anger management course, whose eyes were wide and expectant. Ms. Barnes was in her mid-forties to early fifties, with light blonde hair that hung past her shoulders and a much younger woman's figure, although Alex did his best not to notice.

"Yes, ma'am, I'm sorry?" Alex tried to arrange his face in a way that would suggest that he hadn't heard her correctly—not that he hadn't been listening.

"Grumpies?" said Ms. Barnes.

Alex's mind was as vacant as his expression.

"We're on 'S' of our Anger Alleviation Acronym, Mr. Conway."

"Oh, right." Alex scanned the chalkboard behind her quickly, but to his luck, her lovely-but-who-was-looking figure was blocking the "S." He would have to guess. "So, 'S' would be … 'stop yelling'?"

Several people laughed.

Ms. Barnes tutted. "Let's all remind Alex together … and?"

"'Stay away until you're calm,'" the class chanted at him.

"Right," Alex muttered.

At the end of the session, Alex joined the administrator at the front of the room. He pretended to be immersed in finding the form for her to sign in his bag to avoid her appraisal.

"Is everything okay, Mr. Conway?"

"Yes, ma'am, I'm sorry about earlier," he said. "I was up late because I worked late. But I'm sorry."

Ms. Barnes raised her eyebrows. "You know, I can only sign off on these sessions if you're here. And by *here,* I mean physically *and* mentally."

"I understand."

"Perhaps in your case, less note-taking would be helpful."

Ms. Barnes nodded toward the composition book under Alex's arm. He wedged it more securely into his armpit, afraid she might ask to see his "notes." Then she held out a hand and he had a mini panic attack before realizing that she was reaching for the form.

"Thank you, Ms. Barnes. Really, you have no idea. I promise this won't happen again."

She nodded curtly before turning her back on him to erase the chalkboard. "Make sure it doesn't."

—•—

An hour and a half later, Alex was standing in the doorway of Rosalee's room, which was apparently still "temporarily" downstairs. Rosalee was sitting on the floor with a book in her lap.

"Hey," he said, knocking softly on the door jamb since she hadn't looked up yet. "Can I come in?"

"Looks like you already are."

"Yeah, sorry, Lola let me in."

Rosalee shrugged. Alex walked tentatively into the room and sat on the edge of her bed. Maybe she sensed him trying to read over her shoulder because she closed the book. Since Alex didn't have very much time before his shift at Laurie's, he decided that directness was probably best.

He cleared his throat. "We can't afford to keep Oliver at Engelmann anymore."

Rosalee looked up, startled. "What?"

"We'll have to pay out of pocket if we want him to stay in the program."

Rosalee exhaled slowly, opening the book again to mark her place, then shoving it under the bed. "*God,* Alex. I'm sorry."

Alex joined her on the floor and swept a hand quickly under the bed to relocate the book before Rosalee could stop him. "What is this?" He fended her off with one arm as he read the title. "*Clipped Wings: How to Fly the Coop* ... Seriously, what is this?"

Rosalee shrugged again, this time looking embarrassed and angry.

369

"Because of what I said about growing up? Rosalee ..." Alex set the book down and she snatched it back immediately, shoving it out of sight. "Please don't tell me you took *anything* I said the other night to heart. I was like, the world's most colossal and raging dick."

Regret burrowed like a splinter into his gut as he watched Rosalee busy herself with a loose strand of carpet, eyes too full of tears to look up. He walked the fingers of one hand over to hers until they were touching, and when she didn't retract them, he moved closer.

"Rosalee, I'm so sorry—you have no idea. I didn't mean anything I said. I just ... wasn't expecting the insurance stuff yet."

Rosalee cleared her throat. "Yet?"

"Insurance doesn't usually cover experimental programs. But we were hoping we could, like, renew the medical trial period or something. Apparently not."

Rosalee was watching Alex like she was afraid of giving too much away. He hated to see her eyes so guarded again.

"When did you find out?" she said.

"My mom called me last week. Right after a disappointing conversation with my attorney."

Rosalee sat up straighter, but Alex shook his head. "I can't even get into that right now. But suffice it to say, I kicked off my 'No More AA Meetings' celebration with a bang."

"No kidding."

"I don't know what to say. I'm ... *mortified.*"

Rosalee seemed to be contemplating their fingers, which were still touching. "I wish you could tell me what happened."

"I wish *you* could tell me what happened," said Alex, tapping her index finger lightly with his.

Rosalee smiled softly. *"Touché."*

"I will someday. I promise."

"Yeah, me too."

"It's just embarrassing."

"Yeah, me too."

Alex linked their hands together, immeasurably grateful when she didn't pull hers away.

"I think while everything was crashing down around me last week, I couldn't help thinking that … this isn't where I thought I would be by now. Ya know?" he said.

Rosalee nodded and something in her expression told Alex that she wasn't just agreeing with him to agree. He gave her hand a tiny squeeze.

"But that doesn't give me the right to pile all my baggage onto you." Alex paused. "God, *what* is that song?" he said, staring at the ceiling as though willing the title to fall from it.

"What song?" Rosalee glanced toward her CD player, which was switched off.

"By Madonna? The 'baggage' thing just reminded me …"

Rosalee gave him a blank look. Alex bobbed his head to the song only he could hear and she smiled again and settled against his shoulder, sending a little shiver of hope through him.

"So … where did you think you would be by now?" she said.

"I don't know. In LA? Writing movies?"

"So why aren't you?"

"Because I'm here."

"Well, thanks. That clears things right up."

Alex suddenly slapped a hand against his knee, making Rosalee jump. "'Human Nature,'" he said triumphantly.

"What?"

"The Madonna song."

"Ah."

"Hey." Alex nudged Rosalee's shoulder until she met his eyes again. "I heard you visited my brother."

He watched as Rosalee searched his face, possibly looking for warning signs. "I'm sorry. I should have asked. But Ellie and I collected all this stuff from the attic and I was working on the mural anyway, and you and I hadn't talked since—"

Alex kissed her, effectively pausing her apologetic ramblings. He meant for it to be soft and brief, but the tiny sigh that issued from deep in Rosalee's throat caught him off guard and it was several long seconds before he could tear himself away.

"I wasn't scolding you," he said before she could start up again.

"I still should have asked. Was it weird for him? I felt bad dropping everything off and leaving, so I thought maybe a game of Chinese Checkers ..."

Alex smiled. "It wasn't weird. And actually, *that's* what's weird."

"What is?"

"The fact that it *wasn't* weird. He couldn't stop talking about it. I don't think he'll ever be satisfied playing games with me now—just you."

"Whatever," said Rosalee, although she looked pleased.

"Seriously. I think he might be more infatuated with you than I am."

Rosalee laughed. "He is *not*."

"Okay, you're right," said Alex. "There's no way *anyone* is more infatuated with you than I am."

Rosalee looked up at him again and Alex was instantly entranced by the gilded halos around her pupils.

"Really?" she said softly.

"*Really*. Rosalee, I feel horrible about the other night."

Rosalee looked down at their hands. "You had some good points, though."

Alex grimaced, trying simultaneously to remember and *not* remember what he actually said. "Did I?"

Rosalee made a noncommittal head jerk.

"I was out of my mind." Alex shook his head. "I haven't felt that out of control for a long time. I never want to feel like that again."

"Are you going to go back to AA?"

"Maybe."

He knew he needed to. But where the hell would he ever find the time?

"I'll go with you if you want ... I know you're a 'grown-ass man.'"

"I didn't mean it, Rosalee," said Alex, his eyes imploring. "I like that you worry about me. And I *want* to take care of you."

"I never asked you to," Rosalee snapped, and Alex had a sudden flashback to the version of her he had tried so hard to impress when they first met.

"I said I want to."

"Well, I don't *need*—"

"I know."

Rosalee huffed. "You don't even know what I was going to say."

"That you don't need me, or any man, or any*one.* But could you, please ... for a second? Just ..."

"Just what?" Rosalee eyed him warily.

"Just come here? Please?"

Rosalee's eyes softened noticeably as Alex stood and reached for her. For once, she accepted his hand and he pulled her into his arms, fingers weaving automatically into her hair as his other arm circled her waist.

Alex felt another shiver run through him, but this one was distinctly different from the last. Where the first was hopeful, this felt darker—perhaps a reminder of what he nearly threw away. There was another layer beneath that, though. Something foreboding. *'O god, I have an ill-divining soul.'*

Alex shook himself mentally and tried to focus on Rosalee's hair against his cheek and her body willingly sharing space with his own.

"Tighter," she sighed.

Alex felt himself turning to putty as he complied, reveling in Rosalee's warm breath at the hollow of his throat.

"What are you doing this weekend?" he said.

"I have it off."

"Well, don't make plans. I'll call you tonight about it, okay?"

Alex felt Rosalee nod, but she had yet to relinquish her hold on him—in any capacity. He groaned. "I have to go to work."

At last, Rosalee pulled away to look at him.

"I'm so sorry," said Alex. "And I'm not asking you to forgive me yet, I just wanted you to know."

Rosalee reached up to smooth the frown lines in his forehead, then kissed him gently on the mouth. "I do anyway."

She smiled as he passed her and his fingertips whispered across the fabric at the small of her back.

"Oh, I almost forgot ..." Alex stopped just outside the doorway and turned back, his expression guilty.

"*Now* what?" said Rosalee, and he felt worse watching her face tense.

"How mad are you at me about Pete and Ellie?"

"You *knew?*"

Alex winced as Rosalee's eyes flashed. "A little. We'll talk about it tomorrow. I have to go."

He left quickly, before she could pounce.

Chapter 40

By three o'clock the next afternoon, Alex and Rosalee were packed into his Jeep and headed away from Rabbitbrush. The sky was overcast but as they drove, fat snowflakes like popcorn floated down around them and everything became more still—more quiet. Alex turned onto the highway and Rosalee rolled her window down and tried to catch several of the flakes that swirled inside the cabin and vanished almost instantly.

Alex purposefully synchronized his breaths to Rosalee's. Despite all of the turmoil of the past week, she seemed excited to be leaving Rabbitbrush, if only for a little while. Maybe he could also look at it as a sort of mini-vacation from his life. The problem was that his mind and body were still grieving the things he had dumped down the drain only days before, and that only increased the frequency of his cigarette cravings. By now, he was essentially a walking, human chimney, but he didn't want to smell like one, so before he picked Rosalee up, he chain-smoked until he had to take a shower and then drowned his shredded nerves in half a pot of coffee.

Luckily, Rosalee didn't seem to be harboring any lingering resentment about their ruined plans or Alex's drinking. Instead, she interrogated him about the secret romance between his roommate and her sister while Alex repeatedly assured her that Pete hadn't even mustered up the courage to tell him until his passing-out-and-puking fiasco. "The ... 'POAPF,' as it were."

"What does that stand for?" said Rosalee.

Alex thought for a minute, then sank back into his seat, defeated. "Nothing. I must be losing my touch."

Meanwhile, Rosalee was doing a commendable job of distracting him from his multi-layered cravings with her standard combat boots and tights under a black mini skirt and oversized sweater—even more so when she turned to him, suddenly anxious and fretting about how they should have said goodbye to Oliver before they left. Alex assured her that since he had the morning off, he had spent breakfast and lunch with his little brother and that Oliver was probably glad to see him go. To be fair, that was mostly because he couldn't stand the smell of cigarettes and Alex had trouble hiding the multitude he had to smoke lately to keep himself stitched together.

••••

By the time they reached their destination, the sun was beginning its descent. Alex didn't care how long he lived; he would never get used to the sun setting at four thirty in the afternoon during the winter months—as if they weren't depressing enough already.

Mini vacation, he reminded himself as they climbed the steps with their bags and he fumbled for the keys he had attached to his key chain. He was lucky that they had this place to themselves for the next day and a half. Manny's cousin was in the process of moving, but the condo was still on the market and the cousin's cats were living there to avoid settling problems. Alex was familiar enough with cats to understand how easily upset they were. It was also his job to water the houseplants, which wouldn't normally have made him so apprehensive, except that there was apparently a diagram. Normally, all of those jobs would have been offered to Manny (the pay wasn't bad, either), but he and his girlfriend were still in Colorado Springs.

Alex pushed open the front door and ushered Rosalee in front of him and onto the large mat in the even larger foyer. Rosalee gasped. "It's huge."

Alex laughed. "Your aunt's house is way bigger than this."

"Yeah, but there are four people living in it." Rosalee paused at the sound of voices. "Is someone here?"

"That's just the TV—they leave it on for the cats."

They set their bags down by the door and took off their shoes—the carpets looked like they had just been cleaned. A staircase directly in front of them led to the second floor, with ledges all the way up for the abundance of greenery, and a dining and living room lay on either side. The living room featured large windows and a breathtaking view of the mountains, then led to a small kitchen and what appeared to be at least one bedroom.

"I'd love to have this many plants in my house," said Rosalee, her voice full of longing as she took in the vegetation spilling over the railings.

"Manny said they've already moved half of the plants to the new house."

"Holy cow."

"Hey."

"Hm?"

Alex came up behind Rosalee and kissed her lightly on her sweater-clad shoulder. She sank into him as he wrapped his arms around her.

"We're alone," he said.

"Well …" Rosalee nodded toward the bottom of the stairs, where a furry black head was peering out at them, its dark body winding around the railing as its eyes reflected the light from the entryway chandelier.

"There's another one." Alex pointed out a ginger cat lurking halfway up the stairs. "Manny said they'll warm up to us faster if we ignore them. Cats are so weird."

Rosalee shrugged. "I ignored you and you warmed up to me pretty fast."

"Ugh. *Touché.*"

Rosalee laughed while Alex moved her hair to the side and kissed the skin above her sweater, letting his breath linger. Rosalee shivered and stepped carefully back out of his arms.

"Maybe it looks so big because all the furniture is gone," she said. "Where are we going to sleep?"

"I brought sleeping bags." Alex chose to ignore what could have potentially been an awkward moment. Rosalee would bring it up if it was important. Otherwise, progress was still progress, no matter how slight. "I also saw packing blankets in the garage we can use as cushioning."

"I feel so tired already and I wasn't even driving. I've been sitting all day."

Now that Alex was paying proper attention, Rosalee looked more than tired—she looked downright exhausted.

"You could take a nap," he suggested.

"I didn't come up here with you to nap."

"It's okay, I can work on my movie."

Rosalee looked tempted. "Are you sure?"

"I'll go get the packing blankets."

By the time they were situated, Alex was aching for a smoke. In normal circumstances—before his inelegant tumble off the wagon—he would have loved nothing more than to snuggle down with Rosalee and nap away the afternoon. However, his sudden departure from alcohol left him so raw and off his axis that it was hard to be still for any length of time. He wasn't sure he would be able to write at all, but he thought he should give it a shot, if only for the sake of thinking about something other than booze or cigarettes (after he had one). He kissed Rosalee on the forehead and stood to go outside before she called him back.

"Will you just, um, sit ... with me for a few minutes before you write?"

For some reason, her hesitancy and Alex's heightened feeling that he was coming unglued made him ornery. Why had she paused and said "sit"? Was it to avoid saying something else? He laughed at his own joke.

"What?" said Rosalee.

"Nothing, I just ..." Alex shrugged off the part of his brain that would normally stop this kind of behavior and slipped into the mushy-gushy, icky character from so many months before, talking about horoscopes. "Are you asking me to *lay* with you, Rosalee?" he crooned, sickening himself in the process. "Because I've been waiting my whole life to—I can't, I'm sorry." He laughed at the nauseated expression on Rosalee's face and stretched out next to her, not quite touching. "You okay?" he said in his normal voice.

Rosalee scooted closer. "I don't know. You know that feeling you get right before everything falls apart? Like it's too good and there has to be ..."

"A catch?"

"Right."

"Because of home?"

"Home, us, everything. I just feel like something's coming."

"Maybe it's a good 'something.'"

"It doesn't feel good."

Alex frowned and rolled over onto his side, propping himself up on his elbow to look at her.

"Ellie was gone before we could talk," said Rosalee, staring at the ceiling. "Robin and Lola are constantly at each other's throats. I'm just waiting for the explosion."

"Maybe that's what needs to happen. A good old-fashioned, knock-down-drag-out, come-to-Jesus hoopla."

Rosalee turned her head to look at him. "At this point, I don't know if my family could survive that."

Alex fought down the cravings scrambling around inside him and tried to focus on the warmth of Rosalee's hand as he traced patterns into her palm. "Did I ever tell you about Manny's parents' house?"

"I don't think so."

"So, it was Manny's grandparents' house originally, and it was basically this dilapidated, crumbling shack. But she couldn't let go of it—Manny's mom, I mean—after her parents passed away. Manny grew up there."

"Wow."

"That's what I said. Anyway, it needed to be fixed or it was going to collapse, but the structure was shot and there was too much damage to fix it. So, they ended up tearing everything down to the foundation—luckily that was still good. But Manny said his mother cried for days before they tore it down."

"I can imagine."

Rosalee's eyes were far away and Alex tried to infuse soothing vibes into his thumb as it rubbed circles into her skin and he continued.

"But then it was done and suddenly everything was so much easier to rebuild. Manny said his mother told him the spirit of her parents felt stronger in the rejuvenated house than the one she kept hanging onto that was falling apart. It's, like … therapeutic for people to fall apart, as long as they can hang on long enough to build back up."

Rosalee nodded, but was quiet this time.

"Anyway," said Alex. "Manny tells it better."

He looked over to see Rosalee wiping her thumbs under her eyes and felt his throat tighten. "I didn't mean to upset you."

"You didn't. That was just a nice story."

Alex reached for her and she moved easily into his arms. Who needed cigarettes and booze, anyway? He immediately cursed those thoughts as they saturated his frontal lobe and made him feel like he was underwater. He forced himself to focus on the threads of Rosalee's sweater, scratchy against his freshly shaved face. He moved the blanket to cover her legs in case the tights weren't warm enough.

"Hey," he said suddenly. "You didn't flinch."

"When?"

"Just now."

Rosalee readjusted herself in his arms so that she was facing him. As Alex watched her, a slow smile started at her lips and made its way to her eyes before she dragged him forward by the back of his neck and crushed her lips against his. Alex *let* her crush him—let her be all he needed in this rare moment of lucidity already blurring at the edges as doubt wedged its long, clever fingers into the tiny fissures. Try as he might, Alex couldn't stop himself from wondering if the recent sense of urgency in Rosalee's kisses was more about the exhilaration of testing her limits and less about who she was kissing. Not that now was the time to get into something like that—Rosalee was already upset, and Alex had a strong suspicion that a lot of his dark reflection had more to do with the things he quit cold turkey than the woman currently driving him crazy. *Crazy.*

"What's wrong?" said Rosalee, and Alex only realized then that they had somehow stopped kissing.

"I was just thinking," he said, stalling. *Definitely not the time.*

After all, who was he kidding? Whether she was kissing him to prove something to herself or kissing him because she was smitten, did it really matter? Would it ultimately change anything about the situation? Other than a sizable bruise to his ego, Alex had a hard time believing that he wouldn't allow himself to continue to be pulverized by her until he was a pile of mangled hope and heartstrings at her feet. Somehow, that thought wasn't as depressing as he expected it to be. Instead, he accepted it as something inevitable—as inevitable as Daylight Saving Time and the sun setting at four thirty in the afternoon.

No ... no, that was still depressing.

Rosalee watched him with her eyes narrowed and Alex sighed. No use starting a fight over something he was afraid to mention because it might start a fight.

"So you, uh ... *like* me, right?" he said.

"What?"

He could tell Rosalee was caught off guard, but he still needed to know the answer—as much as he pretended he didn't—so he waited.

"I wouldn't be here if I didn't," she said finally.

"Just making sure." Alex flashed a quick smile—an easy smile. A "no-big-deal-just-wondering" smile.

As usual, Rosalee was not to be fooled and pulled her hand gently away. "Are you asking me to prove it to you?"

Her eyes were cautious again, but Alex met them steadily, though with a bite of impatience. "I hope you know me better than that by now. I just need to be sure that you're not pushing your limits just to prove to yourself that you can. Not that that's bad." He paused. "I think I also need you to … *want* me. For my sake."

For an instant, Rosalee looked at him with something that stung—almost like pity, before her expression grew undeniably smug.

"'*Wanting someone. What does that even mean?*'" she said, in her imitation of his voice.

Alex stuffed down his embarrassment and attempted to keep his face neutral. "Yes, fine. Let us take a moment to appreciate the irony."

"So you're afraid you're my project?"

Alex sucked his teeth.

"How does it feel now that the shoe is on the other foot?" said Rosalee, her eyes twinkling. "Walking funny?"

Alex felt his mouth twitching toward a smile. "How many more of these do you have?"

Rosalee paused, then grinned. "I think that's it."

Alex cleared his throat, his mouth suddenly dry. "I just want to … mean something. To you."

Rosalee looked a little bewildered at the new direction of the conversation. "Of course you mean something to me," she said, her voice barely above a whisper.

Alex was starting to get dizzy from the lack of oxygen—or cigarettes, and he sat up and put his face in his hands, realizing a second later that it probably looked a lot like he was losing his cool. And he *needed* his cool. It was pretty much all he hadn't chucked off the wagon. Except, again, who was he kidding?

"Alex?"

"Yeah, sorry, I got lightheaded for a minute."

"Put your head between your knees. Trust me, it works."

Alex felt Rosalee's hand on his back as he obeyed, and although the dizziness began to lift, the anxious feeling in his stomach only radiated a wider circumference. Somewhere off in the distance, he could sense the dark cloud looming closer, but he still hoped he could outrun it.

"I just got too worked up," he said finally, raising his head again and doing his best impression of a reassuring smile. "I think I need to smoke or something."

"Or something?"

While most of Rosalee's face was the perfect imitation of innocence, the throaty quality of her voice and mischief in her eyes betrayed something else entirely.

It was a mark of Alex's suffering that the potent combination of both elements didn't bring him to his knees, but his aching need for nicotine was too great—plus, he was already sitting down. Still, he gave himself over to Rosalee's magnetic pull, if only briefly, as she kissed him hard enough to topple them backward onto the sleeping bags. Then her fingers in his hair and gripping his shirt were smoothing down the edges of his cravings and replacing them with a different kind of ache.

"Jesus, Rosalee, you're supposed to be resting."

"I know, I must have caught my second wind."

"You're not tired anymore?"

Rosalee paused, looking pained.

"*Nap,*" said Alex. He pushed her down gently and covered her with a blanket.

"Okay, but I brought you something. In the cooler."

"I told you you didn't need to bring anything."

"And I told *you* that I'd bring dinner. It's the least I could do."

Alex rolled onto his stomach and reached for the red and white plastic chest, dragging it over to his side of the sleeping bags and opening the lid. "I can't remember the last time I had shish kabobs. These look great."

"Keep going."

"Um, Rosalee, are these ..."

"Root Beers," she said quickly. "I figured you'd be having a hard time. And since they're glass bottles ... placebo effect or whatever."

Alex felt a faint prickling near the backs of his eyes as he leaned over to kiss Rosalee on the forehead. Maybe he meant something to her after all.

Chapter 41

By the time Rosalee woke up from her nap, it was dark outside. She flipped over onto her back and stared up at the white ceiling, the same shade as the walls, with dark wooden beams that ran across and held it up. The contrasting colors were clean and cozy, and they had given her a sense of nostalgia the moment she and Alex came in the door. Here, in the quiet, she finally realized where the memory came from.

Even though the whole family rarely attended church together, Evelyn liked big family dinners (often including Pete or, occasionally, the Sheriff) on Sunday nights and always baked some sort of scrumptious dessert for afterward. Robin's favorite was a brown sugar angel food cake iced with white, creamy frosting made of whipped cream, powdered sugar, and creme de cacao, then sprinkled with chocolate curls. If it was snowing outside when Evelyn baked it, she also added an extra dusting of powdered sugar or sometimes the clear crystal sprinkles over the chocolate. It was a Betty Crocker recipe, but Rosalee couldn't remember what it was called.

Rosalee afforded herself several minutes of self-assessment before sitting up in her sleeping bag and stretching. She seemed to be alone—Alex must have chosen one of the bedrooms to work on his movie. She padded in her stocking feet over the wood floor, freezing compared to the warmth of her nylon sleeping bag, and found him in the second bedroom, sitting at a small, wooden desk and writing by what looked like less-than-ideal illumination from an overhead fan light. Rosalee assumed that the two large windows overlooking the mountains must have been what drew him to the space.

"So, they left some of the furniture after all," she said, leaning against the doorframe.

Alex looked up from his notebook and smiled. "Just my luck." He closed the notebook and set it on top of two others, both of which had different colored duct tape along their spines.

Rosalee walked to the desk and leaned down to kiss Alex softly. He scooted the rolling chair a few inches away from the desk and pulled her onto his lap. As they watched snowflakes floating serenely past the windows, she could feel Alex's heart beating against her back and nearly drifted off to sleep again. When she righted herself and glanced at his profile, he seemed lost in thought, but Rosalee recognized the need to orient oneself after undertaking an artistic endeavor. He probably needed a few minutes to resurface from his writing. At last, she felt him take a deep breath and watched his eyes focus to a closer point than the distant snowy peaks.

"How was your nap?" he said.

"Awesome." It was true; Rosalee had been afraid that her anxiety about this trip would cause a full-fledged flare-up, but she felt great for now. "How was your writing?"

"Awesome." Alex smiled at her, then looked at his watch. "Are you hungry?"

"Starving."

"I already fired up the grill. I have to throw the kabobs on, but they shouldn't take too long and then we can watch a movie or something?"

"Sounds perfect. Do you need help?"

"Nope. Don't move."

"Why?"

Alex nodded toward the doorway, where the ginger cat was stepping carefully into the room. It lifted its nose into the air, whiskers twitching, then began sniffing at Alex's messenger bag on the floor.

"You can stay with your friend," said Alex. "I'll be back in a few minutes."

Rosalee stayed as still as she could as the cat inspected her boots and tights, then bounded effortlessly into her lap. Tentatively, she raised one hand and let it hover over its back, and almost immediately, the cat arched into her palm, allowing her to pet down to the end of its orange tail and then scratch under its chin. She felt all of her remaining tension dissipate as the cat purred. It allowed Rosalee several more minutes of affection before butting its head against her palm one final time and leaping onto the desk and Alex's notebooks before she could stop it.

One of the notebooks tumbled to the ground, and as Rosalee reached down to pick it up, she was startled to see her name. She looked away quickly, knowing she had no business snooping around in Alex's writing without permission, but it was a little like trying to avoid looking at oncoming headlights. Her eyes strayed to the open pages again and this time, *"Touch me."* jumped out at her. She skimmed further and began to feel a knot in her stomach. *"Kiss me."* taunted her next.

What the hell had she stumbled into?

————•●•————

When Alex returned ten minutes later, Rosalee was sitting, stunned, at the desk. The ginger cat had since abandoned her, which was unfortunate because she could have used the comfort.

"Hey ..." said Alex, concern and confusion etched in his face until his eyes landed on the open notebook in front of her.

Rosalee recognized the expression that followed only too well: *Oh, shit.*

"What is this?" she said.

Alex held his hand out for the journal, which Rosalee passed to him, still open. He glanced down at it briefly and a muscle flexed in his jaw before he snapped the book shut, holding it loosely by his side. "How much did you read?"

"All of it, I guess? I didn't read anything before it."

Alex was quiet for several seconds and Rosalee finally looked up, but couldn't read his clouded expression. Was he angry? Embarrassed? *Anything?*

"Are there more?" said Rosalee. Now that the can of worms was open, she might as well assess the carnage.

"... Yes."

"About me?"

"Yes."

"Why?"

Alex didn't answer, but he also didn't look away.

"I mean ... I guess I'm just confused," said Rosalee.

"What's confusing?"

"Well, none of this happened."

"Right?"

"Well, that's it. None of this happened. I recognize bits and pieces, but you made the rest of it up."

"Yeah, I did. I never meant for you to read it."

"I didn't *mean* to read it. The cat knocked it off the desk and—"

"Carrots."

"... what?"

"The orange cat is Carrots. The black one is Marvin." Alex frowned. "Melvin. Mervin?"

"Got it." Rosalee fought the urge to chew the inside of her cheek. "Well, I saw my name and then I couldn't stop. Reading."

"And now you're upset."

"Shouldn't I be? I mean, I guess I never realized that the movie you're writing is—" Rosalee paused, searching for the right word, "—well, *porn?*"

"Ouch."

"You know what I mean."

"I hoped my storyline was a little more romantic than porn."

Rosalee crossed her arms. "Well, whatever it is, it's—"

"Not my movie."

"What?"

"This isn't my movie." Alex opened the notebook again at random, letting it flop in his hands like soaked butterfly wings. "It's my journal. Or diary, I guess."

"Your ... diary?"

"Yup."

"*Not* your movie?"

"Nope. I hit a roadblock and switched to a different notebook."

"So, this story is ...?"

"A ... fantasy, I guess."

"Oh."

Rosalee squirmed in the desk chair. Alex reached carefully around her to toss the notebook back onto the desk and then sat on the floor, leaning back on his hands.

"Can I ask you something?" he said.

Rosalee nodded.

"What about this was so upsetting to you?"

Rosalee flushed. "I mean, it was just so … raw?"

"Does it bother you that I think about you that way?"

"No …"

Alex squinted up into her face. "Really? Because you seem pretty upset."

"I guess I wasn't expecting … all of it. Everything."

"Sure …" Alex's eyes still hadn't left Rosalee, but she did her best to focus on anything else in the room. "But it doesn't change anything."

"What do you mean?" Rosalee asked Alex's foot.

"I mean, have I ever pushed you or made you feel uncomfortable?"

"I *definitely* do things outside my comfort zone with you."

Alex shook his head. "I'm not talking about things that are *good* for you, like leaving your house or The Goose once in a while. Have I ever made you uncomfortable … that way?"

"No…it's just *weird* that you have all of my reactions … mapped out and explicitly detailed—"

"But none of this happened. I haven't pushed you for any of this."

"No, but it's how you would *want* it to happen. This is how you want me to be with you, right? But it's not how I am."

Something contracted at the top of Rosalee's stomach before settling like a rock.

Alex studied his ravaged thumbnail before turning his attention back to Rosalee. "I'm sorry if it doesn't feel genuine. It's who you are to me—underneath all of the apologies and … I don't know, *fear?*"

"How could you possibly know that?"

"Maybe I don't. Maybe I'm totally off, but sometimes I swear I can see how you want to be with me. You want it to feel good, but not too good, because then it might hurt? Or I might hurt you?"

Rosalee felt a lump rising in her throat and wrestled it back down with difficulty.

"I'm sorry that it upset you," said Alex.

"It's okay. I shouldn't be critiquing your fantasies anyway."

"So ... you never think of me that way?"

"No."

Rosalee watched as Alex's expression echoed the one he wore when they first met and she lied about not liking movies.

"No," he repeated. "But you kiss me."

"Yes."

"Okay, but Rosalee, you, like, *kiss* me."

"I know, I'm there."

"And you're telling me that you *never* think about going farther?"

"No, because I can't. Yet."

Alex's eyes narrowed and Rosalee could see the thought hovering between them, even though he didn't say it: *I don't believe you.* She wasn't sure why she was lying to him, except that it felt like if she admitted that she'd thought about him that way, she would eventually be required to fulfill those thoughts—like some sort of contract.

"You're still afraid I'll hurt you?" said Alex.

"No."

"You're afraid it will hurt even if it's *not* me, then?"

"... Maybe. No. I don't know, I need to think for a little bit."

Alex leaned forward and pulled Rosalee's chair closer by the wheeled base so that her knees were level with his chin. "Well, can you do it out loud, please? *Please,* just let me in."

Rosalee sighed. "I left that part of myself behind, okay? In a heap with all of the bad things I did to escape after the diagnosis and my aunt. And I can't just separate out that little part that was good and risk the bad parts catching up or having anything to do with you."

"So ... the thing you said about not being a nun?"

Rosalee nodded and Alex rolled his eyes. "It's the *nineties*, Rosalee, I didn't expect you to be. So, you've been with other people. So have I. Big fat deal. You're acting like you're broken or something. That's not what you think, is it?"

Rosalee shrugged.

"Because you've slept with people?" Alex pressed.

"Because I *used* people. One person." A sudden vision of Connor's hopeful expression the last time she saw him made Rosalee's stomach clench. "I don't want to use you."

"You mean for my body?" Alex let go of the chair and leaned back on his elbows, tossing his hair out of his eyes and fixing her with an exaggerated smolder. "Because I think I'm okay with that."

Rosalee pushed both hands through her hair and rested her forehead in her palms. "Stop it. This isn't funny."

"I know it's not," Alex sat up again. "But ... you said I mean something to you."

"You do."

"So, then, maybe it's different."

—————•●•—————

Later that night, Rosalee stood in the downstairs bathroom and stared at her reflection. Alex was outside on the back deck fiddling with the hot tub while she changed. She hadn't thought to pack a swimsuit in the middle of winter, but couldn't quite convince herself to go outside in her bra and underwear. On the other hand, the condo was a clump of five units with a small courtyard in the middle, which they all faced, making all of the back patios relatively private.

In the month and a half since she cut it, Rosalee's hair had grown nearly an inch, but still settled above her shoulders. She freed it from its elastic and swiped on a coat of waterproof mascara while she tried to make up her mind. She imagined sashaying onto the deck in her combat boots and oversized sweater and tousled her hair experimentally in the mirror.

"Molly *who*?" she purred seductively, then dropped her arms.

Her eyes landed on Alex's blue flannel overshirt draped over the shower curtain rod. He must have gone outside for a smoke without putting his coat back on. The snow had been the wet and slushy kind until after Rosalee's nap, so it was understandable that it would have gotten soaked through. For a moment, she imagined Alex shivering outside, desperately nursing a habit that only partially satiated a different one, then pulled the shirt down from the rod, holding it against her. Although the soft, worn material smelled a little like smoke, it also smelled like aftershave and coffee, and ... Alex. Rosalee turned back to the mirror and stared at her reflection again, resolution setting in her eyes.

— • • —

Alex turned at the sound of Rosalee's approaching footsteps on the wooden planks of the patio, then did a double take as he took in her appearance. She thought she saw him pale slightly.

"I didn't pack a swimsuit after all," she said, glancing down at her alabaster legs poking out from under the flannel. "I hope this is okay."

Although it was dark, Rosalee saw some of the color return to Alex's cheeks. Still, there was a careful air about him—like he was trying not to look *too* happy.

"So, I saw your deodorant in the bathroom," said Rosalee.

"Yeah?"

"Old Spice. Not what I was expecting for someone so ... *young*."
Rosalee grinned and leaned against the porch railing.

Alex smiled back. "Yeah, my uh ... my grandpa wore it."

"Oh."

"It's okay," said Alex when Rosalee's smile slipped. "It just reminds me of him. I like it."

"I like it, too," said Rosalee quickly. "I wear lavender hand cream like my Aunt Evelyn. Did."

Alex held out a hand, which Rosalee took.

"Aren't you freezing?" he said.

He was wearing his coat again, but Rosalee's adrenaline was keeping her comfortably warm for the time being—except for her feet. She shifted slightly to rest the bottom of one on top of the other.

Alex didn't miss the movement. "C'mon, let's get in before you get frostbite."

He led Rosalee to the hot tub, where she perched on the ledge, contemplating the steaming water. "I can't stay in long. I'm not supposed to go in at all."

"Doctor's orders?"

Rosalee nodded.

"Good thing I turned the temperature down," said Alex.

"How far down?"

"Get in and see."

Cautiously, Rosalee climbed in so that her feet and calves were submerged. It was the temperature of a warm bath. Alex quickly discarded his coat and T-shirt, shivering in the icy air, then started to undo the belt on his jeans. He stopped as he assessed Rosalee's expression, and too late, she realized that she probably looked panicked.

Alex grimaced. "Always the look I'm going for when I take off my pants." He hitched them more securely on his hips as he kicked off his socks and shoes instead.

"Sorry, I wasn't thinking about you. I was thinking about me."

"What about you?"

Rosalee hesitated and Alex vaulted over the side of the hot tub, jeans and all. Rosalee shrieked then laughed as he dragged her into the water with him, his soaked shirt billowing around her. As he kissed her, she felt little tingles of her old self surfacing and mixing with the new.

"Wait," she said, extricating herself from Alex's arms.

"Sorry, did I hurt you?" he said.

"No. I just need to stand up."

Alex stood, too. "Are you okay?"

"Yeah, but could you maybe … not look for a second?"

Alex scrubbed a hand over his mouth and down his chin, and it was only when he had turned his back on Rosalee to face the glittering city lights below the mountain line that she remembered she was technically a flight risk. Eager to reassure him, Rosalee lifted Alex's sodden shirt quickly over her head and laid it on the edge of the hot tub before wrapping her arms around him from behind and pressing her body into his back.

Alex turned slowly in her arms, his fingertips brushing bare skin. His gaze swept lightly over her before meeting her eyes with his full of questions. Rosalee smiled, breathing in the mountain air and letting it fill her up and make her brave. She moved in closer to press her mouth against his naked shoulder, then slid her palms lightly down to the waistband of his soaked jeans. She felt him suppress a shudder as his muscles flexed and he twitched her closer.

"Macaroni and cheese with cut-up hotdogs," he murmured into her hair.

Rosalee pulled back to look at him questioningly.

"Baby carrots with Ranch dressing, and Gushers. The blue ones." He seemed to be talking to himself.

Rosalee frowned. "Did you dip into the catnip?"

"This is your revenge, right?" Alex's voice sounded slightly strangled, "If you're trying to kill me, I demand a last meal."

Rosalee laughed, her hair falling around her face as she traced the muscles in his abdomen with her fingertips. Alex groaned and lifted her chin again to claim her mouth, kissing her with something that bordered on recklessness before bracing his hands on her hips and pushing himself away, eyes tight shut.

"Sorry. I'm sorry."

Rosalee hesitated for a moment, then moved Alex's arms to circle her waist and raised on her toes to brush her lips against his neck. Alex sighed and drew her in again, tucking his face into her shoulder. And then Rosalee was the one being reckless and Alex cradled her face in his hands as they tumbled onto one of the ledges. Alex shook the water out of his eyes and pulled Rosalee onto his lap.

"Is this too much?" said Rosalee, unsure which of them she was asking.

Her heart was racing. She didn't want it to feel like Connor all over again. It couldn't. But how was it different? *Because this is Alex,* said the little voice in her head. She cared about Alex—*that* was the difference. But if she was honest with herself, she cared about Connor, too. *This is different,* the little voice insisted.

"You tell me," Alex said, his eyes cautious—searching, and Rosalee was almost too lost in her thoughts to remember her question.

It *was* different, she decided. Here, she wasn't putting on a show to vent her frustration or get away from herself. Instead, she was open and vulnerable. Maybe that was why it was so terrifying.

Alex lifted a hand out of the warm water to brush Rosalee's hair out of her face, and she captured his hand and held it against her throat, closing her eyes. When she opened them again, Alex looked like he was holding his breath. She traced the outline of his mouth with her fingertips.

"I *do* want you, Alex," she whispered.

She watched his eyes drop to her lips before he flipped them in the water so that he was hovering over her, supporting her weight with one arm while the other hand gripped the side of the hot tub to keep them from floating away. He kissed slowly and methodically down her sternum and she felt heat blossoming over her skin as an unconscious sigh escaped her lips.

Rosalee pulled Alex closer, lifting her lower body to meet his and wrapping her legs around his waist. His fingers at the base of her neck contracted briefly and then he was kissing her with a kind of desperation that stole the air from her lungs and made all of the veins in her body tingle. Still, she wasn't close enough and half-wrestled him in the water until she was straddling him again.

"I was ... thinking about your fantasy," she said, reaching carefully between them. She fumbled briefly before Alex gasped and buried his face in her shoulder again, a moan reverberating deep in his chest and against Rosalee's skin.

His breathing turned increasingly ragged as she touched him, and when he resurfaced, he chanted incomprehensible words against her lips until they were both delirious. Finally, Rosalee paused, waiting until Alex met her gaze. The awe and agony in his eyes almost took her breath away again.

"I want to feel everything you wrote, Alex," she said, "All of it."

———— •●• ————

"Where are you going?"

"Nowhere."

"Then what are you doing?"

"Trying to pull this blanket up. You're shivering."

"I know. Just come back."

Rosalee sighed, snuggling into Alex's chest. "... *Seriously*, Alex."

His laugh echoed in the mostly empty living room. "I'm not cold. That was just ..."

"What?"

Alex raked a hand through his damp hair and blew out a breath. "Intense."

Rosalee drew back slightly and Alex groaned. "Are you okay?" she said, ignoring his continued protest.

"*Ugh.*" Alex flung an arm over his eyes. "Yes, I'm embarrassed."

"About what?"

"Falling apart after ..."

Rosalee tried to pry his arm away, to no avail. "Well, you haven't had your cigarette yet."

"*Mm.* Don't remind me," said Alex. "How are you?"

Rosalee sighed and ran her fingertips down Alex's chest before he caught them and kissed them. "*So* good. I'm boneless. You ... *de*-boned me."

"Nice."

"Really, though, if I'd known what I was missing, I might not have ignored you so long."

"Stop it," Alex groaned.

Rosalee laughed. "I'm serious. That was some mind-blowing stuff."

Alex lowered his arm to look at her. "Yeah?"

Rosalee didn't answer but arched up to kiss his shoulder, then his neck.

"Jesus *Christ,* Rosalee, how are you not exhausted?"

"I don't know maybe ..." *Maybe the medication is working.*

Adrenaline-laced euphoria flooded Rosalee's system and she lost herself in Alex again, forgetting all of her reasons not to.

"Oh, god, you're gonna kill me," said Alex, breaking away but clutching her hair in his fists. "You're *actually* going to kill me. I'm ready to go all over again and I know I can't—"

"Shhh." Rosalee stemmed his rambling with a finger to his lips, then kissed down his chest as his hands worked further into her hair. "You don't have to do anything."

Chapter 42

"I want to be your sister again," Rosalee said quietly to her breakfast. "I just don't know how."

She nudged a soft, bloated blueberry with her spoon so that it left behind a purplish divot in her oatmeal, then scooped it into her mouth. As she ate, she leafed through one of Evelyn's Betty Crocker cookbooks until she reached the desserts. The name of the cake she had remembered at the condo still eluded her, but suddenly, there it was, after Boston Cream Pie—a "Chocolate Alexander Cake." She would have laughed in different circumstances.

Rosalee knew that her sister was awake because she could hear her TV. Ellie liked to have that or her boombox on while she got ready for the day. Nervous butterflies assaulted Rosalee's stomach. It shouldn't be so hard to open up to someone she had known most of her life, but maybe that made it harder.

She wished she could be as brave with her family as she could with Alex, but with him, everything had kind of fallen into place at the condo when she realized that the person he saw and dreamed about in his fantasies was the same person she longed to be and knew that she *was* under all of the protective scar tissue.

The thought of baking still made Rosalee's chest ache, but maybe it was her best option to win Ellie over again. Ellie loved raspberry Linzer and lemon tea cookies, although her all-time favorite dessert was Evelyn's lemon bars. Of course, that would require Rosalee admitting that she had the recipe and had been hoarding it, along with the others, for months.

And there it was: the remedy.

Rosalee felt her body tense as what little oatmeal she had eaten while she talked to herself began to churn. She forced herself to swallow several more bites, which stuck on the way down, the way oatmeal sometimes did before it was chased with coffee.

Ten minutes later, she stood outside Ellie's door, hands clammy around the box that contained everything her sister had been looking for. Still, Rosalee had allowed herself a last act of cowardice and stuffed the recipe box inside a shoebox so that she could at least be across the room when Ellie discovered its contents.

Rosalee knocked softly and heard a muffled "Come in."

Ellie was seated at her vanity, pinning her hair up with bobby pins that she held in her mouth. She glanced in the mirror at Rosalee, then returned her focus to the perfect bun she was crafting. She left a couple of soft tendrils around her face, then admired the effect. Rosalee could tell she was taking her time on purpose, refusing to make the first move.

"Your hair looks pretty," said Rosalee.

"Fanks." Ellie stuck the last two pins in and spritzed a halo of hair spray.

"What's the occasion?"

Ellie shrugged.

"Avoiding me?" Rosalee said, going for a teasing tone to lighten the mood.

"Maybe."

"Well ... I brought a peace offering."

She set the shoebox in a clear space at the end of Ellie's vanity, where she saw her sister's eyes move briefly, then dart away again. It soon became apparent that Ellie was not about to open the box in her presence, so Rosalee saw herself out and trudged down the stairs to slump at the kitchen table again. Then, feeling restless, she decided to get down to some dishes, instead. She assumed it would take Ellie at least ten minutes before her curiosity got the best of her and right on cue, an outraged gasp came from above her as Ellie appeared on the balcony.

"Are you kidding me?" Rosalee winced as her sister nearly flew down the stairs, the recipe box cradled in her hands and tears in her eyes. "I've been going crazy and scouring the house for these, and you've had them the whole time? What the *hell* is wrong with you, Rosalee?"

"I know. I'm so sorry."

Ellie set the box down on the kitchen table with a *thunk* and lifted the lid, fingers trembling. Had Rosalee ever seen her that angry before? She watched as her sister began to rifle through the recipes, now and then emitting more gasps and grumblings.

"Lemon bars, cherry snowballs, monster cookies ... are there any more, or is this it?"

"That's it." Rosalee felt prickling shame spreading to the tips of her ears and turning them red. "The yellow cake recipe is in the back."

Ellie flipped to it, her mouth tightening. "I can't believe this, Rosalee. I can't believe *you.* Maybe you've decided to give up on baking now that Evelyn is gone, but that doesn't mean that the rest of us have."

"I *know.* I just couldn't face her recipes now that she's ... which is why I threw an entire bowl of batter away before Pete and Alex's party."

But Ellie wasn't listening and Rosalee could feel her sister's rage billowing like clouds before a thunderstorm. "You don't get to decide how the rest of us grieve, okay? If you get to pop those stupid Tic Tacs and pretend they're pills and play with Alex like he's some sort of Ken Doll, then I should get to bake my beloved aunt's lemon bars, Robin should be able to go to church if she wants to, and maybe you should get a grip on your own life."

Rosalee tugged on a stray end of her sweater, determined not to let the tears shivering at the edges of her eyelids fall. She didn't need to make Ellie feel bad for *her* mistakes, but she couldn't help feeling humiliated about all of the things she thought she kept hidden from her family, even if she hadn't done the Tic Tac thing in months. She sincerely hoped the comment about Alex was out of anger, though. She had tried so hard to make things different with him. She stared at the table while Ellie continued to fume and flip through the recipe box with almost violent gusto.

"I never said Robin shouldn't go to church," said Rosalee. "I'm just wondering *why* she's going to church. All of a sudden. After all these years."

Ellie rolled her eyes, standing up from the table before scooting her chair out so that it screeched in protest against the wood floor. She slammed the lid shut on the recipe box.

"Look, Ellie, I never—"

"No, *you* look, Rosalee. Maybe you should stop trying to control everyone and every*thing* in your life before you drive everyone out of it."

Rosalee winced as Ellie stomped back up the stairs, slamming her door for good measure. She dimly registered that her breaths were rattling out of her chest and that she had lost the battle with her tear ducts. She didn't bother to wipe them away until they dripped from her chin.

The phone rang several times before it occurred to Rosalee to answer it.

"Hey, you," said Alex.

"Hey." Rosalee tried to sniff away from the mouthpiece.

"Are you okay?"

"I just got in a fight with Ellie."

"Bad?"

"Pretty bad."

"So maybe not a great time for me to ask if I can see you?"

"When?"

"In about an hour and a half. I have a microscopic break between Oliver and work."

Rosalee stared at the clock on the oven, but couldn't seem to make any sense of the numbers. "I really want to. But I feel like I should do some damage control. Plus I'm helping Robin close tonight."

"Do you wanna talk about the fight?"

"Maybe later. I can handle it."

"Okay. I'll call you on my break tonight."

"Yes, please. Talk to you later."

Rosalee hung up and stared around the kitchen. She had half expected her sister to start talking to her again after all the yelling was over. Now, she was unsure how to proceed. She thought about making apple dumplings. Apples sounded good, now that it was fall—not that they weren't delicious all year round, but especially during fall. There were also chunks of rhubarb stashed in the freezer, but rhubarb crisp would almost seem lazy, especially since it was already harvested and sliced. She felt that she needed to labor in her atonement.

Rosalee sorted through the mental Rolodex of recipes she could remember by heart and finally decided on Apple Charlotte as a compromise. She wondered vaguely if she should try to make the bread crumbs without wheat, but immediately decided against that. After all, she had thus far failed to stick to that particular recommendation, although she had cut back on bread, hoping it would count for something. And anyway, this dessert wasn't *for* her—it was for her sister.

After all, who else did she have in the house with the steadily worsening tension? Rosalee and Ellie still hadn't been filled in on the specifics of the loan meeting for the B&B, but Robin and Lola's persistent bad moods and short tempers had since seeped throughout the house like a poisonous gas, reaching out with twisting, ghostly fingers to slide down its next victim's throat. It had been relatively quiet the past few days, but that was only because Lola was on a business trip.

Rosalee set about gathering her ingredients and baking components, willing her mind to stay away from Evelyn and simply allow herself to slip into the world of baking, where it was warm and comforting. She thought of Pete as she ran several thick slices of cinnamon raisin bread through a food processor and then toasted them in butter on the stove. It wasn't an obvious connection, since she couldn't imagine him eating something like that unless he was feeling particularly whimsical. Maybe if Ellie coaxed him into it. That thought made Rosalee smile as she grated lemon zest and was immediately transported to the deli of The Goose. As she sliced apples into slivers, she thought of Evelyn's apple pie ... she hastily and haphazardly chopped the rest of them as she ripped her mind away from that subject.

As Rosalee pressed the soft, sweet-smelling breadcrumbs into a glass baking dish, she heard footsteps behind her and wondered if the familiar smell had wafted up to Ellie's room and lured her back to the kitchen. However, when she turned around, she was surprised to find Robin lingering silently behind her, sorting the mail almost aimlessly.

"Hey, Robin."

Her aunt started.

"Are you okay?" said Rosalee, frowning as she turned down the heat on the sugar, lemon zest, and cinnamon from one of the burners.

"Oh, I uh ... oh, you're baking." Robin looked almost happy, then aimless again. "Did Lola call today?"

Something in the back of Rosalee's mind slipped off its track. *What a weird question.* "No, but I assumed she was at her class. Didn't she come back from her trip last night?"

Rosalee tried not to panic as she saw the telltale signs of Robin shutting down. She heard a *pop* and *hiss* behind her and hastened to take her sugar mixture off of the burner. By the time she turned back, Robin had gone and Rosalee cursed softly, looking at her half-made dessert. As quickly as she could, she layered the apples over the crumbs, poured her mixture over that, and then spooned hasty dollops of apricot jam over the top before shoving the dish in the oven and setting the timer.

Then she hurried up the stairs and into her aunts' room, where Robin was toweling her face dry.

"Aunt Robin, what's going on? Are you guys fighting again?"

Robin didn't answer as she hung her towel back up and took the sweatband out of her hair, then brushed it through several times with her fingers. Suddenly, Rosalee had a horrible suspicion. She had fallen asleep almost immediately the night before, an hour or so before Lola's ETA.

"Robin ... Lola came home last night, right?"

Ellie appeared suddenly in the doorway, eyes round. "What's going on? Is Lola missing? Should we call the Sheriff?"

Robin looked at them before sitting down resignedly on the edge of her bed. "Lola's fine, we're—She's staying with Gwen for a few days."

Rosalee and Ellie exchanged looks of confusion.

"What, like, a sleepover?" Even as Rosalee said it, it sounded ridiculous. "Gwen?" she said, then turned it over in her head. "*Gwen,* oh my god."

Robin clicked her tongue. "It's nothing like that, they're just friends."

"Jeez, Rosalee," Ellie muttered, but Rosalee ignored her.

"Robin—"

"Look, girls, I appreciate the concern, but I really don't want to get into this now. So, if you'll excuse me, I'd like to lie down for a while before I have to go back to The Goose."

Ellie and Rosalee looked at each other—or more, Rosalee looked while Ellie glared then walked away with her nose in the air. Rosalee followed her halfway down the hall.

"I made you Apple Charlotte," she called after her, but Ellie disappeared again with a snap of her bedroom door.

Rosalee walked heavily back down to the kitchen. The timer had seven minutes left, so she set to work whipping sugar and vanilla into heavy cream. When it was time to add the rum, she stopped short. With a sinking feeling, she realized that she didn't want to open the liquor cabinet. Whether she was afraid of finding the empty bottles she was fairly certain she had left behind or new, full ones in their places, she wasn't sure. Either way, she avoided the cabinet altogether and rummaged through the spice cabinet instead, hoping to find an imitation. As she suspected, though, there was no such substitute. Evelyn had always liked to use the "real thing" in anything she baked—real eggs, real butter, real booze.

As Rosalee stared at the pure white topping, she felt her gaze pulled back to the liquor cabinet. Surely a little peek wouldn't hurt—just to see how strong she was and how far she'd come—plus, she really did need it for the recipe. She felt a little bubble of disgust floating upward inside her as she looked around her to make sure that she was alone, then reached for the cabinet door.

It was empty.

Rosalee shut it again, bracing herself on the edge of the stove, warm from the small amount of heat leaking out of the door. Relief, guilt, and disappointment swept over her in equal measure and she was awash in her emotions for several long moments before her thoughts turned to Alex. Alex, who was perhaps the only person in her life who would understand the way she was feeling—the emptiness, the lightness, the anger that no one had thought to replace all of the bottles with something else—*anything* else—to avoid the bare and cavernous space for which she hadn't been prepared.

Rosalee glanced at the clock. If she hurried, she might be able to catch Alex before work. It had been three days since the condo and she got butterflies every time she thought about it. She covered the bowl of rum-less topping with aluminum foil and put it in the fridge as the oven timer went off. She set the pan of hot, spicy apples on top of the stove to cool and hurried to the bathroom to yank a brush through her hair.

⎯⎯⎯ •●• ⎯⎯⎯

Rosalee took Ellie's car without asking (after all, it was Lola's, anyway) and arrived on Alex and Pete's front porch as out of breath as if she had run there. Alex opened the door in his Laurie's shirt and jeans. He paused, the happy surprise fading from his face as he took in her erratic appearance.

"Hey," he said, leaning against the door jamb. "Is everything okay?"

"No. I don't know. I just wanted to see you."

"Okay." He stepped aside to let her in and Rosalee quickly shed her coat and bag.

"Is Pete here?"

"No, he's at work. Why?"

Rosalee didn't bother answering. She felt frenzied and almost manic as she kissed him and her hands worked across his shoulders and down his chest, but he was nearly matching her energy and she hoped that he only sensed passion. Almost in answer to her thoughts, though, she felt him pulling away.

"Rosalee, wait ..." Alex groaned as she jerked him back by his belt loops and attacked his mouth again. After several moments, he managed to push her back to arms' length, although he was nearly panting from the effort. "What happened? What's wrong?"

"Nothing. Everything," Rosalee shook her head at the blatant lie that had come out first. "I don't wanna think about it right now."

"Well then, do you want—"

"You. Just you. *Please.*"

Rosalee watched Alex's Adam's Apple bob as he swallowed then reached out to touch her face. She closed her eyes, nuzzling into his touch before turning her head to kiss the inside of his wrist, where she could feel his pulse quickening against her mouth.

"I missed you," she whispered into his skin.

Alex used both hands to tilt her face toward his, kissing her softly as his thumbs stroked along her jaw and down the sides of her neck. She sighed and deepened the kiss, locking her arms around his waist. When they broke apart again, the dark brown eyes that stared into hers had warmed to the color of root beer, sparking recent fond memories and soothing the chaos in her chest as she gazed back at him.

"How long before your shift?" she said.

When Rosalee arrived home, she entered the kitchen to find Ellie toying half-heartedly with a bowl of Apple Charlotte in front of her.

"I made the whipping, too. *Topping,*" Rosalee corrected herself as she hung up her coat and bag. "It's in the fridge.

Ellie looked at her.

"I'll get it," said Rosalee.

She grabbed the covered bowl out of the fridge, then opened the cabinet for an ice cream bowl. She felt much calmer than when she had left, but the nerves in her stomach sparked menacingly as she thought about the actual idea of eating. She closed the cabinet again and dug in the silverware drawer for a spoon instead, carrying the topping and utensil to the table and placing it in front of her sister, who barely looked up.

"I'm sorry I hid them," said Rosalee, sitting across from her.

"I'm sorry for the things I said after you hid them."

"Well ... you were right. Just because *I* can't stand to make these recipes anymore doesn't mean no one else should get to."

Ellie paused, clearly torn between sympathy and her love of Evelyn's famous baked goods. She pulled the topping toward her and lifted the aluminum foil, digging out a generous helping for her dessert. Rosalee leaned forward to grab the spoon from her sister before she put it back into the bowl.

"Plus," she said, "it felt better than I thought it would. Making them, I mean. Kind of ... therapeutic?"

"That's how it is for me," said Ellie. "That's why I wanted to find them. I feel, like, closer to her when I bake her stuff or even just ... sit in her room."

Rosalee paused licking the topping off the spoon. "I know. I don't know what I was thinking."

Ellie shrugged.

"I don't ... know how to be your sister again," said Rosalee. She couldn't believe she was using her oatmeal speech.

"Don't be stupid," said Ellie, finally scooping a respectable portion of apples and topping into her spoon. "You're always my sister."

Chapter 43

Rosalee had always loved Rabbitbrush around the holidays—especially The Goose.

Transitioning into fall, the deli and meat cases began to feature less coleslaw and macaroni salad and more hearty fare, like roasted fingerling potatoes and Brussels sprouts. Approximately three weeks before Thanksgiving, the cranberry sauce and green bean casserole would appear alongside twice-baked and sweet potatoes and walnut stuffing. Robin had discovered early on that even though people in Rabbitbrush liked making their own Thanksgiving feasts, that didn't stop them from wanting to experience the festive dishes nearly a month early.

Then, of course, there were the smoked chickens. Nearly a decade ago, Robin had acquired two large smokers for the meat department, and Rabbitbrush and the surrounding areas had gone crazy over the smoked birds. They were much easier to manage than whole turkeys, and people loved them all the way through Christmas, when they shared the spotlight with honey-baked hams.

The day before Thanksgiving, Rosalee spent so much time lost in holiday aromas, she almost felt dizzy. Halfway through writing the Day-Before-Thanksgiving specials board, she realized that her arms felt weak and her writing was shaky. Had she eaten breakfast? She couldn't remember, but it felt like she had been having blood sugar issues since

Monday—it was hard to remember to take breaks with everything so crazy at the store. Plus, the harder she worked, the less time she had to ruminate on the idea of the holidays without her late aunt.

Begrudgingly, Rosalee flagged down Elijah to finish her sign, then resigned herself to a five-minute break in the back to scarf a Power Bar. She had been working since five AM but convinced Robin to let her stay until three o'clock since the store was closing early that day. Apparently, she would need all the strength she could muster until then.

After fifteen minutes, during which Rosalee finished her bar, gulped down almost a full bottle of water, and broke down boxes from at least fifty orders, she headed back up to the registers and realized on the way that her foot had gone numb. She must have been sitting on it. She walked as normally as possible to relieve the cashiers for their lunches and was annoyed that her arms and legs still felt weak.

By one thirty, Robin pulled her off the register and into the office.

"Sit," she said, pointing to the desk chair in front of the main computer and shutting the door behind them.

"I'm staying until three, Robin. You need the help." Rosalee tried not to sink too far into the worn leather.

"No, I don't," said Robin. "Per my Thanksgiving tradition, I over-scheduled and underestimated the number of folks going out of town tomorrow, so we're good. Also, you look like hell."

"Gee, thanks."

Rosalee tried to sit up straighter, to no avail. Meanwhile, her foot continued to tingle.

"Have you been sleeping lately?" said Robin.

"Yes."

"Poorly?"

"Not particularly."

"Look ... I know it's the holidays and everything is hectic ..." Robin sighed. "Okay, I'm only going to ask you this once, but *please,* if you value my sanity at all, answer it honestly."

Rosalee felt little beads of sweat popping along her hairline. "Okay ..."

"Have you been ... self-medicating again?"

"Oh," said Rosalee, blowing out her breath in relief. "No, I just haven't been remembering to eat regularly. That's it, I promise."

"And you're remembering your actual meds?"

"Yup."

Robin gave her one more searching look but seemed satisfied. "Well, maybe you should see about upping your dosage if that's possible. You sound exhausted."

"Yeah, maybe."

Rosalee leaned forward to get out of the chair and back on the floor, but Robin held out a hand to stop her. "If I asked you to please clock out and go home, would you?"

"It's only another few hours."

"Rosalee ..."

"What? What's wrong?"

"You were kind of slurring your words up there," said Robin, not quite meeting her eyes. "You still are a little."

"I am?"

Rosalee felt suddenly cold.

Robin crossed her arms and then uncrossed them. "Is that a symptom, do you remember?"

Rosalee felt like she was falling, even though she was still sitting.

"No, I don't—remember." Suddenly, her tongue felt too big for her mouth as her blood pressure mounted. "Oh god."

"Hey, hey." Robin leaned forward and held her by the shoulders. "Don't go there yet, okay? Let's see how you feel after some rest."

"God, I hope the customers didn't think I was drunk."

Now Robin was definitely not meeting her eyes. *Fantastic.*

"I'm gonna go, I think," said Rosalee.

She finally succeeded in emerging from the depths of the chair and forced herself not to wince as she stood on the foot still full of pins and needles.

"You taking the bus?" said Robin.

"Yeah."

At this point, the idea of walking home was intolerable.

Robin checked her watch. "Better get out there, then. Don't worry about clocking out—I'll do it."

"Thanks, Robin. I'll see you at home." Rosalee paused with her hand on the doorknob. "Have you heard from Lola?"

"Not yet."

Rosalee felt her pulse spike unpleasantly as she watched her aunt blink back tears, but forced her face into what she hoped was a reassuring expression. "She'll call, I know she will."

———— •●• ————

When Rosalee got home, Ellie was poring over recipes for the next day. She had already prepped several of the side dishes and Robin would bring the smoked chickens home that night with the pumpkin pie.

"Wow, did you leave anything for *me* to do?" said Rosalee.

Ellie surveyed the counter. "Not really. Oh. Except for the rolls. We can do those tomorrow." She stopped and looked at Rosalee. "*God,* are you okay?"

"Boy howdy, my self-confidence is taking a real nose dive today."

416

"Sorry, you just look ... *bad.*"

"That's much better, thank you. I'm fine—busy. Low blood sugar, yada yada."

Rosalee sank into one of the chairs at the kitchen table, then realized that Ellie was looking at her with a mixture of suspicion and fear. "I'm not drunk. Robin already asked me."

"Then why do you sound so—"

"I don't know, El."

Rosalee couldn't tell if her sister believed her.

"Well, have you eaten lunch?" said Ellie. "Wanna go get something at Laurie's?"

"Yeah, just let me change."

"Why? We can get it to go. *Ohhh*, but Alex might be there."

"I'll be fast," said Rosalee, although her legs weren't quite cooperating on that point. She changed as quickly as possible into jeans and a sweater, trying to ignore how much longer than normal it took.

"C'mon, they're gonna be closed by the time you're ready," Ellie whined.

"Take a pill. I gotta pee."

"Okay." Ellie seemed to be hanging out on the other side of the bathroom door. "You never told me about housesitting—was it fun?"

"Yeah, it was—Oh, *whoa.*"

"What? What's the matter?"

Rosalee gritted her teeth at the sudden, throbbing pain south of her abdomen.

"What's wrong?" Ellie called through the door. "What are you doing?"

Rosalee gasped, doubling over so that her elbows dug into her thighs. "Peeing."

"Uh-oh."

"What? What's 'uh-oh?'" Rosalee said into her knees.

"You probably have a UTI."

"What the *hell* is a UTI?"

<hr>

"Urinary tract infection," said the nurse. "Very common."

Rosalee groaned. Ellie shot her a sympathetic look over the latest issue of *Marie Claire* she had snatched from the urgent care waiting room.

"Is this your first infection?" said the nurse.

"I think so."

"How's your hygiene?"

"Good. Oh, you mean like …? Um, yeah, still good."

"Period?"

"What?"

"Is it regular?"

"I think so."

"I have a few more personal questions," the nurse said. "If you'd like, it could just be the two of us."

Rosalee considered, but at this point, did she have any more secrets from Ellie?

"It's fine," she said.

The nurse flipped to a new page. "Are you sexually active?"

Damn it.

"… Yes."

"Are you on the pill?"

"No."

"But you're using protection?"

"Yes."

"How many sexual partners have you had in the past year?"

"... Two."

At least Ellie already knew about the first one.

"Any other medical conditions not noted on your chart?" said the nurse, reviewing yet another page. "I see we already have ... MS?" She looked up again and finally seemed to give Rosalee her full attention, precisely when she didn't want it. "You're so young."

—••—

"So ... I should have waited in the hall," said Ellie. "Sorry."

Rosalee shook her head. "Don't be. I could have asked you to leave."

"I feel like so much has happened in the last year, ya know? Things we haven't talked about."

"Like what?"

Ellie glanced sideways at her and Rosalees suddenly regretted the invitation in her response.

"I know it's kinda late now, but do you wanna get french fries or something?" she said before her sister could take her up on it. "I have to take these antibiotics with food, and it's the only thing that sounds good right now. We could get them to go."

"Okay. I've actually been jonesing for an Arnold Palmer since last week. It was so warm," said Ellie wistfully. "And maybe we should get dinner since no one will feel like cooking tonight. Laurie's?"

Rosalee chewed her lip. She was sure she didn't want Alex to see her like this and couldn't remember if he was working. Meanwhile, Ellie took her silence as assent and pulled into a parking spot while Rosalee dug some rumpled bills out of her pocket.

"You're not coming in?" said Ellie.

Rosalee shook her head. "Alex."

419

"Are you guys fighting?"

"No, but *look* at me."

"Okay. Well, it could be a few minutes—and it's pretty cold in here."

"I'll be fine, El."

Rosalee watched her disappear into the diner, then suddenly felt claustrophobic. The temperature was barely above freezing, but the sun was shining so brightly that she couldn't stand being stuck in the car. She took the keys out of the ignition and pocketed them, then walked across the dry, late autumn grass to sit on a wooden bench next to a flowerbed that played host to every color of rose imaginable in the spring and summer months. As she sat, she tried to ignore the achy pain in her bladder and will the sunshine to soak into the top of her head and fill the rest of her body. She also admonished herself for not going in with her sister when she realized that she hadn't talked to Alex in days and didn't want him to think she was avoiding him.

Another throb in her lower abdomen distracted Rosalee momentarily from her thoughts and she doubled over in pain. She hung upside down, her gaze unfocused as she peered through the gap between her ankles and noticed that the backs of her legs were wet and dripping into her socks. She twisted around to look behind her, cursing whoever had neglected to shut off the sprinklers in November, but saw nothing to account for the wetness. Besides, the water was warm.

Another pang.

Rosalee winced, still searching wildly for the source of the water. Then she felt her blood run cold with dread. The seat of the bench was wet now, as were her jeans, and she bit her lip to fight back tears as she looked quickly around her again—this time to check if anyone was outside to witness her mortification. Luckily, she and Ellie seemed to have come at a slow time for the cafe, and her sister was already backing out of the front door with a to-go bag and soft drink container.

Even so, Rosalee felt her body going into all-out panic mode. She couldn't keep sitting in her own urine, but even if she got up and pretended to have waited by the car, how would she explain the giant wet spot on the back of her jeans? Ellie reached her before she could thaw the indecision that froze her to the bench. One look at Rosalee's tear-stained face and wet pant legs evidently told her everything she needed to know.

"Can you get up?" she whispered. Rosalee nodded, dying of shame. "Do you remember if we have towels in the trunk?"

Rosalee shook her head. Any minute now, someone was bound to walk out of the cafe, or out of their car. Ellie seemed to be thinking along the same lines. She set the to-go bag down on a curb and then without warning, dumped the entirety of her Arnold Palmer in Rosalee's lap.

"What are you doing?!" Rosalee yelped, jumping up from the bench as the iced tea and lemonade soaked into her jeans.

"I'll get some towels." Ellie raised her eyebrows and hurried back into the diner.

Several minutes later, she returned with a half-used roll of paper towels, a trash bag, and a new drink. She handed Rosalee the paper towels and opened the passenger side door to arrange the trash bag so that it covered the seat.

"Thanks," Rosalee muttered as she began to clean herself up.

If ever the Earth decided to swallow someone whole, this would be the day to do it, she thought. In fact, she wouldn't even wait to get sucked into the swirling vortex—today, she would jump.

Chapter 44

Rosalee stood in the mirror, towel-drying her hair after a shower that she knew was too hot, but not hot enough to scour away the wretchedness of the day. She sat on the edge of the tub to pull her clothes on, her body still too weak to do the daily things she had always taken for granted. She peered into the mirror again at her puffy eyes and wondered if she would be able to slip into her room undetected by her family. Unlikely, since she had used the downstairs shower and was still living in the guest room. At least she wouldn't have to climb the stairs.

The medication wasn't working—that was the only conclusion that made sense for her worsening symptoms. No matter how Rosalee tried to pass off her weakness as low blood sugar, eating never seemed to fix the issue. Plus, no matter how much sleep she got, it didn't prevent the marrow-deep fatigue from seeping back into her bones. She should have known that the temporary relief couldn't last forever. After all, medication was science, not magic. And now, on top of everything, she had experienced her first bout of incontinence since she was five years old, from an infection that probably had something to do with her recent interactions with Alex. If that wasn't a sign from the universe that she wasn't meant to be her old self again, she didn't know what was.

While Rosalee attempted to pull a wide-toothed comb through her hair, she grew quickly impatient at the reluctance of her fingers to wrap around its handle and her arm's refusal to hold itself up. For the first time since the hair curler fiasco, she was grateful that her hair was short now. By the time she had finally worked through the tangles, she heard the phone ring in the kitchen and then a knock on the bathroom door.

"Rose, it's for you," said Ellie's voice from the other side.

"Who is it?" As if she didn't already know.

"It's Alex."

"Can you tell him I'm still in the shower?"

What if someone had seen her at Laurie's besides Ellie and told him? Or what if Ellie got the paper towels and plastic bag *from* him and he found out that Rosalee had avoided him on purpose? Either way, she wasn't about to let him in on her urgent care visit or its revelations—she had enough to be mortified about at the moment.

———•●•———

When Rosalee finally emerged from the bathroom and wandered into the kitchen, Ellie and Robin were sitting at the table with steaming mugs of hot chocolate. When Rosalee sat down to join them, Ellie hopped up to pour her a mug from the stove.

"Everything okay?" said Rosalee.

She was suddenly suspicious that Ellie had filled Robin in about their afternoon, despite Rosalee swearing her to secrecy. But as Robin continued to stare at a space above the table, she guessed that probably wasn't the topic at hand.

"Lola still hasn't called," said Ellie.

"Oh." Rosalee wrapped her fingers around her mug. Her aunt still wouldn't look up. "Should we go over and talk to her?"

Robin seemed to come back into herself a little and shook her head. "She'll come home when she's ready. I don't want to go over there and fight. That's all we do now."

Ellie shot Rosalee a startled look across the table. It wasn't very often that Robin let them in on the disagreements between her and Lola, and neither one of them was very well prepared to respond.

"Is it about the bed and breakfast?" said Ellie tentatively.

"Usually," said Robin. She contemplated her placemat and Ellie shot Rosalee a "your turn" look.

Rosalee cleared her throat. "Why can't you ... I mean, is there a reason you're not using the money from Evelyn's estate for the bed and breakfast? Is that what you guys have been fighting about?"

She looked at her sister again. This was getting close to uncharted territory. She had never seen her aunt so vulnerable—at least not since everything with Evelyn. Months ago, Rosalee hadn't had the energy to weed the gardens properly. Now, if ever there was a digger-type weed cutter job waiting to be tackled, it was whatever was eating Robin, who tended to stuff her feelings down tighter than a garbage compactor. That made the process of drawing out the little pockets of poison that got trapped in the layers all the more challenging. Rosalee knew that she would just have to dive in with the same dedication as total button weed extraction, and those suckers' roots could grow to two feet long.

"Aunt Robin ... you *know* Evelyn would have wanted you to open the bed and breakfast, right?" said Ellie.

"Yeah, she wouldn't have wanted you to give up just because—" Rosalee felt a lump rising in her throat and couldn't finish.

"What if I did it?" Robin croaked. She looked at Rosalee and Ellie at last, her eyes rimmed with red and a tortured expression on her face.

Ellie shared a confused look with Rosalee. "What if you did what?"

"Evelyn and I worried and *bitched* about never having the money to do this and then ... and *now* ..."

"Oh," said Ellie softly.

"Oh my god, Robin, *no,*" said Rosalee. "Are you saying you think you *killed* her?"

"'*He who is greedy for gain troubles his own house,*'" said Robin.

Rosalee didn't immediately recognize the quote, but it sounded Shakespearean. Or biblical.

A tear made its way down Robin's cheek and soaked into her over-shirt, and Rosalee wrestled with her stupid inability to show love for the people she cared about. Lola forced Robin into hugs all the time, but Rosalee didn't know if she took comfort in them. Ellie and Lola were clearly sewn from similar cloth, though, and her sister didn't hesitate to go to Robin's side and wrap her arms around her. Rosalee moved chairs so that she was closer to them and took Robin's hand. It wasn't the most she could do, but for now, it was something. When she felt her aunt return the pressure, she knew it was at least that.

"Robin," said Rosalee, "Aunt Evelyn died because she never should have been on that hormone therapy. Not because you somehow ... *wished her dead* to help your financial situation."

Robin wiped under her eyes with her free hand. "I know. But maybe if I had been more appreciative of what I had ... I *never* wanted this. It feels like both of my siblings are gone."

Rosalee glanced at Ellie again. She couldn't remember the last time Robin or Evelyn had brought up their brother—Rosalee and Ellie's father.

Rosalee held Robin's hand tighter as she cried while Ellie continued to cling to her other side.

"Did you tell Lola all of this?" said Ellie.

"Yes."

"And she didn't understand?"

"She did," said Robin. "We thought we might wait on Evelyn's money for now and see about an insurance claim for Lola's studio instead."

"Oh. That's a great idea," said Rosalee.

"So then, what's the problem?" said Ellie.

Robin stared miserably at the dregs of her hot chocolate when the sound of a key in a lock made them all stare at the front door. After what felt like minutes, Lola entered the kitchen, carrying her overnight bag.

For several long moments, no one moved. Rosalee knew that her sister was probably caught in the same emotional conundrum she was—if they ran to greet Lola, was it a betrayal of Robin? On the other hand, if they stayed at the table, would it look like they were choosing Robin *over* Lola? As a compromise, Ellie stood and looked indecisive while Rosalee waved at Lola from the table and hoped she looked welcoming.

Lola closed the door behind her and set down her bag, smiling tentatively. "Didn't expect to see all my girls at once."

That was enough to unravel Ellie and she rushed to hug her. Rosalee glanced at Robin, who was wiping hastily under her eyes, then rose from the table to join her sister, her adrenaline partially soothing the parts of her legs that still didn't let her walk normally as she crossed the room. Eventually, Rosalee and Ellie stood back to make room for Robin, who had approached silently behind them.

"Hi, love," Lola said softly.

"Hey."

Rosalee was surprised at how steady Robin's voice sounded, especially while her eyes seemed to be asking Lola whether she was home for good, or just long enough to retrieve her belongings.

Lola seemed to know what she was saying without words.

"I'm home." A single tear made a shiny track down her cheek. "Is that okay?"

Rosalee heard a sharp intake of breath next to her and saw Ellie trying to stifle her emotions with a hand over her mouth. When Rosalee looked back at Robin, her aunt's lips were pressed into a tight line, but she had moved closer to Lola and her hand was cupping her shoulder, then the nape of her neck.

"It isn't home without you," she said.

And with two deep, trembling breaths, they were in each other's arms.

———•●•———

Despite Evelyn's absence, Thanksgiving was more tolerable than Rosalee could have hoped. The house and table were full, with the Sheriff and Gwen (who had apparently been an item since a little before Rosalee's tree incident), Mr. and Mrs. Laurie, and several employees from The Goose whose families lived far away. Past Thanksgivings had also included Pete and his parents, but they had since moved out of town and Pete would be joining them in Aspen for skiing this year. Rosalee wondered fleetingly if he had invited Ellie. If so, she was grateful that her sister had decided to stay.

At one point, as Rosalee passed a large dish of steamed asparagus to Mrs. Laurie, she wondered if Alex's mother had come up to have Thanksgiving dinner with her sons. A surge of guilt nearly overwhelmed her as she imagined them eating microwaveable turkey dinners and cranberry sauce from a can on TV trays in Oliver's lonely room or Alex and Pete's empty apartment. She quickly excused herself to calm down in the bathroom and tried to ignore a tingling sensation

427

that started at her fingertips and created static up her arm nearly to her shoulder.

Why hadn't she thought to ask about Alex's plans?

Halfway through pumpkin pie, Rosalee wondered if it was better this way after all. While the chaos of the holiday had partially distracted her from her worsening symptoms, she couldn't help but notice them more in the quiet moments she was forced to sit with herself. If she really was getting worse and the medication wasn't going to cushion her fall, she would rather end things with Alex now, even if that thought made her airway tighten and ache in protest.

As she rinsed plates and silverware to load into the dishwasher, she tried not to think about the intense concentration on Alex's face the first time they touched while dancing, or his feet moving to music she couldn't hear under the table while she ate lunch and he peppered her with annoying questions. More recent memories of ardent whispers in the dark and his hands in her hair threatened to overwhelm her again before Lola and Robin joined her in the kitchen to start divvying up leftovers for their guests.

Lola reached around Rosalee at the sink to hand Robin a leftover pecan pie. "Will you wrap these slices for the Sheriff and Gwen, please, since you're closest to the tin foil?"

Robin took the pie plate from her but put it on the counter behind her and took Lola's hands.

"No, I really need you to wrap these up," said Lola, "they're about to lea—"

"Marry me," said Robin.

Rosalee turned off the faucet, sure she hadn't heard her aunt correctly, then turned to see Lola looking stunned and flustered.

"Look ..." Lola pulled her hands gently away from Robin and wiped them on her apron. "I told you, I thought about it and if it's not for you, it's not for you. I still want to *be* with you."

"I know I said 'no' before—"

"*Three* times."

Rosalee wondered if she should even be here for this conversation. She felt soapy water from her hands sliding down to soak into the fabric of the sweater sleeves that pooled at her elbows and hastily reached for a dish towel.

"I thought the timing needed to be right, or society needed to be right, or something," said Robin. "But none of that matters when I love you the way that I do. And I do."

Lola's lips pursed slightly as she studied Robin's face before turning back to the multitude of dishes on the counter. Robin stood watching her for a moment before walking out of the room, passing Ellie as she came through with used glasses and napkins.

She stopped abruptly as she noticed Lola and Rosalee's tense faces. "Whoa, what happened in here?"

Before anyone could answer, Robin reappeared with a ring box, which she flipped open to reveal a gorgeous art deco ring with a sapphire in the middle—the perfect ring for Lola. Ellie yelped and then covered her mouth with her hand.

"I got this a week ago, when I decided that I couldn't be without you," said Robin.

"And because you don't wanna fight anymore," said Lola grudgingly.

Robin caught her elbow and turned her back before she could immerse herself in leftovers again. "I never wanted you to feel like this wasn't your home. If this is what you need to feel like this is where you belong, I'll do it."

Lola felt behind her for the kitchen counter, leaning against the edge. "I know you think it's silly because it isn't *real*."

"It's important to you, which means it's important to me," said Robin. "I've known I wanted to spend the rest of my life with you for over a decade. I shouldn't mind telling the world that."

"You wanna get married?"

"I wanna get married."

"To me?"

"Is there a 'yes' coming?"

"Can I see the ring again?" Lola winked at Ellie and Rosalee.

Robin tsked and shoved the ring box up near her face, but Lola didn't move her gaze from Robin's eyes.

"*Yes*, I'll marry you," she said, "*Of course* I'll marry you, but boy oh boy, do I wish I could tell *you* 'no' three—"

The rest of her sentence was drowned out by Robin kissing her, and then Rosalee was distinctly aware of Ellie cheering and bouncing over to strangle her in a crazy hug as their aunts unwound themselves and Robin slipped the ring onto Lola's finger.

Chapter 45

Nearly a week after Thanksgiving, Rosalee watched pink cotton candy clouds illuminated by a crescent moon floating across the sky, occasionally wiping away the tears that slid continuously down her chin and dripped into her lap.

The back door opened and Rosalee turned too quickly, causing a crick in her neck.

"Hey," said Ellie.

"Hey."

"Alex called again."

"I know."

"Do you wanna talk about it?"

Rosalee pressed her lips together and turned away so that her sister couldn't see her face all screwed up like a toddler about to lose it. Ellie watched her for a moment before sitting next to her so that their legs were touching. She leaned into her and Rosalee leaned back, her body shaking with the things that she could no longer hold in.

"What the—*hell* am I gonna do, Ellie?" she sobbed into her knees.

"What are you talking about?"

Rosalee shook her head, refusing to lift it. Ellie only hesitated another second before wrapping an arm firmly around her shoulders and squeezing.

"I mean, this is it. This is the end. Next, I'll be in a wheelchair and I'll need someone to help me eat and brush my teeth and—*Oh god,*" Rosalee choked. "Ellie, I can't freaking do this."

Rosalee heard Ellie let out a slow breath. "Okay, first of all, I don't know what about today makes you think you'll be in a wheelchair."

Rosalee hiccuped and tried to steady her breathing. "The meds aren't working anymore. I was doing so much better. *Why* aren't they working anymore?"

"I don't know. But even if they're not, a wheelchair wouldn't be 'the end.'"

"El, do you want to know my worst fear with this disease? My absolute worst fear?"

"What?"

Rosalee looked at her sister, who was pale and nervous, then laughed and buried her head in her hands again. "I can't even say it."

"You don't have to say it."

"I can't stand the idea that I'm going to wake up one morning and—and not be able to take care of myself. Not be able to shower, or brush my teeth, or ... go to the—" Rosalee stared up at the sky, exhaling forcefully. *"I don't wanna shit myself!"*

For a moment, neither of them looked at the other. Then they both burst out laughing and couldn't stop for a long time.

"Oh, god. I think I'm gonna throw up," said Ellie.

"Me—too." Now, Rosalee's hiccups were worse than ever.

"I'm so sorry, Rose, I know it's not funny."

"No, it's not. I mean it *is,* but only because ... it hasn't happened yet."

"Okay, but what makes you think it's *going* to?"

"El, I *peed my pants* last week. In public. I feel like it only makes sense that that's next."

"Is that what you've been out here worrying about?"

"Well, wouldn't you? God, what if I can't work anymore, and then Robin and Lola have to hire someone to help me in the bathroom, and it drains all of our money, and then *they* have to help me in the bathroom? Jesus, I think I'm *actually* going to throw up."

"So, what does Alex have to do with all of this?"

"What do you mean?"

"I mean, why are you ignoring him?"

For a moment, Rosalee didn't know what to say. It seemed so obvious, she didn't think she would need to explain it.

"Because this isn't going to work. Not if my medication won't work, either, and not if I'm only going to get worse. I'm certainly not going to let *him* help me in the bathroom."

"Rose, forget about the bathroom for a second," said Ellie. "I think you're being pretty stupid about this."

"Ellie."

"Look, I'm sorry, but you'd say the same thing to me if I was spouting this nonsense. If Alex wanted to leave, he would have done so a *long* time ago."

"Not necessarily. He only barely found out. It's probably better to end this before it starts."

"I doubt he would agree with you."

"Yeah, well, we're both adults." Rosalee dipped her chin into the collar of her coat and sandwiched her hands between her knees. "Adults break up. He can deal with it."

Ellie crossed her arms over her lap and looked out across the snowy yard. "I'm not so sure."

"Why?" said Rosalee, suddenly suspicious. "Did you talk to him?"

"No, but Pete said he's worried about him."

"*That's* stupid. It's only been, like, a week or something since we've talked."

"Rosalee, come on."

"No, *you* come on." Rosalee turned to look at her sister. "You don't know what this feels like, okay? You don't know how it feels to think about someone who knows you *like that*, seeing you at your absolute crappiest—no pun intended. Okay? What if we got married and then I got worse and we couldn't afford help and my freaking *husband* had to help me in the bathroom? Do you think he'd ever want to see me naked in the romantic sense ever again?"

Ellie didn't appear to be convinced. "Don't you think that's sort of the point?" she said. "You know, of caring about someone that much? Of building a relationship? Don't you sort of have to let them see all of the different parts? Otherwise, why bother?"

"I don't even know if Alex and I are together."

Ellie made a noise of dissent.

"Well, I *don't*," said Rosalee.

"What were you really crying about before I came out here? The MS or Alex?"

"... Both."

Ellie looked thoughtful. "Come inside with me for a second."

"Why?"

"Just come."

"I don't want Aunties to see me."

"They're in their room. Can you climb the stairs?"

"Yeah, my legs seem better today."

Rosalee followed Ellie through the back door and kitchen, then up the stairs and down the darkening hallway to Evelyn's room. Ellie flipped on the ceiling light and sat down at the computer.

"I don't want to email Alex right now, El," said Rosalee.

"I know, relax. I was writing a paper earlier."

Ellie pulled a stack of textbooks next to the computer into her lap while Rosalee perched on the end of Evelyn's bed.

"You know, you never really told me how it was," said Ellie as she skimmed the top book's index.

"How what was?"

"With Alex."

"Oh."

"That good, huh?"

"What? No." Rosalee shook her head and let her thoughts stray for a moment to the night at the condo. Even now, it felt like a dream. "It was ... kind of amazing?"

"Wasn't it—" Ellie stopped, flushing, and set the first book aside.

"Wasn't it what?"

"Um, *weird?* In someone else's bed?"

"We weren't in someone else's bed. They had a hot tub."

Ellie stopped abruptly with her finger in the second book to mark her place. "Rosalee, *oh my god.*"

"We scrubbed it down afterward." Rosalee felt her cheeks heat up.

Ellie shook her head, then looked serious. "Was it scary?"

"No. I mean, not like ... *scary* scary. It's always a little nerve-racking opening up to someone, but—"

"What?"

"Have you ... ever ...?"

Ellie stared at the carpet, cheeks red again. "No, not yet."

"Well, good, you shouldn't. Not when Pete won't even take you to a dance."

"Yeah ..." Ellie twirled the end of her ponytail. "I may have altered some facts there."

"How so?"

"*He* wanted to go. Together. As a couple. *I* didn't want to because I wasn't ready to tell you yet."

Rosalee grabbed a throw pillow from the head of the bed and held it on her lap. "Oh."

"And then I wouldn't let him tell Angela that we were dating when she asked him to dinner, so he had to go."

"Jeez."

"I know."

Rosalee squeezed the pillow against her torso. "But now you're ... in love?"

"Yeah. Crazy, right?" Ellie smiled tentatively before turning back to the remaining books in her lap. "*Finally,*" she said, apparently finding what she was looking for in the index of the second book.

She flipped back to the middle pages while Rosalee argued with herself about whether or not to question her sister further. After all, it was *Pete* they were talking about—how much did she really want to know?

"Here we go. 'Incontinence: Symptoms and Causes,'" Ellie read. As she skimmed, she muttered the list under her breath. "Ha!"

She handed the open book to Rosalee, her face triumphant.

"There," she said, coming around to the side of the bed and tapping the correct paragraph. "Read that one."

"Urinary tract infection. Oh. *Oh.*"

"See? This isn't your body's way of telling you 'it's over,' or 'the meds aren't working,' this is your body's way of telling you not to have sex in a friggin' hot tub."

"*Shhh!*" Rosalee glanced toward the door, which was wide open.

But she couldn't express how light she felt as she shut the book and flipped onto her stomach, whisper-shouting into the pillows. Ellie flopped down next to her and they lay there, facedown, for several minutes, Rosalee engulfed in palpable relief. Eventually, Ellie turned her head to look at her.

"Guess what?" she said.

"What?" said Rosalee, her voice still muffled by the pillows.

"I bought you Pampers."

"What?"

Ellie had started giggling and it was contagious.

"Why would you do that?" said Rosalee.

"I wasn't sure if it would happen again and I didn't want you to have to go in all by yourself to buy them."

Rosalee sniffed, feeling her emotions turning on her again as her eyes filled with tears and she began to laugh. "That's so sweet."

"I even bought some Ensure to pretend it was for Mrs. Edelstein."

"Who?"

"Mrs. Edelst—" Ellie slapped a hand over her mouth as a snort escaped.

Rosalee giggled. "Who's Mrs. Edelstein?"

"I ... *I don't know!*" Ellie screeched, losing her head completely and sliding onto the floor, clutching her ribs.

At this point, Robin and Lola appeared in the doorway looking panicked.

"What the hell is going on in here?" Robin demanded.

Rosalee and Ellie were laughing too hard to answer.

Lola bent down to give the air above them a hearty sniff. "I don't think they've been drinking."

"We're going downstairs to watch a movie," said Robin loudly over the continued mirth.

"Okay," said Ellie breathlessly.

"Yeah, okay," said Rosalee.

"For crying out loud," Robin muttered as she and Lola left.

After they had laughed themselves out, Rosalee scooted up toward the headboard to lounge against Evelyn's throw pillows and Ellie copied her.

"So," said Rosalee, wiggling her eyebrows. "Is Pete a good kisser?"

Ellie tried to hide a goofy smile. "Um, yeah. Is that weird?"

Rosalee shrugged. "Maybe a little, but I'm happy you're happy. Both of you."

"You are?"

"Of course I am. Anyway, I kinda figured he might be good at it. Just watching him do, like, *anything.*"

Ellie nodded. "Yeah, he's pretty much got that down to a science, too. What about Alex? I always wondered if you could taste the cigarettes."

"No. I mean, I can smell the smoke on his clothes, but he's good about brushing his teeth and using mints, or whatever ... Hey, El?"

Ellie looked startled as Rosalee grew serious again. But as long as she was spilling her guts tonight ...

"What is it?" said Ellie.

"I think Aunties not opening the B&B is my fault."

Ellie frowned. "How do you figure?"

"I think they spent Evelyn's money on that stupid camp, and no one thinks it worked, but the money is gone already, so now—"

"Whoa, whoa, hang on." Ellie sat up against the headboard. "Aunties didn't use Evelyn's money to send you to Camp Bristlecone."

"How do you know?"

"Because they used Mom and Dad's money."

"*What?!*" Rosalee sat up, too, facing her sister with eyes that felt like they might pop out. "*Mom and Dad know?*"

"Of course not." Ellie waved a hand dismissively. "I used their birthday money."

Rosalee decided that any guilt she felt about the money before was nothing compared to this seven-layer dip version.

"Ellie, that was *your* money."

Ellie shrugged. "It was just sitting there. Besides, I couldn't bring myself to spend it on anything I had to look at or throw it away because either option would make me feel crappy."

"Okay, sure. I guess that makes sense ..."

"It does. And by the way, no one thinks it didn't work. It brought you back to us. I haven't regretted it for a second."

Rosalee chewed her lip. "Jeez, El, I really owe you."

"Okay," said Ellie cheerfully, "I'll let you cover my rent for the first month after we move out."

Rosalee laughed, wiping under her eyes with her sleeve. "Deal."

"I was kidding. A heaping plate of raspberry Linzer cookies would be perfect."

"How about both?"

"Deal," said Ellie, smiling. "So ... Alex."

"What about him?"

"You really like him, huh?"

Rosalee sighed. "... Yeah."

"So, what are you gonna do?"

Chapter 46

Alex sat slumped on the floor with his shoulders and neck braced against his mattress, staring up at the ceiling and feeling fourteen years old. He had stopped himself from walking to the library nearly twenty-seven times since breakfast to avoid checking his email again and had half a mind to disconnect the phone if it hadn't been the only line in the apartment. Plus, he was waiting for an important call—just not the one he was hoping for.

Without shifting his position, uncomfortable as it had become, Alex rolled his head against the mattress to stare at his clock radio. He had nearly an hour to kill until his shift at Laurie's, but he wasn't quite sure how to summon the energy. Luckily, he was no stranger to completing waitering shifts half dead. He took a swig from the can of Coke on the floor next to him and groped blindly above him for the TV remote, then dragged the TV in front of him by the stand with his foot, nearly toppling the monitor several times in the process.

He was flipping through channels, searching for something mindless to watch when the phone rang. He had already taken the cordless into his room, but this time he was forced to get up to retrieve it from his desk. He was expecting his mother's voice and was mildly surprised to hear a nasally male vibrato instead who introduced himself as her realtor, Simon Klume.

"Oh, sure, how's it going?" said Alex, muting the TV.

"Very well, yes, thank you, Mr. Conway. Your mother asked that I give you an update as she had to return unexpectedly to work."

"Sure," Alex said again.

Mr. Klume treated him to a long and stuffy explanation of appraisals, inspections, and home sale contingencies that all ended in the feeling that Alex's Ramen was about to come back up—they hadn't sold the house yet. Alex gritted his teeth to avoid cursing into the phone.

"I know this isn't the news you were hoping for, Mr. Conway, but I've lined up showings all next week."

"Okay, great." It was all he could muster, considering.

"I or your mother will let you know if there are any new developments."

"Sounds good, thank you."

"Goodbye for now."

"Bye," said Alex, realizing too late that he had already ended the call.

He wasn't sure how much more bad news he could take this week—all he needed now was for Glen to call and tell him that he couldn't get the extension for the final settlement payoff. That would be an excellent choice of straws to finally snap his aching, straining back. And then there was Oliver ... with all of Alex's extra shifts, he was having a hard time seeing him for more than an hour or two at a time, but he at least made sure to manage a couple of hours a day. In the back of his mind (and more recently, the front), he wished that Rosalee would go back to visit his brother, too, but he hated to say that he wasn't surprised when Oliver confirmed that she hadn't. In the meantime, he had completed his last anger management course earlier that afternoon—somehow, he had expected to feel more relieved.

Alex glanced at the clock again. He still had a little over half an hour left before he needed to leave for work. He tried not to think about

Rosalee knocking on his door nearly two weeks ago and ensuring that he wouldn't be able to concentrate for the entirety of his following shift. What he wouldn't give for a distraction like that right now ... although he kicked himself for not seeing their relationship for what it was—a distraction—from the beginning. It wouldn't have kept him from pursuing her, but at least it may not have been so disappointing, especially after everything he thought they had shared at the condo. Meanwhile, a dark corridor of his brain wondered whether he had hurt her after all and she hadn't said anything until she was sure she could get away from him. But ultimately, that didn't make sense considering the enthusiastic reunion she had facilitated in his bed several days later.

Again, Alex managed to force his thoughts away from Rosalee to more tolerable subjects, like how annoying he found his mother's realtor. Why did they even *need* a realtor? How hard was it to put an ad in the paper and then hand over the keys? Rationally, he knew that Mr. Klume's insufferableness was marginally a product of Alex's need to vent his spleen and his utter inability to do it at the person who deserved it. Still, he contented himself with listing all of the habits he found annoying about the realtor, including the one where he *assumed* his clients were doing well instead of asking: "Ah, Mr. Conway. Nice to see you. I *assume* you're doing well?" On its face, the salutation was perfectly pleasant, but in actuality, Alex decided that it was a manipulative way to stifle an explanation, one way or the other. After all, it would be impolite of the manipulated to do anything other than nod, agree, and return the question/statement, would it not?

Bristling with indignation, Alex turned his attention back to the TV and unmuted it when he realized that one of his all-time favorite movies was on. Next to *The Princess Bride, Say Anything* was pretty much the quintessential movie precedent of true love defying all odds. Now, though, with Alex's frustration stoked and his heart rankling, he saw through all of the drivel and decided then and there that Lloyd Dobler, with his infamous boombox at the window, was nothing more than a hopeless and eternal idiot.

Alex pushed the power button on the remote as hard as he could, but Peter Gabriel's "In Your Eyes" continued to play in his head, swelling dramatically as he nursed his pre-shift cigarette on the back porch. It repeated several more times as he dressed in his uniform and he attempted to drown it out with music from his clock radio. To his acute vexation, however, every station he tuned into seemed to be playing love songs. Eventually, he punched the power button on that, too.

It was going to be a long shift.

Chapter 47

Alex strolled with Oliver down their familiar path along the creek, the water of which was covered in a thick layer of ice. Every now and then, a jagged edge or missing chunk revealed the black current beneath. The sky was overcast, with little white flecks standing out like bright ash against the grey, and the temperature wasn't supposed to make it above thirty. Alex shoved his hands deeper into his coat pockets, the stagnant cold deepening his bad mood. Still, he knew he would feel better after their walk, and Oliver thrived on routines. Alex watched as his brother made long swipes in the snow with a pliable fallen branch from an aspen tree, making numerous "X" marks on the powdery surface.

He didn't notice the solitary, red-headed figure winding her way toward them until she was several feet away and Oliver stopped to look up at him.

"Hi," said Rosalee, greeting Alex first. "Hey, Oliver."

"Hey, Rosalee," said Oliver promptly, while Alex stayed quiet. Oliver looked between him and Rosalee for several seconds. "You promised we would look for an American Kestrel," he told Alex.

"I did. We will."

"I wasn't trying to intrude," said Rosalee. "I can go."

She turned to head back the way she came, which would have been exceedingly awkward since it was the same direction that Alex and Oliver were walking.

"Oliver, why don't you go on ahead and find a good birdwatching rock? We'll catch up," said Alex.

Rosalee stopped walking as Oliver skipped past, whipping his branch in a wide figure eight in front of him so that it struck each side of the path in turn with a sharp *thwack.*

"I'm sorry," said Rosalee, falling into step with Alex. "I looked for you at your apartment, but Pete said you were here."

"And how is Pete?" Alex tried to keep his voice casual.

"Um ... what?"

"Pete? How is he? Did you ask, or just get what you wanted and leave?"

Alex could feel his mounting resentment turning him into a hothead, but he seemed unable to temper it. At this point, he was essentially skidding downhill on worn-out brake pads.

"What's going on?" said Rosalee.

Alex watched her stumble in his peripheral vision as she attempted to keep her body turned toward him, but he kept his hands stuffed deep in his pockets. "You really hurt him, you know?"

"When?"

"After your aunt? After the diagnosis? He was really excited when you said you wanted to be actual friends again, but I guess that was when you needed something too, right?"

"Are you ... did he ask you to talk to me? Because he seemed fine a few minutes ago."

"You broke the guy's heart a little, Rosalee."

Alex stole a glance at her while she shifted her gaze to the path in front of her shoes.

"I didn't ... realize," she said quietly. "I didn't mean to."

"Okay ... *well?*"

Rosalee flinched. "I don't—I don't know. What should I do? Should I go back and talk to him?"

"Well, you came to see me, so maybe you should talk to me first."

Still sliding and gaining speed.

"Okay, god, what's gotten into you?"

Somehow, the irritation in Rosalee's voice only spurred Alex on. "Gee, I don't know, where have you been for *weeks?*"

"It's only been, like, *one* week."

"It's been almost *two* since I've heard anything from you that wasn't relayed through your sister."

Rosalee paused and seemed to be counting in her head. "Oh."

Alex felt his mouth stretch into a grim line. "Can I ask you something?"

"Okay ..."

"This? With us? What do you get out of it?"

"What do you mean?"

"I mean, am I just some guy you sleep with sometimes?"

"Jesus, is *that* what this is about?"

The relief in Rosalee's voice was palpable. Unfortunately for her, Alex wasn't about to let her off that easily.

"I get it, Rosalee. It's not like I've never slept with someone just to sleep with them, but I didn't think that was the way it was between us. So if it is, you should tell me so that I can ... adjust my expectations."

He had wanted to say "see myself out" or "let this go," but somehow his mouth wouldn't cooperate. Some lies were harder to say out loud and stay convincing.

"That's not what I was doing," said Rosalee.

"Then what *were* you doing?"

"I ..."

"I know I'm putting you on the spot. I just need to know. One way ... or another."

Rosalee glanced at him as he grimaced.

"You're singing Blondie in your head aren't you?" she said.

"No," Alex snapped. He had kept his eyes off of Oliver for several seconds too long and sped up to compensate.

"Alex."

He refused to turn around. "No."

"*Alex.*"

"*No.* I'm not in the mood for games, Rosalee, so maybe I'll talk to you later. You know, if I need a distraction or whatever."

"A distraction?"

Alex stopped and glimpsed Oliver a little way ahead, selecting a fresh tree branch, then turned back to Rosalee, who had stopped in the middle of the path and was showing every sign of being hurt. At least, that's what Alex would have deduced from those signs before. Now, he recognized them for what they really were: shame at being caught—of being exposed. Still, it was uncomfortable to watch her standing there, looking at him like she might cry. The last thing he wanted from her right now was pity.

"I'm a grownup. I'll get over it," he said, walking backward several steps, his palms open at his sides to show her he was fine. Turn his back and she might think he was about to cry, too. "I just need a little *space* to get over it."

"Alex," said Rosalee, her voice pleading, then more serious as she said it again and stared at something over his shoulder.

Alex turned to find Oliver walking stiffly back toward them, his face ashen and eyes wide. "What's the matter? Oliver, what's wrong? Did you find a hurt one?"

Oliver shook his head and took a sharp, shallow breath.

"What happened, bud? I need you to use your words," said Alex.

Somewhere nearby, a dog was barking. Alex watched Oliver's gloved hands clench and unclench as his lip began to tremble. "A boy fell in. There's a boy in the water."

———•●•———

As Alex and Rosalee raced down the path after Oliver, Alex couldn't keep his mind from conjuring memories of his little brother, huddled and shivering in an empty hot tub, then crouched and sobbing in the corner of the shower in his mother's house. Frame by frame, images of Oliver's water phobia flashed in his head until Alex was thoroughly nauseated and nearly lost his footing as he skidded to a stop at the edge of a hill leading down to the creek. He heard a groan next to him and saw Rosalee sway a little on her feet out of his peripheral vision. He fought the compulsion to steady her, shoving it down with his urge to vomit.

Below them, where the mostly frozen creek split to rush around several large boulders like the wide part of a DNA strand, a small figure in a puffy winter coat, mittens, and knitted hat lay partially submerged in the icy water that rushed past and over him in little rivulets. He was nearly as white as the snow on the bank and Alex had a moment of panic as he looked at the deep crimson stain that spread across the ice beneath the boy's head before he realized that it was a scarf.

As the initial shock faded and urgency snapped Alex's brain back into the world of sound and reason, he realized that the incessant barking they had heard in the distance had grown louder. Across the creek, a golden retriever was making desperate attempts to scramble onto the ice, then scurrying back, yelping and whimpering as it crackled menacingly.

"Stay there!" Alex yelled at the dog, because he didn't know how else to stop the barking so he could think. *"Lay down,"* he shouted, and the dog complied, head between its paws before it raised it again to pant heavily. "Good dog," Alex muttered, raking a hand through his hair.

"Jesus, how do we get to him?" said Rosalee, her voice high with anxiety. "What if he's d—"

Alex gave her a sharp look, but she had already bitten off the end of the word. He glanced warily at Oliver, who was staring at the boy as though transfixed.

"Rosalee, I need you to go get help," Alex said in the calmest voice he could muster.

"But I think I should—"

"Go. Please."

"What about Oliver?"

"I'll help Alex," Oliver said before Alex could answer.

Rosalee looked startled but turned to jog back up the path.

"I'll be right back," she called over her shoulder, and soon, in a flash of red, she was gone. In the same instant, Alex's head became miraculously clearer.

"Oliver, we're gonna climb down to where the bank levels off there, but I don't want you to go any further, okay? We have to go now."

Oliver nodded, his owl eyes round and solemn. However, Alex immediately regretted instructing him to make the treacherous trek down the hill as his own shoes slipped on the rocks beneath the snow.

"Easy. Go slow," he said as his brother followed him.

Alex got to the bank first and reached out his arms. "Jump, buddy." Oliver did and Alex caught him under the arms and swung him down next to him, then pointed to a large boulder jutting out of the bank like a roughly hewn chair. "You sit there and let me know when you see Rosalee, okay?"

"Okay."

Alex was relieved to hear that his brother's voice had regained most of its normal assertiveness as he quickly untied the laces of his workbooks, struggling against the cold that numbed his fingers and left them clumsy. He kept his socks on as some sort of protection against the rocks and tested the ice, which gave way immediately and bathed his entire foot in icy water up to his ankle. Alex cursed under his breath. Ahead of him, the boy was still wedged in a thin spot on the ice, his right side partially submerged in the stream. The water beneath was flowing fast and at least five feet deep—Alex didn't want to risk demolishing the ice so that the boy slipped the rest of the way under the surface and down the creek.

Alex got onto all fours, then felt the thin ice closest to the bank crunch under his knees and soak his jeans as he searched for a spot thick enough to support his chest. He thought he found a place where he could slither onto the surface on his stomach and heaved himself up, only to plunge back into the cold up to his waist a moment later as the ice gave way. His heart hammered in his chest as he watched the boy shift slightly in the crevice, the ice mass bobbing ominously under Alex's weight. He was still at least six feet away, even with the scalloped edge he had broken away.

"I can do it," came Oliver's voice behind him, and multiple scenarios swarmed Alex's brain at once: Oliver plunging through the ice and the unknown boy slipping beneath it as Alex dove after his little brother. Their mother sobbing over Oliver's tiny coffin. The ice cracking mightily in two and bearing them all down the creek to be dashed against the rocks.

"It's okay, bud, I need you to be the lookout."

Still, the more Alex tried to hoist himself onto the frozen slab, the more tiny fissures appeared and the more he worried that he would inadvertently set the whole mass of ice and the boy sailing down the creek. On the other hand, if he could break through and grab him fast enough ... no, that was way too big a risk.

Oliver was lighter and could probably reach the boy. However, Alex's mother would kill him for even attempting it, and Alex would never forgive himself if anything bad happened. He knew he should wait for help. But what if Rosalee couldn't find anyone until it was too late? He glanced up the path. Today was Sunday. Her chances of finding someone quickly were relatively slim, and besides, Alex needed to see if the kid was even breathing. As close as he was, he couldn't look for a pulse with the scarf wrapped around the boy's neck.

Seconds sped by as Alex deliberated. Finally, he waded back toward the bank, every step making his legs protest with the cold that was steadily making everything numb from the waist down. His foot hit something sharp among the rocks, but he ignored it. He would simply have to trust himself to hang onto Oliver. If it got too dangerous, they would stop and wait for help.

"Jump like an airplane," said Alex.

He was grateful that even though he and his mother had stopped playing that game when Oliver was a toddler, he still remembered it. He leapt into Alex's arms with his own outstretched while Alex supported his shoulders with one arm and his hips with the other. He lifted him onto the ice, holding his breath as it descended noticeably with Oliver's weight but didn't crack.

"Okay," said Alex, releasing the breath. "Now spread out your arms and legs like a starfish. Stay on your stomach. That's it."

Alex wedged himself into the groove he had broken through the ice, as close as he dared without making bigger cracks where it needed to stay whole, and redoubled his grip on his brother's ankles.

"Scootch on your stomach. Good," he said. "I'm not gonna let go of you, okay? What can you reach?"

Oliver stretched, his fingertips almost brushing one of the boy's arms. Alex groaned and pushed into the ice a little further, breaking off several more inches to get Oliver close enough to reach the collar of the boy's jacket.

"Do you have him?" said Alex. His teeth had begun to chatter.

"Yep."

Alex watched Oliver's gloved fingers contract. "I'm gonna pull you back. Don't let go, okay?"

"Okay."

Alex began to ease them both backward, but the boy's shoulder caught in the crevice as his body turned, and he had to try several different angles to get him loose. When at last, the boy was on his back, pulled along by Oliver, Alex felt his stomach turn as he realized that the ankle that had been submerged in the water was wrenched at an odd angle.

"You're doing great, buddy. Keep holding on as tight as you can," he said, hoping that Oliver hadn't noticed the boy's injury.

Alex hauled his brother backward until he could reach his waist and the boy was clear of any large missing chunks of ice.

"I'm gonna lift you like an airplane again, okay?" said Alex.

"Should I let go of him?"

"Yep. Okay, now flip around. Good. Can you climb on my back?"

Alex felt Oliver's arms tighten around his neck, then his knees squeeze at his waist.

"Hold on tight," Alex ordered.

He reached for the boy, pulling him the rest of the way across the ice and into his arms, keeping him close to his body and away from the water.

Across the creek, the dog could no longer control its anxiety and scurried along the bank, barking madly. Again, it attempted to scuttle onto the ice, then leapt back onto the bank, its back legs dealing the fatal blow as it launched off of the slab. The ice cracked all the way across and Alex watched in horror as the bottom half wrenched itself away from the whole and began to make its way down the creek, causing more large pieces to break off as it went. Still, the dog continued to whine and show every sign of wanting to swim across it.

"STAY THERE," Alex roared. He only had so many arms—he couldn't save a dog, too. His legs already felt paralyzed and he very much doubted he could swim. *"Lay down!"* he yelled, and again, thankfully, the dog obeyed.

Alex turned and began the trudge back to the other side of the bank, the liberated current making it much more difficult to keep his balance. He tried not to look down or think too much about the blue cast of the boy's lips, which was certainly not a good sign. He tried to remember all of the steps of CPR he had learned during his summers as a lifeguard during high school, but the cold was making his thoughts cloudy as he struggled through the icy, rushing water with the boy and his brother. While initially, it had seemed prudent for Alex to remove everything that might weigh him down, including his boots, he now regretted the absence of the rubber treads. The creek bed was mostly level, but as he continued to slip on algae-coated stones, he resigned himself to shuffling his way across them.

When at last, he reached the bank, Alex could no longer feel his feet or anything below the waist. He stretched to deposit the boy on the snow bank, as far away from the edge as possible.

"Ready to hop off?" Alex called to his brother over the babbling of the creek.

"Ready," Oliver answered, but before Alex could turn to allow him to climb off, Oliver's hand shot past the side of his face, pointing up the hill. *"There's Rosalee!"* he shouted in his ear, and in that brief instant, Alex felt his little brother's hands loosen around his neck before his weight dropped from him completely.

Alex flung an arm instinctively behind him, but too late, and Oliver tumbled into the icy water. Only the pure adrenaline that flooded Alex's veins could have allowed his frozen limbs to launch him back toward the debilitating cold as he dove for Oliver's leg—and missed.

Water surged up Alex's nostrils, burning at the top of his sinuses as he used the minimal friction of his socks as leverage against the slimy creek bottom to plunge after Oliver again. This time, he just missed the cuff of his brother's pant leg, then hurled himself into an aggressive front crawl, kicking desperately with legs he could no longer feel. He nearly gutted himself on a broken tree branch protruding from a log stretched halfway across the creek but managed to drag himself over it. A deep cracking sound came from the log as he kicked off hard and twisted in the water, finally catching Oliver in a barrel roll around the middle.

Alex kicked furiously to stay on his back as they were carried downstream, struggling to keep Oliver's head above the surface. If he could only find purchase in the creek bed with his heels, he might be able to slow them down enough for someone to help. Maybe he could at least swim back to the log, or strike off toward one of the banks. If he could just stand up, they could make it. But as he simultaneously kicked to stay on his back and attempted to drag his heels, the water swept them further away from the bank, the boy, and the hospital.

Alex knew he needed to shift his position to move against the stream, but if he rolled them over, Oliver's face would be in the water. Still, it might be the only chance they got.

"Oliver, hold your breath when I say," he gasped, then began to count. "One, two, three, *hold it!*"

He felt his brother suck in a breath and turned them over in the water, bicycling his legs until a jolt up his legs told him his frozen toes were brushing against the stream bed. Water gushed over both of them as Alex struggled to keep them at an incline, but the stream buffeted him on either side and he had to hop to stay upright. He began to move sideways while urging his leaden legs to pump like they were clearing hurdles. All he had to do now was make it to the bank.

"You can breathe again, bud," said Alex, panting, and immediately felt Oliver's chest rise and fall in quick succession.

Unfortunately, just then, Alex lost his footing and stumbled, pitching them both face-first into the water. The shadow of a cloud passed overhead and Alex didn't have time to shake the water out of his eyes before he launched forward again. Immediately, stars popped in front of his eyes as his skull smashed into something much too hard and unyielding to be a cloud—something solid. He threw an arm out blindly to grab it.

Screaming. Someone was screaming.

Alex vaguely registered the sound as it pealed in his chest, but it seemed to be outside of him. Somewhere in the depths of his throbbing head, the dog was barking wildly again and footsteps raced above him on what sounded like wooden planks before strong hands pulled Oliver out of his arms. His vision swam and he hoped that the figure was at least human and not some sort of angel of death.

Alex registered dimly that his own body was still being dragged by the water, but one of his arms seemed to be stuck to something that wouldn't allow him to float away. He heard shouting above him, but the words came to him slowly and didn't make sense.

He heard a child's voice mingling with a calmer, female voice, and then Oliver's screams cut through the fog in his brain: *"No, I'm not leaving, THAT'S MY BROTHER!"*

A surge of adrenaline thrust Alex back to the present and he realized that an EMT was reaching through the railing of a wooden bridge, holding onto his wrist and yelling at him to reach up with the other hand. After two attempts, he did and another EMT helped to haul him up over the railing. Both of them collapsed next to him as Alex lay on his back, sucking painful breaths of frozen air and trying not to succumb to the sparkling lights that still danced in front of his eyes.

Sudden footfall on the bridge shook the planks beneath him and several people shouted *"Don't run!"* before someone launched themselves onto Alex's chest. He ignored the pain in his ribs as Oliver sobbed into his coat.

"It's okay," said Alex, his teeth chattering so hard he thought they might fracture. "We're okay."

Chapter 48

Rosalee could feel the weight of her tired limbs pressing in on her skeleton and bruising her muscles but somehow, she managed to stay alert. She wondered if that's why hospitals always had fluorescent lights—maybe their almost indecent brightness kept the nurses and doctors from nodding off, no matter how much their bodies and minds begged for sleep.

"Hey."

Rosalee looked up from the speckled floor tiles to see the toes of Alex's work boots poking out from underneath scrub pants. He was wearing a scrub top, too, under his coat and it took her a moment to remember that his other clothes had been soaked.

"You should be a doctor," she said without thinking.

Alex gave her a quizzical look. Perhaps after a near-tragedy wasn't quite the right time to mack on your sometimes/sort-of boyfriend.

"Did his parents ever come?" said Alex. He glanced toward the former boy in the water's room, which was across the hall from the waiting area where Rosalee was sitting.

"Yeah, his dad just left to take the dog back home. Rufus. Kyle is the boy."

Alex nodded and started to get the jittery, "I-need-to-leave" look Rosalee understood all too well but wasn't used to seeing in other people. Maybe Robin.

"How's Oliver?" she said, hoping to hold him there for at least a few minutes.

"Not sure yet. They gave him a sedative so he's out right now. I'll spend the night here tonight. Then Engelmann after that. I should have insisted that they let me stay there to begin with."

"Is that allowed?"

"I don't know. Or *care*, at this point."

"Kyle should be okay. He had a bruise on the back of his head and his ankle is pretty messed up, but they think he mostly passed out from shock when he fell."

"Good." Alex's normally animated features took on a dull, almost grey cast under the lights.

"You got to him in time," said Rosalee.

Alex jerked his head ambivalently as he sank into a chair next to her. She glanced over at him as he twirled a pen between his fingers. Had he been writing? After several twirls, Rosalee realized that it was a hospital pen, so maybe he swiped it from an exam room. Was he still mad? Did he really think she was just in this for sex? Rosalee certainly hadn't looked at it that way, but she also wondered how many opportunities she had missed by spiraling inside her inner monologues instead of having actual conversations with Alex.

"Are you okay?" she said, and this time she made sure to say it out loud.

Alex shrugged.

"Talk to me." Rosalee almost reached for his free hand but stopped herself.

Alex twirled the pen faster, clearly agitated. "I knew I shouldn't have let Oliver help me with that kid. I knew it, and I did it anyway."

"But Oliver's going to be okay. Everyone made it out okay."

The pen flew out of Alex's hand and smacked the opposite wall, then dropped into a chair cushion in front of him. He didn't move to retrieve it. When he spoke, his voice was strained. "That's the thing, though—they *didn't.* Oliver almost drowned today and this time, it wasn't some snot-nosed little shits who almost did it—it was me. I'm supposed to protect him."

"You *did.*"

Alex bounced the back of his head against the wall several times before Rosalee slid her hand between the wall and his skull. He stopped and closed his eyes briefly as she curled her fingers into his hair. Then he opened them again and reached up to remove her hand and deposit it back on the arm of her chair before leaning forward for the pen and wincing.

Rosalee tried to ignore the way her throat constricted when he let go of her. "What's hurting?"

"Nothing," Alex said dismissively.

"You got pretty banged up today, too."

"I guess."

Rosalee sighed. "How long are you gonna be mad at me? Or need ... space, or whatever?"

It suddenly struck Rosalee that that's where they were now. Finally, Alex needed "space or whatever." She had successfully pushed him away, and it felt horrible—even worse when the seconds began to drag and she realized that maybe he wasn't going to answer her.

"I thought we weren't leaving each other behind anymore," he said.

"I wasn't trying to leave you behind, Alex, I swear. I can explain everything. I've been *trying* to explain everything, but you never answer the phone or my emails anymore."

"I needed to think. I haven't had a lot of spare time to get to the library."

"What?"

"To email you."

"... You email me from the library?"

Alex started to twirl the pen again and Rosalee suddenly realized that she had no reason to believe that he owned a computer.

"I'm sorry," she said softly. "I didn't know that."

Alex made an impatient noise in his throat. "What is this?"

"What is ... what? You and me?"

"No, me and this pen."

"Jesus," Rosalee muttered.

"Please just answer the question."

It seemed like it should have been that simple, but the start of every sentence Rosalee tried seemed wrong. Alex huffed in frustration and raked a hand through his hair.

"Can you give me a minute?" said Rosalee. "I'm trying to organize my thoughts."

"Is it that hard of a question?"

"It's complicated."

"Gotcha." Alex slapped his hands against the wooden arms of his chair, making Rosalee jump. Then he pushed himself to his feet, flinching so badly this time that it nearly bent him into a right angle. "In that case, Rosalee, it's been real," he said through gritted teeth. "But I need to get the *hell* out of here, so I guess I'll see you around."

"Mr. Conway?"

Alex and Rosalee turned to see a nurse headed toward them.

"Mr. Conway, I have your paperwork," she said, not bothering to wait for an acknowledgment as she launched into her summary. "Now, the ribs are definitely bruised, so go ahead and use an ice pack and take ibuprofen for the pain. We got that tetanus shot on board for your feet, but make sure you keep those cuts clean and change the bandages every day, and let us know if there's any sign of infection. Oh, and you'll need someone to wake you up every two hours for the concussion. Is she staying with you?" She nodded toward Rosalee, who was still sitting.

"Yes," said Rosalee before Alex could answer. Her stomach sank as he glowered at the nurse's shoes.

The nurse offered several more suggestions and results while Alex nodded politely. Then she hurried down the hall again, and Alex turned to leave.

"Alex, will you wait a second?" Rosalee scrambled to stand up and winced as she realized that one of her feet was asleep.

"No, Rosalee, I can't wait a second, I have to grab stuff from my apartment so I can come back and check on my brother."

"Okay, but who's gonna check on you?"

"Look, I don't need your pity, *I just need to leave.*"

Rosalee looked around them. Alex was talking loudly and had already attracted the attention of the sparse number of occupants in the waiting areas.

"Let's go outside for a minute," she said in what she hoped was a pacifying tone.

Alex shot her a look of pure vitriol that nearly stilled her pulse. Then he turned and stalked toward the exit, slamming the door open as he went and leaving Rosalee to dodge it as she stumbled after him, her foot still full of pins and needles. As soon as they got outside, Alex began pacing the sidewalk in front of the parking lot.

"Alex, please listen to me for a second—"

But Alex whirled around and suddenly, he was yelling.

"LISTEN TO WHAT, ROSALEE? WHAT EXACTLY DO YOU WANT ME TO HEAR RIGHT NOW?! THAT KID ALMOST DIED BACK THERE AND I NEARLY SENT MY BROTHER

WITH HIM, SO I'M SORRY, BUT I CAN'T REALLY DEAL WITH YOUR WISHY-WAFFLEY FEELINGS RIGHT NOW!"

Rosalee reached out to grab his hand or an arm, but Alex flung them out of her reach and kept yelling as he stepped backward off the curb and into the parking lot.

"SO WHAT? WHAT DID YOU WANT TO TELL ME? THAT YOU'RE SORRY? YOU'RE SAD? YOU'RE SORRY IT DIDN'T WORK AND SAD THAT I WAS TOO STUPID TO FIGURE IT OUT SOONER? WHAT, ROSALEE? SPIT IT OUT, ALREADY!"

"Damn it, Alex, will you shut up for a second?!"

"WHY?!"

"Because I—"

"WHAT? BECAUSE YOU—*what?*" Alex's voice caught on the last word as his whole body sagged. "Just get it over with, okay? I can't do this anymore."

Rosalee moved toward him as he backed away, matching him step for step.

"Stop coming," he growled.

"Stop going."

"Okay, seriously, Rosalee, just—"

Alex tripped on a cement block at the top of a parking space. He threw out an arm to catch himself on the brick wall behind him, then swore, doubling over to clutch his ribs. Rosalee reached out instinctively.

"CACTUS!" Alex shouted, practically in her face.

Time froze as an invisible barrier materialized between them. If it had been glass, as close as they were, their breath would have fogged it up. Also, if it was glass, it might have explained the sudden ache somewhere beneath Rosalee's ribs—like somehow a shard had come loose and pierced her between them.

"Alex," she said softly, waiting until he finally met her eyes. He looked so ... *lost.*

She fought the urge to reach up and touch his face as he looked away again, focusing on something across the lot. Should she keep talking? They had never specified—only danced (literally and figuratively) around the issue and never, in all of the scenarios Rosalee had envisioned, had Alex been the one to use their code word. But she would have expected him to respect it if the situation were reversed.

"Do you want me to go?" she said.

Although in the past few months, she had nearly memorized the eyes that stared back at her, at that moment, they looked like a stranger's. When he didn't answer, she turned to leave.

"Wait."

It wasn't a command, but Rosalee obeyed as though Alex's fingers had closed around her wrist. Instead, she felt them clenched inside her chest at the vulnerability in his voice. She turned back.

"Why did you come here today?" said Alex.

"Why?"

"Yeah, *why,* because I'm not an idiot. I can figure out when someone's done with me. I don't need a formal exit interview."

"I'm not done with you," said Rosalee, bewildered. "That's not what I was coming to say."

"Then what was it?"

"I thought you wanted me to stop talking." Rosalee gestured at the invisible wall between them.

"I wanted you to stop *moving,*" said Alex. "I can't think when you're that close to me."

"Why?"

"You first."

"I feel like I shouldn't say it now."

Rosalee paused and Alex shook his head, the merest trace of a smile flickering like sunlight through storm clouds. "Boy, if this headache doesn't kill me, the suspense might."

"I know, I'm s—" Rosalee frowned. "It just feels … manipulative."

"Is it true?"

"Yes."

"Then how is it manipulative?"

"Because I'm falling in love with you."

Alex froze.

"Actually, that's not true," said Rosalee. "I'm done falling. The falling has already happened. I'm … *in* love with you. Already. Alex?"

She reached out tentatively to brush something wet from his cheek. Alex blinked and wiped at his eyes with his palms. "Well, fuck."

Chapter 49

"Kyle says Rufus knows fourteen commands so far." Oliver swung his arms while he and Alex walked back through the sliding glass doors and past the reception desk at Engelmann. "He wants to teach him more, but only in even numbers."

"Maybe he's related to Pete. He likes even numbers, too," said Alex, when Oliver looked up at him questioningly.

"Well, Kyle doesn't have any brothers," said Oliver.

He led the way to his room and shrugged off his coat to hang in the closet, then reached for Alex's.

"Thanks," said Alex, sinking into the sofa.

His head had been pounding on and off all day and he could feel another headache coming on.

"Kyle's mom and dad said that it was nice of me to visit and I can come over when he gets out of the hospital," said Oliver.

"That's awesome, bud."

Oliver walked over to the couch and collapsed next to Alex, imitating his slouch and making him laugh. He was in a better mood than Alex could remember seeing him for a long time, and definitely more than he had ever been at Engelmann.

"Should we eat in fifteen minutes since you have to work at two o'clock?" said Oliver. "No, sixteen. *Sixteen* minutes?"

"Sounds good." By then, it would be almost acceptable for Alex to take more pain meds.

"What time is Mom coming tomorrow?"

"She's not sure yet."

"Yeah, that's what she told me, too." Oliver rolled his eyes toward the ceiling and then up at Alex.

"Are you excited that she's coming?"

"Yeah. Then maybe I can get out of this place."

Alex felt a tightness in his chest as he thought about all of the ways Engelmann had helped Oliver, and all of the ways that it had only made him feel more alone, despite everyone's best efforts.

"Looks like you found some new books," he said, trying for a lighter subject.

"Yep." Oliver jumped up from the couch and retrieved the stack from his desk. He read the titles and handed them to Alex in turn. *"Birds of the Rocky Mountains, Diving Birds of North America,* and *How Birds Fly."*

"Wow, this is an excellent haul," said Alex, examining the covers. "How'd you manage this?"

"Rosalee brought them."

Alex paused. "She did?"

"Yeah."

"I thought you said she hadn't come to visit you again."

"She didn't. She left them while I was at school and the nurse told me."

"Oh." Hope bloomed in Alex's chest faster than he could tear off the petals.

"Have you told her yet?" said Oliver.

"Rosalee?"

"Who else?"

Alex shook his head. It was a full-time job trying to keep his brother from turning into a total sass box. "Not yet."

"When will you tell her?"

"Probably tonight."

"Do you think she'll be mad?"

"I don't know, bud." Alex watched his brother carry the stack of books back to his desk. "So ... since we have some time, do you wanna talk about the other day?"

Oliver flopped down next to him again. "What other day?"

"Sunday. When Kyle fell in the creek?"

"Oh. What about it?"

"I wanna know what you think. How are you feeling?"

Alex had purposely held off talking about the incident right after it happened, afraid it might retroactively cause a panic attack. Oliver looked thoughtful.

"It was kind of a big deal—what you did for Kyle," said Alex.

"It was?"

"*Absolutely* it was."

Oliver shrugged. "I just did what you told me to do."

"That's true, but you also overcame your fear of water."

"What fear of water?"

Alex felt something in his brain stutter. "What?"

"You said 'you also overcame your fear of water,'" said Oliver. "What fear of water?"

Alex leaned forward on the couch and rested his elbows on his knees. He rubbed the light stubble on his chin and willed the cogs in his head to rotate again.

"Oliver, why don't you like to take baths or showers?"

Oliver's posture stiffened immediately.

"It's okay, bud," said Alex. "I'm not gonna make you talk about what happened in Denver, okay?"

"I took a sponge bath yesterday. I also was in the creek. I don't have to take a bath today."

Alex shifted in his seat to face his brother. "I'm not gonna make you take a bath, Oliver, I'm just trying to figure something out."

"Figure what out?"

"… What don't you like about showers and baths?"

Oliver glanced toward the bathroom door, a nervous glint in his eyes as he began to twirl a piece of hair at the base of his neck.

"Is it the water?" Alex pressed.

Oliver stared at the opposite wall for several moments, then nodded.

"It *is* the water?"

Oliver twirled the piece of hair faster.

"But you weren't afraid of the water on Sunday?"

"I'm not a liar."

"I know you're not." Alex sat back again. He had to be missing something. "Do you remember when we went to visit Meemaw in Florida?"

Oliver nodded.

"Did you like *that* water?"

"You mean the ocean?"

"Uh-huh."

Oliver shifted his eyes to one of the nature photos on his wall—a blue-footed booby on a beach in the Galapagos Islands. "Yes."

"How come?"

"The roseate spoonbill, the ring-billed gulls, the laughing gulls, the great blue heron …"

And then it hit him and Alex nearly laughed. All this time, the answer had been right there: *the birds.* Oliver wasn't afraid of water, he was afraid of being trapped, and Alex felt astoundingly dense for not realizing that distinction sooner.

"You said you wouldn't make me take a bath today," Oliver reminded him.

"You're right. I won't." Alex reached over to ruffle his brother's hair and sneakily stop him from pulling it.

"Good, because we have to go eat in twelve minutes."

———•●•———

The last half of Alex's swing shift at Laurie's passed quickly and before he knew it, he was driving back to his apartment to clean up for his date with Rosalee. It felt good to be driving again, and he was grateful that this time, he hadn't had his license taken away. Per Alex's request, Pete had held onto his keys for the past few weeks to avoid the temptation of driving to the liquor store, which was just far enough past Picket to dissuade him from getting there on his bike.

It was nearly seven thirty, so Alex barely had time to shower and down a couple of ibuprofen for his head. He managed both of those things in record time out of necessity after chain-smoking three cigarettes in a row on the back porch.

The ten-minute drive to Rosalee's house took no time at all, and Alex was only consciously aware of the road when gravel crunching under his tires told him that he had pulled into her driveway. He had prepared to knock on the door and walk her to the car, but as he switched off the ignition, she appeared in the doorway.

If he was a cartoon character, Alex's jaw would have been embedded in the gravel, and he struggled to close his mouth before Rosalee noticed. It was only the second time he had seen her wear a dress (not counting his fantasies) and this one nearly left them all behind, even partially obscured as it was beneath a black wool peacoat. As she closed the door behind her, the burgundy velvet fibers sparkled in the porch light and the slit down the side opened just enough to show sheer black tights and a dressier version of her usual combat boots.

He watched her come down the steps in slow motion. Somehow, everything around her—the night, the stars winking behind wispy clouds, and the branches of trees that hung overhead—paused as she walked toward him. Then Alex was opening her car door for her and driving again, and he could barely keep his eyes on the road or suppress his wild desire to pull over as soon as possible and show her how restlessly he had been missing her.

"You're so quiet tonight," Rosalee said eventually. "Are you still mad at me?"

Alex pumped the brake as they approached a stop sign and looked over at her. He noticed that her breath caught a little as he did and tried to assess his expression. He forced a smile that didn't quite reach his eyes but hoped it was dark enough that she didn't notice.

"No, sorry," he said. "I'm just tired. I didn't sleep very well last night."

"Oh." Was it his imagination, or did Rosalee sound disappointed? If she was, she seemed to recover quickly. "So, where are we going?"

"There's this place downtown I've been wanting to try."

Rosalee nodded.

"So, how did you sleep? Last night?" said Alex.

"Um ... great. Like, exceptionally great. I think just from everything that's happened the past few days. The good things."

She shot him a nervous glance, as though afraid that bringing up the "bad things" would send him into a blind rage.

"I'm not gonna start yelling again, don't worry," said Alex, the corner of his mouth twitching.

"Thanks for agreeing to start over with me," said Rosalee.

"As if it's some great sacrifice on my part? I still owe you a proper date."

"How about this one's on me, considering?"

"We can fight about it later."

"Deal." Alex heard the smile in Rosalee's voice before she fidgeted in her seat in his peripheral vision. "So ... how's Oliver?"

"He's ... actually really good."

Rosalee turned her head to look at him. "He is?"

Alex smiled, letting relief flood his system all over again. "Yeah. I think I may have figured out how to get him to take a shower, too."

"No way. How?"

"I have a few ideas, but I'm gonna start with one of those shower curtains that's clear on top and a CD of bird sounds."

"Oh." Alex took his eyes off of the road briefly to look at Rosalee, head tilted back against her headrest and laughing at the ceiling. "So it's enclosed spaces with water."

"I think so. He doesn't mind 'outside water,' just 'inside water.'"

"That's so great, Alex. Something good came from that experience after all."

For what felt like the thousandth time since the "experience," Alex steered his thoughts away from how badly things could have turned out. He still wasn't sure he made the right decision when he thought about the risks.

"I think watching that kid pull through really helped him," he said.

"I think *you* really helped him," said Rosalee. "Not that Oliver didn't already hero-worship you, but maybe this proved to him that even in scary situations ... there are always helpers."

"Mr. Rogers?" said Alex, fiddling with the temperature dial.

Rosalee stared at him. "Do you know *all* the quotes? Like, *ever?*"

"Just the good ones. On a completely unrelated note, you're *killing* me in that dress."

As they approached Picket, a rare passing streetlight illuminated the inside of the car enough for Alex to see the blush that colored Rosalee's cheeks. For once, it looked like it came from happiness and not self-deprecation. Unfortunately, it also further hindered Alex's ability to concentrate.

When they reached the restaurant, Alex hopped out of the car first, jogging around it to open Rosalee's door. He bowed, adopting a suitably posh accent. "There you are, miss."

Rosalee laughed. "Why, thank you, sir," she said, wafting herself with an imaginary fan.

Alex offered her his arm and they began to make their way to the front entrance when he was seized with an unshakable feeling of guilt. How could he possibly go through an entire dinner without saying what he had to say? How could he give a passable performance of okay-ness without tipping her off?

"Shoot," he said, thinking fast. "I left my jacket in the car."

He doubled back, pulling Rosalee gently along behind him, and unlocked the door. He searched for a moment in the back seat and then closed it again. As much as he didn't want to wait until after dinner, he also didn't want to take her to the actual doorway of what should have been their first date and then make her freeze into a human popsicle in the passenger's seat of his Jeep instead. He would just have to deal.

"Huh," he said. "Not here—I guess I didn't bring one."

Now what?

"Do we need to go back?" said Rosalee.

Alex leaned against the car, shrugging. Maybe he should grab a smoke before they went in. That would be as good an excuse as any.

"Whatcha doin'?" said Rosalee, a smile playing on her lips.

She thought he was being coy. Should he let her think that? Was it wrong, in his desperate attempts to act normal, to let himself enjoy the relationship that had taken months to build and was still only in its beginning stages? Outside of the car was obviously colder than inside, so he certainly couldn't tell her here. Really, Alex's only option was to play along for a little while and push away the reality speeding inevitably toward him. Besides, as he considered his options, doubt was creeping into Rosalee's eyes and he didn't think he could stand it.

"Come here," he said, *"Please."*

Now that he was letting himself forget, he was pretty sure if he didn't touch her in the next ten seconds, he would physically combust. Luckily for him, Rosalee didn't hesitate to close the space between them, lifting her arms to circle his neck and gazing up at him in a way that nearly undid him right there. Alex leaned in carefully, brushed her lips softly. Somehow, even now, he was afraid she would pull away.

But then Rosalee's fingers were in his hair and she was pressing her body into his so that he could feel the frozen condensation from the car melting into the back of his shirt. He tasted her strawberry lip balm and felt almost lightheaded as he inhaled something flowery that must have been her shampoo. Then his knees bent involuntarily, almost threatening to give out as her tongue swept over his bottom lip.

"Wait." Alex pulled back to rest his forehead against Rosalee's, trying to catch his breath. "We should go eat … before I'm not hungry anymore."

Rosalee bit her lightly swollen lip and stared into him with eyes like liquid amber tinged with jade.

God.

Alex shook his head, trying to undo the magic she was weaving through all of his senses, and grabbed her hand again, pulling her toward the restaurant.

—•●•—

At dinner, Alex hardly noticed what he was eating. He was too wrapped up in the impossible beauty sitting across from him and the fissure that threatened to break him every time he reminded himself how hard it was going to be to say goodbye.

Chapter 50

"Watch out for deer, will you?" said Alex. "I don't think I'll ever get used to driving this road at night."

As he and Rosalee made their way down the long, winding road back to Rabbitbrush, the mile markers reflecting the Jeep's headlights and stars that stretched for miles were the only lights to guide them. The moon wasn't visible at all, but that was fine with Alex, as he had decided that he was no longer on speaking terms with it. By now, he knew what Rosalee would do to him under a full moon. Suddenly, she wouldn't be Rosalee, the human—she would become an overwhelming, iridescent, unfathomable creature with more power in one glance and toss of her fiery hair than your average nuclear detonator.

She was already distracting him enough with the way she was looking at him, and he needed to focus on the road and getting them home safely. Besides, he didn't *want* to notice her looking at him. Where was that look a couple of weeks ago, before everything got ripped to hell—before he gave up? Of course, Alex thought he'd seen at least a variation of Rosalee's expression before—at Manny's cousin's condo, in Alex's room, in the moments after they kissed. But at this point, he wasn't sure he could trust his judgment, and he *certainly* couldn't tell if he was reading her correctly.

Alex shook his head as he pulled into Rosalee's driveway and she didn't miss the subtle movement.

"You okay?" she said.

Again, Alex hoped the dark would hide the smile that only manipulated his mouth. When he parked and finally turned toward Rosalee, she fixed him with a look that was half Bambi and half Medusa, instantly turning his brain to mush.

"Jesus Christ, you're beautiful," he said before his brain could catch up. He groaned and let his forehead land in the middle of the steering wheel, which let out a short *beep* in response.

Rosalee laughed and Alex couldn't help raising his head to witness the miracle that had taken so long to manifest. Now, she took full advantage of his face turned toward hers and kissed him—not in the timid way she used to, but like she *needed* to. Alex thought he might never get used to that, either, after so many months of tiptoeing. But now, here was Rosalee—in his life, in his Jeep, in his arms—and before he could so much as unclip his seatbelt, she was already in his lap, her kisses moving up his neck as her fingers deftly unfastened the buttons of his dress shirt.

Alex knew he shouldn't kiss her back the way he was, or lose track of his hands as they slid from the velvet material of her dress to her satin skin, then into the immeasurable softness of her hair. He knew that she would never forgive him for crossing the line tonight—even if she dragged him over it. Then again where *was* the line? Rosalee sat back in Alex's lap to loosen his tie and shimmy it over his head. Then she was back to her magic, subtly tugging him inside her trajectory and binding him there in the darkness.

"Rosalee," he said, clinging to the edges of his equilibrium. He tried to infuse some sort of sureness into his voice, but her name came out as a supplication and he could feel her practically purring in response.

For a moment, Alex let himself get swept beneath the current, where the only thing real or tangible was his breath mingling with Rosalee's and fogging up the windows as her touch transported him and made him lose track of his hands, too. But he couldn't—not tonight.

"Rosalee," Alex tried again, physically pulling himself away, and this time, she stopped to look at him. That's when he realized that what he saw in her eyes would ruin him if he stared too long.

It was a deeper nuance of what he had read there at the hospital after her confession. It was an affirmation and a question, and he knew she wanted him to say it back. She would never understand how much he couldn't.

"Rosalee, I need to talk to you about something."

Alex's voice in his head was accompanied by a buzzing that threatened to drown it out. He swallowed to release the pressure in his ears as Rosalee's eyes searched his.

"Okay," she said. She looked apprehensive, but there was still a glimmer of hope that nearly hollowed him.

"It's um, *Jesus*." Alex pressed his palms into his eye sockets, trying to figure out how to explain without rambling. "You know the 'incident' I got in trouble for? Back home?"

Home. Somehow, after all these months, that word didn't sound right for Denver, either.

"Not really," said Rosalee, "Besides the bottle swinging and your arm, I mean."

"Right. Well, I thought I should tell you the whole story."

Rosalee cocked her head, smiling quizzically. "Right now? If it's stressing you out, maybe we should talk about it later." She leaned forward to nuzzle his neck while her fingers explored the skin below his waistband. "...when you're not so stressed out anymore."

Alex shook his head and, as gently as he could, gathered both of Rosalee's hands in his, kissing the tips of her fingers before leaning back in his seat. "I need to tell you now, I think."

He watched Rosalee's smile fade. "Oh. Okay."

She pulled her dress back onto her shoulders, then her coat as Alex buttoned his shirt. He kissed her again as she handed him his tie, hoping to be reassuring. Still, the awkward silence pressed in on them, so he cleared his throat and began, holding her hand on the center console.

"So, I was a waiter at this restaurant downtown, and they had these live music nights on the weekends."

"That sounds cool."

"Yeah, it was," said Alex. "But everyone got soused on those nights—customers, owners, everyone. Probably where my drinking problem started."

Rosalee winced and rubbed his arm.

"Anyway, this one night, it was just the owner's son in charge because everyone else had gone home, and that meant that all the employees were trashed—myself included. So, at the end of the night, when all the customers were gone, I was taking the mop back to the utility closet, which was near the dishwashing station. And on the way there, I saw Marcus—that was the owner's son—ragging on our dishwasher, Adam, who's mentally retarded and deaf, so obviously Marcus figured he could get away with it."

Rosalee made an angry noise in her throat, her fingernails curling briefly into the back of Alex's hand.

"I know," he said. "That wasn't the first time, though. I might have told Marcus and his cohorts to knock it off a couple times, but I also really needed that job, so I didn't push it." Even now, that revelation flooded Alex's insides with guilt. "I should have, though. They called him 'Grapes,' 'Grape Boy,' 'Gilly,' what have you after that movie came out. Not that any of them ever *saw* it."

"Jesus. Bunch of assholes."

"Right, but like I said, I hadn't exactly done anything about it. That night was a little different, though, because the week before, Oliver had been trapped in a jacuzzi for half a day. And that morning, my mother decided to send him up here, which meant I had to come up here, too, and I was *pissed.* At those kids, at Oliver, at Mom ... and I guess you can say I kinda lost my shit."

It was embarrassing to admit how immature he had been as a twenty-four-year-old man. Rosalee's eyes were wide with concern or distaste—he couldn't tell which, but there was no point in stopping the story now. After all, she knew (more or less) how it ended, and whether or not she didn't want anything to do with him after this wouldn't change what was coming.

"I can't remember how long I stood there watching that asshole taunt the guy—I only remember that somehow, Marcus' shirt collar ended up in my fist and I was twisting it until his face was purple. Lucky for him, though, he got in a pretty solid kidney shot, and I was down for a few punches before I could get any in. At one point, I looked up and saw that Adam got away, which was good at least, but Rosalee, I swear, I've never felt more out of control in my life. If you can blow out your vocal cords, I just about did it, and then he had this soapy butcher's knife in his hand, and I don't know if that was before or after I grabbed an empty wine bottle off the counter, but I swung it as hard as I could."

Alex tried to slow his breathing, all the while assessing Rosalee's reaction. Although, again, *did it really matter?*

"Thank god you missed," she said after a while. "How did you guys not kill each other? How did you not get *arrested?*"

"I don't know." Alex shifted in his seat to face her again. "I think some of the employees panicked, but they didn't want to call the cops because some of them were underage, so they called Marcus' dad."

"Was that better or worse?"

"In hindsight, it was probably worse for me. Obviously, I had to pay for the damage to the restaurant, which I've been doing for the past several months, but then to appease my dad, I also had to take the classes—"

"Which you finished."

Alex nodded. "Which I finished. But there was an extra settlement on top of that, which has been harder to pay off since I've been helping my mom with her mortgage payments, and now that neither one of us can afford to pay for Oliver ..."

Rosalee looked down at the hand still holding Alex's and brushed her thumb across his knuckles. "I wish I had known all that—I would have helped you. Somehow."

"I didn't want anyone to know. I was a little bit afraid Pete would tell you, but I should have known he wouldn't."

"Pete knew?"

"Not about everything. About the money, though. He tried to get me a loan at the bank—mostly to be polite."

"You still have your job at Laurie's, though, right?"

"Right, but ..." Alex took a deep breath. "I have to go back. To Denver."

Rosalee's fingers went still in his hand. "What? Why?"

"I only had until the end of last week to pay off the settlement before the restaurant pressed criminal charges. I didn't make it."

"Oh my god," said Rosalee, her fair complexion paling further. "Oh my god, *are you going to jail?*"

"*No*, no," Alex said quickly. "My att—My ... dad ... paid it."

Rosalee stared at him. "All of it?"

"Well, the rest of it—which was still a lot."

"Wow."

"I know." As frustrating as it was to be indebted to the man who abandoned his whole family, he had saved Alex's ass—*big time.* "But now I have to pay him back, so ... he offered me a temporary job at his firm to work it off."

Rosalee nodded and Alex tried not to focus on the line of moisture that clung precariously to her lower lashes, a shiver away from sliding down her cheeks.

"But where will you live?" she said.

"My mom's house. I'll stay there and help her sell it so she can move up here."

"She's moving up here? To be with Oliver?"

"Tomorrow, actually."

"But where will *she* live?"

"She's taking over my lease with Pete and then she'll find somewhere close to the hospital. She got a nursing position there, so we think Engelmann might give us a break on Oliver's program fees, especially if he can live with her."

Rosalee let go of Alex's hand to grab her purse and put it in her lap, then looked down as though surprised to see it there. She didn't reach for Alex's hand again. "So, you'll work with your dad, pay off your debt, sell your mom's house ... and then what?"

"I thought about coming back," Alex admitted. "But I was also thinking about film school. In LA."

"Oh. Really?" Rosalee's voice was definitely higher than normal.

Alex pulled a thick envelope from between the front seat and center console and handed it to her.

"I got in right before 'the incident.' I'll have to apply again, but I thought I might as well."

Was it mean to say it like that? Alex figured it was better to be honest about this whole mess of a situation. Besides, no matter how he sliced it, he couldn't figure out any future for himself in Rabbitbrush.

"Wow," said Rosalee. She slid the acceptance packet carefully back into the envelope and handed it back to him. "Yeah, might as well. That's great, Alex. Good for you."

Chapter 51

Rosalee was only vaguely aware of her feet as Alex walked her to the door and kissed her goodnight, his lips lingering hesitantly at her temple, then her forehead. She nodded absently when he asked if he could call her the next day, then slipped quietly inside, jumping when the screen door banged against its frame.

The kitchen was dark, but Rosalee sat down at the table in her coat, her purse still clutched under one arm. She lost track of time as she stared into the darkness where she knew the usually comforting parts of the room were. She wished she had something hot in a mug to wrap her hands around—not that she was physically cold, *per se*—she was more numb than cold, but it was a different numbness than the tingling associated with her flare-ups. This felt empty. Like someone had taken her insides out and replaced them with still, frigid air. It was only when she got to 325 in her head that she realized she had been counting.

A creak of floorboards, a flickering pop, and Rosalee was suddenly blinded by the kitchen light. Next, her eardrums nearly gave out as someone strawberry blonde and wearing pajamas shrieked.

"Good lord, Rosalee, what are you doing sitting in the dark?!" Ellie hissed, pressing a hand to her heart the way Evelyn used to. "Where's Alex?"

"He dropped me off."

"Why, what happened?"

When Rosalee didn't answer right away, Ellie inched closer to the table, her eyes wide. "Did you sleep together again? Was it bad? Did he hurt you?"

"He's leaving." *Empty. Cold.*

"Right now?" said Ellie, suddenly flushed. "I'll kill him."

She was halfway across the kitchen before Rosalee caught her by the sleeve and pulled her back to the table, although she couldn't convince her to sit down. Then she gave her sister the short version since her lips didn't seem to want to move efficiently. When she finished and looked up, Ellie's mouth was hanging open and she looked close to tears. Rosalee sincerely hoped she would fight that urge. She could already feel various muscles in her own face twitching.

Ellie sank into a chair across from Rosalee. "When is he leaving?"

"Next week."

"And there's no other way to pay off the debt? No one else to sell his mom's house?"

"Apparently not. He said they've been trying for months."

Ellie's eyes darted around the kitchen like she was looking for something. "But isn't he worried Oliver will get worse without him?"

"He thinks he needs their mom more. I guess she's been going crazy without him. Plus ... Alex is convinced he made everything worse with the near-drowning incident."

Ellie was quiet for a moment. "He doesn't have the tightest grasp on reality does he?"

Rosalee shrugged.

"I mean if anything," Ellie continued, "it seems like the whole thing made Oliver more resilient. Plus, now he has a friend."

"Preaching to the choir." Rosalee finally released her purse and shoved her thumbnail into the familiar crack in the table.

"And then ... *film school?*"

Rosalee nodded. "To write movies."

"Oh." Ellie unknitted her eyebrows. "Well, he'd be really good at that."

"Yeah, he would. And he's wanted to do it for a long time."

"So ..."

Rosalee knew the questions that were coming: *"How do you feel about it?" "Are you staying together?" "Did he tell you he loved you?" "Do you think he will tell you he loves you?" "Do you think he does?"* They hung between them like strings of alphabet refrigerator magnets, but neither Rosalee nor Ellie seemed ready to grab any of them down for examination.

Instead, Ellie got up from the table again. "I actually came down here for a snack—I made lemon bars. I can make tea, too. We need something hot to hold."

While Ellie bustled around, Rosalee shrugged her coat off, then pulled it back on. Somehow, it made the deep cold inside her more manageable.

"Hey, El?"

"Hm?"

Ellie set a plate of lemon bars on the table and took their mugs of hot water out of the microwave.

"Is Pete ..." Rosalee nearly said "mad at me," but that seemed childish. "Uh ... okay?"

Ellie slid a chamomile tea bag across the table to her. "What do you mean?"

"Well ... Alex said something. About him being upset with me." *So much for that.*

Ellie took her time selecting a lemon bar and putting it on her plate, then carefully licking the powdered sugar off of her thumb and forefinger before looking at Rosalee. "I wouldn't say *upset.*"

"What *would* you say?"

"I guess he's a little … disappointed that you don't spend very much time together. But he seems a lot happier since you talked about your portfolio."

That had been ages ago.

As much as Rosalee suspected that Alex's outburst was more about him and less about Pete, she couldn't help the subtle twist in her gut that confirmed that his accusations were still mostly true. She also suspected that it wasn't the steam from her tea making her face hot.

"Maybe I'll call him tomorrow and see if he wants to have lunch next week."

Ellie smiled. "That would be nice. I know he'd like that."

"Yeah, me too."

Mostly, though, the thought of "next week" made her nauseated.

———•●•———

When Rosalee finally dragged herself to bed, she couldn't sleep, and again, she found herself thinking about three different men. This time, however, they were all Alex. First, there was the infernal pop-up book version that she couldn't stand, who launched movie quotes at her with the vigor of a batting cage pitching machine and left her to wonder if he had any original thoughts while forcing her into ridiculously awkward lunches.

Then, there was the Alex who crept unbidden into her thoughts. The Alex who challenged her and made her want to be better—who made her feel out of control at times, like a balloon caught in a high and tumultuous wind. But somehow, he was always there to reel her in, tugging her gently back into herself. By the time Rosalee realized she was in love with this Alex, it was too late to back out or stop or assess. It was undeniable.

And now he was leaving. Somehow, through all the turmoil, Rosalee had convinced herself that she and Alex would always find their way back to each other. After all, Rabbitbrush was a very small town. It never occurred to her that he might leave it, although now that it was true, it seemed so obvious—he didn't belong here. So, then, Rosalee was forced to think of the third version of him—the version he was before Rabbitbrush and the version he would be when he left. The version that would kiss another girl—maybe several other girls—and eventually forget about the basket case he met in a very small town in the mountains.

It was almost unbearable to think that this would be the end of their story, but deep down, Rosalee knew that she had pushed him too far. Despite everything that made Alex seem like some sort of superhuman entity, he was still a man—a *human* man, not the kind that only bowed before kryptonite—and he had been stretched too thin.

Leaving would be better. Rosalee knew that there was no future for Alex in Rabbitbrush, and it would be selfish to try to make him stay because of her. Besides, what was she supposed to do—run through the airport after him and beg him not to go? Although that definitely seemed like a romantic gesture he would appreciate, it wasn't exactly practical; there were no flights from Rabbitbrush to Denver, and he wouldn't be leaving for LA for months.

And finally, there was the fact that Rosalee had already told him she loved him. If Alex loved her back, wouldn't he have said it? Maybe not right away, but ... by now? As Ellie pointed out (after adding another trauma to Rosalee's eardrums when she found out about her confession at the hospital), he could be holding off because he was leaving.

"I've seen the way he looks at you. I can't think of any other reason," she had said.

But Rosalee knew the truth. No matter how many romantic excuses she made to make herself feel better, she knew that Alex needed someone to take care of him, too, and she hadn't fully considered that until she had abandoned him too many times. And now, he was ready to move on. After all, they hadn't even talked about staying together after he left ... or had they? Rosalee had struggled to focus through the thrumming in her head while Alex talked about all of the plans that would soon carry him away from her. But he did say he'd call the next day. Maybe they would sort it out then.

Somehow, the pit of Rosalee's stomach told her otherwise.

Chapter 52

The original Denver and Rio Grande Western Railroad Depot was erected in Grand Junction, Colorado in 1905, but had since been replaced by a newer building in 1992. The original structure stood nearby, its once-magnificent stone walls and red roof sad and derelict. Rosalee noticed wreaths around the sconces on the new building and faux pine garlands lining the windows, but nothing festive on the old structure. Would it have been such an inconvenience to stick some of those battery-powered candles in the windows or a wreath over the main entrance? Even with its holiday trappings, compared to the subtle majesty of the original depot, the new one looked corporate and bland. Or maybe Rosalee was more irritated than usual from the long drive with nothing to occupy her brain but indecision and negative thoughts.

Because it was Tuesday, Ellie was back at school and Pete was at work, although he had probably driven Alex to the station. Again, guilt settled in around Rosalee's throat like a too-snug turtleneck. *She* should have offered to drive him, but it was too late now. Besides, she hadn't even been sure she wanted to see him off before that morning.

As she walked through the front doors, her stomach filled with butterflies and dread in equal measure. She wanted to find Alex before he spotted her, to get her bearings, but she was underprepared for how empty the station was. Even though all of the benches were filled, it was a much smaller space than she had expected, and almost disappointing in its plainness.

Rosalee dug in her pocket for the sticky note with the train number she had scribbled down the night before and cursed herself for the umpteenth time for not writing down the departure time. However, she realized she didn't need it, as the set of tracks she could see from several windows on the back wall clearly only allowed one train to arrive or depart at a time. As her eyes scanned the faces in front of her, she felt an unpleasant little jolt behind her belly button every time she noticed someone else's dark blonde hair. Eventually, she found herself not twenty feet from Alex.

Rosalee stared at him and considered turning back. Alex appeared to be lost in thought, his elbows resting on his knees and head bowed in a position of prayer. After several moments, he reached for a notebook tucked under his legs and began to scribble purposefully, oblivious to her approach. Several strands of hair fell in front of his eyes as he wrote, and Rosalee was reminded of the first time she'd been close enough to see the warmth that infused his dark brown irises with golden tones … the Ferris Wheel. Had she had any idea that night how much her annoying, interfering seat partner would come to mean to her, maybe she wouldn't have been in such a hurry to come back down to earth.

As if on cue, Alex glanced up, the end of his pen lodged firmly between his back teeth. His smile was sad as he stood up from the bench and took the pen out of his mouth, notebook at his side. He waited patiently while Rosalee stood still, awash in a sea of regret. She felt almost dizzy, either from nerves or low blood sugar, but somehow she made it within a foot of Alex without passing out, and then she was in his arms, feeling the tightness in her chest receding and letting her breathe again.

"You're here," he said when they finally broke apart, and the smile closer to Rosalee's favorite confirmed for her that she had made the right decision, whatever the outcome.

"I couldn't remember when your train left," she said.

"In about an hour."

Rosalee nodded stiffly. She wished she had given herself more time. Or less. She couldn't decide.

"You travel light," she said in the meantime, indicating the shoulder bag and backpack stowed under the bench.

Alex glanced behind him. "I took most of it down a few days ago."

"Right."

The past week had been mostly a blur, but Alex had sent an email on Friday to tell Rosalee his plans to drive down to Denver in his Jeep, then drive a U-Haul back from his mother's house while she followed in her car. The train ride back to Denver had been an early Christmas gift from her.

"You wanna sit down?" said Alex.

"I don't know."

For now, hovering felt less scary. Alex stayed standing, too.

"You're not gonna leave before I board, are you?" he said, moving closer and shaking his head in mock disappointment, although he was still smiling. "Cruel woman."

"*I'm* cruel?" Rosalee reached out to tug distractedly at the zipper pull on his winter coat, unable to look at his face. "You're gonna make me watch you leave."

She tried to laugh then—make things lighter—but the laugh turned into a hiccup as it caught in her throat, and she shifted her gaze to the ceiling in an attempt to master herself. Soon, she felt Alex's fingers thread gently through hers.

"I'm sorry I haven't been around very much this week," she said, grateful for the familiar gesture.

"At least I understand why this time. I think."

"I wanted to see you. I just … couldn't."

The truth was, she had thought of going to see him dozens of times over the past week, but she never made it further than the front door (and three times, the driveway). At night, she tossed and turned, thinking about calling him and then waiting until it was too late, then fantasizing about driving over in the dead of night to see if he was sitting on the back porch. If so, she imagined she would join him in a cigarette, and lay her head on his shoulder, and beseech him in hushed tones not to go. Then maybe he would take her to bed and forgive her—and then stay.

She felt her eyes fill with tears again as Alex squeezed her hand.

"This doesn't have to be 'goodbye,' you know," he said, then cleared his throat. Did she imagine that his eyes were over-bright?

"It doesn't?"

"I'm willing to try long distance if you are. If you want to be together, we'll find a way to make it work. If you don't, then … no hard feelings. My mom and brother are still here, so I'm sure we'll still see each other from time to time."

Rosalee felt the glacial air inside her again, but this time it was stirring and making her even colder, worrying at her over-sensitive nerves like ice water to exposed tooth roots. How could he be so cavalier about all of this, especially knowing how she felt? Unless maybe … he didn't believe her? She searched his face for a sign—anything to give her a clue as to what he was thinking behind what she hoped was a false calm and cool exterior.

"You don't have to decide right now," said Alex. "I was gonna get something to eat. Are you hungry?"

Rosalee avoided his question. "I'll come with you."

She doubted she could chew food right now, let alone swallow it.

Alex let go of her hand to retrieve his bags and stow his notebook and pen inside the shoulder bag. "I saw a place down the street. How do you feel about pizza?"

———•●•———

"Alex, I don't think they serve pizza here," Rosalee whispered as they waited for the man in front of them to pay for his jerky and cigarettes.

It turned out that the "place down the street" was a convenience store, and Rosalee was already getting a headache from the fluorescent lights and sickly sweet smell of slushies and processed food.

Alex didn't respond but squeezed her hand as they stepped up to the counter. "We'd like to order a pizza, please."

Rosalee waited with her eyes downcast for the cashier to laugh at him.

Much to her amazement, though, he nodded. "Let me ring up this lady behind you and I'll get that going for you. Go ahead and wait over there by the restroom, if you don't mind."

Again, Rosalee surveyed their surroundings, unable to detect any clues to suggest that the convenience store sold anything related to pizza, or even cheese made with actual dairy. Still, although she was sure she was imagining it, she could almost *smell* pizza.

About five minutes later, Rosalee and Alex were the only people in the store besides the cashier, who ushered them into a utility closet next to the restroom, then flipped on the light.

"Thanks for your patience, folks," he said, then slid back a curtain on a rod in the back of the room to reveal an archway.

493

Rosalee gasped as Alex thanked the cashier, who closed the closet door and turned off the light before he went back to manning the register.

"Okay, well I can't see anything," said Rosalee.

"Our eyes should adjust soon. Or this is how we die."

Rosalee blinked and looked down the staircase, which was carpeted in a deep crimson and surrounded by painted brick walls. As she and Alex made their way slowly down the stairs, more lights seemed to glow from the room below until the whole thing came into view.

A polished mahogany bar with stools stood at the center of the room, surrounded by a handful of round tables with high chairs, where less than a dozen people sat chatting over their food or reading newspapers. Rosalee noticed a payphone next to the kitchen, a hallway leading to the restrooms, and a jukebox and pool table on the opposite wall. She let Alex lead her to a table in the corner.

"How did you even find this place?" she said.

Alex reached for his backpack, which Rosalee had on her shoulders, then put it and his shoulder bag on the back of his chair and shrugged off his coat.

"Manny told me about it. But I have to admit I was a little afraid he was messing with me."

"Guess not."

"Nope, guess not. Too bad they don't have stuff like this in Rabbitbrush. This should have been our first date."

"I liked our first date," Rosalee said quietly.

Alex reached out and almost touched her face, then dropped his hand to her arm instead. "Yeah, me too ... I'll go get us some drinks."

"Just seltzer for me, please." The bubbles might soothe her stomach.

"What kind of pizza do you want?"

"Oh, I'm not very hungry. Thanks, though."

Alex returned several minutes later with two thick, translucent plastic tumblers. He handed her a straw and sat across from her, his knees nearly touching hers under the small table. "It'll be ready in about half an hour."

"Cutting it kinda close."

"I'll take it to-go if I need to. Are you sure you don't want anything?"

Just you. "I'm good, thanks."

Rosalee unzipped her coat to have something to do and noticed Alex's eyes lingering on the off-shoulder sweater she knew he liked. She glanced around the room again to avoid his face.

"We could play pool." Alex hooked a thumb toward the table, which was currently unoccupied.

Rosalee began to feel like a pathetic loser as she followed him to the table and watched him rack the balls. He handed her a stick and she wondered if this is what he had felt like during all of their lunches—the agony of being awkward and unsure if the other person wanted you there or was just being polite. Rosalee was pretty sure she never gave Alex the impression that she wanted him there, though. Apparently, she had no idea what she wanted. *Would long distance be so bad? YES,* came a quick voice inside her head. After all, it seemed to be an undeniable fact that they were terrible at being apart.

They made their first few shots in silence, then Alex crossed behind her to get to the white ball, his hand brushing lightly against her lower back as he passed. Rosalee watched across the table as he took his turn and the look of concentration that furrowed his brow turned to triumph.

"Please tell me you saw that." Alex's expectant smile wavered as Rosalee shook her head.

She immediately cursed herself for missing the shot, especially since it had been a fairly difficult one, and celebrating it would have been an excellent way to break the ice. She could feel herself spiraling inside her head as the pain in her body began to surface, too. Her legs ached and exhaustion from a week of crappy sleep reminded her again that she was no longer the superhuman being she had once believed herself to be.

She braced herself against the table as Alex came closer in her peripheral vision. He collected her stick with his, leaning them both against the wall, then took one of her hands and led her back within a few feet of their table.

"Are you thinking about looking at me today?" he said.

Rosalee glanced at him quickly, then away again. "I've looked at you. I missed that spectacular shot because I was looking at you."

Alex guided both of her hands to his shoulders, then wrapped his arms gently around her waist and began to sway to the R&B music Rosalee hadn't immediately noticed.

"We didn't used to be able to do this," Alex said, resting his forehead against hers.

Rosalee tightened her arms around his neck, reveling in all the smells that were now vying for spots on her list of favorites. The haze of cigarette smoke in the room was making it harder to detect the scent of Old Spice under Alex's shirt, but not impossible, and she could just distinguish his preferred flavor of mint on his breath as it lingered, warm on her face and the nape of her neck. Without thinking, she reached up to slide her fingers into his hair, anchoring herself to him as they moved together and she felt his breath catch, his lips whispering over the skin of her shoulder. This wrapped up in his warmth, Rosalee's legs barely ached, and Alex's hands drifting from her waist to her ribcage melted away any tension she held there, too—until she thought about the fact that he was leaving and that the end of her time with him was approaching faster than she could stand to think about.

Then the question remained: did he truly not believe how she felt about him?

"Alex?" she said, looking up into his face and then unflinchingly into his eyes as if it wasn't the hardest thing she'd done all week. "I hope you don't regret the time you've spent here. In Rabbitbrush, I mean." She shifted her focus to the plaid collar of his overshirt, tugging and smoothing it straight as she struggled to find the right words without letting the ones she swore to herself she wouldn't use today escape with them. "I mean, I hope you understand the impact you've had ... on Oliver, especially. He would have been lost without you. Like, *truly*, utterly lost. But you were this *force* and you helped him be brave ... I just don't think you understand how much he's going to miss you."

Alex looked away as they continued to sway on the spot, and Rosalee realized how much substituting "Oliver" for "I'm" and "me" probably sounded like a lecture. Still, Alex tended to observe and comprehend more than she generally gave him credit for. When he drew her in again, she knew he understood. At least partially.

"I'm gonna miss him, too," he said into her hair. "You have no idea how much."

Then don't go, Rosalee almost said.

The words were ready on her tongue—all she had to do was open her mouth, but she clamped her teeth together, hard. When Alex finally released her back into their casual dancing position, her jaw was aching.

"Whatever happens between us after I leave is still up to you," said Alex.

"I just need to think about it."

If she was being honest, Rosalee wasn't sure how much longer she could stand to drag this out—especially if the relationship was doomed, regardless.

"No pressure," said Alex.

His arms still circled her waist and Rosalee wondered if he wanted to drop them but was afraid to hurt her feelings.

"Alex, I'm afraid I can't do long distance," she said in a rush. "I can barely do *this* distance. I'll screw it up, I know it."

Alex was looking at her with a strange expression. Was it relief? "Is that your decision, then?"

Rosalee's vision blurred and she stared at Alex's shoes.

"It's okay if it is," he said quietly.

On the verge of shaking her head "yes," Rosalee changed course halfway. "It's not okay," she whispered. She could feel her composure unraveling as tears stung the back of her eyes and the tightness in her chest threatened to close off her throat. "Either way, it *sucks*, okay? And I'm sorry if that's selfish. I'm trying really hard to not be that today."

Alex gave a low laugh. "I know the feeling."

"You? Selfish? *How?*"

Rosalee realized they had stopped moving and wondered if she had initiated it. Her arms were still around Alex's neck until he unwound them and led the way back to their table, where he moved their chairs next to each other. He gathered her hands in his lap, wrapping one arm around her waist.

"What's this?"

His fingers tangled in several threads poking out of Rosalee's pocket. As he pulled, the friendship bracelet from weeks ago tumbled into his hand, safety pin and all.

"Oh. I started that a while ago and forgot about it. It must have gone through the wash."

Alex smoothed out the threads. "I like it. Who was it for?"

"You," said Rosalee. "I mean, I hadn't decided if I was going to give it to you or not."

"Why not?"

"I wasn't sure if you were a bracelet guy."

Alex smiled and looked like he did when he was about to quote something, but seemed to change his mind. "Is it finished?"

"Almost."

"*Could* it be?"

"Why? Do you want it?"

"Of course I want it."

"I still need to braid the end."

Rosalee took it back from Alex and pinned the loop at the top to the knee of her pants. She combed through the threads with her fingers, acutely aware of Alex's eyes on her as she braided the remaining length and tied off the end.

"What do the colors mean?" he said.

Rosalee cleared her throat, but couldn't bring herself to answer.

"Do you have your pocket knife?" she said instead.

She pulled the threads taut so he knew where to cut, then unhooked the pin for him to cut the safety pin loop. He slid the knife back in his pocket and held out his wrist.

"Tie it tight, I don't wanna lose it." They both admired it for a moment. "Thank you."

Alex put his arm around Rosalee's waist again. She smiled as he tucked a strand of hair behind her ear, then leaned in to speak low so that the rest of the room nearly disappeared.

"Do you have any idea how many times I almost came to see you this week? Even though I knew it was unfair and that if you didn't want to see me, you shouldn't have to?"

Probably not as many times as I almost came to see you, Rosalee thought. "What would you have said?" She tried to make her tone as casual as possible.

"What would you have wanted me to say?"

"You first."

Alex sighed. "I would have wanted you to tell me to stay."

Rosalee looked up, startled. Was it really that simple? All this time, was that all she had to do—ask him to stay?

She searched his face and found the answer in the sadness in his eyes.

"Would it have made any difference?" she said at last.

"... No."

"Good to know."

The arm around Rosalee's waist tightened briefly. "I just mean that it wouldn't change that I have to leave anyway."

"Pepperoni and sausage pizza for Conway."

Rosalee was spared having Alex see her wipe her face on her coat as he went to retrieve the pizza and put it in a to-go box, but too soon, they were bundled up again and Alex had both bags slung over his shoulders. He held her hand as they walked back toward the depot, then stopped at an empty bench so that he could shove the pizza box into his shoulder bag. He gave up on the zipper after several tries.

"That's gonna leak all over," said Rosalee.

Alex shrugged. "So my notebooks will look a little gory."

Rosalee wrinkled her nose, then glanced at the clock. "What would you have said after I asked you to stay?"

"I would have asked you to forgive me," said Alex, fastening the clasp on his bag, "and then begged you to distract me." Rosalee felt a shiver go through her, but it was warmth pulsing against her frigid insides. "Rosalee, all I've wanted for days is to touch you, hold you, make foolishly reckless love to you ... even if it was the last time."

Rosalee couldn't say anything back, so she just watched as a shadow passed in Alex's eyes. "See? I can be selfish, too."

"Train 165 to Denver Union Station is now boarding..."

The voice that echoed through the depot dragged Rosalee back to reality, and then Alex was kissing her hair and saying "That's me."

Her heart dropped into her shoes as he readjusted his bags, possibly stalling for time and wondering whether to leave her there or on the actual platform. Then she couldn't stop the words that tumbled out of her mouth:

"Stay. Alex, *please* stay. I'm so sorry for the way I treated you and I know you don't believe me or trust me, but *I love you* and I want to do better. I *know* I can do better. Please, just stay."

She watched as Alex's shoulders slumped, watched as he blinked several times and looked away, then shook his head. It was too late. Rosalee knew it was too late, but something stubborn and masochistic inside her had to exhaust all of her options and, apparently, ensure that she came out of this experience utterly eviscerated. She felt herself mirroring Alex's defeated posture, crumbling in on herself.

Now what? She was already out of time.

"Well, then ... kiss me goodbye at least," she whispered, and with the surrounding noise, she was sure it wasn't loud enough for him to hear.

Luckily, Alex had always been an excellent lipreader and didn't hesitate to drag Rosalee back to him, roughly enough that she stumbled.

"Sorry," he said, but Rosalee shook her head and flung her arms around his neck.

Alex countered with fierce intensity and she nearly let herself forget where they were and where he was going. She kissed him desperately, clinging to him even as he all but crushed her. Then someone in the crowd wolf-whistled and she was suddenly self-conscious and annoyed, then empty again. Her lips were still only a second before Alex's.

Rosalee trained her focus on the tile floor, slick with various wet and muddy footprints.

"You should go."

"Deja vu," Alex muttered.

But he didn't move away and Rosalee looked up to see him chewing the skin next to his thumbnail and glancing behind him at the window where his train waited. He looked conflicted, but when he met her gaze again, she could see something else—something determined and sure.

"What if you came with me?" he said.

Rosalee stared at him, sure she had misheard or misunderstood. "What, to Denver?"

"To Denver, to LA, wherever."

"So not ... to Denver and then catch the next train back?"

Alex smiled. "No, that's not what I meant."

Just then, a busy-looking attendant appeared around the door Alex was supposed to be going through. "Sir, are you boarding?"

"Yes," said Alex, although he didn't move.

"You need to get on the train then, please."

Alex glanced at Rosalee, then back to the attendant. "Is there any way you could give me, like, five minutes? It'll make *such* a good story, I promise."

The attendant looked him up and down, apparently not in the mood for humor. "No, sir, you need to get on the train right now."

"Okay, look ..." Alex dug in his pocket for his wallet. "I have ... eight dollars and this coupon for a free slushy at 7-Eleven. Can I have *two* minutes?"

The attendant glared and Rosalee knew they would be able to hear her foot tapping if there wasn't so much commotion around them already.

"Please?" said Alex, and Rosalee had to look away, mouth twitching, as he tried to gain the attendant's sympathy. "Look, just tell the engineer that my friend here is helping me with my, uh … cast."

"You're not *wearing* a cast."

"You're telling *me.* It's a real problem. So we're gonna need a few minutes to put it on. *So* quickly."

"Two. Minutes," the attendant said through her teeth.

"You're *crazy,*" Rosalee hissed as they moved aside for several stragglers to pass through the doors and onto the platform.

"You're *scared,*" said Alex. "But we should probably at least move in the direction of the train, in case my astonishing charms have a shorter half-life than normal."

"I'm not scared." Rosalee stopped walking as Alex limped slowly past her. "What are you doing?"

"Two minutes," he reminded her. "*Less* than."

Rosalee huffed, falling into stride with him. "Where would we even live? Neither one of us has a job there. Well, I guess you do."

"Jobs are easy. Places to live are harder and we have that, too."

"Your mom's house?"

"For a little while, anyway."

Rosalee studied Alex's profile for signs of teasing. It would be an awfully mean joke, and she knew he didn't have that kind of mean in him.

"You're *crazy,*" she said, this time in awe. "And you limp too fast."

They were already at one of the doors and Rosalee could see the attendant from before making her way toward them, shoving in baggage and closing compartments under the train as she went.

Alex hitched his bags more securely on his shoulders, then jabbed his hand at the space in front of Rosalee. "I really think we can do this, Rosalee. I think we're finally on the same page."

"Are we?"

Why wouldn't he say it? Why didn't he *feel* it?

A nerve jumped in Alex's jaw. He looked like he was grinding his teeth. "'Something persuasive,'" he said.

"Oh my god."

Rosalee could hear the blood rushing in her ears. She needed more time. This was all too much, too fast.

"'Something romantic,'" said Alex, his smile full, and real, and her absolute favorite as it finally reached his eyes. He climbed the first step onto the train, his hand still extended, palm up, waiting for her. "'Something insane and *earth-shattering* and—'"

"Alex."

"*Come with me.*"

Acknowledgements

This novel has taken approximately 14 years to come out—like, *literally* come out. Sometimes it felt like physically yanking it out of a clogged vacuum cleaner.And because its toiling has extended over a decade, I've felt incredibly guilty not including everyone who has had even a passing hand in my writing career thus far. However, to avoid adding another 500 pages to what is already a substantial book, I've only included those individuals who have gone above and beyond in their gestures of support for this particular endeavor.

Thank you, sincerely, to everyone who provided cherished encouragement, whether through research assistance, beta and/or ARC reading, celebrating milestones, and commiserating with me, listed in alphabetical order, as follows:

Krystapher Ardrey, Lynn Bodnar, Debby Cranor, Jan Cranor, Ellen Cruz, Jennifer Cupich, Vivien Falk, Shawn Gillespie, Tim Gillespie, Justin Gorney, Heather Hein, Kara Jacob, Russell Jex, Catlyn Ladd, Reid Maulsby, Leah Morris, Meg Murray, Michael Pickard, Anna Powell, Evan Snedeger, Ashley Sponsel, Sarah Worley, and Ruby Sue.

Finally, thank you to everyone who answered research questions on social media and interacted with my posts, everyone who asked about the book's progress, and everyone holding this book in their hands. I am incredibly grateful for your support.

About the Author

Kaitlin Cranor is a lifelong day-dreamer with a bachelor's degree in creative writing and an affinity for collecting TV and movie quotes to sprinkle into everyday conversations. Kaitlin lives in Colorado with her husband and fur baby. This is her first novel.